Midsummer in the Tanami Desert of central Australia. Tally No_____ _____ She's an expert in r_____ _____ the elements. But i_____ _____ she must test the li_____ _____ known about living _____ believed _____ herself.

LEAVE NO TRACE

Red sand stretched like an ocean in every direction. Pale green clumps of mulga and other bushes dotted the swelling sand. But I wasn't looking at the scenery. I've spent too much of the last couple of weeks doing just that. The view never varies. Nor do the facts. I'm still stranded 322 kilometers from the nearest settlement.

Doesn't matter that I've helped anchor a Search and Rescue team in the Rocky Mountains for the last ten years. Working SAR has nothing whatsoever to do with this level of survival. Park rangers are just as mortal as any tourist on the planet.

I, Tally Nowata, smell death. Again.

Only this time it is my own.

"That rarest of birds—a memoir truly worth the telling and an adventure worthy of the name. Unflinching in her observation, Hannah Nyala follows the track of the truth—her own and ours."
—Jacquelyn Mitchard, author of
A Theory of Relativity

"[A] poetic, beautifully written memoir."
—*Chicago Tribune*

"An arresting tale of courage and hard-won wisdom."
—*Booklist*

"Beautifully rendered. . . . The gripping chronicle of a tracker finding herself as she looks for others."
—*Kirkus Reviews* (starred review)

"A story of hope, survival, and the human spirit."
—*Los Angeles Times*

LEAVE
NO
TRACE

Hannah
Nyala

POCKET STAR BOOKS

New York   London   Toronto   Sydney   Singapore

An *Original* Publication of POCKET BOOKS

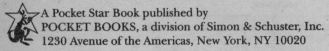A Pocket Star Book published by
POCKET BOOKS, a division of Simon & Schuster, Inc.
1230 Avenue of the Americas, New York, NY 10020

ISBN: 0-7434-5171-6

First Pocket Books printing June 2002

10 9 8 7 6 5 4 3 2 1

POCKET STAR BOOKS and colophon are registered
trademarks of Simon & Schuster, Inc.

For information regarding special discounts for bulk
purchases, please contact Simon & Schuster Special Sales
at 1-800-456-6798 or business@simonandschuster.com

Cover design by Lisa Litwack
Front cover illustration by Shasti O'Leary Soudant

Printed in the U.S.A.

For all the Tally Nowatas in the world,
and all the Rayburns.
And all the rest of us in between.

ACKNOWLEDGMENTS

Only in fiction, I've always believed, do we ever really tell the truth. The courage to tell it, for me anyway, comes from the people who stay close at hand no matter how rugged the going gets. I have been blessed with an extraordinary human community who knows, above all, how to *stick*.

Pat May, sister de jure, believed in this story from its conception and offered unstinting support as I sweated it into being. Vicki Wilson and Ronni Kern, sisters de facto, did the same, proving that family is as much a decision as anything else. I cannot imagine living in this world without these three women. Not a day passes without me saying at least one prayer of gratitude for each of them.

C. Michael Curtis read repeated early drafts and offered ongoing encouragement. Irene Goodman discovered Tally Nowata and me in her massive stack of unsolicited mail and had the grace and nerve to see what this story—and its storyteller—could be. Then she proceeded to believe in us strongly enough—and practically enough—to get us there. Through Irene's efforts, Amy Pierpont came along, with her cheerful spirit and enormous talents, and helped not just to bring Tally's story to life but to deepen and enrich it. Deirdre Dore handled all the futzy details of checks and contracts and author photos with enthusiasm and efficiency. Linda Minton endured my insistence on defying the rules of English grammar in favor of truer language and still managed to copyedit with style. Alex Kamaroff tossed out story ideas and hope in equal measure. I am fortunate to have such a slew of great colleagues.

Through the four years this book was being birthed, many others befriended me, but some deserve special mention: Molly Rose Teuke, Jacqueline Mitchard, Pam English, Nancy Karbo, Pete and Marty Freeman, Reba Whittenborn, Craig Patterson, Melanie and Rick Yaeger, Lois Rushing, and Dennis Wilson. These are the sort of folks who make the world a better place simply because they breathe in it. What each of them gives of themselves on a daily basis boggles my mind even as it inspires the rest of me. But what each of them has done for me personally makes me both humble and yet terribly proud to know them, every last one.

And, finally, we come to the center of my soul: Ebenezer, my canine companion, who did not live to see the book finished so that we could return to our long walks together. Eb is still one corner of my touchstone. Brent, my son, who fought back from a malignant brain tumor with guts and good humor and showed me what kind of man Paul O'Malley could've been, is my second corner. Taliesin, my daughter, who fought tooth and nail and endured even my obstinacy to help make Tally Nowata both more humane and more honest than she ever could've been otherwise, is my third corner. And Stewart West, my dearest husband, who gave me the courage to love once more and proved it well worth the gamble it never actually was, is my fourth corner. We none of us get out of this life alive, but surviving while we're here is at times a delicate balance. If I manage that, it'll be because my four-sided touchstone stays intact. No matter what life throws at us, we *stick*.

The survivor is one who has finally learned
That survival itself is beside the point.

—Tally Nowata, Day 39

DAY 1

I worked my first search for the National Park Service the day I turned nineteen, and found my first dead body three days later.

Her name was Loren Blair, young and athletic and as good on a mountain as anybody ever gets— a first-rate climber in a class of her own—but she wasn't climbing the day she disappeared. She was simply out for her morning run, tall and blond and beautiful as always, looking more like a model than a nature rat, when she stepped off the trail, slipped, and fell to her death. Five days passed before anyone even reported her missing. I didn't get to her till two weeks later, far too late to do anything but call in the 11-44 and bag the body for transport and try desperately not to throw up in the process. Loren no longer looked like a model or a climber. She belonged to the dead, not the living. Nothing and no one could bring her back. This is the bitter edge of the work I do. The smell of death never lets up.

The next day the Chief Ranger made me a permanent part of the Windy Point Search and Rescue

Team, and since then I've been stationed in the Grand Tetons, mountains that draw plenty of people who are a lot less prepared and fit than Loren Blair was. I've been trained to rescue these people, dead or alive, clothed or not, in all kinds of situations and all kinds of weather. I can rappel off a rock face carrying a grown man and do a solo rope rescue without backup, if needed. I can ski an injured climber off a pass in a blizzard and control the descent. I have been well trained to do these things.

But I have not yet been trained to deal with myself at the smell of a three-week-old corpse. They can't train you for something like that.

And I certainly wasn't trained for this.

Nobody can train you to die.

My name is Tally Nowata and this morning, for the first time since I was ten, I remember my dreams.

———

I dreamed of rain and then of dying and then of rain again and woke in a cold blind sweat, reaching for my half-finished net like a drowning person lunges for a line except my net was on hot sand instead of water. Red desert sand that hasn't seen rain in at least a year to boot—which puts the lie to the wet part of my dream and punches the death part home. Hard.

It's the bird, the songbird, that brought me to this, not the situation, not the sand, not the fear, not even the raging hunger. It's just the bird. My very own personal last straw.

Two months ago I wouldn't have eaten a songbird to save my life. Today I did exactly that. Stranded in a strange desert 10,000 miles from home, starving, alone, and beginning to come unraveled at my seams, and still, the worst of it is having to eat bird.

"When you get down to the end of your rope, tie a knot in it and hang on," Grandmother Nowata used to say. She never said what to do with the nausea that comes with hanging onto your own rope that tight. Or what you're supposed to do if you discover your neck in the noose. Pray for double joints from the waist up and squirm free if you can, I suppose. That is Oklahoma's answer for anything a gun won't solve.

Never was much for a gun. Ropes are more to my liking, but a rope here would be overkill. The best tool I have for this job is a hank of flimsy hemp twine, and its rough edges did a number on my fingers this morning. Every knot I tied in my homemade net left its mark on me, but I squared them off anyway, four by four out from the middle until it was the size of a small tablecloth. My hands are still raw and shaking and look like they belong on somebody else—one of the dead tourists we pulled off the Skillet Glacier last year maybe. Minus the bloated pallor, mine look just like theirs did when we zipped them into the body bags: blue-gray, chapped, and battered from the struggle to survive.

On the carryout, Jed quipped that if only they'd prepared their *minds* for the backcountry as well as they had their fancy, color-coordinated, Goretexstudded gear, we might not be having to tote them and it out.

"Any man who can say tote *and* hold up his end of a litter at the same time might be worth keeping around," I muttered, easing my way down a section of scree while trying to keep my side of the litter stable, and Jed shot me the bird with his eyes and almost tripped in the process.

"People pick some of the most inconvenient places to die, don't they?" Jed grumbled, regaining his feet and making do with a gloved finger my direction. I grinned and winked at him. Jed's been my best friend, colleague, and climbing buddy for nine years. We've shot each other the bird so many times we can do it without moving a muscle, so one of us going to the trouble of raising a finger is like shouting through a bullhorn. (And winking back is the rough equivalent of poking the bullhorn inside his eardrum and hollering at the top of my lungs.) I could feel Pony Sutton grinning at the back of our heads. The Windy Point Search and Rescue crew has been together so long now we know each other's every last quirk. That is handy for the kind of work a SAR team does: total equality, total comprehension means we don't have to waste words unless we just want to. Jed shook his head. He could feel Pony's grin on us too.

Laney Greer piped up from the head of the second litter. "Bet the jackets these blokes're wearing cost $500 apiece. Pay my rent and part of the super's with that kind of dough. And just look at all the good it *didn't* do them."

We got quiet then, the way you do on a carryout sometimes—not tense, just focusing on the job, no longer able to leave issues of mortality to someone else.

Pony broke it up. "New gear's a dead giveaway, Lanes," she deadpanned, and we all groaned at her bad pun, then laughed not just because it was true but because every last one of us needed a break from knowing what we were toting right then.

It's a fact. People who pitch up in the wilderness sporting the latest outdoor fashions are a SAR team's surest customers and biggest nightmares. We used to bet on how fast it would take them to need rescuing after they left the visitor center at Moose and how big the callout would be for each one. Ten dollars a head for every SAR crew member called in to work the gig; two for every body put on standby. Since a big search can sometimes have more than a hundred people on the ground and that many more packed and ready to show up, our bets got lucrative fast. I paid for a two-week vacation in Yosemite that way one time, and the rest of the crew groused about it for three years in a row, but that didn't stop us betting on the tourists.

Paul once said it was arrogant the way we did that. "Save people's lives and bust your sides laughin' at 'em all the way home." When Paul is annoyed, the Louisiana bayou baptizes every word.

I tried to explain it—how if you don't laugh when you're scraping somebody's body off the rocks and hauling it down the mountain you'll go right round the bend in your own head—but couldn't, so finally agreed, "Hell yep, it's arrogant. Got a right. Let me tell you one thing for sure, O'Malley, one thing for damn certain. You ever see *me* needing the services of a SAR team, you can count on it—bet the farm you don't own and your next girlfriend's pretty blue eyes too—it'll be a cold day in hell proper. *Very* cold, like switching that brimstone for this blizzard, poof!"

"As if one little Indian girl could change the whole ecosystem of hell," he drawled, and I retorted that if you spend enough time anyplace you eventually get around to working on the decor.

"And please don't call me Indian because I am only half." This has always been a sticking point with us. Paul puts more stock in ethnicity than I do. He can afford to. He's Cajun and Irish. I am something a good deal more complicated.

So here it is. Midsummer in the Tanami Desert of central Australia and hell gone twenty below zero. Paul has disappeared and I am alone, have been for fourteen days, eight of them without food. Hence the plan to trap that lonesome little bird. Necessity is the mother of everything.

He started whistling from his favorite perch just inside the supply tent at dawn. I heard, tried not to, and kept layering in the knots. Soon the blistering summer sun ricocheted off the sand and parched every single inch of my exposed skin. At 11:00 A.M., the ground thermometer hit 124 degrees Fahrenheit. I tried to ignore it, kept working.

Around noon, I finished the net and stood up, startling the songster into leaving—by the exact same route he always used, I noted, with a certain amount of grim satisfaction. It's our loyalty to routines that makes us most vulnerable to predators. Balancing on two metal crates, I stretched the snare across his flyway, lightly hooking the middle and one corner between the tent frame and canvas, and stepped down trailing a long piece of twine. Then I crawled back up and readjusted it four more times before I was satisfied it was ready—in theory. There was nothing else to do but wait.

The pores on my sunburned neck seeped sweat, I could feel it rise, but the hot winds off the spinifex plains sucked the salty mist away before it even broke the surface. Heat shimmers rose and wavered. Tussocks of yellow spiny bushes marched endlessly to a lost point where this aching empty land finally meets the endless sky. My skin was taut and tired, stretched over my bones like a dirty piece of old cellophane, my long hair heavy with grit, my throat scoured by dust and thirst. My stomach bucked and kicked every few minutes from hunger pangs or the knowledge of my situation or both. Breathing hurt.

Red sand stretched like an ocean every direction as far as I could've seen had I been staring at it instead of the net, waiting for the bird to reappear. Clumps of acacia and other trees whose names I neither know nor care to dotted the swelling sand, struggling to recover from the bushfires that swept through last season, hardy shoots of pale green poking out through hectares of charred stubs and roots. A few mulgas, so dry their leaves looked silver, hugged the drainage near the waterhole. Fire does the spring cleaning here. It's the desert's housewife, more interested in culture than ecology.

But I wasn't looking at the scenery or paying much attention to the Tanami's living arrangements this morning. I've spent too much of the last couple weeks doing just that. The view never varies. Nor do the facts. I'm still stranded over 300 kilometers from the nearest human settlement and it's still gone twenty below blessed zero in hell. Half-breed Okie lost in the heart of a continent that's losing its ozone—now there's a bit of cultural data for you. It's easier to get skin cancer here than anywhere else on the planet today. As if I didn't have enough to worry about already.

Worse yet, none of my skills as a wilderness ranger back home in the Tetons make one whit of a difference here. It doesn't matter that I'm an experienced climber with peaks like Denali and Rainier scratched off my Must Climb Before I Die list. Doesn't matter that I know how to dig a snow trench with skis and wait out a blizzard in relative comfort. Build a warm fire out of wet wood, spot an avalanche slope and grizzly spoor. Rig a Tyrolean traverse and guide a loaded litter to the ground on it. Doesn't matter that I've worked with a SAR team in the Rocky Mountains for eight years, helping to save the lives of 47 tourists who got themselves lost or injured in the backcountry. Or helped schlep out the bodies of a slim dozen more who didn't survive despite my crew's best efforts. Doesn't matter that I've stood at the feet of way too many three-week-old corpses, preparing the body for transport and reeling from that terrible smell. Doesn't matter. None of it matters here, and that makes me sick to the stomach. Literally.

Anyway, enough of that. The bird finally returned. The trigger loop of twine sat limp in my fingers. I waited, nervous, sure he'd see the line snaking its way from the saggy tent above his head down to this woman below and depart by the back way on principle if nothing else. I could see it in living color, him somersaulting backward off the perch, neatly avoiding my trap, doing some solo avian version of a Flying Garibaldi move, way out of reach or need of a net.

But he didn't. He just sat there, trusting and simple, surveying his little world, scratching his head. I wanted to leave and started to. He opened his beak to sing me off, in a routine we've pretty much perfected over the last month, and somehow, accidentally, I yanked the line. Tripped over it, I believe.

Then I simply stood there, trapped as a deer in headlights, shocked that my hairbrained plan had actually worked, not knowing quite what to do next. I've never killed an animal before, not even for food. None of my years of training are worth one red hill of beans here. Working search and rescue has nothing whatsoever to do with this level of survival.

Park rangers, it hit me dead center, as the bird

struggled against the coarse mesh, fluttering and chirring in terror, are just as mortal as any tourist on the planet. Skills be damned.

Especially if they're the wrong ones.

When that thought landed on the warm feel of the suddenly limp, feathered body in my hands, I pitched forward, heaving, crying, and the fingers that just wrung the tiny neck went numb and clutched at my stomach. The songbird, still secure in the knotted twine, tumbled to the sand and lay still, quiet at last.

Last straw. I, Tally Nowata, smell death. Again.

Only this time it is my own.

DAY 2

This wasn't supposed to be about dying. It was supposed to be a vacation, a four-month furlough from a stressful job, joining the man I love in a place I knew nothing about on purpose. I came for fun, relaxation, sex, and companionship—and not necessarily in that order, either. Before exiting the plane in Alice Springs, I'd never set one foot in a desert, never had a hankering to, wouldn't ever have done so if it hadn't been for Paul. I like trees and mountains and cold, rushing rivers. I like valleys tucked away in the shadow of tall granite walls, plants without spines, and freezing wind and rain. Deserts were too much like the plains—you can see for sixty miles any direction either place and that's just too damn far—so I intended to leave them well alone and die someplace temperate and green and preferably wet. Now here I am in the middle of a hot, red, sandy land, staring death down the nose and gagging so hard it hurts, and all the stuff I came for is gone like it never existed. Even him.

What I know about desert survival you could put in a thimble and still have room for a big man's thumb, so what I think about my chances of surviving here are unthinkable. But I'm not a needy woman, clutching at any man in sight to help steer my boat or shoo the mice off my terrain. I'm as capable of taking care of me as anybody, more capable than most. I'm worried about Paul, yes, but I can stand on my own two feet till he gets back, and he knows that as well as I do.

This is something I've never said to another living being, but here I've taken to saying it right out loud several times a day. Convincing my own self maybe. Talking tough to keep the truth at bay.

Truth is, though, it's not working, because in spite of all my talk the last few days, I am a little unnerved at this exact moment.

The worst of it, I think, is that after all the trouble I went to yesterday—snaring, strangling, plucking, beheading, gutting, skewering, and roasting that damn bird—I still haven't managed to keep a single bite of it down. Tried again last night and erupted like Mount St. Helens minus the ash. My unfinished dinner went flying into the bushes and I tumbled onto my hands and knees, sick as a dog. Sicker, actually, than any dog I ever saw.

Back where I'm from they shoot dogs that get this sick. It's the Okie version of the good neighbor: put the unfortunate out of their misery so the rest of us don't have to watch 'em suffer. That way we can all pretend we're exempt from the rules, forget them a little while longer, play God with a stick and a smile. But, then again, maybe that's not quite right.

Grandmother Nowata used to say, "Life's a terminal disease and nobody's gettin' out of it alive. Okies are tough, but Indians are made of four-ply steel granite. They have to be." I never crossed horns with my father's mother over that. She was dead by the time I was old enough to have the nerve to cross her. But, for my money, genetics are almost beside the point in the Sooner state: the whole damn population takes a stiff upper lip to the extreme. That used to bother me. I felt trapped by all the adults' strength.

Today, though, I wonder. Maybe their forgetting is done to remember and they aren't so much playing God as figuring out how to survive *and* not kill him— or anyone else—off. Maybe the thing we all know best about death is the one we lie about last. Maybe, when you get into the business of saving lives like I have, you forget the most important point: we none of us are gettin' out of this gig alive. Maybe people like me fight too hard to beat the odds and people like my grandmother walk nearer the truth.

May be.

Can't say. Wouldn't know.

All I know is my own truth: If you're still breathin', you're still a candidate for my services. SAR isn't a job so much as an attitude: So that others may live. Save a life no matter the cost. We come onto every gig willing to give our own lives if necessary. There's a certain folly in that, but we're well trained, well equipped, and deadly effective when we show up, so people rely on us. Even *we* rely on us, me perhaps most of all. But then, I'm usually on the good side of bad situations in the outdoors. Here everything's changed, like a pair of die flung high and no telling where they'll land.

Enough. Just work the gig as if you picked it, Nowata, and keep your head in the middle of now.

It took a long time to pull myself together enough to retrieve the bird's carcass and begin brushing sand off the greasy meat with fingers so dirty the effort itself was moot—but necessary. When a person shrinks inside herself, effort alone becomes part of the point, a big part. If you can still struggle you know you're still alive, that sort of thing. Lies become articles of faith.

Spoken aloud, truth.

Where are you, Paul O'Malley? I've run it down in my head a hundred times and am no closer to knowing now than I was the first time through.

Supply run to Alice Springs, four days tops. You were supposed to pick up your daughter at the airport, get that worthless base radio repaired again, buy another month's stock of food, fill the water dolly, and come straight back here. You are the most reliable human being I ever met. Never late for anything, not even by a few minutes.

But you're overdue now, for the first time ever—and by way too many days to count yet again—and I don't know why. And the worry is starting to eat at my edges.

Stay put, stay calm.

This is what I used to teach the tourists in my

campfire talks on wilderness survival. "If you get into trouble in the out-of-doors, folks, stay put and stay calm. Survival here—*anywhere*—is 95 percent brains and 5 percent circumstances, so the smartest thing you can do if you get hurt or injured or just plain lost is to *stay put and let us come to you*. If we come and you're gone, wandering, a miss is as good as a mile. Could mean the difference between us taking home an empty body bag that day or a full one a week later. Your choice."

It is good advice, unvarnished and useful, and I have followed it to the letter in this heat-scoured place. For two weeks now, I have lived each day a little smaller than the one before—trusting that if I stretched the food and water supplies carefully enough and conserved my strength, Paul would somehow make it back, and we would laugh about whatever misadventure delayed him. I am not given to fretting. But nine days ago I finished the last half of the last granola bar; four days ago I stirred the last packet of fizzy Vitamin C into a cup of water and sipped it all afternoon; yesterday I killed a songbird and today I'm still trying to eat it. There is no more sidestepping these facts.

I'm in serious trouble, stranded in one of the most remote deserts on earth with summer in full swing and no hope of rescue. No radio, no vehicle, no weapon, no backup plan, no food, and nobody expecting me home for three more months so nobody to come looking either. It's 322 kilometers to the nearest village, 115 degrees Fahrenheit at dawn and dusk, 125 in the shade at noon waist-high, ten degrees above that on the ground. I could try walking out, but probably wouldn't make it to the halfway mark. Or the quarter. If that. I have a little over a gallon of water, which buys me one thirsty day—resting. Walking, I'd need twice that in this heat to cover 30 k's, so 322 might as well be 3,000 for all the good it does my sorry little unprepared multicultural behind.

———

History. Half a planet and two decades away and it's still dogging my every step. Back home in the Tetons I joke about my mottled heritage. Not here. History's a damn sight more entertaining if your nose hairs aren't scorching, I think. When they are it gets on your nerves. Like family.

Little brother Dixon used to tell me Indians couldn't get lost on the land ". . . if somebody paid 'em to, Tal, because we all have an inner compass, sort of a thin little needle in our hearts that always points north." Dix had navigation issues. I will always believe that was because the state of Oklahoma put us in a foster home in Guthrie the year our mother died and our father went to prison for it. I was ten and Dix was eight, and our new parents were white, educated, and rich enough to have three meals a day and not save the leftovers.

Artis and Elaine Jones were good people and meant well. They wanted to do right by these mottled little part Potawatomi, part Lakota, part gringo orphans. I wanted to forget I was Indian;

Dix wanted to remember. So they compromised and took us to powwows and rodeos and national parks and circuses every summer in their Lincoln Continental, read *Black Elk* and *Pretty Shield* and *The Phantom Tollbooth* at bedtime, made fry bread and Navajo tacos and apple pies á la mode. For two kids whose daddy was in the state pen and whose mama was in the strange red dirt outside Shawnee we were living high on the hog, but we stuck out like sore bloody thumbs and, at best, felt like a couple of charity cases. Which is exactly what we were. No state government can give you a family. I tolerated the Joneses and found some solace in horses and books. Dix hated them and focused on things like innate Indian navigational skills and, later, the curative powers of hallucinogens and alcoholic beverages. Inner compasses and Jack Daniels. Bad mix.

"So?" I ragged him mercilessly when we were teens, always worried that his habit of clinging to his bloodlines and social history was jeopardizing his chance at a decent life. "Who cares if you know where north is? If you're not prepared you're a goner anyhow, bro—don't matter which direction your damn nose is pointed. Knowing north ain't gonna make you any the less dead." I had preparedness issues.

Make that *have*. Of all the things that could've taken me out, you might know it would be this one. I am not prepared for this place. If Dix was sober enough to know where I was and what was going on with me today, he'd bust a gut on the rightness of that little footnote to our family history: the one who always preached being prepared no matter what *ain't*.

The singed smell in my nose, I just realized, is a sign of worse problems than ambient air temperature. That didn't do it, though Lord knows it's hot enough to. I did it. Leaned too close in to the campfire last night and that's what singed my nose hairs. I was hunching over the tiny flame, sweating like a stuck pig but shivering, trying to comfort my innards with the innocence of a familiar camp habit, and I got too close. Just got too close. This desert didn't singe my nose hairs; habit did. Habit on a hungry stomach and the weakened limbs and judgment that come with that territory. More of me is unprepared for now than I care to admit. Dix would have a field day.

———

I've been over this a hundred times already, meticulous, point by point, and always end with the beginning: Paul, for whatever reason, is gone. I am sitting in the middle of the Tanami Desert of central Australia and the one person who knows I'm here has disappeared from the face of the planet. God help me.

More words echo inside my head. Enraged words, partially formed, bent on sapping strength and gumption. They need retracting before they escape. I swallow hard, and gag again.

God's not in evidence at this moment anyway. No sense wasting spit on him.

A shadowy canine figure slinks past the open tent flap, and I forget all about God and saliva. They're just not basic enough to worry about at this exact moment. I have more pressing things to consider.

Like predators.

The local dingo band that Paul came here to study usually lays low in the daylight hours, but since I cooked that bird they've been skulking about camp, watching me with fearless eyes. I've been trying to make myself look as big and intimidating as possible, but it isn't working very well anymore. One of them, an albino female, has even taken to lying in the shade of a nearby bush. When I feel her calm gaze on me, I shiver.

Dingoes don't attack people. I keep saying it. They don't. It's practically a law. The only problem is I'm not sure I look like a convincing human anymore, and I know they can smell my fear because even I can. It's like a sweet musk tinge to my sweat.

Stay put, stay calm, Nowata. The dingoes aren't your problem. Your own head is. Nose over your toes, focus on the known.

Water.

I'm on the end of the water we trucked in. One good sip and it's less than a gallon. But I've seen this coming for a week and I'm ready. I'll start using the spring this evening, doctoring the water with iodine tablets or boiling it, and as long as that holds out, I can hold on here. Humans can survive without food for up to six weeks.

So that's it. Two down, four to go, and I still have a bird to eat.

That's better than even odds.

DAY 3

The odds went to zero sometime in the night.

I knew the spring here was seasonal, that it would eventually dry up. The water level has been dropping slightly over the last few days. But then last night it disappeared completely, faster than I thought it could, and my best chance at survival—staying put until Paul shows up again—went with it. I no longer have a choice. If I live any smaller, I'll disappear into the bowels of this place. That's it then.

I move out tonight.

It is noon now and my pack is ready. My note to Paul is written and secured under a heavy rock so it'll be the first thing he sees on entering the sleep tent. He's still my best chance. If he knows where I'm headed and when I left, he can come find me, so I laid out my intended route (and my backup) and told him exactly what gear I'm carrying and how much water I have, to the drop. He'll know what that means.

If he gets back, that is—no, *when* he gets back. *When Paul gets back.* Because he will be back. He would never leave me out here to die. He will be back for me.

Still, my mind wants to linger on the questions: Where are you, Paul O'Malley, goddammit?! And where is Josie? Did something happen to her? To you? Did you ever reach Alice at all? How the hell could we let something like this happen?

I cannot linger. Mental games of Twenty Questions will get me deader than a doornail out here faster than anything else, so I flat out cannot waste energy asking questions that have no answers. Focus on the known, Nowata. Lay this thing out backward and run it just like a search, only solo and no support. Leave the questions to the gods and the folks with full enough bellies and hydrated skins to answer them. You work with the facts.

322 kilometers. A few less, if I was a crow and could fly, but I'm not and I can't, so 322 it is. 161 miles, give or take a few. Miles sounds shorter. I'll go with that. The distance isn't my biggest problem anyway.

Water is.

I dug a hole near the spring and managed to get enough to top off all my canteens—ten quarts total. That's twenty pounds of liquid alone, way more than I need to be carrying out here and way less than I need to make it to the next waterhole. If Paul's research maps are accurate, there's a small permanent spring fifty-one miles to the southeast and a much bigger one ten miles beyond that. Once on the move, I will just have to drink as much as I can.

"Belly makes the best canteen, Tal," Paul always said. "No sense totin' it on your back."

I don't know jack fucking shit about deserts, but that much makes good sense to me.

— — —

Stay put, stay calm. That's only good advice if somebody else on the planet knows where the hell you are and is reliable enough to send in the cavalry if you don't show up as scheduled. Pony, Jed, Lanes, the Chief. They'd all show up if they knew I was in trouble. Even Dix might, though after our last falling out he'd be in the right not to. Artis and Elaine would come, too, woefully ill-prepared for this place but determined to find their "girl," if that drunk driver hadn't taken them out together eleven years ago. Another ten-second slice of time that changed my whole world. I've had way too many of those. First my father's mother, then Mama, then Elaine and Artis. They all would've come if they could've. And since they're family they would've been expecting regular news from me and when it didn't arrive they wouldn't have waited three months to see why. Jed and Pony are different. They may get miffed at me for not writing, but it wouldn't occur to them that I'm in trouble if I don't.

It wouldn't occur to anybody who knows me. And that's my own damn fault.

The stay put, stay calm rule has no failsafe for people like me in a place like this. Mainly because I've spent a lot of years convincing everybody by my actions that I would never be here.

Yet here I am. Worse than lost because I know where I am and exactly how insane it is to think I can get where I need to be on the limited resources I have. Only a fool would try what I'm about to try. Only a damn fool.

So be it. There are worse things to be than a fool. A coward, for instance. Can't nobody ever accuse me of *that*. They might find me deader than a doorknob, laid flat out in the sun, toes curling upward, buzzards picking my eyeballs clean—but they won't find me curled up somewhere whimpering. If I'm going, I'm going upright and feet first. Kicking, if I can manage it. I just have to get with this desert, have to figure it out and sidle alongside it for a ways.

The land does not look inviting.

The closest burn area stretches as far as I can see, with intermittent unburned patches throughout. Fire mosaic, they call that back home. No one can explain the logic of wildfire. It runs a line of its own and takes what it will clear to the ground, and under, leaving the rest standing untouched. Paul said it made for fascinating ecological puzzles. I'm less fascinated than overwhelmed.

The thought of walking through all that scrub soot in this heat—trudging over the miles of sand ridges that lie between me and that village—makes me tired. And if I miss the waterholes he has marked on these maps I won't last long enough to remember the feeling, and that makes me tired too.

Enough. Can't talk of tired when you feel it, Nowata. You know that. Focus on the known. Bend the details to your will.

Okay, water's as set as it's going to get. So what's next?

The route.

I have two choices, both equally unappealing. There's a dirt track cutting through about three miles from the first spring, but Paul's maps don't show any other water sources along it. Given my druthers I'd pick the track to walk on—even though Paul said almost no one travels it this time of year. But it's human-made, mostly free of spinifex, flat, and shorter by a good forty miles. I could move fast and I wouldn't have to worry about losing my bearings. If water wasn't an issue, that would be the best way out of here.

Actually, if water wasn't an issue I wouldn't be needing a way out of here, so I can lay that one to rest. The other option is cutting across the big middle of this desert, south-southwesterly in general, traversing miles of scrubby sand hills and hoping I hit the few water sources Paul has mapped. One is big enough to be named. Lake Surprise. Even if I miss some of the others, I shouldn't miss a pool of liquid that big. So that's Plan A. If something changes and I can use the track, good. If not, I'll go cross-country. Won't be the first time I've had to do that.

So, back to the details. Water's set, route's set, what's next?

Food.

Before leaving I intend to finish eating this bird. After all, I did kill him—a helpless little creature that's done nothing worse than sing for a living. Already damned, might as well have the nutrition. I ate half last night—all of two whole ounces, I'm guessing—and put the rest away for later. It's a good feeling, being able to plan a day around a meal again and having a portion size big enough to measure mentally. I like having that much control. It helps make up for everything else spinning way out of it.

The hunger's the worst, I think. I've never been this hungry. Not even as a young kid. Then there was always somebody somewhere who'd share a bite of something with us on those long, empty days before the end of the month. A couple stale crackers, a slice of dry white bread. An orange on the verge of spoiling or a dollop of homemade peanut butter if we were lucky. Until you've been a child whose adults are on the government dole, you don't know shit about monthly cycles. I hated the end of the month the first ten years of my life. On the rez or off, it didn't matter. It was a bad time of the moon.

Shame and starvation fighting for first place in your body and your mind all the damn day. Town kids laughing and pointing and throwing rocks and singing redneck songs about bums on welfare. Father drunk and out of a job *again* and mother defeated but doing her deadlevel best to cope and smile and stretch two pounds of potatoes so it would feed a family of five for eight days, and everybody else we knew caught in the same deadly cycle. Here at least there's one thing in my favor. The end of the month can't make one whit of a difference. There's nobody here to see my shame.

Which is almost beside the point today, because the hunger is driving me to my knees and I'd be there even if the whole world was watching. That little dab of meat made it worse, I think. I'm pretty sure I was doing better before I had anything to eat. Two bites of bird and I'm ravenous, eyeing the dingoes and not planning to bother with a cooking method, chewing on an acacia pod, watching a string of ants with more than passing interest. I'm more predator than person, judging everything by its potential nutritive value.

One thing's clear. Hunger opens a bigger hole in you when you're older. I get dizzy when I stand up now and I shiver at night, even in the heat. Plus I'm weak all the time, so moving takes not just thought but planning, and if I'm not real careful I drop things and stumble. I never remember any of that from when I was a kid. The most I can recall of then was the way my mouth would water when the ice cream truck warbled its way through town, always one street over from ours—never on it—the three sweltering summers we lived in McAlester. Just the idea of those cold sweets gave me chill bumps. I'd sit on the porch stoop and chew on a stalk of raw wheat and rage against my own slavering, craving spit. One week I was so angry about it I came up with a plan to hijack the truck by hitting the driver over the head with a board, but Dix ratted on me to Mama and she showed up to confiscate my board. Hunger has always taken me out of my right mind.

Even here. Especially here.

It made me mad at first, but mad takes too much energy and I don't have any to spare, so I settled back and dreamed up luscious meals in my mind like we used to do on the rez the years we lived with Grandmother Haney. Over the last week I probably fixed my favorite dinner ten times: icy cold chunks of watermelon, chicken basted in honey and shoyu and grilled, couscous with roasted mangoes and chili peppers, and a fresh garden salad piled high with tomatoes and carrots and broccoli and chickpeas and mung bean sprouts. Then, all of a sudden, what I was doing hit me like a sucker punch to the gut and I quit it cold.

Knucklehead city. Dreaming like that in a place like this.

"The desire for comfort is one of the deadliest dangers in a survival situation—so, whatever you do, *don't go there*. Sink inside wherever you are instead. Now just think about it, people. What kind of sense does it make for your mind to go wandering off to McDonald's for a Big Mac and fries when your leg's broken and you're stuck in a crevasse ninety miles from a town too small to have a Mickey D's? No sense, I'm tellin' you, no sense a'tall. *Use your energy to be where you are*. That way, when we come looking for you, you'll be there to help us instead of mired up to your damn middle eardrums in two all-beef patties, special sauce, and the likes." I've probably said that a thousand times in training sessions and campfire programs, and it's the gods' own truth. People who come to terms with their current situation usually last long enough to be rescued. People who don't die. It's really that simple.

The problem is, I don't have any real hope of rescue. Unless Paul shows up, it's just me and this desert for a long, long time, and time is on the desert's side, hands down.

But that's the gig. Didn't pick it, didn't plan it, only have to deal with it. Sort of like childhood and I survived that just fine, now didn't I? Aim for the finish line, Tal, and don't look back.

The dead finish. A shrub that's earned its name. The one next to the supply tent just brought me up sharp, its needles brushing against my arm as I crossed between it and the tent.

Dead finish. Paul grinned when he told me about it. I did too. It was funny then. Today it isn't. *Acacia tetragonophylla*. Paul likes those Latin names. I would too, if I could ever remember them long enough to get fond of them. But they have too many syllables, so they usually go in one ear and right on out the other without leaving so much as a dent in my brain. This one I remember because it was so easy to tease Paul with. Tetra what? Four-sided gono what? Venereal disease? For bushes only or are grasses susceptible too? Reckon it ever crosses species? Paul was trying to regale me with the plant's horticultural characteristics, and I was doubled over, cackling at the irreverent things you could do to tweak the Latin name for the dead finish.

I quit laughing when he told me the reason for its common name. This shrub is the hardiest plant in central Australia; it survives drought, fires, floods, and time. "If you ever come on one that's dead, you're finished. Because when these shrubs die, Tal, it's all over but the shoutin' till the rains come through." It was always ominous when Paul went Biblical on his analogies.

This dead finish is *dead*. Graveyard dead, I'd say. I just stand and stare at it and wonder how funny its Latin name would've been a month ago had I known I'd see its common one get this relevant this fast. Details. I wish now I'd paid more attention to all those ecological details stored in Paul's brain.

"I'm on *furlough!*" I moaned at him once in the middle of a long disquisition on the desert raisin. "I don't want to learn *anything else* about *anything else* today!"

Raising his wrist, he made a big production of laying it against my forehead, checking for a fever. I stuck my tongue out at him and stalked off, snapping, "I'm a tourist! A *departing* tourist, no less. One that's leaving you old scientific types to your studies right this exact second, that's me. Departing."

"And what a nice view she affords her scholarly audience from here," Paul said, stopping me in my tracks.

We made love right there in the sand and when we'd finished, Paul pulled me into his arms and whispered, "One of these days you're gonna beg and plead for me to tell you something about the desert raisin, Tal, and I might do it, love, but it's gonna cost you. *Dearly*."

Man, I hate it when he's right. If I could recall what he said about the desert raisin, I might be able to find some. But my mind's as blank as a freshly minted penny. Blanker actually, because at least the penny remembers the shape of Abraham Lincoln's head.

I'd pay every cent I ever laid my hands on to have Paul here to tell me where to find desert raisins.

I need to remember to admit that to him when we make it out of this mess.

———

One thing is on my side. The decision to leave has put some steel in my backbone, and steel counts when you're in a mess.

Even the dingoes recognize the change and have moved back a respectable distance. Only the white is still hanging around camp. I thought seriously about trying to trap her, but decided I can't afford to waste the energy. Need water way worse than I need food. Hunger makes you thirsty, yes, but digestion uses up a lot of liquids, and I can't spare any of them right now, so I'll just have to deal with the hunger because everything I do from this point on has to be geared toward conserving my fluids.

That's precisely why I'm forcing myself to stay put till the sun goes down. Now that I'm packed, part of me is raring to go and say the hell with the sun, but the part that's still sane knows that would be idiotic because the sun here is high and tough and it sucks water out of anything it can lay a ray on. I can't fight the sun. Have to wait for dusk and go by the moon. All I can do till then is sleep, think, or plan.

I *must* make it to that next spring. Paul's notes say there's standing water in that gully year-round. If I can just get there, I can regroup and maybe, just maybe, manage to march my way out of this godforsaken land. Then my biggest problem will be finding out what happened to Paul and Josie.

<hr />

Josephine O'Malley. Bright, articulate, stubborn, and tough as tempered nails. Looks at the world with unblinking eyes and knows how most of it ought to be fixed on any given day. Will tell you how, when, and why in a heartbeat too. Loudly, if necessary. She is the center of Paul's world, the brightest flame at the core of his being. But she scares the ever-living daylights out of me. Always has.

Did it from the first time I laid eyes on her too, hovering near the door of Paul's office one afternoon, shades of innocence and mischief slipping across her tiny, perfect face, clearly trying to figure out how to get her father's attention without asking for it. Seconds later she succeeded. Raw power—in a package roughly the size of a flea and about half as old. There ought to be a law against that somewhere. I have never seen to beat it in all my life.

"Josie comes at the world on her own terms," Paul always says. "Just like somebody else I know," he tacks on with his crookedest grin. I'm too stubborn to agree out loud. It's a moot point anyway. Fact is, Jo has about as much use for me as she does for a toothache. And, in the interests of total honesty, I'd rather get a root canal any day than have to spend time with her. We take one look at each other and break out in hives.

Paul's mostly unfazed by the whole thing, laughs at us sometimes and says we only strike sparks because we're so much alike and one day we'll see that and be inseparable for good and then "Look out, World!" Paul always sees the world in one lighter shade of rosy than it ever could be. That probably comes from being raised in Louisiana. With so much swampland about, I expect you need optimism.

Oklahoma's dry as tinder. We're realists. So I worry there's something deeper, more confusing, going on for both of us. For Jo, feelings of guilt maybe—that if she likes me she's somehow being disloyal to her mom. Or anger—that I've stolen her dad, which isn't true but I'm sure it looks that way. And for me, since I never had any kids and never intended to, I'm just not very good with them. That's the short side of my end of it anyway, and I'm not interested in looking at the long side. The Nowatas don't need to be procreating, that's all, and I aim to comply. So Jo's and my relationship has been tenuous, to put it mildly. This visit was supposed to help change that.

"She's older now," Paul said, "Ten full years." Like chronological age actually means anything when you're dealing with a prerational being, I thought loudly, biting my tongue on the words in my head. Drew blood but I did manage to keep them to myself. There are certain advantages to being raised the way I was. Like a high tolerance for pain.

Still, no amount of tongue-bitten silence on my part can change the facts. Josie may be ten by the book, but it's ten going on forty-seven in the real world, and there this child absolutely believes she is the Queen of Everybody's Universe. Throws a world-class hissy fit. "Makes corporal punishment look like self-defense," I once told Paul, during one of her tantrums in the grocery store checkout line, and he said, "Then it's a good test for all your notions about nonviolence, Tal, isn't it?" Test, my eye. He was so right about that one it hurt.

Ever since I was ten I've tried to keep my promise to my mother: no violence no matter what. I've slipped a few times but haven't hurt anybody seriously. Yet. But Josephine O'Malley is a temptation. A big one. Pony put it best one day at Dornan's three years ago. Jo, as usual, was pitching a fit over something on her plate (or not on her plate, I can't remember which). Paul, as usual, was cajoling her. I, as usual, was wanting to leave. So bad I could taste it. Even Jed was eyeing his dinner way too close, and all the waiters were huddled together in a corner and it didn't take a rocket scientist to know they were laying dibs on who had to ask us to vacate the premises. Josie howled louder and every adult in the room blanched. Pony finally raised her eyebrows and drawled, "Now I understand why the wild eat their young."

Jo skipped a beat and then bawled more fervently. I gave up thoughts of leaving and laughed out loud. Paul frowned and suggested that we go. We had a huge raging argument about that set of responses on the way home. Paul thought his and Josie's were appropriate, mine and Pony's out of line. I disagreed to the last detail. "I don't believe in violence but if that child was mine she'd have felt the palm of my hand on her sassy little rump tonight—right out in front of God and everybody. I wouldn't have tried to kill her or maim her or anything, but I'd have made her think twice before bellowing in public again in my presence," I snapped. Paul was furious. I didn't apologize. Wasn't sorry.

What that says about me as a human being I don't know, but it for sure means I don't need a child. Ever. It's bad enough loving a man who has one.

So that's been the rub. No question, Josie's been my biggest personal challenge since Paul moved in with me four years ago. But she lives with her mother in New Orleans, so we only have to see her twice a year and I learned really fast to just be gone when she came to Wyoming. Went rockclimbing in the Shawangunks one summer. Volunteered for wildfire duty out of Redding, California another time, working on a hotshot crew, swinging a pulaski like a second arm. Helped with a wolf census in Glacier National Park this last spring. Then Paul headed here for his research.

Joining him, I knew it meant coming to terms with Josie, since she would spend part of this year with us and we'd not only have to provide bed and board, but homeschooling for the duration. I knew it, prepared for it as best I could, and came anyway. I made a commitment to this man four years ago. His daughter was part of the package deal. It was high time for me to pay up.

The week Jo was due to fly into Alice, Paul understood I had to stay behind here at the camp. It was only a four-day trip but I needed the break, every last minute of it, to get ready for my first real go at quasi-stepmotherhood. I was nervous and tense and needed to take the edge off my own hide before this child arrived. A few days' reprieve was the answer.

Paul agreed and teased me about spending four days alone in the desert. "Indian's notion of the Jesus stint, huh, Tal?"

"Not much sense in staying forty when four will do," I snapped, turning away so he wouldn't see me smile.

Laughing out loud Paul settled the ailing base radio onto the passenger seat. Then he blew me a kiss, warned me not to go mental or tourist and beat up any of the small mammals in the vicinity while he was gone, and drove off, calling his usual farewell out the window, "Don't you ever marry me, Tally!"

I waved and yelled, "Don't worry, I won't, so don't you ever ask!" And turned my back on him because that was the way we always said good-bye. Crisp and clean, no frills, no fuss. Fussing's for people who're worried about what's coming. Frills are for people who plan to head it off at the pass. Paul and I have never worried and never headed anything off. We just are. Even with that one big wedge of his daughter between us, there has never been any doubt that we wouldn't make it. I intend to love him till I die. The child thing we can just navigate. So when he left to pick her up, I was determined to do whatever it took to be calm and collected when she arrived. I'd read a whole stack of parenting books on the plane. This time I had it all figured out. I just needed a couple days to center myself and get ready.

I had no premonition of trouble then. None. Not a whiff. Those first three days went great. I slept a lot, read a couple trashy adventure novels, moseyed down to the spring twice a day and watched its few residents show up for water, feeling no compulsion to learn anything whatsoever about them. There was no point. The natural history of the Tanami belongs to people like Paul who need or want to know it. People like me, I thought (tickled clear out of my right mind that I was on vacation and didn't have to *do* or *learn* one damn thing), could afford to be curious or not as the mood hit, and mine didn't give a rip about this place. I was just a tourist, focused on rest. Rest and preparation for a visit from the Queen.

By the fourth morning, I was steeled for Paul's arrival. And Josie's. Ten hours later, anxious for it. By the evening of the fifth day, worried sick. On the sixth, praying—which is saying something for a half-breed Potawatomi who hasn't ever been on speaking terms with any god of any sort.

On the seventh day the food ran out, and I marked the event by doing yoga at sunrise—in the nude for good luck. On the thirteenth morning, I was measuring the last of the bottled water and heading to the spring not to spy on its remaining residents but to figure out how best to collect its warm, bug-strewn liquid. By the time the fourteenth day rolled around, the songbird was looking downright tasty. I started building the net at noon from a ball of twine I found in one of the supply cases and started a new journal for good luck with Day One. My early morning striptease last week clearly didn't even nudge the fates. Now I'm back to more mundane efforts at stirring my own luck.

So here I am at Day Three. No Queen, no Paul, no sad little bird to sing me through the long hot days. Only me, the hapless tourist who's done way too much dwelling on everything but the kitchen sink recently. To get out of here alive, I have to let go. Stop worrying about Paul and Josie, stop thinking about my family and friends and the goddamn past, stop hoping I'll be rescued. It is time for me to unhinge from all that and put every cell into smart, forward motion.

I reach for the locket Elaine gave me when I turned 12 and snap it open. My mother's kind eyes smile back. I haven't opened this locket or taken it off my neck since the moment I put it on. Even when we climb I tuck it way down inside my shirt and refuse to leave it behind and that's knuckle-headed, because swinging gold chains get in the way when you're inching your way up a vertical rock wall with nothing but a rope and the steadi-ness of your own muscles and nerve between you and the ground.

Now I lift the chain free of me at last and set the small oval on the sand and stare at the woman smil-ing back at me from inside. I quit dreaming two days after she left. But I started again this week. Perhaps that is a sign. Perhaps it is time to leave my mother behind for real. I need to travel light. As light as possible. This locket carries all the weight of my past, dreams and hopes and shattered reali-ties. It is the heaviest thing I own. I can't afford to have anything slow me down. So that is it then. I go alone.

DAY 4

No, I do not.

But I did try. Left the locket at camp and started out strong at dusk, determined to move at night to conserve my body fluids. About twenty yards away, I wavered. At fifty I stopped, dropped my pack, and went back for the locket. I feel naked without it, that's all, and it doesn't weigh *that* much. I'll be sensible on everything else, but not this one. I just can't walk away from this much of me.

I felt better after that, almost like a backpacker on a self-designed solo trip, traveling light for the challenge of the journey, and the night passed well and quickly. Walking through the long hours of dusk let my eyes adjust and a sliver of a moon made up the difference. Night vision is close in, but once you settle in to it and let your other senses pick up the slack, you can really see almost as well as in the daylight.

The sun is beginning its long climb up the sky now. I stopped walking as soon as it rose and made a shelter from a piece of cotton sheeting. Sunburn I do not need. Sleep I do, but I plan to get it in the hottest part of the day.

As near as I can tell, I probably covered 25 miles through the night. Paul's maps are disturbingly vague, nothing at all like the detailed topo maps we use back home, so I can't be certain of my exact location. Judging by my pace, though, which isn't up to par but not dragging yet either, I'm pretty sure I've put at least twenty-five behind me. Long forced hikes are the norm for my team. We've just never been dumb enough or unprepared enough to do one without adequate food and water.

Even so, I'm in better shape than I'd expected to be. Went on adrenaline the first half of the night and stubbornness the last, so I'm tired, but none of me is any the worse for wear yet. No blisters, but I didn't expect any because my feet aren't swelling and my boots are well broken in. No scrapes or bruises either, since I was careful not to trip or fall. That actually is a really big deal. As long as you can stay unbloodied your chances are better than even. Fall and get banged up and they drop to fifty-fifty or worse.

People never think about little stuff like that when they're talking wilderness survival. It's more fun to focus on the window dressings—starting a fire without matches, building ingenious little traps for mammals and fish. Problem is, the average lost person doesn't last long enough to get that damn creative, much less curious enough to window shop. They trip and fall and get busted up and then their chances drop out the bottom. So I paid attention to the basics last night. Keenly. Don't want to be done in by missing one of them.

I also didn't ever get very thirsty. On purpose. Even in the mountains, by the time you feel thirst, you're already five percent dehydrated. At about ten, you start to lose it mentally, and by fifteen you're dead or verging on it. So I'm doing my deadlevel best to stay below that five figure. Sipping hot, foul-tasting iodined water every few minutes. Keeping my mouth closed to conserve my spit, breathing through my nose the way I do when I ski. Wearing my long-sleeved cotton shirt and full skirt so they'll catch my sweat, allowing the wind to wick it away from my skin and cool me some. Urinating onto my cotton bandanna and rubbing it over my neck and throat and wrists for the same reason—nasty, but it works. I never laid eyes on a desert survival manual, never wanted to either, truth tell, so all of this is strictly common sense, but since that's the only thing I have in my corner out here I'm going with it.

Common sense and attitude. Two days ago I would've described last night as unbearably hot and miserable. The temperature stayed above 105, so that wouldn't have been far off the mark. But somewhere along the way from camp to here, I decided I couldn't afford that kind of accuracy anymore and started chanting inside my head, "It's cooler than it could be. And very easy to bear. Keep your nose over your toes, Nowata."

This helped. Calculated lies always do. I refuse to consider the possibility of failure. Everything's gone too well so far. That has to be a good sign. All I have to do is cover the same amount of ground tonight to get within striking distance of that water. I may not be prepared for this place, but I've got enough of the basics to see me through if I'm careful: common sense and attitude in abundance.

And wits enough to live by. The wits come in when the rest of it leaves off. Paul's not here, but a few of the things he told me about the desert are slipping back in—like how to deal with black flies. Three months ago I shuddered on reading his descriptions of them in a letter. "Bush flies come in swarms," he wrote, and I vaguely imagined a few heavy-bodied black bugs buzzing past his head in tiny tornado formation like the gnats do over the long grass in southern Wyoming. When I'd been here a couple weeks and none had shown up, I teased Paul about desert fever.

"Fried your brain a bit, did it? Had you conjuring up bug storms and such?"

He grinned and assured me that one day soon we'd run into the flies and I'd better save my worries about fried brains for myself on the day we did. Paul's from Louisiana. He exaggerates. So I took his warning with a fist-size grain of rock salt.

Until last night.

Shortly before dusk a thick cloud settled around me, its dimensions so dense I couldn't see my arms or legs and sure as hell couldn't make out whether they were flying tornado formation or not. Bush flies don't bite, they just crawl, but crawling is enough. I'd barely get them brushed off one side of my face before they were back, hundreds of tiny feet combing every inch of skin, clambering down into my ears and over my neck and into the corners of my mouth. Thirty seconds of that and I was half-crazed, digging frantically through my pack, searching for elastic bands and safety pins. Paul's letter recounted how he'd dangled pins from braided hair to keep them off his face, and for two whole days back home in Moose I'd smiled at the image of his long curly hair yanked tight into forty braids. Last night it was not remotely funny.

Verging on stark raving mad, I walked and braided for two hours straight and ended up with about a third of my hair functioning as fly deterrents. I probably look like a half-wit now with these heavy brown ropes swinging in front of my face, but it works—which means my wits are still intact and on my side of the equation, and that is important out here.

Everything is important out here, it seems.

So many tiny details for surviving never crossed my mind before because they were just too fundamental. Now I'm noticing everything, analyzing and explaining what I do, how I do it, why and when—attaching myself to the world by what I know about how it's supposed to function. Laying it out to the bare bones. Talking it through to remember. One hair shy of senility.

Fine. If that's what it takes to make it out of here in one piece, then that's exactly what I'll do. I need practice for old age anyhow. I don't think senility comes natural to most folks.

So. Common sense and attitude and wits. Three keys to survival. What's next?

More attitude. All those rules I used to preach to visitors around campfires most of them would never venture far enough away from to actually get lost. Stop, think, observe, and plan. Avoid the desire for comfort. Avoid a passive outlook. Think positive. Keep busy. Maximize your resources and minimize everything else. Improvise. Right.

I used to be good at this. Improvisation used to be my middle name. But that was in the Rockies—where I knew the wind and the weather and the trees and the way the ice left the glacier and exactly what that all meant. Not here. I can improvise ten ways to Sunday in this blessed place, but it won't make water flow from a rock, and flowing water is the one thing I could use the very most. So much for that one. So what else is there?

Proper gear.

Ah ha! Finally. The one thing I've got covered like a duck on a June bug.

———

My pack and its contents are laid out neatly on the ground, and the sight alone is reassuring. Gear dweebs, they used to call my crew in the Park Service, and it's a fair assessment. People who work SAR learn to keep close track of their equipment, even in times like these when there isn't much to keep track of. *Especially* in times like these. If you ignore your gear, one day you'll turn around to find it ignoring you.

It could be as innocent as a rip in the seam of your pack you didn't notice when you set out on the trail, so you lose your first-aid kit and compass. Or maybe you didn't tighten the lid on a canteen, so you empty half a quart of cherry-flavored ERG inside your pack and attract every yellow jacket in the county on the way home. Then again, it could be something a good deal more ominous. One of your slings was frayed, so you take a nosedive off a rock wall. Or the snap came loose on your shake 'n bake—that tiny silver lifesaving shelter we carry on our belts when we fight wildfires—only you didn't realize it was gone till now, when the fire's running hard your direction, so you get barbecued on the hoof. Innocent or not, I don't like curves in the field. So, nary an apology or excuse, whenever my crew had any downtime, on searches or fire camps or simply out back of the ranger station, we could always be found sorting and cleaning and checking our gear.

There isn't much to do along those lines now. I brought only the barest essentials. Two changes of clothes—skirt, slacks, a bra, another T-shirt, and one more cotton long-sleeved shirt. My shorts are comfortable, but the skirt's the best garment of all out here. Very versatile, just like Paul said it would be—a natural air-conditioning unit, thorn deflector, tent, and pallet all in one—so I'll wear it and switch off to shorts in the daytime when I stop to sleep. Bras and undies are dispensable. I only have two pairs of each. But six pairs of socks. Socks are more important than anything else in the outdoors. It's my first rule—if your feet aren't happy, the rest of you's mad—so I brought every pair I have. Everything else is pretty basic.

An old flannel shirt of Paul's I've carried everywhere I've gone for the last few months, a stripped-down first-aid kit, flashlight and two extra batteries, tiny compass and thermometer, two plastic garbage bags, one piece of rope, a dozen safety pins, toothbrush, the homemade bird net and some extra twine, one tube of sunscreen, big packet of matches, signal mirror and flare, two candles, one map, three bottles of iodine water purification tablets, Swiss Army knife, that piece of cotton sheeting, my pen and journal, locket, binoculars, tin bowl, and the canteens. Three empties, one full, and the one I'm drinking from, which means my water weight is down to five pounds.

One gallon to cover twenty-six miles. I don't like those numbers. In these conditions, they add up to death by dehydration somewhere about halfway between here and the closest spring.

But I will not panic. I will lay this thing out straight and run it just like a search, only backward with no support. Which means the numbers have to stand aside.

Take another gulp of water, ignore the taste, focus on the task at hand. Iodine is hard to ignore. It punches nausea into overdrive.

—————

It's time to reload the pack, each item stowed in exactly the same spot as when I started. That way I can find things even in the dark. Once it's closed, I'll lay my bandanna on top and use it as a pillow. Packs always double as pillows in the field.

So there. I may not control the big picture but I have the small one by the nose on the front of its scrawny little noggin right now. I *refuse* to die out here. Simply refuse to.

———

The sun's at my ten o'clock—broad daylight for everybody else in the southern hemisphere but midnight for me. I'm still not sleepy, but I know I need to start winding down. That, at least, is easy enough to do.

Anybody who works SAR has to be able to detach from everything and sleep on demand no matter what's going on, mainly because we know there's no telling when we might have a chance to be horizontal again. All I have to do is lie on my left side, put my head on my pack and my mind on off, cover my face with my hat, and I'm gone. Pony sleeps on her back with one hand over her eyes. Jed sits up against a stump or tree trunk. Laney lies flat on her stomach no matter what the terrain. Every last one of us is a master of the five-minute nap.

Today, though, I believe I'll sit a while longer. Partly because I'm not tired yet and partly to convince that white dingo that I'm not the easy pickings she clearly thinks I am.

Damn dog stole my dinner while I was tying my shoelaces last night. Slipped into the cook tent

behind me and snatched it right out of my bowl—
one measly little bite of greasy bird, but it was all I
had, so I came unglued for a minute or two and
cussed like a sailor just dropped off the boat in a
town with no women. Too late. She didn't even
have the decency to disappear to swallow it. Stood
there in full view and licked her chops when she
was done, no less.

I cannot believe she followed me all this way. I
thought I saw her in the moonlight a couple times
but figured I was hallucinating and shook my head
and kept on walking. At daylight she ended all that
by pacing alongside me about thirty feet to the
west. Must've decided, "Hey, I'll just stick with this
sucker—she makes home-cooked meals."

"News flash, girlfriend," I tell her. "You stick
around me very long, you'll be the main dish at my
next dinner. I need protein and I ain't picky right
now. Just you wait till I get to that waterhole."

She stares at me, curious and defiant, ears
perked. I am not afraid.

But then, neither is she.

Nodding to her, I crawl into the patch of shade
I've concocted for myself, reach for my hat, and get
ready for bed. Twenty-six miles to cover tonight.
Ten hours to sit tight till I can start covering it.

I'm better off sleeping than thinking in this
meantime.

DAY 5

Dawn again. I didn't make the twenty-six miles. I didn't even make twenty. Or fifteen.

Around midnight I stumbled and fell flat on my face. Couple hours later, stumbled again and broke one of my lower left ribs, same one that got cracked when I was ten, I think. Self-assess is tough, they didn't teach us those skills in EMT training, but it's definitely broken. Shit.

Pain severe. Worse than I remember. Hard to breathe through it. Slowed me down. Way down. Ripped a section off the cotton sheet and wrapped it around my middle to stabilize the rib, but it didn't help with the pain. Or the fury.

God *damn* it! I *know* how to fall so I don't get hurt. It's the first thing you learn in Brazilian jiu-jitsu—which I have been doing for nine years. I have a brown belt, am getting close to the black, which means I know about 600 different ways to take down and disable an unarmed opponent in under fifteen seconds. *So I know how to fall*. But look at me now!

Sniveling in my patch of shade. Busted rib.

Three quarts of water left. So thirsty I could cry. Urine output down and bright orange. Trouble concentrating. Not good signs. At least twenty miles to go. White dingo watching my every move.

Must sleep but cannot seem to make the disconnect. Nightmares of childhood, long forgotten and lived down, I thought, rage hot again, and I doze only to wake minutes later in a cold, clammy sweat begging Dix and Mama to forgive me, throat so hoarse I can barely breathe. My feet and hands are swelling, from dehydration maybe. My eyes feel sunburned. My neck aches as bad as my ribs. A big part of me wants to just lie down and sleep till this is over. The rest knows I cannot.

I pray that Paul will make it back to camp, find my note, and then come find me.

DAY 6

Dawn. Again. One quart of water left. Still nauseated, so it wasn't the iodine.

I did the inhuman last night. Walked almost 18 miles, hurt every step. Couldn't have done it if it weren't for that snake.

Eastern brown. One of the deadliest on the planet. Takes out more Australians than any other poisonous snake. Don't know much about the desert, but I do know that.

Woke yesterday, late afternoon, hot, hurting, and stiff. Dragged myself onto my knees and reached for my water. Froze. Fingers inches from his nose. He was draped over the canteen, neck raised, heavy head poised to strike. Nausea vanished. Every hair on my body stood straight up. Forgot I even had ribs, much less a broken one.

All I could think was, I'm way inside his striking range. *Way*. If he wants to hit me, I'm done for.

Didn't dare move. Not that I could've. Tried to remember what Paul told me a month ago. "He doesn't want you, Tal, you're too big for dinner and he knows it by your heartbeat. He'd rather wait for meal-size prey, hon, so if you just don't startle him, he'll leave you alone."

It was a bit too late for that not-startling business. My knuckles were in his goddamn face.

"Just give him a chance to disengage and he'll take it every time," Paul's voice intoned, steady, knowledgeable, quiet, and I remembered how carefully he eased that last brown snake onto a shovel and carried him out of the supply tent into the desert.

My arm cramped, I wanted to draw it back but couldn't. The brown was hyper-alert, tension crackled between us. If I moved a hair, he might strike out of sheer instinct. If I stayed dead still, he might do the same thing. Everything was up to him. Nothing to me.

I waited. Locked inside a lethal game of wait and see with a creature that had no earthly reason to want me to win it. Heartbeats pounding in my throat, temples, the back of my head. Thighs and knees, burning. Feet and hands, numb as posts, too numb to even tingle anymore. Brain processing the facts. The brown's fast and ferocious when cornered, often inflicting several bites. Carries neurotoxins in his head. Second most toxic land snake venom in the world. Rapid acting, too. Even with antivenom, I'd be in trouble. Without it, I'd be dead. No two ways around it. No one way either. The only way to get out of this thing alive was not to have his fangs connect with my hide. Period.

Out of desperation I tried to get humble: relax every single muscle and look as submissive as possible—with one arm stuck bizarrely out in the air, yes, but no longer appearing to be reaching for anything in the snake's vicinity—*especially* him, I hoped. I slowed my pulse the way we do it when we're running the physical fitness leg for firefighter qualifications every spring: took a shallow breath and held it thirty seconds, then breathed slow and deep. Softened my whole body, skin to center.

The snake didn't follow suit. He stayed arched in a wide S-curve, like a heavy strand of high tensile wire, set on kill.

I waited.

When his head finally dropped a hair, I went on instinct. Swung my hand up and out and back toward my body. He struck, swift and sure, toward my moving arm. Missed it by a slim inch, but I felt his upper body pass because the air between us emptied. I froze again. White-hot pains tore at my ribs.

We stared each other down, him swinging forward, nose almost touching my knees, tongue flicking steadily, then drawing back. Again and again.

There's no accounting for where your mind goes when your spine senses death. Mine careened wildly for a few seconds and then went to a debriefing from a search six years ago. We were propped up inside the maintenance shed, half of us on upturned crates, the rest on backpacks or the floor, Jed standing in front of the topo map and walking us through the last few days' events. The lost hiker had long since boarded a plane for home, but his rescuers were going over his trail one more time because the debrief is one of the most important tools we have. In debrief we study the victim's route and motivations, plans and detours, successes and mistakes. We also critique our own performance, assess our strengths and weaknesses, and figure out how to function better as a team. This one was a no-brainer. The guy got mad at his girlfriend, walked off, and left her. She had the compass and the map and the good sense to head back to the car immediately. He didn't.

Windy Point was coming apart as a crew that season. We'd had several big failures in a row. The latest one was the boyfriend. We put our resources in the wrong quad, nowhere near him. So nobody was happy at the end of the gig, but that went double for the ranger who'd overruled me early in the search. I'd guessed from the boyfriend's footprints that he was crossing a canyon headed away from their planned route. Our search boss, a newbie from the Smokies named Tony Taylor, decided I was wrong and sent us all the other direction. We stayed out three days and three nights. The boyfriend went right where I thought he went. We didn't find him. He stumbled out onto a side road the fourth morning, cold and hungry and blaming the whole thing on his girlfriend. The debrief was tense because Tony Taylor was embarrassed and called me on the carpet to explain what signs I had used to make my initial recommendation.

As the snake swayed and settled in front of me, I watched his body leave sinuous tracks beneath him. That boyfriend did the same thing. He kept pausing on the trail and turning slightly toward the valley to the west. It was the long way out, the wrong way, but he kept looking at it and thinking about it and his feet told the tale. So I read that and radioed into base and, after a heated discussion about the uselessness of trackers, Ranger Taylor sent me and everybody else east. The boyfriend covered a lot of miles in those three days. The snake didn't look as if he ever planned to move that far again. His heavy body dug deep furrows in the sand, but none away from me. I wished I was back in the park being called on the carpet for an educated guess. I hurt all over.

Suddenly, a long time later, how long I don't know but it felt like aeons, the brown looked for a way out and as soon as he took it, I broke camp and started walking, shaking like an aspen leaf in a straight-line wind. Didn't wait for sunset, just set out.

It wasn't a wise move. It's a waste of fluids to walk while the sun's up. I know that. Couldn't help myself. Had to walk. Walked all night long. And I didn't stumble once. "Adrenaline enhances performance," Jed always says.

I'm in bad shape now—hands and feet swollen, legs cramping, tongue thick, beyond thirsty—but last night I didn't stumble a single time. That has to be a good sign.

I see the line of trees ahead where the water should be. The white sees it too, looks that way, then back at me. Too far to reach now. Two miles at least on one quart, full sun. Can't do it. Must sleep the day through. Pray I wake able to get there tonight. And no snakes. I can do without the snake's help this time.

I was born in Oklahoma, for crying out loud, and batted back and forth between McAlester and Shawnee and a tin hut on the Yankton Reservation for the first ten years of my life, and I managed *that*, didn't I?

So yes, I *will* do this thing.

Nose over your toes, Nowata. Let's get this gig into debrief.

DAY 7

Dawn. My last.

There is no water here. Not a drop. Went underground. Long time ago. Paul's info outdated.

Or just plain wrong.

At least nobody can say I didn't put up a good fight. Fifty-one miles at plus-100 degrees on ten quarts and sheer willpower. Insane. Impossible, but I made it. Not in good shape, but I am here. Dug a trench two feet deep with just my hands as tools. Dry as a bone even there. Gave out. Crawled over to this tree and curled up. The white sits alert nearby. She's just about to have dinner served up without even a fight.

I dream of icy rain and shiver from fever. Legs look like toothpicks, knobs for knees. Hands and fingers swollen double, red and puffy. Everything hurts. Nothing to cool myself with. I've gone LCD. Every scrap of me reduced to its lowest common denominator.

Dry tears. Swab out my mouth with the bandanna and rub it on my throat and face and wrists.

Let the wind blow against the damp places. Do it again. Slow. Again. Must cool off.

I think it helped. I think I'm not so hot. I miss you, Paulson O'Malley. If only you were here. Or Pony. Jed, Laney, anybody else on my team, Dix— little brother Dix would do if he knew I was here which he doesn't since we haven't spoken in two years, but Dix does like deserts so if he was here he'd be some real help. Wish someone would show up. Someone with some skills and equipment. Somebody, anybody. Anybody breathing.

Anybody besides a white ghost dog that reminds me of my father's mother this morning and sends a chill up my neck. Grandmother Nowata cooked a dog once. An ugly yellow mutt with a bad tendency to bite kids. Bit Dix one day so she shot it and cooked it and fed it to the other dogs. I'd forgot all about that, but the albino remembers. She looks in my eyes and remembers the whole. She remembers Mama and Dix and what I can't forget. She knows Paul and Josie and everything else. She knows me and what is happening right now. She waits, unafraid.

I am so scared I can't breathe. I try to get up and run but can't, so I huddle and whimper and all that's best about me turns loose inside.

The struggle's on, I feel it. I'm starting to unhinge. Mind and body one piece at a time.

It's always the unhinging that kills you, Nowata, not the desert, not the heat, not even the lack of water. Lose your head, lose your life, you know the drill. Stay put, stay calm.

Sleep.

No, *think*. Think till you can't. Words, your last link to existence.

And the dingo. I look around for the white ghost dog. Just seeing her helps. I remember to breathe without thinking about it. She is so alive some of it has to rub off.

She ignores me, face buried in the wallaby she just killed.

No water for six days—she's still able to run down a meal. Gets enough liquid from it to not need drinking water a while more. Eats anything— wallaby, rabbit, songbird—with no moral qualms supping at her innards in return. She is at peace with this land in a way I can never be.

And yet, perhaps that's not quite so. I hear Grandmother Haney's story about the albino grizzly who helped make the world and the parents who never leave, but stand silently by while you choose the path you must walk for yourself. Like a faint tuneless whistle it grows still in my mind and I remember the connections I've so long denied. She told me that story when I was sixteen and starting to believe I could live down my roots. I stood in her tarpapered shack and watched her eating a ketchup sandwich and listened to her talking, toothless and old and distant, and thinking how glad I was not to live on the rez anymore and how lucky I was to be able to get inside my birthday present—a shiny new Ford Mustang—and drive wherever I liked. Grandmother Haney wouldn't take us in after Mama died. She let the state have us. I don't even know why I went back to see her that day. To appease Dix, I suppose. Or maybe to show off my new car. Bess Haney sat in her broken-down chair eating that ketchup sandwich and telling me that story. I hated it till today. Hated its message of eternal life and dead parents and animals becoming guardian angels.

Today I hear it with a different heart. The dingo and I are not enemies. We are kin.

For my flesh will soon become albino flesh. Muscle, tendon, bone, skin, fur. I'll be the glint in her eye when she spies her prey, the sudden twist backward when she lunges sideways to catch and break its neck. I'll run swift with her across these reddened plains, recycled as new cells on the pads of her feet to claim a piece of this harsh dry land as my own. It will be a clean death, an honest one, tied closer to the planet than it ever could be at home—the best you can hope for back there is to fill up another bunk at the morgue. Bagged and toe-tagged. Iced and diced. Body bag to slim steel casket in the States.

Carrion on sand for the white here.

One thing's plain: she won't get much liquid out of me. I'm drying up by the second.

———

It is time to let go, but I can't. Life is holding onto me strong, like a snapping turtle to a stick. They say a turtle won't let go till it thunders or you break its neck. One bit me once and didn't turn loose till Dix pried its jaws open with a stick. So we always knew a farm kid with a stick is the equivalent to one good clap of thunder. Or a broken neck.

At least I did one thing right. Broke my family's circle of violence in my generation, stopped it all with me. Spent the last eight years saving lives, even studied jiujitsu so I could effectively disable an opponent without having to hurt him too bad. Vowed nonviolence and lived it, all except that one last thing with Dix anyway and that was sheer instinct, I think. I just snapped.

I never have figured that out. Buried it like I did every other hurt and refused to even think of it again. Until now.

Mama was right. We have to end the cycle. If I could just get out of here, I'd look Dix up and apologize and see if we could start over. I should never have let him leave that day. I should have called him back and straightened it out. Just like I should've turned my red Mustang around and gone back inside Bess Haney's shack and put my arms around her neck and hugged her. Instead I stayed up on my high horse and spent my energy straightening everybody else out.

Like Pony? Lovely, crazy, scrappy, *tall* Sutton. How many times have I dragged her out of the Rancher or the Wort or the Million Dollar Cowboy Bar to keep her from decking a cowboy who'd had just enough to drink that he couldn't see trouble looming over his head even when it stood six-foot-one and was staring him straight in the eye?

"If it weren't for me, Knothead, you'd spend *every* Friday night in the Teton County Jail!" I always tell her, relying on moral certitude and seniority to get my reckless friend into a vehicle and headed out of town before she breaks body parts on some unwitting man. She always snaps back, "You're too damn short to play God, Nowata." Then, the very next day, without fail, she slaps a Post-it on my desk with a scrawled message: "Tal. Sorry. Thanks. Again. P."

I have a whole stack of those notes.

Paul teases me about being Pony's personal savior, Jed calls me the park's own portable bomb squad, and though I've never let on, I always liked that feeling—of being the one that doesn't lose it, *ever*, the one people can count on to defuse tensions, *always*, the one that values nonviolence enough to live it, *no matter what*, the one that grew out of her childhood urges to brain the ice cream truck man with a two-by-four and put all that energy into saving people's lives. It used to make sense, that story. Now it feels hollow. Empty. The one time it really counted, with the one person who is closest to me of anyone—joined by blood, no less—I lost it.

Fingers straying to the little neck pouch of tobacco Dix gave me the last time I saw him, I see my brother's diffident grin and his bowlegs easing his gangly body into a saddle with no more effort than the average man uses to land in a recliner. Dix goes quiet inside when he's on a horse or a bull; you can't tell where the animal stops and the man begins anymore. Little brother Dixon. He has a good heart. Probably hit that girlfriend of his on instinct. Didn't need me to knock the living day-lights out of him for it. Didn't need me to make him learn nonviolence. He would've gotten there on his own soon enough. Quicker, I expect, without my interference. Hypocritical as all get out.

He did get me for it, though. Never said a word, never raised a finger to hit back, just stood up and walked out the door and left his girlfriend sitting there at my kitchen table. I had to drive her home to Minot, 1,200 miles round-trip, and by the time I dropped her off I'd come close to slapping her a few times myself, but I couldn't admit that then. I was too busy being a one-woman antiviolence squad, the big sister who'd for damn sure not let her little brother turn into her father without a fight. I didn't reckon at all with the fact that Dix could do that on his own. He has a good enough heart to figure that out without my help. I was out of line. I wish I could tell him that.

———

My locket burns the skin between my breasts. Above it my small tobacco pouch hangs loosely, rawhide strips no longer coloring my neck to match and worn almost clear through in places. The tobacco is from Sun Dance two years ago. Dix always brought me an offering. It was his way of making up for my irreligion, his way of keeping me safe in a crazy world. I was so busy being his savior that, until now, I never understood he was mine. Saving him was a huge part of how I stayed upright and sane all these years. When you save somebody else, you have to function. Well. But it's a lie.

I must hurry for there they go and I am their leader. That was me before here. Saving everybody who crossed my path whether they needed it or not. But there are blinders to this business of saving lives. I got so used to cheating death for everybody else, I never realized how arrogant it all was. Never knew how undone I could come without all my props—and how fast. Or how much I needed all of those people to need me.

Take Pony. I can see her draping one long leg over the edge of my desk, hands slapping yet another of Headquarters' senseless orders on her thigh, eyes flaming, every cell ready to pick a fight with the Chief Ranger for this latest bureaucratic insult. She storms into my office several times a month, mad and spoiling for a fight with somebody from the top, but always leaves laughing, and the Chief never knows how close he just came to the center of the tornado. Pony either. I was their defuser—small, quiet, and effective, a natural leader. They needed me to keep the place humming. But now I'm gone for good and I understand it different from before.

With me not around the crew will function just fine. Dix will figure out how to get mad at the ditzy women he dates without slugging them. Pony'll handle the idiocies of bureaucracy with finesse. She'll probably toss HQ's new edicts into the trash can and follow them fast with a lit match. I do wish I could see that one for myself though. It would be worth the price of admission. Jed promised to write down "the good ones on our Sutton girl" so he could tell me about them when I got home, only now I won't be back to hear them.

Home. The thought is a dull ache. Jed and Pony and the rest of the crew, the Grand and her sisters watching over us all, the Snake River winding its way down the valley, elk and moose strolling through alpine meadows during the only two seasons we get—winter and July 4th—and sometimes it snows that day too. How I love Wyoming.

But it is not home. Not anymore.

Home is not a place to me now. It's where Paul is—no, where *we* are. The exact where of it never mattered. In cities, tents, campgrounds and backyards, rugged mountains, the north woods, even this godforsaken desert: I never cared. Wherever we have been together over the last four years, I have always known I was home. And now, suddenly, I am not.

Where could you possibly be, Paul O'Malley? If I'd known you were leaving for more than four days, I'd have done it different. Hugged you good-bye. Said something profound. Stared after your truck. *No*. Gone with you. If I'd known then what I know now, I'd have gone with you for sure.

Or at least sent along another batch of letters for home. Jed and Pony, they'll be waiting to hear from me. If I'd known I was coming here to die, I'd have said good-bye better and written every single day.

Ifs. I hate ifs. There is no fixing anything once

it's over or before it arrives, and the word "if" just fools us into thinking there is. If I could somehow miraculously survive this place, I'd strike the word "if" from my vocabulary for good.

So this is it. I am ending with a lot undone, but life itself will continue. There should be something reassuring about that, but I'm not reassured. Not calmed. Not soothed. Ninety-five/five. Brains and circumstance. Like hell.

I'm fed up with my own philosophical bullshit.

And very, very tired.

I will mark this day in my journal just for the principle of the thing. Sign my name to it for spite, like a world leader affixing a signature to a peace treaty she never intends to keep. I don't want to die. I'm not ready to die. Why pretend I am?

Tally Nowata, Day 7

———

So tired I can hardly breathe.

But my mind will not detach and let me go to sleep. Even that basic skill's gone. I should already be dead by now. Why am I hanging on?

No answers. It's a question no human should ever ask anyway. I watch the white eat and a small thought begins to grow large in my mind.

DAY 8

I took the wallaby meat away from her last night. Not all of it, just the heart and liver and intestines. She growled and postured but let me crawl up and steal them and retreat to my tree. Then she settled down to eat while I sucked on the heart and swabbed the intestines on my face and neck. I was trying to get cool enough to fall asleep. Didn't want to die awake.

Turns out I didn't die at all, but nobody could've been more surprised than I was to open my eyes and see the world still here and me still in it this morning.

The white woke me with a howl—the first time I ever heard her make any sound other than a low growl—so I thought surely I must be dreaming or dead. Everything was blurry, she was trotting out into the desert, looking at something, then trotting back, close, to stare at me. Over and over, she came and went. I finally hauled myself up to follow her. It took four tries just to get on my feet and by the time I did, blood was running down my arms from hanging onto the tree trunk so tight. Bleeding is a good sign; you can't do it unless you're breathing. Reassured, I staggered along after the white ghost dog.

Seconds later I saw the Land Rover, tipped up on its left side, with Paul still trapped in his seat belt, hanging there limp, suspended behind the steering wheel, and something drop-kicked my adrenal system into high gear. I thought maybe I could save him, that it wasn't too late, so I charged forward, dizzy and disoriented but half-crazed to reach his truck. A few yards out, I hit the smell and stopped stone cold.

Human death. There's no scent on earth like that one, and you never get used to it. Never. I ducked on reflex, kept walking. One foot in front of the other. No thought.

When we reached the truck, the white circled warily as I dropped my pack and stumbled the last few feet in, holding my urine- and sweat-soaked bandanna over my nose. The driver's window next to Paul's head was broken, and thick sheared glass edged the frame. His body hung motionless from the seat belt. Through the windshield I could see his arms mottled dark, purpling under sallow grayish skin.

Avoiding his face, I stared at his shirt. I gave it to him for Christmas last year.

Plain white T-shirt with an Onion slogan on it:

End Racism.
Kill Everyone.

I got one just like it from him, not because we wanted to match or anything but because Jackson is a pretty small town to shop in and we both have the same sick sense of humor. Now dark muddy blood covers the front of Paul's. It will never come white again. Never. That's all I could think.

That and "This truck is headed for Alice Springs. So he never even made it that far."

———

The white paced the perimeter like a rookie cop at a crime scene until I could get hold of myself. Half crawling, I finally made it to the back of the Land Rover to look inside.

One rear door was flung open. Sand and dust had formed a heavy coating over the interior, but a few of Paul's things were strewn about—his canteens, two small portable water tanks, a pile of bedding and clothes. I grabbed the closest canteen. Water. Blessed water. Wanted to guzzle it down but knew better, so didn't.

The scorching heat of midafternoon felt almost comforting. Still crouching at the back door, I stared inside again. Details I missed moments before started to coalesce. Wireless radio, gone from its metal frame ahead of the wheel well. Steel-sided equipment chest, pried loose from its mountings on the floor. The rifle Paul always kept strapped between the two front seats, missing.

Somebody else made it here first. Took Paul's things and left him to die.

Who the fuck would steal from a dead man? Three sets of footprints crisscross the area, no attempts at concealment. Two adults, probably men, very large feet wearing lug-soled boots. And one child. Barefoot. Shit. And who the double fuck would ever let a child steal from a dead man?

Or run barefoot in a spinifex desert?

Bastards.

I closed the canteen and headed back around the vehicle and stood staring at the windshield, half blind with grief and rage and helpless to fix any of this.

Paul. Goddamnit. Why couldn't you be late for a better reason?

Then I saw the windshield, really *saw* it—and the small hole punched through right in front of the driver's seat.

No more avoiding Paul's face. Had to know the extent of this, so I wrapped my hands inside my sleeve cuffs to shield them from the scalding metal and pulled myself onto the driver's door. Paul's body was slumped forward against the belt. I've seen this twice before in the field. Two strangers killed by bullets. Bullets intended strictly for killing humans. Hollow points that explode on impact. A small hole matching the one in the windshield entered Paul's forehead just above his right eye and opened his skull on the way out. A second one through his right temple.

There is nothing left behind his ears anymore, just a mass of dark dry blood and the decaying matter that used to be his brain. Red curls matted and still. This terrifying smell is nothing like the man I know and love. This lifeless thing cannot be him. Just cannot be. There must be some mistake.

But even as my mind denies it, my heart knows the truth.

Someone murdered Paul. Shot him. *Then* took his radio and rifle and drove away.

DAY 9

Late last night, long after the moon began inching its way up the star-pocked sky, I stretched my cramped legs and stood quiet at first, then began screaming into the darkness. No words, only guttural noises, like an animal dying. I could hear it, but couldn't control it. Images of Paul's bloated body mingled with my mother's on our kitchen floor that last time, bloody and warm but still, me pulling on her arms and begging her please, please to get up. The awful silence of then and now brought rough waves of nausea. I heaved until I couldn't stand up, felt the truck that entombed my lover's body against my back, and jerked away, crawling sick and half-crazed toward nothing, just wanting it all to end. Suddenly everything stopped.

A scuffling, whimpering sound was coming from the Land Rover. The white alerted too, leaping to her feet in one seamless movement and standing with her ears and eyes trained on the vehicle. I scrambled toward my pack and fumbled around for the flashlight, then dragged myself to the back door. The whimpering continued, and my light beam followed the sound to a clump of blankets and bedrolls behind the front passenger seat. Easing inside, I edged forward, holding the light like a club, half expecting a rabid mammal to come charging out at any moment. None did. The whimpering subsided to sniffles.

Lifting one of the blankets, I pulled it away—and promptly fell backward, screaming when my sore rib slammed against the wheel well. The flashlight crashed onto the floor and went out.

Scrabbling furiously, I finally came up with it and switched it back on in the direction of the sniffles. Curled up inside the pile of bedding was a small child with flaming red hair. Tangled like her father's. Josie. Alive. Barely, but alive.

Shit.

I swallowed the word, but not before it was out. The shit. Can't swear around children.

"People who cuss are scared shitless and it shows, Taliesin, so you keep a clean tongue in your head around the little ones"—it was one of my mother's two moral rules. Mine too, I guess, which is a big part of the reason why I don't like anybody under the age of puberty.

The rest of it is that I just don't understand them. They are strange little creatures. Confusing. They make me nervous. I'm never quite sure what you're supposed to do with them. The way I look at it, parenting ought to be left to the folks who are willing to dive headlong into the short end of the pond no matter how skanky the water. People like me are better suited to carry the float and administer CPR when they hit bottom and need pulling out.

—

Despite the warm wind, I'm freezing. Shaking uncontrollably. Operating on willpower alone. The smell is acrid, strong enough to take me to my knees. I see the Land Rover and think there should be some familiar scent of Paul about it, but there isn't. This smell has nothing to do with anybody I know. Knew. My mouth starts to form another scream. I press it closed with both hands. Sheer raw terror rises like bile. I can't start screaming now. I would never stop. Josie needs me. I have to save this kid. I glance at her tousled hair and the bile turns to vomit and I wind up on my knees again.

Sometime later I drag myself to where I can lean back against the truck and stare into the desert at the white. She is watching me, still unafraid. I am grateful for her company. I cannot do this alone.

Still out cold, Josie whimpers from her pallet. She didn't wake all night, not even when I hauled her out of the truck and forced water down her a few sips at a time. I hung a sheet between her and the wind, kept it damp, and swabbed her whole body with wet cloths every fifteen minutes. It took a lot of water, but it did pull her fever out of the critical range. She was at 105.2 when I found her—not in heat stroke, but in bad shape, definitely on her way out of here. It's 103.4 now, so I believe she will pull through, but how well, I've no idea.

The truck rolled more than one time, judging by its roof and the tracks. I can't believe she survived that, let alone the men who killed her father, but maybe they figured she was dead and not worth a bullet. Clearly they didn't know Josie or they'd have double-checked her pulse. She's a stubborn little cuss.

"Won't quit till *after* her heart does," Paul once said, proudly, in the middle of one of her more memorable fits.

"That's a very admirable trait unless it's you she's aiming it toward," I replied, looking pointedly for an excuse to leave the house. Paul noticed and asked if I'd mind doing the grocery shopping by myself that week. I was out the door before he finished the sentence.

She moans again now. Did that all night. Restless patient, spoiled rotten even when unconscious: now *that's* saying something.

Dear God, forgive me! What am I saying? I can't do this. *Cannot do this!* I am something less than human myself right now, yet entrusted with the care of a child? A child who's just watched her father die? A child who didn't like me at all when everything in her world was going *well*? A child who—yes, might as well say it straight, was spoiled flat rotten in the real world—how in hell am I supposed to save her life?! How am I supposed to get the two of us out of this desert alive? To do that I need her cooperation and Josie doesn't cooperate with anyone on anything ever, on principle. She's as muleheaded as they come.

Oh Lord, I have to figure out how to be more maternal before she wakes up. Shi—God bless America.

And a few other places too. Starting with this one.

I force myself to watch Josie sleep, breathing my nerves back from the edge of my own terror. Paul called us his "de facto twins." He saw so many similarities in us. I thought he was just being perverse. It seems like he ought to be here. Rounding the corner of the truck with a cup of tea or something civilized like that. I can't relate him to that body hanging in the front seat. My mind thinks it is a sick joke, that it's somebody else. Somebody dressed up like Paul and any minute the real Paul will step out of the brush and say, "Hey hon, did you miss me?" And I'll retort, like I always do, "Hell no—you have to be memorable to be missed." And he'll laugh and kiss my cheek anyhow and I'll be glad he's back because when he's gone I always miss him, tough talk notwithstanding, and he knows it too.

The warm wind sucks the memories away and I'm left exhausted, drenched in this hateful odor of death. I decide to drag Josie away from the truck far enough that we don't have to smell that. It takes every ounce of strength I can muster to get her into a little gully about twenty feet toward the trees. She moans, but doesn't rouse. I rig a shelter for us and then collapse underneath it beside her. Haven't slept in twenty-four hours. I need to sleep. Here, now.

Otherwise I'm not worth a hill of beans to her or me.

One thing's clear, I do have to give her credit for lasting this long. Best guess this happened a week ago or so, and she's been conscious most of the time since. It's her barefoot tracks I see all over. She's scrounged the granola bars Paul kept stashed in the glove compartment, emptied several canteens, eaten all the cheese and jerky snacks in her back-pack—and every wrapper's neatly stowed in its front pocket, just the way her dad always did it. How she could manage all that with him hanging there and without going stark raving mad I'll never know, but the last thing she needs is to wake to another scared adult. Have to hold up my end for the species.

No cussing.

At least it's not like *that's* entirely new for me. The first thing I learned on the first search I ever worked was that the team members doing the swearing were the ones most likely to get them-selves or the rest of us hurt. Mama was righter than she ever knew. Her name burns like a brand in my heart. How hard I've tried to forget! How long I've shrunk from the memory of her last days. How deeply I buried it all, deep enough it couldn't break me in two, I'd hoped.

But now I need to think back, remember what she did with Dix and me, how she dealt with us, all those things I've tried so hard to block from my mind for seventeen years. I try it and draw a blank. Maybe when you bury a memory long enough it finally dies.

DAY 10

The night passed quickly. I set the alarm on my watch and woke every hour to swab Josie's body with wet cloths. Her temp has dropped to 102.3 now. She is going to make it. I am determined that this child will survive.

To balance my terror, I work on a plan. While she sleeps, I'll assess our situation and figure out how to get us out of here. Children see through adults quicker than anyone else, so Josie will know if I'm really confident or if I'm bluffing—which means I have to get all our ducks in a neat tidy row. Ducks. Right. We're nowhere near enough water to be making duck analogies. Camels, more like. Camels it is then. I need to get our camels hitched up and ready to move out. Have to remember that one. Josie might like that. I have to find things that will make her laugh. She might laugh at camels. Paul did.

There's something about this child that makes me forget everything normal. Somehow when she looks at me, all my reason and intelligence flies right out of my head and I feel like a numskull.

So what. It's certainly not the first time I've been a numskull and I doubt it'll be the last. I can do this, numskull or not. Plan, Tally, make a plan. A good plan is 90 percent of the battle. Assess the situation and your resources, then bend the whole to your will.

Our situation is grim any way you cut it. The Land Rover is pointed toward Alice, but only because Paul made a wide loop toward the southwest. He was being pursued at the end. I don't know why he turned back—maybe in an attempt to lose them—but by then it was too late. His tire tracks were steady up to about 200 yards from here and then they cut in deeper, speeding up, it's clear, swerving wild and frantic through the brush like I've never seen Paul O'Malley drive. The other truck came from the east and bore down quick. There were two men inside (judging by the size of their footprints, that is—eleven and a half and thirteen—either men or some really *big* women), armed (judging by what they did with that gun), dangerous (goes without saying, but I will say it anyway to keep me alert). The tracks are blown over some, not much detail in places, but I can still deduce their movements from what is left.

They didn't waste any time once the Land Rover turned over. One man stood outside the driver's door of their vehicle, staring off into the desert, while the other one walked to the front of Paul's vehicle, shot him, verified that he was dead, and then stepped back and just stood there. I looked everywhere for signs that they ransacked the Land

Rover then, but there wasn't so much as a single track close to the back of it, so I was wrong before when I thought they took the radio and rifle here. They didn't. As near as I can tell, the one guy took a shot at Paul, moved to the window, took another, stepped back, and then the second man joined him briefly in front of the truck and they both turned around and left. So when did the Rover get sacked? Earlier? But how? Surely Paul didn't know them, right? He never mentioned any friends out here. So then they're strangers. Strangers with a gun and an itch to use it.

Did Paul have some sort of run-in with them on the dirt track south of here? It's only a couple miles now. Maybe he crossed paths with these men by sheer accident? "Desert tends to draw the unsavory types, Tal," he once told me, adding, with a big grin, "That's why I fit in so well, babe—I'm an unsavory!" The feel of his smile and the sound of his slow Louisiana drawl takes my breath, and I sit here with one hand on Josie's head, feeling her daddy's wiry curls against my palm, fighting nausea and vertigo, and plain out sick to the heart. I should be able to smell the warm male scent of him, but there is nothing on the air but the lingering odor of death.

Suddenly frantic, I reach for my pack and fumble inside it for Paul's shirt and draw it to my nose, trying to drink in his smell. His real smell, the living breathing Paul who made me laugh and cry and love again.

The day he left for here, I drove home from the

airport and walked inside to find a care package on the table and his favorite shirt—and mine, the old blue flannel I stole from him regularly—hanging on the chair on my side of the bed. It still had his smell. Without thought, I let my own clothes fall to the floor, slipped inside the worn, faded cloth, crawled onto his side of the bed, and cried myself to sleep. I never washed that shirt. Never. Would've clobbered anybody who tried to. Lugged it everywhere I went, no matter what the weather. Dragged it all the way from Wyoming to here and wouldn't let him have it back. It's the one totally useless thing I brought along from camp. Useless. No need for flannel here.

But necessary. Necessary as air.

It still has his smell. I fold it close, burying my nose in its softness, drinking in what is left of the only one who ever walked through the last wall of my heart.

I can almost feel him, he's so near. And then it comes to me, in the deep, generous voice I'd willingly kill to really hear again. "It's going to be okay, Tal. It really is."

He said that all the time, all the time, and the funny thing was, no matter what was going on, I always believed him.

Even now, here, some part of me still does.

Then, without warning, the wind shifts and that hateful smell of death surrounds us again and I thrust the shirt away deep into my backpack, scrabbling furiously to keep it from being tainted by the truth. I have the pack half buried in the sand before I stop, sobbing, heaving, shocked at myself. I'm trying to keep the live smell of Paul safe from the dead smell of him. How insane is that?

Stop it, Tally! Just *stop*. You can't afford to wallow! Get your goddamn nose over your fucking toes. You have a child's life to save. And something a good deal more deadly than a little red desert to save her from too. You cannot fall apart.

Josie sleeps peacefully, unaware of my torment. I can plan later. Dragging my pack out of the sand, I lie on my side with my head on it and stare into this child's tiny face. I reach out to touch her cheek but draw back at the last second. I shouldn't risk waking her. Sleep is healing. You need to sleep, baby girl.

I lost your father. I will not lose you.

—

The nap helped. I feel more like myself now. I can think things out more clearly. Work the case like the ranger I am.

So that is probably what happened. These men were most likely up to no good and Paul happened along with Josie. Paul always did trust people too much. Maybe they feigned car trouble and flagged him down. Paul would've stopped to help. He always did. Knothead. I knew that was going to get him into trouble one day. He'd just laugh at me and say he'd rather get in temporary trouble being nice than endure the permanent trouble of being mean. Damn you, O'Malley. God*damn* you for leaving me—*us*—like this!

Stop, Nowata. There's more to survive here than a drought-scarred desert. You don't have energy to waste on a rant. Take the facts to the basics and build your case from there.

Paul is dead. Somebody shot him. Somewhere before that someone looted this Land Rover. It would've been loaded down with supplies; now it isn't. Paul's been gone more than two weeks. Even allowing for a delay in town, that leaves a week unaccounted for. Did he get waylaid and trapped with these men for more than a week? Why? Whatever for? What would they want with a geeky ecologist and a kid? There are easier ways to get a month's supply of food, a temperamental radio, a dart gun, and a rifle. How did Paul manage to get away? Are there more of the men somewhere close? Some kind of base camp for poachers or something maybe? Or only two guys on the run from the law? Maybe the law doesn't know about them yet? I don't know.

All I know for sure is that they caught up with Paul. I don't know anything else. Like why did they leave Josie alive? And why didn't they take the Land Rover? Paul bought it almost new when he arrived and then spent most of his grant money outfitting it for desert travel, so it's worth some money. With a winch, it would've been fairly simple to right it and drive it out of here. So why didn't they at least do that? Maybe they didn't have a winch. The Rover isn't going anywhere. They have time.

That's it. They have time. So they'll be back.

They won't leave this $50,000 vehicle lying here to dry rot. They'll come back for it and when they do, we need to be long gone. I have got to let this situation alone in my head and plan in earnest.

———

Resource assessment.

If I had time to be depressed, this would bring it on. I don't see any way I can get the two of us out of this desert alive. None.

Water is still the key problem. There's just not near enough. The radiator's intact, so I punched a hole in it and drained several quarts of liquid to use for Jo's cooling cloths. That at least saves our drinking water, which is the real crux of all this. The water dolly Paul took in to be filled is gone. The two twenty-gallon tanks he had mounted in the Land Rover are still intact—clipped inside their welded frames—but one's empty and the other's on the way. So we've got maybe ten gallons tops, twelve if we're lucky—and nobody in their right mind could accuse us of that right now—so ten it is. Those tanks were full when Paul left Alice, I'm sure. He is like that: anal retentive, always prepared. But it looks like Josie tried to cool off by draining some of the water onto herself and her clothes. Many times. About thirty gallons worth of times.

Every inch of fabric in the back of the vehicle has the strained, wrinkled look it gets from repeated air drying. Some have watermark stains in several places, too. When I see them I feel sick. That extra thirty gallons might've given us the edge we need on this desert. But then, the kid might not have survived the last week without it either, and anyhow, who's to say: bent as my mind was a couple days ago, I might've decided to take a long warm shower when confronted by 40 gallons of water and we'd be no better off. But I wonder why those men didn't take the tanks? Maybe it was too much trouble. They were probably nothing more than opportunists, scavenging whatever was valuable and easy and not bothering with anything that would take effort.

No, more likely, they planned on getting the tanks when they came back for the Land Rover.

I have to get us out of here ASAP. If we're not gone before they show up, everything else is moot.

DAY 11

Back in control today, not at the top of my game but close enough to it I can smell my own strength. I'm still nauseated and weak, and for every ten minutes of work I have to take a ten-minute nap, but I'm calmer now, more me, and hydrated, which feels a hell of a lot better than I ever realized it could before. That old cliché about not missing the water till the well runs dry is a hard cold *fact*. I'll never take water for granted again.

I have seven senses now. Thirst is first. The rest fall way in line, because without water, nothing else matters very much. It's a good lesson, high time I learned it, and I'm pretty happy about that. If you're coherent enough to learn something, you're still in decent shape. Learning is a higher order skill than breathing or bleeding. Learning means you're participating, and if you participate very long you just have to get a handle on things.

So I may not be in total control yet, but I'm getting there, and that is *progress* any which way you cut it.

Josie's temp is 99.4 and she's sleeping soundly at

last, so even our physical situation is nowhere near so grim as it was twenty-four hours ago. Technically, I suppose, a rational person could argue it's worse. I had a slim fighting chance to escape this desert when it was just me, next to none now. How I'll get a child out of here too, I can't imagine. But Jo's alive and I'm alive and to me—or any SAR nut worth her salt—that means our odds have come back to even numbers again. Jed used to tease me that a fifty-fifty setup was my cue to overachieve. We'll see if that's still the case.

Last night I made a sturdy waist wrap from one of the sleep pads in the truck, and the extra support is helping my rib situation. The pain's still bad but more manageable, and my scraped arms are sore but already healing. The less I whine about it, the less trouble it is—pain is like that, I think.

Having water and some food sure changes your outlook too. I found a packet of powdered chicken broth in the Land Rover and reconstituted a cup of it at midnight. It took me four hours to drink, but I believe it was the best thing I ever tasted. I also dug a hole in the sand, lined it with plastic, and poured some water in for the albino. She lapped it all up and waited patiently for more. Since we're even on the dinners—songbird for wallaby—and I got the best end of that deal, I figure the least I can do is share the water. She seems to approve. One thing's certain: we're less wary of each other today than when we started.

I don't know exactly what to think about her. I never had a dog, never really wanted one either, after seeing what my father did to the only one my mother ever had, but every now and then I look at this wild white girl and know an unfamiliar twinge of union. When she is near, I stand a bit straighter and relax somewhere deep inside. When she's gone, a part of me is always waiting for her to come back. With her here, I am not alone. Maybe if I share the water, she'll think of me as home. And what little she takes won't be enough to make the difference between life and death for Jo and me anyway. Even if it did, I might still share. That wouldn't have made any sense to me three weeks ago, but today it's as clear as the nose on my face.

It is a strange thing, this having a pet. I've heard people talk about it and I see now what they mean. The white lets me be real—tired and angry or cursing and crying or falling and failing or striding strong ahead—and it's all good enough. The heck with less wary. I am flat out glad she is here. Together I believe we can get this child to safety.

———

This morning I scavenged everything from the Land Rover and laid it out. There's not much.

For food, we have two packages of powdered soup and a small one of freeze-dried strawberries, one box of raisins, a handful of trail mix, and a fist-sized pack of homemade kangaroo biltong, oven-dried strips of seasoned meat. Paul loved that stuff.

For equipment, I found a lightweight shovel, which'll beat digging with my hands. There are several cotton sheets and a couple pallets—far more bedding than we need or can carry. A rope and roll of clear plastic sheeting. Two quarts of motor oil I drained from the vehicle. Two side mirrors. A couple short hoses and some wire from the engine. Paul's equipment sled and harness and the two 20-gallon water tanks.

That sled is a godsend. Paul sawed a SAR litter in two and welded light runners and a set of retractable wheels on the bottom so he could pull his gear along behind like we do for injured folks when we're on backcountry ski patrol in the Tetons. It works pretty well on this sand with just the runners. In heavy brush, I can drop the wheels for easier going. The weight's the only question now. The weight and the harness.

The water alone weighs 100 pounds. Then there's my pack and Josie—probably another eighty or so—a rough load when I'm at my best, much less now, and Paul's harness has only a light waist belt. On me it lands on my hips, which is actually a good thing, given my injured rib. If I had to pull from my waist right now I'd lay right down and cry. Hips are bad enough.

I've rigged the belt with shoulder straps made of rope covered in cotton wraps to distribute the drag better and take the pressure off my middle, but it still hurts to pull. Too bad I can't train that damn white to haul a load—now *that* would be a good use of a dog. I eye her, scheming how to make a dog-pack or travois to turn her into a beast of burden. She ignores me and stretches out flat for a nap. That is oddly comforting.

I've calculated our chances. The dirt track's there and awfully tempting, and if it was just me I'd go that way for sure. With the water we have now I could get out of here or so close to it I could smell the town. But pulling a kid? There's no way. The water wouldn't hold out long enough for that. We'd also be sitting ducks for those men, and it wouldn't take a good tracker to see our footprints. And if they have night glasses, they could be on us before we even knew they were coming. So no. We'll stick to the desert. They won't expect us to do that. It's too insane. Nobody in their right mind would choose to cross-country this on foot. Which is exactly why we have to do it.

There are three more mapped water sources between us and that settlement. Five if I'm willing and able to veer off the route by ten miles or more each time. I'll aim for the straightest line out, but if the water's not turning up, we may have to detour. There are old homesteads marked in two places too, but both are about thirty miles out of our way and I can't risk them. If they're abandoned, their water's probably long gone anyhow or unreachable. And if they're occupied by men like the ones who did this, we definitely don't need to pitch up on their doorsteps.

I just have to think myself inside this place better than I've been doing the last couple weeks. Quit resisting. Stop comparing it to high alpine and bemoaning my lack of skills. It is different, yes, alien even. But it's still the same planet I was born on and there's no reason I can't function here.

Must sink inside the place and think outside my boxes. Mine the corners of my own mind. Relax into this desert. Stop fighting the land, like Grandmother Haney used to say. Lay out a plan and follow it through.

But that will have to come later. For now I need a nap and the courage to take care of Paul.

Can't just leave him hanging there like that. Must come to terms with it. Steel myself for the job. When dusk falls, I have to get him buried. Can't just leave him hanging there. The thought makes me sick. Cannot seem to get my head around it. Scenes of my mother lying bruised and bloody on that cold tile floor mingle with Paul's face and this red sand and the shaking starts deep inside. I turn away from my father's angry hands. I thought I'd lived all that down, let it go. Half a world, a whole lifetime away, and it's back strong as ever.

I need to get him buried. Break it into single jobs and tackle them one at a time. Nose over your toes.

DAY 12

I dreamed of rain and floods waist high and dragging Paul's body and Josie along behind me in a
canoe, trying to get to higher ground. My mother
kept whispering in my ear, "You can outlast your
past, Taliesin," and then the wall of water took her
voice and the canoe and I went under and woke up
choking.

I intended to bury Paul this morning. It is the
right thing to do. I even started digging a hole, but
then realized I couldn't afford to use what strength
I had left to cut him down and drag him out to the
grave. Burial is a luxury. They never tell you that
back home, but it is. It takes a lot of work.

Besides, if those men come back it'd be better if
they didn't know I've been here, so burial's out of
the question. I've spent the last several hours trying to make it look as if I don't exist either. Packed
our gear and moved it off to the south, ready to
move out at dusk. Crumpled the sheets in the vehicle and dusted sand on them, brushed out my footprints, scattered dead leaves and sticks around the
whole site, strewed the litter from Josie's pack onto

the floor of the truck. Maybe they'll think she scrounged around a couple days and then wandered off on her own—to certain death. No little girl has a chance in this place. They won't follow her. There's no need.

Just to be sure my version of things was the one they bought, I went to the trouble of laying a fake set of Josie's footprints out into the brush. A good tracker would know that an adult was halfway in those shoes. The soles are leaving too heavy a track for a child, and in some places my feet slipped sideways and I had to redo the print. A good tracker would see all that, but an ordinary person wouldn't have a clue. I was praying these two men were ordinary and doing my best to lay a lie for them. Josie slept through it all. Then, at the worst possible minute this morning, she woke. Child always did have impeccable timing.

I was on my hands and knees at the edge of our shade, heaving one more time, when I heard her voice, weak but demanding.

"You shouldn't throw up your food. We don't have much left." Jo was sitting up, staring at the little stash of groceries on the pallet.

Just like that. Wake from the near dead, assess the situation, and start issuing orders to a grown-up you haven't seen in six solid months. It took a couple minutes to compose myself enough to answer and by the time I had, she'd repeated the order twice more. *This* is why I don't have children, I thought crossly, but bit my tongue on that and simply said, "Well. You appear to be feeling better."

"I'm not. I'm hungry."

"Okay, there are six more strawberries, some biltong and raisins and trail mix, and some soup right next to your knee. Take your pick."

"I don't like powdered soup."

"Then don't pick it."

She scowled at me, reached for the dried kangaroo meat strips, and started sucking on one.

The albino rested in the shade of an acacia nearby, watching this tiny human closely. Josie caught sight of her and said, "I didn't know you had a dog."

I shrugged and mumbled something inane like, "She's new."

Cocking her head, Jo stared at the white a long time, then ripped off a piece of the biltong and held it out. The white sat perfectly still.

Josie frowned my direction. "You should teach your dog some manners."

I didn't even know what to say to that, so I just watched as she crawled toward the dingo and placed the strip of meat near her front paws. Then she crawled back to her mat, sat down, brushed off her hands, and waited. The albino sniffed the offering, looked at us both for a long thoughtful moment, and ate it. Jo nodded.

"So are you gonna teach her some manners?" she asked.

Before I could come up with an answer, she continued, "Well, are you?"

"Actually no," I replied, out of sheer instinct. "I was thinking maybe you'd be a better teacher of manners than me."

Josie pursed her lips, considering that, and then

nodded again. "*I* have manners," she said, in a way that left no doubt as to my lack of them.

I'm just sitting here now, feeling like a knot on a log. Jo has the unique ability to make me tongue-tied and simpleminded in nothing flat. Here I am supposed to be comforting her and I can't get an adult word in edgewise. She hasn't so much as glanced toward the Land Rover. Doesn't she remember what happened? Trying to decide whether to bring it up or let it alone, I watch her watching the dog and have what seems like a brilliant idea.

"Actually, Jo, she's not my dog. She's just been hanging around. Why don't you take her and train her? That'd probably be a good thing."

Josie wrinkles her nose and stares at the dingo, ignoring me for so long I finally say, "Well? What do you say, kid?"

"Don't call me a kid! I'm not a kid! A kid is a baby billy goat, not a person!"

I start to mumble an apology, but Jo cuts me off short. "I don't even know if I want a dog."

"Oh," I say, subdued. I truly don't know which way to turn next, so I blurt out, "I thought you were wanting a puppy last year."

"Yes. A puppy. I want a *puppy*. Not a grown dog with no manners."

"Oh, I see."

Josie sniffs and squints her eyes at the white, who sits up on her haunches, curious now and almost friendly.

"I'll think about it and let you know tomorrow," she says, never taking her eyes off the albino.

I sigh in relief, careful not to make any noise. We are through the first hurdle—both in one piece, and nobody has yelled. That, at least, is something.

A few minutes later Jo fingers the strawberries, munching one in between bites of the biltong. That leaves five. I can't help counting. It is small of me, but I can't help it. Mouth watering, I'm wracking my brain, looking for something motherly to say and not finding a single thing moving there but the down-count for our strawberries. Josie doesn't stop eating until there is just one left.

"That's yours," she says. "I don't want it so you need to eat it so it don't spoil."

"It's freeze-dried. Can't spoil." I say the absolute dumbest things to this child.

"You need to eat it anyhow."

Little snit. I just stare at her, not knowing what to think. Josie, unfazed, simply sits gazing at me until I finish swallowing the berry. Then she lies down again, turning on her side, and says, "Would you be quiet now because I need my sleep."

It doesn't seem as if a reply is necessary, so I pick up my journal and pen. Josie declares, "Well, would you?"

"Yes *ma'am*, I will," I retort, undone entirely by this point.

"I'm not a ma'am either. I'm a girl."

There is nothing whatsoever in the world to say to that.

This is the thing about this child and me. She breaks me out in hives. For the last two days I've been planning for when she woke up. I was going to comfort her and hold her tight while she wailed out her grief over her dad. I was going to nurture her when she cried for her mom and show her my plan for getting her home to Louisiana safe and sound. I was ready. Then she wakes up and axes my preparation in a slim heartbeat. All she wants from me is a promise to be quiet.

Which I will honor. I'd like to sleep too, but have a feeling it's going to be fitful. I'm edgy as a long-tailed cat in a room full of rocking chairs right now. No wonder parents go mental.

———

Parents. I feel the old tug within, the long suppressed yearning to be held in my mother's arms once more. For a year after she left us, I prayed every day to the sun. Bring my mama back for one day, just one. I could live the whole rest of my life on just one more day with her. I would make her smile and keep her safe from him. We would laugh and dance and sing and cook and the house would echo and swell with happiness until it burst out and healed the whole world. Mama was that good. She could've healed the world. I believed it so hard it made my head hurt every single day for one solid year, but on the anniversary of her death, when she still hadn't come, I cursed the sun and swore never to speak of her again and I haven't done it either. Not once, not even the day Artis gave me the locket. Mama's name hasn't crossed my lips until now, here, in this desert stained the color of blood, where I'm talking to myself to make sure I'm still breathing, so her name slips out like commas riding on the wake of other, safer words. I used to be hardheaded enough to keep my vows.

Now I'm just tired and grasping for something, *any*thing, to hold onto.

Joy was her name. Joy Haney Nowata. She was friendly and kind and quiet and cheerful, the sort of person who gave all of herself to anyone she met and didn't expect—or seem to need—anything in return. The only thing I ever heard her ask for was from me, late one night just before bed.

Two hours earlier I had threatened to use the ice cream man's two-by-four on my father's head if he came in drunk and hit her again. My gentle little mother shook her head sadly, picked up a hatchet and set to work on the board. She didn't stop till it was split into kindling, and every last shred was piled into the woodstove. Then she sat down on the floor and pulled me onto her lap and, without a single word, we watched the flames eat my erstwhile weapon of justice. A board, I thought then, could fix the wrongs, could make things right and fair, could straighten all the mean people up and make 'em fly right. And there my mother was, burning mine up the chimney like it was an ordinary piece of stove wood. I wanted to fix the world. She was cooking my sword.

"Violence isn't the way to fix violence, Tally. You don't fix anything by breaking it again. To end this circle you have to be bigger than your pain and step outside it. Promise me you'll do that," Mama whispered, kissing my cheek and pulling my ragged afghan up beneath my chin the way I liked it. Hypnotized by the love and the kindness in her eyes and an almost desperate desire to be as good as she was, I listened with my heart. "Promise me you'll end it."

"*Promise me, Taliesin,*" she begged—and I did. Kept my word firm too, even that horrible night two weeks later when his regular Saturday night beating of her took her down and never let her rise again. I wanted to kill him then and would've, except for Mama's pleading eyes. When they went still, my father was gone, raging through the night as usual, blaming the world for the pain he caused and daring somebody to stop him, and there was nothing I could do to save her anymore.

Except keep my word. End the circle. I've lived by that vow all these years no matter what, except for that one thing with Dix two years ago and if I get out of this place alive, I'm going to look him up and fix that. Joy Nowata.

The name alone softens the hard wall I've built between her memory and me. If the dead still know us, surely she can see I did keep my word in the big places, the places where it really mattered, and that if I make it out of this desert, I'll fix that little one with Dix too. Ending the circle. Honoring my mother's life. I am too tired to forget her anymore.

Josie flinches in her sleep, her body remembering some horrible part of her recent past, I'm sure. I hope she can speak her father's name soon. I will help her learn to do that. Maybe that way my own past will count for something besides pain.

The day is burning hot around us, no wind, no clouds. This land asks nothing. We sit empty-handed and quiet, waiting for the sun to rest so we can walk toward home. No one in the world knows where we are.

A small cloud of dust is gathering to the east. And moving this way fast. I stand up to see what it is. Raw terror rises like bile.

That is the quickest I have ever broken camp, bar none, not that it was much of a camp to break. I simply dropped the sheet and rolled it up and dragged the sled over the edge of a small gully about twenty-five feet from the Land Rover, nudged Josie awake and down into the ditch, then hurried to sweep out our tracks and scuttle backward to Jo's side. She had my binoculars in her hands, and her eyes answered my unspoken question. The steel blue truck barreling toward us belonged to the men who killed Paul. The white dingo disappeared.

There are times when you feel targeted by death, caught in its crosshairs like a squirrel in the scope of a cannon. This is one of those times. I rue the day I ever heard the name Tanami and curse the whimsy that drew me into its angry heart.

The blue truck keeps coming. We huddle together, Josie with her back to the wall of the wash, me on my knees facing it, head slightly above the lip so I can keep track of the men's movements when they arrive. I try to reassure Jo, tell her there's no way they could've seen us yet, they are too far out for the sheet to be visible and we got it down in plenty of time, plus I wiped out our tracks. "So this low place'll keep us safe if we just stay quiet. No sound."

Jo says nothing. I hear all my lies and feel sick. It would take an act of God for these men to miss us here. We're too fucking close—the Land Rover is barely a stone's throw away and the vegetation here is sparse.

"Low places are good for hiding in," I say out loud, trying to sound casual and strong like the ranger I used to be. "They're coming back for the Rover, I'm sure. All we have to do is stay hunkered down till they finish. We'll be okay, you'll see."

Josie doesn't look convinced. I reach to put my arm around her shoulders in an awkward attempt to comfort her. She pulls away and clasps her arms over her stomach.

"You have to be quiet, Jo," I say, worried that she's about to pitch one of her fits. If she does, we're done for. "I *mean* it. Not one sound. Do you understand me?"

Josie stays hunched away. I hold my breath. If she breaks and starts screaming, I don't know what I'm going to do. Go after one of the men, I guess, and see if I can even the odds some.

But they have a gun. I don't stand a chance against a gun.

Now the truck draws level with us and sputters to a stop in front of Paul's truck. We freeze. The passenger door opens and a stocky older man walks to the front of the blue truck, releases the winch, and pays out cable to the hook on the left front bumper of the Land Rover. Raising his hand to the driver, the man steps back a couple feet as the winch engages and pulls the Rover back onto its wheels. It lands in the sand with a dull, muffled thud, and I see Paul's body jerk down with it, seat belt still holding him fast. Want to stop watching but can't.

Shutting off the engine, the driver steps out, recoiling from the smell a step or two, saying, "Nice." He looks like he wants to be somewhere else.

"Yeah, pretty rank, but a hell of a shot, eh mate?" The stocky one replies, proud. He is happy to be here.

The driver stares at Paul's body a few seconds, then says gruffly, "Need to get that in the ground."

"I ain't touchin' the stinkin' motherfucker."

"Look Foy, you took the shot and you left him hangin', now you're gonna drag him out. I'll dig a hole."

At that the driver reaches into the truck bed, grabs a shovel, walks off a few yards, and starts digging. The man named Foy stands silent for a minute, then grins suddenly, trots back to the winch, and starts paying out the cable again.

Something about his face sets cold and hard inside me. Josie pulls at my shirt, wanting to see, but I put my hand on her head and push her back down at my side, my eyes saying in no uncertain terms, Not another move. Her eyes flash angry and she opens her mouth. I shake my head in a warning. This is not the time for a fit. She struggles to peer over the edge again and I hold her down, determined.

It was the right thing to do. No child could've watched something like what happened next and stayed sane. It was straight out of hell.

Foy fished the cable around Paul's body, hooked it in front, drew out a knife and slit the seat belt, then hurried back to his truck and climbed into it, revved the motor, and slammed it into reverse in one terrible motion that jerked Paul's body out onto the ground and my soul right out of my chest.

I didn't need to see that.

Didn't need to see how Foy then dragged Paul's decaying body around in circles after the truck like some drunken hunter pulling a prize trophy around a local bar, yelling out the window on both passes, "Hey Bodley, got 'im out!"

I could not look anymore then, could not watch another thing, just slid down into the gully beside Josie, back to the wall too, gripping her tiny hand for all I was worth, both of us sitting there staring at the far side of the world.

<hr>

As the evening turned in on itself, Jo and I stayed huddled in the wash. She didn't scream or pitch a fit or pull her hand away from mine. When I crouched upward to check on the men, she reached for my sleeve and held on. When I eased back down beside her, she held my hand. We haven't dared even whisper.

The men made camp noisily, tension enough

between them to cut with a dull knife. They seem unfazed by the smell, which is still strong. Foy hauled out a case of Victoria Bitter beer and got into the middle of it fast, tossing his empties all over. Bodley started a fire and put on water for billy tea, then kept tinkering with something under his truck's hood. He didn't say two words the whole evening. Foy never quit talking.

Until he got up to take a leak, that is. Stumbling our direction in the faint light of late dusk, cursing as he tripped over a bush. Josie held her breath. I did too. At first it was because of Foy, but then we both saw her at the same time—the white dingo, pale as a ghost shadow, a few yards away on the other side of the gully, upwind, between us and Foy, I thought. And then he shot a stream of urine into the ditch not fifteen feet to the west of us and I knew. The albino was between us and him.

Josie gripped my arm till it tingled. We sat frozen, staring at the white. Finishing with a curse, Foy lit a cigarette and walked our way, calling out, "Got that shit piece o' lorry fixed yet?"

Bodley grunted in disgust. Foy kept walking. The smoke from his cigarette drifted over our heads, and I abruptly remembered that Josie was allergic to tobacco smoke. Severely allergic. She buried her head in my right side, clutching my shirt to her face, trying desperately not to cough or choke.

Suddenly something slammed and we both flinched.

It took a few seconds to register that Bodley had shut the truck hood. Josie was shaking like a new-born foal. I held her tight and prayed. Foy kept pacing along the top of the gully.

Suddenly the dingo ran out into the open where he couldn't miss seeing her. Everything inside me screamed *Leave! Get out of here, you damn mutt!* but I couldn't yell, couldn't warn her, couldn't even risk moving to wave her away, and then it came clear, she was doing this to draw Foy away from us, he was so close he was almost on us, no way he'd miss us but for her.

And that was how it went. The instant he saw her, he muttered, "What's this shit?" The white turned heel and ran the opposite direction, west and out—away from Josie and me—a few yards, then stopped and turned and looked at him again, deliberate, waiting. Foy ran stumbling toward his truck and his rifle and then back to the wash above us and took steady aim. I couldn't see him, I could only see the white standing there fearless in the half light as I sat with my palm pressed tight over Josie's eyes, but I know his aim was steady because he hit her on the first shot. Red blood stained her chest, she wheeled and disappeared into the night. No sound.

Except from Foy. He howled into the night, "You see that, Bod? Some shootin', hey mate?"

I do not know what Bodley said. Both Jo and I just sat there in the deepening darkness, trembling. Josie dug her fingers into my skin so hard it brought tears to my eyes. We are numb from sitting here, numb from hearing, from seeing, from thinking, numb from knowing what we both know about the world tonight.

"Wonder how far that professor's kid got, Bod? The little redhead—what'd he call her, Joanne or something?"

Bodley shrugged. Josie leaned against my side as I crouched on my knees, watching the men. I was looking for weaknesses, places that might yield on our behalf with the right kind of pressure. I wasn't seeing much. These men were hardened. Foy especially. He was staring at the place where Jo's fake trail bent into the bush, backlighting it with a flashlight. I didn't like that. He was a good enough tracker to know to backlight a trail. That meant he was good enough to figure out a much bigger person was in the shoes that laid that trail.

"How long you think she lasted out here?" he asked.

Bodley shrugged again.

"Not long, I'd say. A day? Two? Three? Not more. Three tops. Place's too mean for a mite."

Bodley stared into the fire and said nothing.

Foy went on, "You shoulda let me shoot her too, mate, just like the boss said. Put her outta her misery."

A shadow of something like disgust flashed across Bodley's face and he said, "Didn't sign on to kill kids."

Foy flicked off his flashlight and walked back to the fire, chuckling. "Soft, that's what you are, man. Soft."

Josie leaned against me and held on. I patted

her head and kept watching. Somewhere, somehow, these two had to have a weak spot. I intended to find it.

———

Before long Jo fell asleep, exhausted. Over and over she whimpered, lost in some nightmare of all this that will probably never leave her. I covered her mouth with my hand and whispered close in her ear to shush. Without waking she responded to the warning touch, and slipped away quiet for a few minutes more before the dreams crowded in again.

I finally let my hand rest on her small face and the feel of her skin on my palm twisted my gut. It's like Paul's always is after he shaves. Soft as spun silk, warm and yielding. Without fail, twice a week, every Monday and Thursday, or sometimes in between if we have a special date, he'll disappear into the shower with whiskers and come out with a face that begs to be touched.

"I always liked a man with a five o'clock shadow," I told him the very first time, "But the first five minutes after it's gone, well—"

Never did finish that sentence. And now I can't even remember what I was going to say.

Josie moans and I'm glad for the interruption. I hold her close and shush her gently and she falls silent again.

The men are settling into camp and seem not to have any idea we're here. Once they go to sleep I intend to carry Jo out a ways so we'll have better odds of keeping it that way, but as long as they're awake I have to stay put and keep her quiet. Won't be able to take the gear. It'd make too much noise. Just have to leave it and pray they don't find it. We'll come back for it as soon as they're gone. Surely they'll leave tomorrow morning.

I've had crazy thoughts about stealing their vehicle, but that's all it is. Crazy idiotic ideas. It'd look great on a movie screen. A movie star could probably carry it off. Some midget of a woman with flawless makeup, bee-stung lips, doe eyes, and a six-inch waist encased in a leather bustier. I can't. I'm no movie star. One crunching twig and one of those men awake and it'd be all-she-rote for us. I'm no woods-smart Indian, either. Even grass breaks when I step on it and anybody without need of a hearing aid can hear it from fifty paces out, so there's hell all way I could get Jo and me into that truck and gone without reckoning with those two men. We will have to rely on the original plan, provided we can evade them long enough to do any relying on anything.

Their fire blazes high. Bodley's still sitting there staring into the flames, quiet and motionless. Foy's half sprawled on the ground across from him, leaning back against the case of beer, cleaning his gun, eyeing the other man but saying nothing for a long while.

Suddenly he asks, "You know why Rayburn took me on, Bod?"

Bodley says nothing.

Foy nods and goes on, "Because I know how to get a man's attention."

Still nothing.

"You know how to get a man's attention, Bod? Well, the first thing you do is, you bed his wife. Or, if you're lucky, his daughter."

Bodley stirs at this last remark, and for the first time his eyes meet Foy's. An instant passes between them before Foy continues.

"If that doesn't work you stick a gun in his face. And then, if you still don't have his attention?"

Bodley stares, silent.

"You pull the trigger. Because a man who won't give you his attention? Well that's a man you just don't need to know."

Foy wipes the gun barrel one last time and sets the cleaning cloth aside. Reaching into a box of shells, he lifts one and, with a quick flip of the action, chambers a round and lets the rifle come to rest across his legs. The muzzle is pointing straight at Bodley. The two men's eyes are locked.

"So that's how you get a man's attention. And that's why Rayburn took me on."

Bodley slouches back against a pack, holding Foy in his gaze, and says, too quiet, "Nice."

Josie jerks violently in my arms and we both struggle to restrain her dreams. I turn around and slide down to a sitting position again, legs tingling from having crouched so long. Back pressed against the gully wall, I lift Jo's heavy little head onto my lap and close my eyes, listening for the men to sleep and searching for Paul.

DAY 13

Jo woke at dawn, eyes crusted with sleep but wide and alert.

"It's okay, Jo," I whispered. "I put some distance between us and them last night."

She nodded and sat up, arms clasped around her knees.

We're a good tenth of a mile from the Land Rover now, with enough ground cover to keep us relatively safe. We've each got our packs and three canteens of water, but everything else is sitting in the gully where we left it when the men arrived. So far they haven't wandered that direction. Actually, so far they haven't even gotten up.

Josie picks at the trail mix, choosing raisins, cashews, and pecans and avoiding the sunflower seeds and almonds. She has to be hungrier than that.

"I'll get us some more food soon, Jo. Promise."

"It's okay. I'm not very hungry."

"Me neither," I lie, and we sit silent, our eyes straying out bush every few minutes until we remember and draw them back to stare at the ground or our hands or our shoes or the seams on our shorts or simply the backs of our own eyelids.

We keep looking for the white dingo and Paul. It's automatic, like breathing. Only not as productive.

The men took their time about leaving and when they did, they left the Land Rover sitting exactly where it was and headed north. At first I didn't put it together. Delighted to see their dust trail moving away from us, I nudged Jo, and she took my binoculars to watch while I gloated, saying something along the lines of, "See there! Didn't I tell you it'd be okay?"

Then it hit me where they were headed. And why they'd left Paul's truck behind for the time being. I felt sick.

Two minutes later, after I'd extracted a blood oath from Jo to stay put at the base of an acacia while I went back for our gear, I was running toward the Land Rover. Two minutes after that I was bent double, hands on knees, losing my last thoughts of breakfast into the sand near the mound that held Paul's body. I hadn't meant to come all the way in, but at the last moment I couldn't not. I wanted to say something to him, something that would make a difference, but no words would come and time was not waiting for Josie and me. We had to move, and fast.

Torn between that knowledge and the dull fact that the only man I ever loved was lying beneath this heavy smothering sand, I broke a stick in two and tied the pieces together with the short piece of ribbon I always wear braided in my hair and then caught my breath, impaled on a memory. Paul liked my ribbons. He used to trail them between his fingers and rest his chin on my head.

Just before he boarded the plane for here, I gave him the blue ribbon I had in my hair that day. The first thing I saw on entering the sleep tent when I arrived four months later was that ribbon, carefully stitched to the tent seam above his bedroll.

Paul saw me looking at it, shrugged, and said, "First thing every morning, last thing every night."

"That's really sick," I retorted, pushing the ribbon aside with exaggerated indifference, but secretly delighted that he cared so much.

Now my fingers feel numb over the makeshift cross in my hands. The ribbon makes no impression on my skin. I see it but don't. That blue one hanging above his bedroll sways in my mind instead, a simple remnant of a steady love. I want to stay but cannot.

Knowing I can't leave this grave marker above ground—it would be a dead giveaway—I bury it near the head of the mound, vowing to return for Paul when this is over, promising to take his ashes to the ridge above Jenny Lake like we always said we'd do for each other back when either of us dying was about as likely as the sun falling out of the sky. I tell him not to worry about Jo, that I will get her out and I promise not to swat her bottom either, no matter how much of a little pilljerk she is. Shaking, most of me wanting simply to crawl beneath the sand and lie quiet beside my lover till the earth ends, I remember his daughter is waiting and turn to go.

Then I see it. Paul's journal, lying in the sand near the Land Rover. Paul always tucked it into his visor, and I've been so upset I forgot all about it. The men must've found it when they went through the vehicle this morning—and decided it wasn't worth keeping. Reaching for the worn leather book, I hold it close. When Paul was with me, stuff didn't mean much. Now that he's gone, it does. I am so grateful for this book. My fingers trace its familiar edges and something jars. The big map he kept inside the front cover, the one marking his intended campsites, is gone.

So that is really it. My instinct was dead on.

Only one thing could lure those men north. The research camp. Where my note to Paul is still sitting right out in the open, waiting for him to return, follow my mapped route, and come rescue me—so all my careful planning's been for naught. If they find the camp, they find the note, and once they find the note, it's only a matter of time till they figure out this child didn't wander off at all. And once they get to that, they'll be back here—motivated to find us—within a matter of hours. By then we have to be somewhere else and we have to leave as confusing a trail behind as we can, circles and backtracking and brushing out in places. Hard work. Especially in full sun, but we don't have a choice.

Without so much as a backward glance, I hurry back to Josie. She hasn't moved an apparent inch, so I make a point of congratulating her on that. Obedience has never been her strong suit.

Minutes later, with Paul's journal now stashed securely inside my pack, I step into the harness and we move south. Jo agrees to ride on the back to sweep a limb across our tracks. For almost two hours I walk and she sweeps, and then I glance back to see that she's dozed off. I shift my part now, drag the sled about 200 yards, step out of the traces and go back to brush out our trail, then walk on again. Over and over, sun beating my head into submission.

Whenever Jo wakes, she helps. I keep waiting for her to bring up Paul, but she doesn't. There's a quiet blank sheet in her eyes that was never there before, so I know on some level she knows what has happened, but she shows no sign of being conscious of it. I've finally found something she wants to talk about, though: practical stuff. Rules for survival. Keep your clothes on no matter how hot it is and your skin out of the sun. Think positive thoughts. Stay put if we get separated.

That one intrigues her. She asks, "Did you really do like daddy said and tell kids to hug a tree if they got lost?"

"Yep. Get lost, stay put, that's the rule. For children we make it concrete. Hug a tree and stick with it like a tick on a dog till somebody finds you."

"But what if there's hardly any trees, like here?" she asks, worried and subdued but as civil as I've ever seen her and verging on cooperative. I need to try to keep her this way. Participating, not balking. So I put all the ranger I have left in me into the reply.

"Then you hug a bush, Jo, or a rock. Crawl

under it, keep your skin out of the sun, be quiet, and stay still."

She nods solemnly, then curls up on the sled for another nap. I start walking again, trying to evade the backside of my advice. Stay put, stay still. For that to do Josie any good, somebody would need to be coming to rescue her. But if something happens to me, no one ever will. The thought makes me nauseous. I'm the only human that stands between this child and death. How wrong is that?

I can't let her down. Just can't. Turning my face into the sun, I walk on.

This heat saps us, makes us drowsy, beyond thirsty. I've had more than a gallon of water already. Josie's had half. We can't keep this up on any level very long.

My plan is to tank up at that next spring, then head east, the exact opposite of my mapped route. If we have to, we can hole up a couple days till these men decide we're not worth it, then come back through and refill our water tanks before going on. That's the closest thing to a backup plan I've had in three weeks. Feels good.

Paul used to tell me I had enough backup plans for everybody in the entire western hemisphere and a good chunk of the east too. I took that as a compliment.

I don't believe that's how he meant it.

Ah, Paul. The differences between us only made our love more true. Now you are gone and I am here, and that one difference can never be overcome.

If we could only know the angle of the path

ahead, sometimes we'd step different. But life doesn't give us a view until the foot's already down, committed, heart hauled along behind like a puppy on a leash.

Why did I stay in camp when he went for Josie? I should've gone with him. Maybe the two of us together could've headed things off at the pass, outwitted those men or just plain avoided them. That's one of my more highly developed skills— avoiding people. Paul's never been any good at it. He trusts everybody too much, but me, I read the lay of the land from a distance and walk a long, long ways around if things look squirrelly. Paul doesn't know squirrelly from squat. Never did. That was my department. I should've gone with him. We could've handled this fine together.

Together we were always good, good enough for anything that came our way, more than good enough for most stuff. And just look at us now.

Nose over your toes, Nowata. Move this gig into debrief.

Josie stirs and whispers in her sleep, "Daddy? But why did he kill the dog, Daddy?"

My eyes search the surrounding land. The white is gone and I don't know what to say to this child. I have no words for now.

——

We saw the trees where the spring should've been from a mile out. Half an hour later I saw the tents and barrels this side of it and hit the ground instinctively. Something's bad wrong with this picture. This is Aboriginal land. You're not supposed to be on it without a permit. It took Paul eight months to get his. Whatever's going on down there, it's not legit.

Josie is still groggy from her last nap, so I shake her awake and order her to stay put with the sled. To be on the safe side I drag it down into a small depression, cover it with a sheet, dust sand and brush over it, and make her a pallet in the shade. Then I cut around to the east and up the backside of a rise where I can scope out the place through my binoculars. Now it's more than a hunch. Something's definitely wrong here.

It's hard to make out in the lengthening dusk, but there's a makeshift camp down there. No vehicles, but three large canvas tents, two open-sided, and something producing steam from one of them. Two portable generators. Several fifty-gallon drums sitting around, a nurse tank off to one side. Familiar. Too familiar. Substitute the tents for a couple travel trailers and it's a dead ringer for a meth lab we busted in the Wind Rivers last year. Low profile drug op, one four-wheel drive to pony supplies and product in and out, round-the-clock production in an out-of-the-way place manned by three or four men. We hit that one in the Winds with an interagency crew—DEA, FBI, local sheriff's office, and us. All of us. They even roped Paul and the rest of the naturalists in to sentry a fire road on that one. It went down without a hitch, mainly because we had twenty-five M-16s to their four, but still, it's not my idea of a fun way to spend an afternoon. This is even worse because it's just me and a little kid to whoever the hell's down there. And they're between us and the water.

One man's all I've seen so far. Large, not portly, just big boned. On the long side of middle age. Blond hair, heavy features, good skin, well cared for. Khakis and cotton shirt, white, clean. The kind of clothes a rich man would wear. He's relaxed, comfortable even. Moves like he owns the place. Probably does. Gets up from his chair every so often and goes into the tent to check something, comes back and sits down with a thick book and a tall glass of red wine.

A glass of wine. *Out here*. That one stops me cold. And gives me an idea.

If I play this right, I might be able to sneak in after dark and lift some food. Jo and I are out of everything.

Josie, goddamnit you little shit, what the fuck do you think you're doing?!

—

She walked into the left field of my binocs, no warning, no sound. I nearly choked. God*damn*it! I *told* you to *stay put!* How hard is it to sit on your sorry little behind for a few minutes anyway?

There is nothing for it but to move in closer, try to catch her eye, figure out a way to extract her without him knowing. Little shit. I'd wring your scrawny little neck if I could get my hands on it right now.

There is no chance of that.

The man tensed the moment he saw Josie. Like a metal coil contracting into itself, then easing a hair's breadth, assessing the situation. His eyes scanned the bush to both sides and landed on her with no sign of nervousness, but slightly unnerved just the same. It was in the way he held his head so still, watching this tiny child walk toward him, drowsy and unknowing. I don't think she saw him until he spoke.

What he said I couldn't hear, but Josie paused, wary. He used the instant to rise from his chair, still innocuously scanning the area, like someone whose world has just changed and he's not sure quite how. Or how much. In one supple move, he stepped to the table and made as if to offer Jo some water, poured it even, but his left hand reached for a revolver at the same time and slipped it into place near his lower back.

My mind races. No options. If he goes at her, I have to yell or something, draw his attention, get him focused on me. I'm too far out to be any real use. Have to get in closer. "Think, Nowata. Lay it out in your head," I whisper, as much out of terror as anything, trying desperately to talk myself down off the edge.

There's no need to yell, Tally. That gun's not for Jo—not yet anyway—it's for whoever's with her. You. Josie's safer if you lay low. The man's assessing his exposure, wondering who's out here, who brought this child in, who's seen what, and setting himself up to meet them on a level field. He's not going to hurt her until he finds out what she knows and who she's with. You just have to get in close and pull her out before then. Come off the edge, put your energy toward handling this thing if it goes down, Nowata. You're not worth a red hill of beans to that kid if you lose it up here now.

The mental lecture helps rein in my panic. Every muscle alert, I watch for several minutes.

Jo isn't talking. She drinks greedily, downing three cups of water with hardly a pause to breathe in between. When the man reaches for a sack of fruit and offers her some, she fills both hands with grapes and starts eating. Good. She'll be sick as a dog in a few minutes from all that on an empty stomach. That's good, real good for us. Can't talk much when you're puking out your guts. Eat up, kid.

It is time to quit watching and start moving. I need to be a whole lot closer than I am.

———

I've edged my way to one end of the camp. No sooner do I lay eyes on the man again than I realize he's looking at something. A churning dust trail aiming for here.

The blue truck. Josie sees it and erupts on cue like a little volcano, half-chewed grapes and water spewing all over. The man steps neatly aside and looks disgusted, but right now he is more interested in the truck than her. It isn't strange to him. He knows it, knows those two men inside, is expecting them—it is written in his stance. Something about the way he holds his head reminds me of my father and raises chill bumps on my arms. This man is deadly. I have to get Jo away from him.

But now is not the time. Three men against a woman and a kid. No way can we win that one. We have to wait, Josephine. We just have to wait. Stay calm, stay still. Josie cannot hear my thoughts. Her eyes are locked on the blue truck, glazed with terror. Hold on, kid. Just hold on. I'm coming.

The man flicks on a light strung between the tents. I wait.

So that's it then. Has to be. Paul must've stumbled into this camp on his way back. He probably stopped in to check out this spring since it was his next research site and their setup's a little too north for him to have seen it before he was already out of the vehicle. He must've realized what was up, tried to make a run for it, and they ran him down. That's the rough of it anyway. Fucking goddamn coincidence.

The other two men cross the sand, Bodley slow and deliberate, eyes on the ground, Foy charging ahead, belligerent.

"Bit of a problem, sir," he says.

"It would seem so."

"Got one loose out bush."

"I thought you told me you took care of that little problem last week."

Foy skips a beat, acknowledging Josie's presence. Clearly he had orders to kill her too, and now this man knows he didn't follow through. "We found another Yank out there," he says to cover.

"And?"

"Seems she's the professor's little cunt."

"And?"

"On the hoof, can't be far."

"Well," the man says, releasing Foy's gaze and looking very deliberately at Josie before turning to Bodley.

Staring at the ground, Bodley says, "Sorry about that, Mr. Rayburn."

Rayburn makes a small dismissive motion with one hand and half turns away, looking out into the desert and saying, "Mr. Bodley, we have product due at Melbourne in three days, which means it needs to leave here at dawn. I wonder if I could prevail upon you to make delivery since it seems I must stay behind."

Bodley nods and walks toward the second tent.

Rayburn turns to Foy and says, nodding toward the blue truck, "Mr. Bodley will be needing some assistance loading that."

Flicking his cigarette onto the ground, Foy starts past Rayburn without a word.

Rayburn lets him go, but then adds, "And Mr. Foy, I expect our little problem to be resolved by morning."

Foy hesitates, his silence thick and angry, then steps toward Josie, saying, "I'll take care of this part of it right now."

Tensing, I start forward by instinct and stop a hair ahead of too late when Rayburn raises his hand and says, "No. You won't."

Foy pauses, his mouth working but silent. He is furious. Mean and angry. He could kill Jo with his bare hands. I can't breathe. I won't let him hurt her. No matter what, I will not let this maniac hurt that child.

Rayburn shifts his feet slightly and faces Foy again. "I believe I asked you to help Mr. Bodley."

Foy's eyes meet Rayburn's, dark fury on cold steel, but he says nothing. I feel weak at the knees. Josie slumps down onto the ground. Rayburn places the fingertips of one hand on the table. The way he moves—it's sinister. Calculating. Deadly. That's what it is most of all. Of these three men, he is by far the most dangerous. So familiar to me. Dead ringer for my father. Shaking, I grip my elbows with my hands, arms pressed tight to my stomach, to keep from crying out. I should've stayed with Josie. Should've skipped this spring entirely. Should've done something besides what I did. How can I ever fix this?

Foy and Bodley start lifting wooden crates into the back of the truck. Jo sits silent, sweating and spent. Rayburn looks hard at her for a moment, then reaches for a rag and hands it to her.

She's still of some value to them. He won't hurt her till she's not.

They will try to put me out of the picture before they do anything to her.

So I have to suck it up. Move back, lay some tracks, confusing, circling, misleading on purpose so that when Foy comes looking for me the trail will work in my favor. And Jo's.

DAY 14

Long morning. I retrieved our gear and laid tracks half the night, then circled around and camped in a ditch about a mile north of the spring. No, camped is too fancy a word. Dropped my pack and landed on it, more like. No fire, no food, just water and shut-eye.

Slept till dawn, then got up and moved in close enough to surveil Foy. I've been huddled on this little rise ever since.

The blue truck left early. It worries me that they may've put Josie in it, but surely they wouldn't take a kid to a drug drop. I'm overworking this thing in my head. Have to back off some. The last thing I need right now is to make this situation worse than it already is. Worry is useless. I can't afford useless today. I will work only with the known.

Rayburn's still here. I'm betting he's still trying to wheedle info out of Jo, but it'd make me a lot happier if I could catch a glimpse of her. Maybe she's sleeping. She's exhausted from yesterday, from the past few days, from everything, exhausted and scared, so maybe she's just sleeping late. I hope she knows I'm out here trying to get to her.

But I also hope she keeps her mouth shut. Rayburn knows about me now, technically doesn't need Jo, but details would be useful to him and she's the only one who has any. As long as that's the case, and I'm still at large, he'll keep her around. I keep talking this thing through. It helps me focus. Comforts me some. I thought we were in trouble before, when it was just us and this desert, but what's going down now makes that look as easy as blinking when somebody's aiming an open fire hose at your head.

A few minutes after Bodley left, Foy found my tracks at the back of the tent, where I was crouching when the truck came in last night, and called out to Rayburn that he'd have the Yank bitch in no time, "No time at all!" and started out fast.

I had to grin at that one. Wished I could say to him, No time hell. I ain't a Yank or a bitch for nothin', asshole. Time's fixin' to stretch out a ways for you.

Paul would've laughed at that. He always thought I was funny. Only person breathing who ever did, I think.

We laughed a lot. From the very beginning. Everything was just funnier when he was around.

I've been torn today, waiting up here, wanting to read his journal but feeling I shouldn't. That was one thing I always liked about us. We always trusted each other. We never violated each other's space. Never went snooping. Never felt the need to. We shared pretty much everything anyway, but it never would've crossed his mind or mine to meddle in personal things.

Like our journals. About as personal as you can get, as much a part of the two of us as our own skins, except skin sluffs off every day and gets replaced and neither one of us could ever bear to part with a journal.

That's actually how we met—on a climb up Teewinot with two rangers and the whole Great Basin crew a couple weeks after they arrived to help our park biologists with a bald eagle count. There were eight of us in all. We hiked the approach from Lupine Meadows together at dawn, then split up into two groups. Jed took four members of Paul's team up the fourth-class East Ridge, an easy route with spectacular views that could be done without even roping up. Laney and Paul went up the 5.8 Direct East Ridge—a route that required both technical gear and skills—with me. I led, intent on making sure we didn't lose this greenhorn on my watch and not paying a whole lot of attention to him otherwise. Teewinot's a long hill—5,600 feet, base to summit—and there are several variations. I had to pay attention or risk getting us off course.

Our trio was quiet and focused. The other crowd was in high spirits, joking and visiting and pretty much never shutting up, their laughter echoing down the valley. Paul didn't say much. He was new to rockclimbing but nimble and careful and the lessons he'd had with Exum Mountain Guides the week before showed. His four colleagues had forgotten it all clean, and I doubt any of them had seen a piece of granite since their first—and last—Exum lesson ended, but they were all strong and willing and capable of powering their way up behind Jed. Paul was different. He'd clearly spent some time on the rock, bouldering in the evenings and at lunchtime, I learned later, practicing his new skills. More important, to me anyway, he moved with finesse—which I consider the ultimate sign of class in a climber. From the instant he took up the end of the rope, slipped it through his seat harness, and knotted a bowline, smoothly, deftly, with no hesitation—and the bowline is a complicated knot that almost always frustrates beginners—I was intrigued. The sight of his hands so large and lean and capable, with those impossibly long fingers, so dexterous and understated—well, they hit me like a kick in the chin and I turned my back on him and walked off, weak at the knees. He told me later that I left a sentence half said when I went. I still believe he made that up.

So there was something between us from the very start. It was the journal, though, the journal and the shoelaces, that did it for me.

At the end of the day, while the others swigged ERG and wolfed down cheese and nuts and jerky, he and I sat a little apart, scribbling in our journals. His was old and worn, mine downright bedraggled. He propped his on his knees, still and centered. I sat cross-legged for a few minutes, then paced some, then plopped back down to write again.

Usually when I write I'm focused. Moving helps me stay there. But that day my gaze kept wandering to this tall, curly-headed man across the way.

Our eyes had met and skittered off each other several times since daylight. We'd passed the Crooked Thumb and reached the summit and made it down with everybody in one piece and unbloodied, which is the measure of a good climb for most people. We'd hiked part way to the Meadows and stopped for snacks. Jed and Laney were stretched out in the grass. I was sitting on a stump, pleasantly tired and mildly annoyed. At my hiking boots. Once again, they'd come untied. This has been a constant running battle for me since the first time I set foot in a shoe, a lifetime battle. The blessed things won't stay tied. So I was sitting there frowning at my Hi-Tecs, about to bend to tie them again, when suddenly I looked up and there he was.

"So good at everything else," he said, shaking his head, "But so challenged by shoestrings."

Without another word he knelt at my feet and snugged each lace tight, then tied it in a double knot, letting those impossible hands rest for the briefest of seconds on my feet.

"I'll probably never get them untied again," I quipped. But deep inside my heart was whispering, I could love this man for life.

Sure enough. We started talking then and our conversation never ended. By phone or in person, it never mattered. We'd pick up where we left off every time. When the rest of the crew headed home a month later, Paul applied for a seasonal position with the naturalists and stayed in the Tetons. He'd been separated from Miriam for a year by then. The morning after their divorce was finalized, he moved into my house at Moose. Aside from three short work details, we were inseparable until he came here for his dissertation research. We were for life, I thought. We really were.

And now he's gone.

And his daughter is trapped in that camp and I'm no closer to getting her out now than I was eight hours ago. God help me, please. I cannot bear it if they hurt her.

Stop, Tally. You can't go there. Can't think about Jo. Just let it rest and play this out careful. Best hope—no, our *only* hope now—is to wait for an opening and then be ready to strike. The men will slip up. They are just humans. They will make a mistake, miscalculate something, forget, break concentration. When they do, you will move in. Until then, wait and watch.

———

Foy has been threading his way through the spinifex on the plain below all morning. Around and around.

He's long since figured out what I was up to, and he's a lot better tracker than I hoped he'd be. But he's tired and hot now, mad too, I imagine, and the sun's beating down on his head. He pauses to take a long drink from his canteen, resting his rifle in the crook of his arm. Squinting at the sun, he comes to a decision and stomps back toward camp. He'll sit out the midday there, which means I have a few hours' reprieve. A nap. That's what I need.

And then a few of Paul's words, from this journal.

Not many, Paulson. Not enough to count as snooping. Just a few words so I can pretend our conversation's still going.

———

The everyday smell of him was strong about me when I woke and I jumped to my feet, sure he was home, sure we both were, sure the dream of this desert was just that—a mean nightmare visited briefly and departed the moment your eyes open on the world again. But the sun told the lie of it and the vast, empty plain below echoed the truth, and when I saw Foy, still out there, still working my tracks, the everyday smell of him vanished and the one from him hanging in the Land Rover swept over me again and drove me back to my knees. Dry heaves. Nothing left to throw up.

I admit it, I'm scared. I never could have admitted that to myself before. Before Paul.

One evening at our place in Moose I was lying in his arms after we'd made love. He had one long arm folded around me and the other was caressing a trail that followed my hair across my shoulders and down my back, and each stroke brought me one step closer to home. I began to cry. Paul noticed and stopped.

"What's wrong?"

I couldn't speak.

He took his arms away and I was frightened until I felt his hands firmly on my shoulders, the thumbs laid tenderly against my collarbone. Eyes searching, again he said, "What?"

By now my tears were pursuing each other in earnest. "You're so good it hurts," I sniffled, a little ashamed.

He chuckled softly, pulling me back in and folding his arms around me. I felt him smiling as he murmured, "Okay then, next time *you* can drive."

"That's not what I meant and you know it," I retorted, nudging him in the ribs.

"I know, I know."

"I'm afraid I won't have this. I'm afraid I won't have *you*," I said.

He sighed, "Oh Tal, how many times do I have to tell you I'm not going anywhere, babe?"

That's what he always said. Four years of promises made and kept. Till now.

So what about now, Paul O'Malley? You back there beneath the sand, Josie trapped in that camp, and me stuck up here on this hill. What about now? Who went somewhere and never came back? Look over these plains at that man out there and tell me what the hell I'm supposed to do without you today?

Foy has stopped again and made another decision, one that doesn't bode well for me. He stalks straight out into the desert, no pauses until he's at least a quarter mile away from camp. I know what he's doing. He's decided to up the ante by moving out past my confusing signs far enough to work a perimeter. It'll take him some time, but he'll eventually get my real tracks. One of us isn't going to leave this desert alive.

I'm sickened by what's coming. To have it all come down to this. To have my whole life, all its busted-up, abandoned pieces and its joys so big I can't imagine them much less think myself around them, to have it all come down to this, here, now. God *damn* this desert, this crazy fucking place, this Tanami! I can't do this thing, Paul. Can't do it. It's too much.

Part of me wants to surrender. Close my eyes and dream of a tall man with a crooked grin lacing my shoes or nuzzling my neck just behind my ear or emptying half a quart of sugar into his one cup of coffee every morning, which meant we had to buy sugar in industrial-size bins—close my eyes and dream until it's over. Just slip away and let it all end.

The rest of me sees that man in Josie. His warm brown eyes, his curly red hair shot through with the gold of the sun, his sidelong smiles and the way they lit up his whole body, his entire contrary self. She's the spitting image of him. There's no way I can let this child down. Or her father.

He taught me that feelings—all of them, the good, bad, the indifferent—were meant to be a communal thing among people who cared for one another. He reached for my hand and pulled me out of the dark isolated shell I lived in after my mother died. With him I finally thought life was possible. If he was here, he could help me know that even for today.

My eyes land on his journal. I feel him close and

understand. "How many times do I have to tell you I'm not going anywhere, babe? You're under my skin, sweetheart. I'll never leave *you*."

So that is it. The body under that mound of sand is only half the truth. The man I love is still here beside me, under my skin. He will never leave.

Somehow I will find the strength to do what I must do.

I open the journal, carefully. This book has to last me the rest of my life.

But the sight of his untidy scrawl straining to leave the page brings quick hot tears and I shut it again.

I used to tease him about his handwriting. All those cherished, scribbled notes he left on the pillow when he had to leave for work before I was up—we both knew I was faking sleep so he'd have to write one. What we knew of each other without having to say it always stunned me. Always. So right. So honest and safe. So lifetime.

So not.

I try to open the journal again. There's sustenance here, I know it. I know Paul. He'll have left words that trace the fear to its source, marking yesterday's boundaries of me only long enough to point to tomorrow's.

I'll start with the inside cover. That's benign, simple enough.

And oh, so very not. I shut the book again, put it away from me, onto the ground even. His name and home address. *Our* address, the old Mission 66 house we shared at Moose with its tan exterior walls and ugly green tile floors, plain rooms and snow piled to its eaves some years, the house that went strangely quiet the day he left for here and I knew he wouldn't be back for two years. I wasn't worried about us. Not really. We're solid granite. But I was lonely well in advance of his departure, and that was new for me. I don't usually mind if people leave. Actually I'm often glad when they do. Paul has always been different. He matters to me, not in a needy, clinging way, but in the way breathing is important.

Stripping off my top, I reach for his flannel shirt and pull it on, taking care to button it all the way to the neck. Taking up the journal once more, I let it fall open in my hands as it will.

> *One true thing.*
>   *What we evade becomes what we fear.*
>   *What we fear becomes what we are.*

A small death adder slips sideways into the lee of a bush. I feel a chill and then nothing as he settles into place, small and deadly and only a few feet from me. A few days ago my blood would've run cold at the sight of him. Now it does not. Everything has changed.

The wind rises warm off the plain, drying my tears and lifting a strand of hair that's slipped its way free of my braids. I see Foy, bent slightly over his task, rifle shouldered but at the ready. He's still coming, bringing his war to me. I must cross my Rubicon.

DAY 15

Moments past midnight. Red lens on flashlight. Sitting to steady my soul, what's left of it. I must go on soon, but I'm too numb to walk right now. Mama's eyes follow me. I shrink from them. I have broken my vow to her and am about to do it again. I cannot face her now. Just can't. Must finish what I have started.

Near dusk I closed Paul's journal and took off his shirt, folding it with care, laying it inside my pack, as still within myself as I've ever been. Unsheathing my knife, I raised a handful of my hair and slid the blade beneath it. It fell heavy to the ground. Again and again, I repeated the action until no more than an inch of covering remained anywhere except along the front where I left several thin braids intact in case the bush flies come back. I can't remember ever having this little hair. It's been growing, untrimmed, my whole life—twenty-seven years. I always thought it'd make me sick to ever cut it. Once it was done, I felt nothing.

Gathering the shorn hair into a bundle, I tied it together with twine, tucked it into my pack, and headed down the hill to intersect the line Foy was on. About 500 yards in front of him, I laid a clear set of tracks into the desert. Half a mile later, I stopped and made camp. Deliberate. Visible. Bedroll set out, pack open and contents strewn about, small fire laid and ready to light when he got within seeing distance. He thinks I'm a stupid Yankee bitch. He'll buy this scene. I was sure.

Then I bundled the sheet so it looked like a person and splayed the hair on it, propped a canteen up next to the roll, and headed back toward Foy. Night bit the sky and from its growing darkness I paced along behind him for the middle half of his trek. When he picked up my tracks at the turn, I slipped back to the camp and lit the fire. Took the length of wire, wrapped it once around each hand with a crossed loop in between. Retreated into the shadows to wait.

It didn't take long. He came on fast, flashlight beam bobbing above my footprints, drawing him to me. About 200 feet from the bedroll, he paused and looked around, then clicked off his light. At fifty feet out, he eased his rifle from his shoulders and trained it on the sheet. At twenty, he stopped and scanned the site, stepped forward a couple yards into the circle of firelight, and stopped again. Suddenly he grinned and relaxed, looking right to left, lowering the rifle, moving as if to set it aside, slipping his knife from its belt scabbard at the same time, crouching toward the lifeless lump wearing my hair and that's when I hit him. Knee to the middle back, arms high to drop the looped wire over his head and down around his neck, hands pulling outward with every cell and holding on.

He crumpled to the ground, taking me with him. We rolled several times, him thrashing, trying to break my grip, then with a crazy lunge backward, he spun me into the fire and fought free, elbowing my ribs, punching and kicking me away, scrabbling onto his knees and then his feet, grabbing at his throat, clutching for his knife, hoarse and shouting, "You crazy bitch! You wanta have some fun?" Punching me in the face, ripping skin with a jagged metal ring he wore on his pinkie, flexing his hand before doing it again. "There! How's that? That fun?" Stomping his boot into my stomach. "Wanta have some more fun?" Pulling me up by my shoulders, then driving my head back into the ground, standing over me, panting, ragged spittle hanging from his mouth, spreading one hand slow and deliberate for his belt buckle saying, "Now I'll have *my* fun."

I went inside my training then, back to the dojo, back to the floor mat where we practiced, where hundreds of times I've waited out my opponent till he was in my guard—between my legs, close in. Jiujitsu's all about ground fighting. Having someone in your guard's the best possible place to have them. But in jiujitsu it's never for real, only competition. This was for real. When Foy knelt on the ground and stretched his knife hand toward my throat, I went for an arm bar—seized his wrist, swiveled on my back, passing over his head with one leg, pinning his arm between my thighs, and then drove my hips up, wrenching down on his arm. It broke his elbow clean and slammed him onto his stomach, knocking the knife loose. He howled and I kept moving, up onto my feet, pulling his useless arm high behind his back, then laying two sharp front kicks to the base of his skull with my heel. At the first one, his neck snapped. At the second, he gurgled and stopped yelling. At the next, he stopped gurgling.

And at the last, he stopped everything.

The night went silent and I fell down and away from his heavy body, bloody and sick and crazy with the pain of it all. Not pain you feel, pain you wear. Pain you are, skin to core.

I crawled around and gathered his things. Rifle and knife mainly. Broke camp. Went back to collect the sled and came partway to the spring. Stopped. This thing is only half done. I have to carry it through.

The easiest is over. The hardest is right in front. I have to do this. I have to get Josie away from that man.

A dingo howls, close. I see a vague silhouette of her in the moonlight. White, I want to believe she's white. She howls again, wavers, disappears toward the spring. Toward Josie. And the other man.

And Mama's eyes. They pierce holes through me, knowing my shame, my inability to draw back from this fire I have set. Violence feeds on violence. Once you start it, you cannot withdraw.

Dawn. It is done.

I walked in on Rayburn cold, sliding the bolt action of the rifle into line sharply. Clear threat. No point in subtlety by then.

He froze at the sound, halted in midstep and waited, back to me, hands in view. Josie was nowhere in sight.

Steel for voice, I asked quietly, "Where's the girl?"

Immobile for a moment, he stared at nothing, jaw muscles clenched. Then he nodded toward the closest tent.

Right hand holding the rifle trained on him, center mass shot if he moved a hair, I took a few steps toward the tent and clicked on my flashlight. Red curls plastered to her forehead, Josie was hunched against a duffel bag, sound asleep. I held the light steady until I saw her chest rise and fall twice. Then I set it on the table and stared at Rayburn, steel meeting steel. He was not afraid.

Without a word I walked to his back again and removed his revolver. Beretta 9mm. Full clip. Safety off. Decided it was less cumbersome than the rifle and set that aside. Weighed the heft of his gun in my hand. Tested the action. Rayburn flinched at the sound, but said nothing. The bare lightbulbs shed an eerie glow over us. I felt numb.

I should've shot him then. Point-blank range, no chance of missing.

Couldn't do it. Dragged a chair to the center of the clearing instead, tied him in it, one ankle to each chair leg, hands together in back and laced to the frame all the way to the elbows. It hurt. I could tell by his face and the way he drew his breath in sharp when I cinched the slipknots tight against the chair, but he didn't say anything. Words don't matter anymore.

I ransacked the place then, rummaging for supplies that we could use. And carry. That ruled out almost everything but I did get us some more water and food. Enough for five days, eight if we stretch it and we will, so eight. Ammo for the revolver, but not the rifle. Never have been able to shoot a long gun. Not very good with a short one either, but rifles and shotguns buffalo me. So I busted the barrel and stock of the rifle with a maul, then took all the bullets and scattered them for a quarter mile out. They'd be better off buying a new gun than trying to get that one functional. It's strange that I didn't find more weapons, though. I expected an arsenal.

I thought hard about staying put, waiting for Bodley to show back up with the truck, trying to get the drop on him so we can drive out of here, but decided Josie and I have a better chance with the desert. There are too many variables I can't control with these men. Bodley might not come back alone. Any of them are probably better shots than me. If I missed or miscalculated or simply didn't follow through fast enough, we'd be in way worse trouble than just stranded. So no, we'll stick with the original plan. After all this the desert looks downright friendly.

The last thing was to deal with Rayburn. I

worked it through in my head the whole time I was plundering the camp. Should've killed him, but in the end couldn't. Instead I set pans of water and food close enough that he could get at them even without hands and intended to leave him tied to the chair. Decided at the last minute that he needed one foot loose in case the dingoes came in. No hands, but at least one foot. That would give him a chance. He could tip himself over and scuttle to the food and water. When the other guy got back he'd be in bad shape and might need medical care, which would give them something besides us to focus on, so I wouldn't have to kill him. Just cut one leg loose, Nowata.

I knelt to cut his right one free.

He thanked me, straight out. Said, "Thank you. That's neighborly."

Then I noticed his trouser leg and reached for the outseam and pulled it up. He had a peashooter strapped on him. All this time I thought he was unarmed, and he was sitting there with a loaded gun. Enraged and terrified, equal parts, I ripped it off, emptied the bullets into the sand, and beat the bloody hell out of it with the maul. Then I made a decision. Nose over your toes.

"Can't have you following me," I said, cold and still inside, my tongue thick and full of the metallic taste of adrenaline. Walking to him, I kicked his chair over in the sand, picked up his right foot, and drove Foy's knife straight through the back of his ankle, just behind the bone, then turned it and cut outward—severing his Achilles' tendon. Blood soaked my hands. He screamed once, writhing on the ground like an animal. I felt sick, empty.

"Just can't have you following me," I said again, shaking, trying to explain something I could never explain in a million years.

His eyes met mine, steel gone to pure malevolence, and I knew before I turned away that I should kill this man because he'd hunt me to the ends of the earth if he survived and I might've done it, I was so queasy and so close to the edge. But just as I reached for the gun I saw Josie, standing there in the doorway of the tent, sleepy but suddenly, terrifyingly awake, hair tousled, little girl eyes like Mama's, stunned, staring at me and the bloody knife in my hand and the Beretta on the table as if she'd just stumbled into hell and Satan himself had strolled up to say hello. I winced.

She didn't need to see that. Godfuckingdamnit, she didn't need to see any of that. She's seen enough for a lifetime already without having to see that too.

Wordless, she followed me to the sled and we set off at a slow but steady, ground-eating pace. The lights of the camp burned behind us for two or three hours and then we lost sight of them. While Josie slept, I kept walking. A while ago I stopped and dug us into the side of a small ravine, spread sand and brush over our gear so we can't be spotted, and laid out the pallets so we can sleep through the day.

"Night travel's our best bet. We'll stick with it," I told Jo.

She said nothing, just turned on her side and curled up, trembling. I want to touch her, hold her close or something, but don't. She's afraid of me now, with very good reason. I think about trying to explain what I did to Rayburn but can't come up with any words that make any sense.

Mama's eyes are silent.

———

It's noon now and every time I close my eyes I see Foy standing over me with his hand on his belt buckle and then I feel his neck snap beneath my boot and the sound compresses my spine. I hunch away from it, trying to get away from me, I think, but cannot escape. Desperate for something solid, a tether to hold me to the ground, I stare at Josie. She is still sleeping. I'd cry if it'd do any good.

I hurt all over. One eye's swollen shut, the other one is puffy and runny and half closed. My stomach and arms are bruised and raw. There's a deep gash in the palm of my left hand and a nasty gaping wound on my right thigh. One jaw tooth's broken right down the middle into two neat pieces, both still attached at the bone. Two, maybe three ribs are out of commission. I have a burn the size of my head between my shoulder blades. All of it makes sense to me but the stab wound in my left palm. I can't remember getting that. Not that it matters. It doesn't hurt any worse than anything else. Can't sleep on my left side. Or my right. Or my back. Or my stomach. I'll have to sit up.

Okay, fine then. At least it's done.

We made it this far. Almost sixty miles down, one-hundred-some-odd to go. If we can just cover five miles a night we can make it out of here in twenty days. We have some food, some water, a decent shot of getting more along the way, a gun and serious knife, the basics. Life hurled the fiery lakes at us and we surfed their leading waves, well, not quite, but we took those men on and came out better at this end of the deal, not counting the shape my body's in of course or what Josie thinks of me right now but it's not like I had a choice. It's how Grandmother Nowata always said it: Just do the best you can do and let the rough end drag. Stuff heals given time, if you just don't wimp out.

So maybe this kid never did like me much. And now she's scared of me to boot. But she's still breathing and that's the point. I don't need her to like me anyhow, just live. So maybe it's not actually surfing either—never saw the sense in that, water that big was meant to be left strictly alone—but it's a damn fine balancing act above a foul stretch of water on a skinny board, if I do say so myself, and I do.

We're going to beat this place yet.

Between Paul's journal and my willpower, we'll get this child out of this desert alive.

I take out my knife and start cutting the dried skin from around the wound on my thigh. Josie opens her eyes, sees what I am doing, and starts to crawl away from me, screaming at the top of her lungs, yelling for her daddy.

DAY 16

I'm going to lose her if I can't find a way in. This child is breaking in two on me and I don't know what to do to hold her together.

She screamed last night until she was hoarse and couldn't make a sound. It went on for hours. If I moved toward her at all, she sobbed and tried to scramble away. I wanted to hold her, to make it better somehow, but she wouldn't let me anywhere near. After a few attempts, I stopped trying and just sat on the ground and talked till I was blue in the face, trying to explain what I did and why. She kept calling for her daddy. When her voice went, she whispered his name. Over and over and over again. I don't think she heard a word I said.

I thought it was the thing with Rayburn that set her off, but now I'm sure it's more. She remembers Paul, remembers losing him. Seeing me use that knife to clean my wound somehow broke open her memory, and I am afraid we may not get it closed again. She's cried so hard her face is swollen and blotched. Spit is trailing from her mouth. She is shaking so bad her teeth are chattering. I keep hoping she'll fall asleep, but her eyes are wide open and terrified. She is hyper-alert, afraid to sleep. If she doesn't soon, I don't know what is going to happen.

I took Paul's shirt out sometime during the night and laid it on the ground near her, thinking she might want it. She hasn't moved a muscle its direction. I offered to read from his journal this morning. She ignored me. She's coming unhinged from the world. I have to do something to bring her back. Surely there is something I can do. I've offered her water and food. She draws further into herself with every breath.

I am losing her, Paul. Losing her. You have to help me here. I don't know what to do. I sit quiet, wrapping my left hand in a strip of cotton sheeting, mind a blur. I'm scared and sick.

Suddenly I remember again what Grandmother Haney tried to do for me the last time I saw her and I know what to do. I will tell Josie a story. A true story about how parents and white dingoes never die, but only walk beside us invisible for a ways so we can choose the path we need for ourselves. I have had no need for this particular grandmother's stories for seventeen years. They made me angry, my mother's mother's tall tales. They made me remember everything I wanted to forget. But today I am at the end of my rope. Maybe somewhere in the stories I can find a lifeline for Jo. And me.

DAY 17

Grandmother's story is helping. Josie is finally listening. I have been sitting here in the sand facing her and telling about parents and white dingoes over and over. I must've told it twenty times by now. A few minutes ago, I stirred some noodles into warm water and offered Josie the broth. She took the cup from my hand and sipped it. I told the story again while she did. A Story of the Truth, I call it.

Now I sit here gripping Paul's journal and waiting for what comes next. Jo is so tired she's about to fall over. My eyes land on the ground between us and I see dingo tracks. Unmistakable. How did they get there and when? I have no idea, but I can use them for the story. Visual aids.

Leaning forward, I set my right hand next to the tracks. "Look, Jo. See? I told you. She's been here, keeping watch, just like I said in the story. Look at it, hon. See the signs she left for us?"

Almost imperceptibly, Josie leans toward the prints. For a long time she looks at them and then at me.

"Jo's sleepy," she finally says, reverting to the language she used to use with Paul when she was little. Tears spring into my eyes and I hurry to the pallet I've made for her and dust the sand off it.

Josie lets me hold onto her arm and help her walk to the mat. Settling her onto it, I lift off her T-shirt and put Paul's shirt on, buttoning it all the way to the neck. Her hands press the fabric close to her skin as I ease her onto her side. Head on her pack, she finally closes her eyes, and I kneel beside her, one hand smoothing her back through the shirt, crying in earnest.

"Tally, tell me a story," she whispers.

My heart feels full for the first time in days. We are going to be okay.

"Once upon a time, in a place like this one, there was a white dingo—"

"No," Jo interrupts. "Tell me a story from Daddy's book."

Closing my eyes for a brief moment, I reach for Paul's journal and let it fall open. Then I start reading.

DAY 18

Jo is coming back to herself. Still weak, she rides on the sled most of the time, but she is paying attention. We both see the albino now and both search for Paul's words. Josie remembered his letters— she saved every one he sent her and brought them to Australia in her daypack—and has started reading them to me while we walk. It is a valuable use of a flashlight. I read to her from his journal on our breaks or at dawn before we sleep.

We both have the same favorite. The story about Josephine and the Rodeo. Paul and I took Jo to see Dix ride in Rock Springs for her birthday one year. Josie tried to beat up a cowboy before the day was over. Paul was appalled. I was tickled. The tale makes for good memories. I have a feeling we'll be reading it so much we'll learn it by heart.

———

Resource assessment.

I brought as much water as I could carry from Rayburn's camp. Filled both water tanks but couldn't budge the sled with them, so had to leave one behind. We had twenty gallons two days ago, enough to get us a long ways down that dirt track if we could've used it. But I was afraid to get on it. We'd just be too damn visible and there's no way we could hide our tracks well enough. I'm sticking with my plan to go cross-country—only now I'm crossing a different way, toward a different village. There are fewer water sources, but it's safer. When Bodley comes back, Rayburn will send him after us. They'll follow my mapped route. We need to be somewhere else. If we're careful and replenish our water at every spring, we should have enough water to make it to that village. It's 110 miles or so, a little farther than the other one, but still reachable, I think.

The food I took from their camp has made all the difference. It's not enough for our whole trek—I simply couldn't carry one more thing—but it's enough to keep us going for a while. Two bananas, some grapes, a small sack of apples, three bags of dehydrated spaghetti sauce and noodles, a few packages of soup powder, and a pack of cookies for Jo. If we stretch it, and we will, it may last us more than a week. I'm still so nauseated I can hardly eat anyway, and Jo's appetite isn't as hearty as I remember it being in Wyoming. Eating is a chore, but at least we have food for now.

The albino appears in the distance, a wavering white spirit looking after us, I would like to believe. And so will. Reality may be a tad overrated anyhow.

DAY 19

Subtlety is not her strong suit.

I trust instinct. Though part of me wants to seize this tattered book and read it word for word cover to cover, no breaks, the rest of me knows better. The whole would kill. Pieces sustain. We've read Josephine and the Rodeo about ten times. It helps. But for the long hours of sunlight when Jo is asleep, I need something for me. I am weak and wounded, evading my mother's eyes, sick to the core, but in a situation where I have to be strong and cheerful and efficient. So, once a day, first thing every morning, I'll let this journal fall open at will and read whatever my eyes land on, and that'll be my touchstone for the next twenty-four hours.

It's a good thing I never got religion. This sort of behavior could be dangerous in the real world. That's the kind of thing Dix leans to. And a big part of the reason he's always in trouble.

Man. Now if that's not a case of the pot calling the kettle something a little less than white, I don't know what is. Dix is probably right. I could use a little religion out here. I'm half mad, seeing a white ghost dog and dragging a kid on a sled through a desert not meant to be traversed on foot. Who am I to judge anybody else?

Subtlety is not her strong suit. Well hell, Paulson, doesn't exactly take a rocket scientist to figure that one. I couldn't do subtle if my life depended on it. Come at life straight on, that's my rule. Always has been. Fear something? Walk right out into the big middle of it and breathe. Hate it? Stroll on out there into its belly and swallow as big a mouthful as you can get. Love someone? Dive high and hard into the deep end and drown if necessary to stay there. That's how I live it. Straight up. No games. If I ever tried to take life sideways, I'd get dizzy for sure. Subtle's for folks who can live on an angle and not fall over and that's a whole lot of people in this world but it's not Tally Nowata.

I don't think Paul ever knew quite what to make of me. I'd look up sometimes to catch him staring at me with this puzzled look, like he was wondering, How the hell did I ever wind up with *her?*

Maybe he was looking for subtle when he bumped into me that day. Someone subtle and tall and so beautiful it aches to look at them. Instead he got plain and short and blunt as the dull edge of an old butcher knife. It never crossed my mind to wonder about any of that before. And I don't really think either one of us was looking the day we met, either. We were just living, and after that first day, we just *were*, period, with a certainty so deep you don't have to think about it. Couldn't if you wanted to. It's beyond thought.

And that's where I have to leave it. Paul never breathed a word to me about needing tall or beautiful. Or having problems with my lack of subtlety. So that's where it has to rest. If we were good enough for no worries then, we're good enough for it now.

What would he ever have done with subtle in a woman anyhow? That would've bored him to tears in under zero. So there. At least I never bored him. That I know for a fact. Aggravated the whay out of him maybe, but bored? Never.

———

We made good time last night. Josie crawled off the sled after an hour and announced she was tired of riding. I was so grateful I nearly cried. Had to readjust to pulling the sled without her on it, though. The rhythm was off. I hurt like hell but in different valleys. Stepped off into a rabbit burrow once and the whole load crashed into me from behind. Turned too sharp at another place and it tipped over. Wanted to cuss so bad I could taste it. Jo just stood there staring at me.

"If looks were spit, I'd still be swimming." I muttered grumpily. "Or long since drowned."

Josie broke into a laugh. I kept muttering. She likes it when I'm grumpy about little things. She thinks it's funny. I intend to grump about everything I can think of for the rest of this trip.

We took two breaks for naps, one after each of

the wrecks, but managed to put several miles behind us anyway. We're going on willpower alone, I'm amazed we can move at all—would've argued it was impossible back home where we think we've got the limits of human endurance pretty well mapped out—but we're moving. Not fast, not efficient, but covering ground, and that's the whole point right now.

Each hour we walk, we widen the search area exponentially; this is a basic law of search and rescue. "Makes it harder and harder for those men to find us—if they even try," I explained to Jo, trying to take the edge off her fear of the men by speaking of them just as casually as I would a stick of firewood. It's starting to work. She doesn't shake now when I bring them up.

We're aiming for another pocket of water. Should reach it in a couple days. It wasn't marked on Paul's research maps, but it shows up on the topo. I wish we could've gone by the route I plotted using his notes. I'd have felt better about that. I'm worried that this next spring may also be dried up, but I don't know what else to do but push forward now. Our water's going fast.

I have been watching animal trails too, trying to make some sense of them. Have to figure out how to get food from this land. The stab wound on my left hand is deep, angry, hot. Hurts like hell clear up to my elbow. It's getting infected, I think. Just looking at it makes me sick to the stomach. I rewrap the hand and try to forget about it, like I'm trying to forget everything else here, but my mind is a traitor, seeking out the darkness, dragging up what I have buried, searching for Mama's eyes in spite of how hard I'm trying to run away from them.

Subtle my foot. If I was subtle right now, this place would chew me up and spit me out. Subtle couldn't skin a songbird, roast and eat it. Couldn't steal raw meat from a dingo and watch in strangled silence as that man dragged my lover's body around behind that truck. Subtle couldn't do what I did back there to him and Rayburn. Couldn't drag this kid one ratty little inch, much less twenty goddamn miles. Couldn't collect fresh urine—which is sterile—and use it to wash out my wounds in order to save water. Subtle can't do any of that.

If you ask me, subtle's overrated. Not worth a pocketful of sundried shit in a crunch.

And I'd tell you that too, sure as shootin', Paul O'Malley, if you were just here. I sure the hell would.

———

It's time to bathe and sleep. Jo's already down for the count. This heat makes her tired.

Stepping out of my clothes, I hang them on the low branches of a bush to air dry, then scrub the uninjured parts of my skin with handfuls of sand. It's a strange echo of an old habit—there is nothing I like better than a long soak in a warm bubble bath at the end of a sweaty day—but when Paul first suggested substituting soil for water a week after I arrived here, I was horrified at even the notion.

"Sand cuts body odor, Tal, and gives some protection from the sun. Plus it just all round makes you feel better," he explained patiently, dousing his armpits with red dirt and grinning like a kid on a ride at the county fair.

Muttering something irreverent about my sanity (and his), I joined him in the bath and was surprised to find he was right. I *did* feel better. Cooler. Cleaner. Less out of place. So daily sand baths are part of the routine now. Habit, yes, but smart. They help center me enough to sleep. Maybe tomorrow I'll get Jo to take one before she goes to bed. Yes, that's what I'll do. That'll be a good thing.

She's still not talking about Paul. The rodeo story seems to be all she can handle. I read it every morning, like a bedtime fable, when I tuck her in. She doesn't smile. She just listens. But she listens with her heart. Sometimes I wonder if I should try to get her to talk about what happened, but I think not. Not now anyway. She's so fragile. I don't want to push. Kids probably talk when they're ready. I wasn't ever ready to talk about Mama and when people tried, I just shut down further. I don't want to do that to Jo. I'll let her choose her own time and place.

My heels are dry and cracked from all the walking and too little water. Reaching for the bottle of motor oil I drained from the truck, I coat the soles of my feet with it and, despite everything, feel a brief flash of satisfaction that I've at least done *something* right. That has to count in our favor. Just has to.

For good measure I rub some oil on my elbows too. There's no earthly reason I have to come apart at my literal seams out here. I can do this.

———

A little success fuels big efforts.

The sand bath and motor oil gave me an idea. Well actually, that's not quite right. They didn't give me an idea, but they did let me feel good enough about myself to come up with one on my own. Well no, even that's not quite right. I didn't come up with this idea on my own. All I did was get comfortable enough not to miss it when it flew over my unsuspecting head.

We've come into a band of low hills, dotted with silver-gray mulga again. The yellow spinifex seems to hold sway on the flats, but every so often a line of mulga hills and rocky outcrops will show up—not quite an oasis, but welcome just the same. Today, feet and elbows greased up good and the rest of me feeling pretty relaxed, I glanced up to see a small bee hovering nearby. It made a short loop past my ear and zoomed off. The sun was coming on strong, but I got up and followed the bee, no longer sleepy. Or tired. About twenty yards from our camp it slipped into a rock crevice.

Honey.

There had to be honey in that rock. Closing the distance between it and us, though, would be a pain in the neck. And other places.

I backed away a few feet and sat down to study the situation. Bees came and went, unaware.

The first problem was how to get to the hive. The second one was how to do that without rousing the bees. Jo's seriously allergic to them. We can't risk a sting for her. She's got one shot of epinephrine in her pack, thanks to Paul, but we can't afford to use that. Have to keep her in the clear.

Maybe not, though. Maybe these bees are like native North American honeybees: stingless? But how could I know that for sure? Test it on myself? Okay.

Waking Jo, I moved her out another thirty yards or so, figuring better safe than stung, and left her sitting there looking about equally cross and worried. She couldn't decide whether to be mad at me or scared. I said something reassuring, or something that passed for it, and came back to the rock with a stick. The time for thinking and planning was over. Too anxious to get at the honey to worry about finesse or being stung, I jabbed the stick into the crevice.

The hive stirred, buzzing and swarming out of the crack as one swirling mass, dozens of legs and feet and wings on my face and in my hair and under my shirt and up my skirt. I meant to stay put no matter what, but when they hit me, I couldn't have stood still at that rock to save my soul or anybody else's. Stumbling backward, I cussed and slapped and stamped seven ways to Sunday, trying to shake the bees.

They wouldn't shake. But somewhere in the middle of my hissy fit, I suddenly realized that nothing new was hurting. No stings. They *were* stingless.

Laughing out loud, I stood completely still, bees stuck in my hair and crawling on my clothes, and raised my arms to the sky to show Josie it was okay, calling her to come see. "Praise the Lord and pass the biscuits, Josephine—we have *honey*, baby girl!"

That was a little premature.

We didn't have honey. Not for a long time. I broke the one stick clear off trying to reach the hive and wound up going through three more before I found a limb flexible and long enough. It took twenty-five minutes to draw it back with a dab of sticky yellow liquid on the end.

I could've cried from sheer exhaustion by then.

Instead I handed it to Josie and we each took a swipe with our fingers. Nothing ever tasted so good. Ever. We lay flat out on our backs—my burn hardly hurt right then—so happy we hummed. Onward Christian Soldiers was what came out. I'm not a Christian or a soldier and I don't feel the least bit holy or military, but for some reason that was the tune we hummed. Jo smiled and clapped her hands a couple times when we finished. I decided to try to remember more hymns.

After a while Josie agreed to nap again. She was never this peaceable about daytime sleep back home—she fought it tooth and bloody nail there—but here she is willing. The heat makes her tired and eases the transition into unconsciousness. I went back for more honey, carting my little tin cup along with some silly notion of filling it to the brim with the golden liquid.

The cup never got used.

Perched at various places on the rock, I probed repeatedly for another hour, more careful now not to disturb the bees with the end of my stick, but each time drawing back a few more bees than honey. The total haul for all that effort and time was less than a teaspoon: robbing bees isn't even remotely cost-effective as a survival strategy.

Trudging back to camp, I tried to remember how pleased I was with myself for having motor oil along to rub on my cracked heels and elbows. Somehow it didn't seem like all that much to celebrate anymore. Success may breed big efforts, but it doesn't guarantee more success. Nor does it improve your general attitude.

When another bee swung past my head this afternoon, I thought about his home and forgot my vow not to desire comfort out here. More than anything else right then, I wished we could be near a grocery store again so I could buy honey in a jar and eat it raw. By the spoonfuls.

And I still wish it now.

I reach for Paul's shirt and hold it close. Jo took it off before she went to sleep. I found it folded on top of my pack when I returned from the hive. The worn flannel offers a measure of comfort. My left arm throbs clear up to my neck, taking the edge off my comfort. Bush flies coat our skins. Sweat stings our eyes. Comfort flees. Everything good here has a whole slew of polar opposites.

DAY 20

It's not where Tally and I climb that matters. It's where we wind up.

Walked time out of mind last night, those words pacing every step. Then opened the journal to read them this morning. I feel an eerie chill in my bones in spite of the heat. It's uncanny how we did that, knew in advance what the other one was going to say.

It's not where Tally and I climb that matters. It's where we wind up.

He said this to Miriam the last time she called, ostensibly to set up the 500th final detail of Josie's visit here. That woman called every day for two months. She was always calling for something. I've never known such a needy human.

Actually, that's not quite right. Miriam was a lot of things, but needy wasn't among them. She didn't need Paul. She just needed to control him. And his guilt over leaving her and Josie for me was the biggest hammer she could've ever had over his head. She whomped him with it every time we turned around. Subtly, yes. She was *very* subtle. No outright attacks. Simple tears and such. She'd call crying, claiming she just couldn't *deal* with Jo another instant, threatening to send her to us. But the second Paul would say, "Great, let's do that," and I would adjust my life to try to welcome this little girl child—we even bought a plane ticket twice and Josie got to us once—Miriam would dissolve into the pitiful mother who'd miss her baby too badly to actually do something that heinous, the sad but courageous little mother who would somehow find a way to bear up under it all, if Paul could just help her get through this one particular altercation with Josie. Or the next one tomorrow. Or the one after that.

Then she'd set up the altercations so her daughter had no choice but to play into them and we all got to ride on Miriam's merry-go-round. Indifference and deliberate unhappiness disguised as innocent need is a bad mix, amounts to meanness posing as love. Slices and dices everybody close. They're paper-thin cuts, though, so you can't complain and sometimes you don't even notice till it's way too late.

I used to get so mad at her games I could've spit sixteen-penny nails straight through a concrete wall, watching Paul go through the pain of walking out on her and Josie all over again, every week, sure as the sun came up and set on Sunday. He never figured out how to stop it. Point-blank refused to back her out of his corner. Let her walk all over him and Josie at will and excused it. It's the way Miriam was raised, he said. She didn't know any better and didn't mean anything by it, she was just hurt and tired too now, from having to rear this child alone—after all Josie really was a handful as I'd seen for myself—and anyhow, supporting Miriam was the very least he could do after leaving her that way. I snapped once that no child is ever that big a handful without a hell of a lot of adult supervision, and he said that was easy to say from where I was sitting.

We had a couple raging arguments about it and I finally let it go and listened in silence. Four years of watching the man I love get charbroiled daily on the fires of another woman's anger at her life. Damn near broke my heart.

Then something happened, I never knew what. Just before he left for here, he'd taken a different tone with her. Said things like *It's not where Tally and I climb that matters. It's where we wind up.* And to Josie, *This visit I expect you to put a little effort into getting to know the woman I love, Josephine. She's here to stay and it's time for you to accept that.*

We were entering a new phase of us, coming here to the Tanami. We didn't talk about it or plan it or anything, it just happened. Deepening the mystery. There was a sureness about us in those last few days before his departure that we'd never had before. A sureness about me. When he reached for me tender and then savage in the nights before he left, I knew he was the end of my journey. The one I was born to find, born to love with all that I am, all I can ever become. I was healed and whole at last and the past let me be. No nightmares, no screaming regrets, and the vow of nonviolence I took at ten finally felt doable—all because of a tall, curly-headed man who had kind brown eyes and a good heart. Just like Mama.

I came to this desert knowing I was finally walking into the reason for my existence.

We had three weeks. Three astonishingly perfect, intoxicating, sensual weeks together. We loved so wild and hard, so intense and loud, and then so gentle and languid and soundless long into the starry nights and well beyond sunrise. We cried and laughed, we read poems aloud and trailed tepid spring water down each other's spines in the simmering heat of the late afternoons. We lay flat in the sand and sketched out a dream home for three, planned family vacations enough to last a decade. We teased and talked and argued nonstop for two days straight and then worked side by side without a single word one whole afternoon and none of it was separate from any of the rest. No pretense, no artifice, no guile, no games. By the time he left to pick up Josie, I couldn't have said where I stopped and he started anymore.

And, the very hell of it is, I still can't.

It is near noon and 127 degrees in Tanami. I am waiting out the heat of the day in the heart of a red desert. A slender blue ribbon dances above my head in the afternoon breeze.

That blue ribbon. I close my eyes and remember my way back to Paul and me.

Standing at the terminal gate as the final boarding call was announced, both of us having said all there was to say, he let his hand stray, as usual, to my braid. Reaching up, I untied the ribbon and gave it to him, closing his fingers around it with my own. Then, like always, I kissed two of my fingertips—the first and second together—and pressed them lightly to Paul's lips. Eyes locked on mine, he backed down the jetway. A month later he lay in his tent here in the Tanami, missing me and staring at that ribbon, telling the whole to his journal.

For four weeks he carried the ribbon in his pocket, buried in a bunch of Australian and U.S. coins, his Leatherman, and copious amounts of sand. One morning he drew the narrow length of satin out, took a needle and catgut, and stitched it to the peak of his tent. Then he lay down and watched it dance awhile before trying to capture his love in words.

Now there it sways above my head, a reminder of an incredible woman with sun-streaked hair and dark green eyes. This flimsy little ribbon is a 10,000-mile tie that binds her and me to us.

I cling to Paul's words, using them as a buffer between me and the truth. I cling to my anger against Miriam too, letting it run hot in my veins in a way I never could before. Every movement now is a struggle. Rage and desire hurt back home, but here they kindle a flame, a desperate energy, the kind that can keep me on my feet, pulling this load, cajoling this child and myself forward.

Josie sleeps, restless. The day burns hot about us. Our throats are raw, parched by wind and dust. Our eyes weep, not tears of any import, but ones sucked from us by exhaustion and the beginnings of sun blindness. I keep thinking I see the albino. Must be losing it. Worried what that says about my state of mind. Josie thinks it too, though. I am afraid for us.

We keep watching for the truck to return. The camp is a good twelve or thirteen miles behind us, but we can see much further than that. There's nothing here but shimmering heat waves over patchy clumps of pale yellow bushes, a few trees, and endless ocean swells of sand. Fire mosaic runs hard down some sections and disappears in others. For an instant I feel Foy's head roll away from my boot, again and again. The nausea rides strong over me and I tumble back to my knees, rivulets of spit connect my retching body to the sand. The divide between who I thought I was seven nights ago and who I am now yawns wide ahead, and I cannot see a way to bridge these two halves of myself. I am sickened by the jolt of that moment, my foot kicking the life out of that man. Sickened too by the thud of Paul's body hitting the ground to be dragged over bushes and dirt like an insensate log, like mother at my father's hands all those years ago. Sick to the bone of this desert and its pounding, angry heart.

Nose over your toes, Nowata. Too far to go to lose it now. Focus on the details.

Food. We're getting low. I have to figure out how to mine this place better than I have been. Seeds, leaves, bark: people ate that stuff before they got around to growing corn and wheat and cramming themselves into cities, so I ought to be able to feed us from this land. The problem is, absolutely nothing here appears edible. Everything's burnt to a crisp and has thorns and looks like it would take out a good chunk of your innards on the way down, cooked or raw. Then too, I have no clue what's poisonous and what's not, and that's a pretty big hole in a knowledge base to fill in by trial and error. It'd take me months to taste test all these plants for toxicity.

But if I find any that look worth eating, I will do it—if I can remember how. It's been six years since I attended that one-hour seminar on field vegetation. And exactly six years since I thought about it. Never in my wildest dreams did I ever imagine I'd need that information. So much for the utility of dreams.

Or the good sense to plan ahead before pitching up in a place like this. If I just knew some of these plants, this might be easier. We'd have a better chance. So much for that too. Hindsight's 20-20 or better every time, but it won't do me any good now to be staring back over my backside. Only direction to look today is straight ahead.

At least I know the acacias, so I picked up a few more pods yesterday afternoon. The beans inside were hard enough to break a tooth. Eventually I remembered making lentil stew back home and got the notion to soak one in water. After about five hours, it was still pretty tough, but I pounded it with a stone into a pulpy mash. Aside from a few busted fingertips and a bland taste, it was okay, so I gathered some more pods and set the beans to soak and then sat staring at the closest land feature to us: a tall termite mound—four feet high and nearly three wide. They are all over out here, but until today, I never really looked at them.

Lizards eat termites. Birds eat termites. I have eaten a bird and if I get half a chance to catch a lizard, I'll eat one of those too. But right now, I might as well cut out the middleman and go straight to the source. Trying not to think too much about what I was actually doing, I tackled the mound.

The rest of the morning was spent with me poking long stalks of dead grasses into the mound, waiting a few minutes, then drawing out the plump creatures, trapping them in my tin dish, and setting them out in the sun to toast. A fire would've been quicker, but we can't risk the smoke. After I got over the idea of eating bugs, and adjusted to their nutty, rather bland taste, this new food source went down reasonably well. Wrapping my hand in a bandanna to shield it from the sun, I set in to trapping more, roasting extra for later. Josie watched the whole affair, disgusted, and finally agreed to eat a package of the soup.

"That is a huge concession for someone who thinks powdered soup is the exact equivalent of dirt," I said to her, and she almost grinned but caught herself and didn't.

I want her to like me. Not bosom buddies or anything. Just some—enough so when she looks at me, I can tell I'm finally a little above pond scum on her list. That would be nice. Once she almost let herself like me, the first time Miriam sent her to live with us. She even made me a birthday card that week out of construction paper and yarn. But as soon as her mom changed her mind about the living arrangements, Josie changed her mind about me. I became their enemy, the woman who came between. It was a rough time for everybody.

By the next year I simply ceded the house to Jo and Paul during her visits. They loved each other too much for me to risk coming between them, I told myself, lying through my teeth. I wanted to be part of them so bad I could taste it. The rest of me was scared stiff at the very idea. Having Josie not like me made it easier because I didn't have to risk ruining anything they had with my Nowata genes. Now there is no longer a chance of that.

But I always hoped that one day we would find common ground, a way to make a family of three that wouldn't always feel like a betrayal of her mother to Josie. I thought maybe when Jo got grown, she would accept Paul and me. The concept of her as an adult was easier for me to take too. I am pretty good with adults. I hoped one day the three of us could work something out. There's no longer a chance of that either.

The emptiness of these truths stretches into the future. One hand lies useless in my lap, swathed in pus-laden cotton, swollen and aching and fiery hot.

The other one gathers termites in a newly remembered, ancient motion.

Fifty-fifty's the score of this gig. But no matter the numbers, I am wresting an existence from this land. Holding fast to Paul's words and my anger, coaxing insects from the ground. The seeds of survival, for Josie at least, still remain within me. I can do this. I can get this child out of here alive.

Crying dry tears, I bury my head in Paul's shirt, trying to erase the smell of his death with what's left to me of the smell of his life.

DAY 21

Yesterday's anger, nonspecific and brooding, faded as the heat rose and I slept undreaming until Josie nudged me awake at sunset. Part of me wanted to summon the anger again, immediately, but the rest was too tired for lies.

Fact is, I never disliked Miriam. Wanted to. Hating her would've made it all a lot easier. I couldn't.

She and Paul were about as wrong for each other as a duck and a dingo. One made for the water, the other just as happy without. One content in mud puddles, the other in a hot sand bath. One feathered, one furred. One web-footed, one padded and clawed. One lays eggs, the other eats them. One predator, one prey—though which was which in this particular union, I'd be hard pressed to say. Whenever the O'Malleys were in the same room, they raised the hackles on everybody else unlucky enough to be there. It was a visceral thing, physical. Duck and dingo, somebody's getting munched. Count on it. Death's in the air. It makes people nervous.

The one thing they still had in common was Josie. I always used to wonder about her chances.

What scars will she have to show for having lived her whole life in death's shadow? Paul was right, more so now than ever. Jo is a lot like me. She saw the death of her parent's marriage before she was six, the death of two beloved grandparents before she was eight, and now the death of her father. Her scars may never fade. Some don't.

The faint smell of my mother's kitchen lingers close today. Desperate not to have to reckon with her now, I cover my nose and will the past away, and she is replaced by the smell of Paul's death and the greasy odor of Foy and finally, the bitter stench of my own vomit. My body cannot accept my mind's denials. It speaks truth in spite of my evasions, my frantic efforts to forget my mother's one request. With a mother in the wings, no one's soul can long be a stranger to its self. I will have to answer to her soon, but not now. Not today. I can't explain it yet, not even to myself. My left arm hurts all the way to the bottom of my feet. I think I can feel it throbbing in my teeth.

Almost blind with pain, I open my leather tobacco pouch and take a pinch to chew. When it is thoroughly soaked with saliva, I roll it into a ball with my tongue and then use it like a compress over the infected wound on my left palm. I remember watching Dix do that at the incision site after he lost the middle third of his spleen.

"Natural pain reliever, TJ," he said, "Best money can buy."

I laughed at him then, but had to call and apologize a year later when I read about the same technique in a wilderness survival manual.

Dix chuckled, then reminded me that not many people have tobacco from Sun Dance. "Strong medicine. You have to keep it with you, TJ. Promise me you'll keep it with you wherever you go. You might need it sometime."

I promised. And kept it. Every year when Dix showed up, he took my old tobacco and replaced it with a new stash newly blessed at Sun Dance. The last he gave me was two years ago, and I wore it all the way here. As things have turned out, I did need it. I must remember to admit that to Dix.

The throbbing in my hand, sure enough, is easing. If I get out of here alive, I'm going to make sure Dixon knows about that too. I may even give in and go to Sun Dance with him one year.

But then again, maybe not. One religious Nowata is probably enough. I don't think the world is ready for two of us yet.

———

We had our first stroke of unsullied good luck this morning. Beneath a rock boulder we found a cluster of green plants—altogether, not more than one cup's worth. Still, one cup is better than none, *if* they're edible, that is, and we won't know that for twenty-four hours. I wracked my brain, trying to dredge up some more helpful facts from that one-hour seminar six years ago. It takes twenty-four hours to run a taste test. But there was something about eight hours too, wasn't there? I mulled that figure. There was some sort of rule about eight hours.

Then it came to me. Fast for eight. You can't

start edibility tests on plants until you've fasted for eight.

"Well, at least that's not an issue here," I say loudly, grinning at Jo. "Unless you count half a teaspoon of termites as food, that is, and I don't. So there. I get a head start on the test. Cut it from twenty-four hours to sixteen. More good luck. Oh my. I can barely contain myself."

Josie looked at me like I'd lost my mind and then began dragging Paul's letters out of her pack.

I started to yank the whole plant out by the roots, right hand extended on go, but my left hand grabbed the right one back and clutched it tight against my stomach until better sense could prevail. Temples pounding, left palm throbbing, I made myself sit still until the shaking passed. Then I reached out and broke one stem off at the ground. Josie was poring over her letters.

She still is, reading and setting some aside in a separate pile, organizing them, I guess. Every now and then she sneaks a look at me and then goes right back to work. I concentrate on my test.

The rest of that seminar's been coming in snippets. PCP Gods. The PCP GODS. There's a rule about them too, but what is it?

Avoid them. If in doubt, avoid anything resembling the PCP GODs. Parsley, carrots, parsnip, G— G—what's the G for? *Garlic,* that's it, parsley, carrots, parsnip, garlic, onions, dill. But what kind of leaf does parsnip have? I can't remember. Not even real sure I know what parsnips are. Five out of six will have to do. So what else? Stuff about the sap.

There are rules about the sap. No milky sap or sap that blackens when air hits it. *Yes!*

It is too small a feat to celebrate, but I do it anyway. I reach up over my shoulder and pat myself on the back. Catch Josie looking at me. She rolls her eyes and shakes her head and turns back to her letters without a word. In the distance behind her, I could swear I see that albino. I'm losing it. Nose over your toes, Nowata. Stick with the job.

Now I tip the leaves over, inspecting them. No animal has chewed on them yet or even tried to. That worries me. If wild animals don't eat it, isn't that a bad sign? Pondering that for all of ten seconds, I plunge in. No choice. Have to try. Maybe other species can afford to be picky. We can't. I don't like dill pickles back home either, but here I'd eat 'em in a slim heartbeat.

The rest of the seminar comes clear in my head, like a moving picture on a giant screen. I remember the instructor standing up there, feet splayed and turned outward, hands demonstrating all the levels you have to check before you put a piece of vegetation in your mouth. So next I tear one leaf apart and wait for the sap. Clear as resin. That's a good sign. Murky or dark liquid means trouble. Rubbing the leaf on my left wrist, I break open a stem and wait again. Clear again. Another good sign. Rub the stem on my right wrist and, while I'm waiting this time, I dig another stem out of the ground, skinny roots and all, easing the displaced soil back around the remaining plants. Cannot risk losing them to the air.

Split open a root. Rub it on my left ankle. Check

my watch. Any reaction may take up to fifteen minutes to appear. Lying on one side I pull my hat down over my face like I'm in the field on a search, only I'm not. I'm still in the Tanami, stranded with a kid and no supplies, hurt ribs and other parts, but the act itself is calming. When you lie on the planet with your hat covering your face, the worrisome parts of the world have to stand aside. Even my ribs don't ache as bad right now.

Exactly fifteen minutes later, I sit up and peer at the skin on both wrists and the one ankle. No redness, no rash. Other than a little dirt, well, a lot of dirt, it is all normal. So that settles it. In a cool crevice deep beneath a large rock, I build a small fire, hanging our sheet so it will diffuse any smoke before it gets into the air. Then I pour half a cup of water in the bottom of my tin dish, drop only the leaves in, set it on the fire, and put on the lid. The second part of the tests is under way. Josie has almost made it through her stack of letters. I can't figure out what she's doing. Now she has three different piles. No matter, at least she's busy and content. That is a good thing. I'm glad she's well enough to be busy and content.

As the greens simmer, mnemonic devices from the seminar come flooding back. Touch lips three. Tongue and chew fifteen, Do Not Swallow. Swallow and wait for eight. I intend to follow these rules to the very letter. The last thing we need now is me getting taken out by a plant. If I do the tests right, there's no chance of that, so I won't cut a single corner. Removing the dish from the fire, I take a pinch of the stewed leaves and touch it to my lips. Wait three minutes. No burning or itching. Then I place it on my tongue and set the timer on my watch for fifteen minutes and lean back against the rock to wait, every muscle poised to spit out the bland mush if I start feeling sick. Nothing happens.

When my watch chimes, I reset it for another fifteen and start chewing, then sit still, staring blindly at the rock, willing myself not to swallow until the alarm sounds, thinking about Jed and Pony and the last climb we did before I left for here. Winter ascent of the Grand Teton. Fast, down, and dirty. We did it in under twelve hours from Lupine Meadows. Good memory. Strong. I can almost feel the sting of the snow on my face, my ice ax and crampons dig in, my skis pick up speed on the descent. The tasteless greens begin dissolving inside my mouth, slimy, heavy with saliva. I almost gag. Fight it. Breathe wind off the mountains, stand at the treeline and watch the world go silent below, grab one elbow with each hand and hold on, force myself to sit still and quiet, breathing into the pain of my throbbing left palm, watching for any signals that the plant is poisoning my body. Tell myself it's no worse than spinach so if it turns out to be nontoxic, we'll at least have a side dish for dinner. I'll pretend I'm doing all this on a childhood bet with Dix. The prize was always the last orange in the house. Oranges. Citrus. Fruit. What luxuries they were. Then and now. Go figure life.

Fifteen minutes later, I swallow the greens, doubting they are actually green any longer, and check my watch, calculating how long the "wait for eight" rule will run. Eight hours of no ill side effects and I can eat a small portion of the steamed greens. Eight hours after that—again, with no ill effects—and I can gather and cook the rest. Then'll come the big challenge: coaxing Josie to eat some. She puts the last letter on the third pile and dusts her hands off on her shirt.

All I have to do now is wait. Wait and watch for symptoms.

We have a window. Narrow, foggy paned, not much to recommend it. Except what it lets us glimpse of our chances.

———

Josie, bless her heart, just threw the window open wide.

Then she reached out and brought Paul inside. We are going to make it out of here in one piece.

She got up and brought the letters to me, saying, "Look, Tally. Look here."

The sight of Paul's handwriting, neater than the scrawl in his journal, big block letters printed for his daughter on every page, turned my heart over. Tears came unbidden and words were slow to follow. Jo took that for general slowness on my part and nudged me. "Look!"

I took the first letter, but my tears blurred the paper so badly I couldn't read a thing. Josie sat down beside me and put her hand on mine. "There's stuff about the plants in here, Tally," she said, pressing through my grief. "Lots of stuff."

Sure enough. Each letter had at least one little

nugget of information about edible plants and animals. Paul was educating his daughter, teaching her how to survive in a desert, from 12,000 miles away. Tanami to Louisiana. At home she'd never need any of this information. He told it to her anyway, just like he tried to tell it to me but I wouldn't listen.

"I used to cover my ears with my hands sometimes when he'd tell me this stuff, Jo," I admitted, sniffling. "So many facts. They made my brain hurt."

Josie grinned and laughed. "He used to do that in the swamps next to Gram O'Malley's. Talk and talk and talk. I covered my ears sometimes too, just sat in the canoe and covered my ears. Like this." And she showed me how she did it so no sound could get in.

We giggled a bit then. Actually giggled. It felt good.

And then we got up and conducted a groundbreaking ceremony for the Tally and Josie School of Desert Plants and Animals. Josephine O'Malley was hired as the TJ's first headmistress and instructor. She scheduled classes for 10:00 A.M. and 6:00 P.M. each day. The letters are the course text. I will have homework assignments and get sent on detention if I turn them in late or incomplete. Now *this* feels like progress.

Six hours down, no symptoms. Two more to go before we have fresh greens for breakfast. We are going to make it out of here.

Once that is done, I can deal with my mother.

DAY 22

Yesterday's momentum came to a screeching halt when we made it to this waterhole. We're down to less than twelve gallons now. We need more. When we came in sight of this place, we dropped our gear and ran for it. Only to stop and stare in horror. Salt.

There's plenty of water here, but it's salty. White brine lines the edges of the pool. It isn't good for anything. All of a sudden I remember standing in the kitchen at Moose a year ago, making dinner while Paul sat at his desk finalizing his research plans. After faxing the prospectus to his adviser, he mentioned, almost in an aside, that most of the standing water in the Tanami was salty so the animals here had to be pretty ingenious. I wasn't paying much attention to him. I was worried about my quiche. I forgot all about that conversation before it was even over, and it never came up again. Till now.

I don't have a desalinization kit. As far as I know, Paul didn't either. Now I know why he marked his study sites so carefully. Fresh water isn't easily had out here. My knees buckle from exhaustion. And disappointment.

So that's it. We have to backtrack and follow my original route. I laid it out using Paul's notes. There will be fresh water along that course. I can't count on it on this one. I'd rather take a beating than go back. I thought we had a chance of escaping those men, and going back puts us directly in their path. But there's no way we can cover ninety miles with twelve gallons of water. We have to have more. So back we go.

As if on cue, dust rises in a small plume east to west. A vehicle is heading toward Rayburn's camp.

Josie doesn't need this much information. She's not tall enough to see over the highest brush anyway. She won't see the dust—or the fact that we're going to be walking toward it—unless I say something. So I will keep my mouth shut. We need to double up on our miles today. That'll keep me busy. That and finding things to make Josie laugh.

I am walking her back into the belly of hell and looking for ways to make her laugh on the way. God help us. My left hand starts to throb in my elbow. The rest of me is numb.

DAY 23

Four miles from Rayburn's camp. The truck that came in yesterday went out this morning. I'm betting the family farm on the fact that Bodley returned and took Rayburn out for medical attention—which means that camp is unattended right now. If we can get there while they're still gone, we can start fresh again with a full tank of water. And more food.

So we are walking in the middle of the day and we are making good time.

When the truck left, I told Josie what was up, figuring I should prepare her some. She looked alarmed, but listened quietly and nodded when I was through. The closer we get the quieter she is, but she is not coming apart. I recognize these signs. This is a child gearing up for a battle. It has nothing to do with a fit. No wonder Paul said we were de facto twins. I could never see that in Jo before because I couldn't see myself.

As we travel, Josie looks at plants. She found a fistful of desert raisins a couple hours ago. They were too hard to eat, so we dropped them into a canteen and covered them with water. Then she walked along reading from Paul's letter and reciting facts. *Solanum centrale* or desert raisin, common in the Tanami and comes in two kinds, bitter and sweet. One grows on the sand hills; one grows in the mulga flats.

"I think these ones are the sweets," she said, gazing around at the sand and the lack of mulgas.

"Good guess," I agreed, proud of her.

"Solanaceae family," Josie said, stammering over the word, folding the letter and putting it into her pocket.

"Sola family? You mean they have kids?" I asked, taking this slim opportunity to tease her.

Jo stopped walking, looked at me a long moment, and shook her head. "Of course they do, Tally. All things have kids." Without waiting for a reply, she set off again, small feet hitting the ground with no hesitation. Maybe I was wrong to keep that information from her yesterday. She knows exactly where we're going right now— straight into the men's camp, the functional belly of the beast—and she's moving as if it was a Pizza Hut or something.

Perspective. It's all perspective.

Come to think of it, the camp may well be our local version of a pizza parlor. If it is unoccupied, we can help ourselves to anything we like. We stride strong ahead. Dinner awaits.

Every few minutes Josie pats her canteen, pleased with herself, checking to see if her raisins are still sloshing around. I catch her eye and smile.

She smiles back. We aren't giggling today, or even laughing out loud, but we can still smile. What we have between us is strong enough to see us through whatever lies ahead.

Jo glances to the south and smiles even bigger. I look too. The albino is back in earnest, walking apace about fifteen feet to our left. I think my left hand feels a bit better now and my ribs don't hurt at all.

Yes, together we are strong enough to take this gig into debrief.

DAY 24

We did it.

Off-loaded our gear about a mile out, then slipped in close with the empty sled and watched the camp for about thirty minutes. No one showed up. Hearts pounding, Jo and I made ourselves stand tall and walked in like we owned the place. I had wanted to leave her behind with the gear. She flat out refused to stay. So we walked in together.

For a few minutes, we spoke in whispers and crept about, going through the men's things as if somebody was watching and taking notes. All of a sudden Josie chuckled. She was standing near the spot where she threw up. Her footprints, blown over in places, were still visible. Most of the half-chewed grapes were gone, eaten by ants I expect, but a couple were dried out and still lying there.

"What's so funny, kid?" I asked, holding a bag of cereal in one hand and a box of crackers in the other, trying to decide if we could take them both.

"Me," Josie grinned, pointing at the ground. "I puked grapes on that man's shoes, Tally."

I doubled over with laughter. Jo stood still, both

hands on her hips, looking first at the ground, then at me, and suddenly she burst into giggles too. For a couple minutes we felt safe and free. Then we remembered where we were and went back to work. And I remembered my gaffe and apologized.

"Sorry for calling you kid, Jo. I didn't mean that."

Josie was quiet for a few seconds and then she said, "You can call me kid, Tally. I like it."

"You do?"

She nodded. "I like nicknames."

"Then it's a deal, kid. Kid Jo. Kind of has a nice ring to it, like an outlaw or something," I said and stuck out my right hand to shake on our deal. Josie smiled but shook her head firmly and put her hands behind her back.

"Your hands are filthy, Tally. I might get a germ."

"Why you little—"

Jo giggled and raised her eyebrows at me. I pretended my feelings were hurt for five whole minutes, which she finally ended by sidling up to me and sticking out her hand for me to shake. She had it wrapped in a sock.

I held my nose and refused to touch it. Josie laughed and hugged my waist. I put my arms around her tiny baby body. We stood there quiet for a long time then, drawing strength from each other. I could feel the bones of her shoulder blades. This child is too thin. *I* am too thin. I vowed to take as much food from that camp as I could possibly carry.

It is daylight now and we have put three miles between us and the camp. Three good miles. We did an excellent job of covering our tracks and even laid a good false trail about a quarter mile the other direction. There's been no sign of the men. I'm hoping they stay wherever the hell they went till we get out of here.

We have a full tank of water again plus eight canteens—twenty-two gallons—and another week's stash of food. Josie helped me load the sled and took one item off at a time till we got it to a weight I could pull. Then she mashed the desert raisins into a pulp and rolled them into tiny balls and we ate them with crackers for supper. They weren't the "sweets" she'd predicted. They were bitter as quince. We ate them anyway and were happy to do it and, as soon as we'd finished, Jo pulled out another letter and got us both looking for bush tomatoes. It's not the right season for them to be fruiting, but she's convinced we might find one dried on the stem.

"All these bushes look alike to me, Teach," I said, and I wasn't just being cute. They really did look alike. Without flowers or something distinctive, bushes are just bushes. Josie sighed, exasperated, and pulled out Paul's letter. Showing me the line drawings he put in the margins, she ordered me to help find and identify the *solanum chippendalei*, or bush tomato, shrubs. Survival is 95 percent brains, 5 percent circumstances. I think I'll leave that reference to Chippendale's alone. Josie is probably not old enough to appreciate me tweaking that particular Latin name. The concept of a male strip show might sail right over her head. I'll leave it alone.

We're doing this, though, better than I'd expected we could. We really are.

DAY 25

97 miles to go, 20 gallons of water left.

The main difference between a camel and a woman is the weight.

I cannot believe he actually wrote that down.

A week after I arrived in the Tanami, Paul loaded our backpacks with two gallons of water apiece and enough gear to stay out overnight. Then we marched ourselves out into the desert—a very, very long way—and propped up to watch dingoes.

Ten minutes later I'd seen about all I ever needed to see of wild dogs. They lick their nether regions a lot, lie out flat on the ground, pant, and snap at flies. This was not, however, the sort of thing I could exactly say to Paul, so I turned my observations to something more mundane.

"Okay, so you're studying the effects of drought on the estrus cycles of alpha and subordinate females. What's your theory again?"

"Well, if drought's a stressor, it should affect their ovulation cycles, perhaps even suspend them temporarily, so they don't come into heat as often."

"I could've told you that. Just watch what this heat does to me in a day or two."

"Didn't notice it bothering you last night."

"It's cumulative. Put that in your theory."

Three days later we headed back out again, another two gallons of water in each pack. Mine felt heavier this time and I said so.

"Take a lesson from the feral camels, Tal. Everything you need is here, it's just up to you to find it. And if you focus on the finding, the load's not near so heavy."

Paul grinned over his shoulder at me, as happy as if he had good sense, then laughed and kept walking.

By the third trip, six days after the first but repeating it to the letter—same exact trail, same exact two gallons of water in my pack, but it felt like fifty this time—I'd figured out that hot weather makes me irritable.

"You know, all Moses had to do was hit a rock with a stick and he had enough water for the whole tribe of Judah. You've been out here what, four months now, and you still haven't sorted that one out?"

Paul shook his head with a grin and kept walking.

"Bet Moses never had to carry any water."

"I could take some of that load for you, Tal, if you like."

"Wasn't askin' you to take my load. Did you hear me askin' anybody for one blessed thing? Nope. Wasn't askin' for a thing. I was just *sayin'* I bet Moses never had to carry any water."

"Well no, 'course not. He had women to carry it for him."

"Would you care to repeat that?"

"Ah, think I'll pass."

"Damn straight you'll pass, know what's good for you."

Paul had enough sense not to laugh out loud, but his shoulders shook a bit and he was careful not to look in my direction for a while. We walked in silence for another half hour or so before I picked it up again right where we left off.

"Women weren't meant to carry water. If God'd meant me to carry this much water, he would've put humps on my back."

Paul didn't even have the courtesy to skip a beat. Plunged right in. "Now *there's* a concept. A woman with humps on her *back,* too? Man, I'd be so eager to get to bed—makes me hurt just thinkin' about it! Imagine how long foreplay would take—I'd be there all night! Regular ménage à trois without having to go to confession. But tell me, Tal, which side would you sleep on? Not that it matters, hon, I'm just curious."

"Side doesn't matter. *You* should sleep with one *eye* open for the next few days."

"Take a good man to hold down a woman like that, wouldn't it?"

"Be afraid, Mr. O'Malley. Be very afraid."

Paul laughed and said, "You know how long a camel can walk without taking a drink, Tal? Six hundred miles."

"You know how long a man can go without having sex?"

"Well no, can't say as I do, but it's probably not 600 miles. Seriously though, Tal, camels were made for this kind of climate. I mean, they weren't indigenous here, but after they got loose on this land they just thrived. Perfect for them, if you think about it. A camel can walk for weeks without water, carry 500 pounds no problem, lose over 30 percent of its body weight without hurting vital functions, drink twenty-one gallons of water in three minutes flat, and wait out a sandstorm chewing a cud while grown men are crying. Great companions in the desert, camels are. A lot like women, come to think of it."

"You aimin' to test that 600-mile celibacy theory of yours?"

"Not exactly. Just pointing out that there are certain similarities between the two."

"Mile marker number one. You better come up with some differences fast, Jack."

Paul chuckled, "Really?"

"Really."

"Well, let's see. What's the difference between a woman and a camel? Hm. Pretty simple actually. Camels can be trained. That's one thing. A big one, don't you think?"

I turned my head the other way. Paul took that as a request to continue.

"Then too, camels aren't bothered by the fact that you're not talking. Camels kick and spit for good reason. Camels are more frail and less frightening. And camels *occasionally* walk away from a fight. How'm I doing, love?"

I ignored him clean. He went on, pleased with himself, I think.

"Camels don't ask if you like the way they look. Camels don't insist on stopping to ask for directions. Camels don't tell you how to drive or offer to do it for you."

I kept walking. Paul lobbed a question after me.

"But do you know what the main difference between a camel and a woman is, Tal?"

"No, I certainly do not. And you're already down by 600. You sure you want to risk adding some more road to the end of your long dry spell?"

Paul laughed and trotted out in front a few feet, walking backward so I had no choice but to look at him. There ought to be a law against a man looking that good in a sleeveless T-shirt and cutoffs.

"The main difference between a camel and a woman, hon, is the weight."

I grinned in spite of myself, but stared at the horizon, threw up my hands and said something snippy like, "And there he goes, folks. Just like a man. Had to do it, didn't he? *Had* to. Just could *not* leave well enough alone. Already at 600, gotta try for 12. Fine by me, you and your tired old camel theories, the whole lot of you're fixin' to be in the middle of a long hot *dry* summer. *Real dry*. Make this damn desert look like the goddamn Pacific Ocean."

We stopped for lunch then, me pretending to be angry, stretching out in the shade with my hat over my face. A while later, I woke to hear him saying quietly, "Ata Allāh."

"What?"

"Ata Allāh. It's the Bedouin name for camels."

"Oh. We're back to them again, 1200's just not enough of a challenge, that it?"

"Ata Allāh. Means gift of God."

Lowering the hat off my face, I sat up. Paul had my backpack open, three-fourths of its water transferred to his own pack. Zipping mine closed, he handed it over with a small smile, "My very own Ata Allāh."

His drought was over and he knew it. Twelve hundred miles traversed in two seconds flat. Beats even the camel's record for rehydration. We spent the rest of the afternoon mostly quiet, walking in silence to the dingoes, Paul watching and taking notes while I read or napped or just watched him watch the dogs. I was as happy as I'd ever been.

And now all that's left of that crazy wonderful time is a single line. *The main difference between a camel and a woman is the weight.*

———

And a child who is starting to accept me, but still periodically thinks I'm the spawn of Satan.

Jo took one look at my spinach this morning and declared she'd rather die than eat it. I told her she might well wind up doing just that, given our food situation, and that if I could eat her bitter old raisins, she could share my spinach. "After all, the food we filched from the camp won't go very far, kid. We need to supplement it."

She finally agreed to try some greens, provided I cooked them together with a few noodles, so I did and she did, which meant we were even for all of about one minute. Then, as if it was the first time it'd crossed her mind, she said, "You cut your hair off—it looks funny with those straggly braids in front. I think you looked better with it long." And then, without a pause, "And how come you don't have black hair if you're Indian. I thought all Indians had black hair."

Little snit. I almost asked her why she was so grumpy, but stopped myself. I know why she's grumpy. She didn't find a single bush tomato or desert raisin yesterday. It's hotter than Hades and dry, dry, dry. Our skins are parched and thirsty. Our eyes burn. Our feet are sore and we're doing our best to be cheerful in a place that took the man we both loved best and would take us too, in a heartbeat, if we gave it half a chance. So she's a bit grumpy. For that matter, so am I.

So be it. There are worse things we could be right now than grumpy. Amendment to Paul's line: *The main difference between a camel and a Josie is the weight and the red hair. And the camel's probably not nearly so obstinate.*

But why I showed up on the planet looking like a damn gringo is anybody's guess, I suppose. Blond hair, green eyes—a throwback to someone on the Nowata side, maybe—nothing like Dix or Mama. It used to trouble me, especially on the rez where I stuck out like a sore thumb, but I don't pay it much mind anymore. It's gotten darker over the last few years, and time'll turn it white before I'm done anyway, but it's so short right now that color is moot. Damn, but it's *hot* in this desert!

DAY 26

93 miles to go, 19 gallons of water.

Figured it out, the mood swing yesterday. We didn't drink enough water. We have to be more careful about that. My left hand is throbbing hard again, pain pulsing up my arm. I bumped it a few minutes ago. I need to be more careful about that too.

> *Pain is your friend; it teaches you lessons you can't learn any other way.*

Right. Like get your fingers out of the damn fire. Duck when the fist is incoming.
And take cover in a sandstorm.
That's a big one, that lesson. You won't forget it but once.

When the winds stir at the far edge of the horizon and don't lie down again, you know the air is planning to take new shape about you. The sand resting beneath your feet at this precise moment is on the verge of swirling fifty feet aloft. Dead leaves, small branches, and dust will pelt anything standing. Breathing will be difficult, painful. Any skin left uncovered will sting.

The second week I was here, Paul and I got caught out in a sandstorm. We spent one full afternoon huddled together, backs against a rock that I'm quite sure lost half its substance in those few hours. Erosion in high gear, pain in slow motion. Paul was philosophical about the whole thing, said, "At least this isn't the Sahara where they get *real* sandstorms." I gave up philosophy and comparative geography entirely and just prayed it would end.

So when the sky rolled toward us this morning, heavy orange going to brown, sucking strength from the land, I knew what we had to do. And I'd had the foresight to bring along the perfect garment to do it in. There wasn't time to congratulate myself on that, but I thought it just the same.

Slipping out of my skirt, I sat, legs crossed, on the ground, pulling it over Jo and me like a tent, snugging the open waist closed with a shoelace above our heads. There is no good way to do this.

"You might as well use me for a backrest," I said, and after a moment's hesitation, Josie leaned her head against me. Breathing into my protesting ribs, I reached out to retrieve a canteen, tucked the skirt hem beneath us, wrapped my arms around her, and we waited.

The cotton weave of the fabric filtered sunlight into a murky pattern in our cave. The air inside grew humid from our sweat as the wind began to press against us. My eyelashes brushed my face, wet and salty. Silt seeped through the skirt and coated our skins, filled our noses and ears like a thin, moving blanket.

"I'm smotherin', Tally," Jo whispered.

"Close your mouth and eyes and breathe slow through your nose. I've got you, kid. It's going to be okay."

Josie cringed backward, scared and helpless, her sturdy baby body flattening itself against mine. My ribs hurt like hell, the burn on my back felt like fire, my left arm was numb, but I held her tight.

For four hours and nine minutes.

When it was over, we dragged the skirt off our heads and shed our clammy, grimy shirts, then collapsed flat in the sand, too cramped and tired to move another inch. I dozed, only to wake with a start. Josie had soaked my bandanna in water and was gently washing the bruises on my face. It stung like the very son of a gun, but I gritted my teeth and lay still. So much like her father. I couldn't stop the tears.

Seeing them, Josie said, "Mommy says water makes bobos better so you have to wash them every day."

"That so?"

"Yep."

"Your mommy's a smart woman, Jo."

"Then why don't you like her?"

I didn't know what to say to that, didn't have a clue where to start. How do you explain adult idiocies to a child? Josie rummaged through my pack looking for something to use to dry my face and came up with Paul's shirt. Slipping one hand inside a sleeve, she wiped my skin with the worn fabric. That was more than I could take. I mumbled thank you and sat up, reaching for my T-shirt. The tears kept coming. I turned away, sparing Josie the sight. Or myself, I don't really know which.

Josie saw the burn on my back then and caught her breath.

"You need a doctor," she said, fear edging her words.

"Oh, I'll be fine," I replied, as cheerful as I could make it.

"A doctor could fix you."

"Well, actually, a hot bubble bath and a soft bed and a cheeseburger and strawberry shake could probably fix me best. I aim to have it all too, soon's we get out of here. You want to join me?"

"Nope. They don't know how to make good strawberry shakes in Australia."

"They don't?"

"Nope. I tried one at the airport and it was *bad*. Made me puke just like you do all the time."

"Oh. Yuck. Must've been *real* bad. Now I wonder why that is? It's just ice cream and milk and you mix it up. How hard can that be?"

Jo shrugged, fingering things in the first-aid kit. When she reached a tiny tube of aloe gel, I said, "That's it, kid. If you'll wash my back and then spread that on the burn, it'll fix it. Better than a doctor could."

She nodded, determined, and set to work. I winced and shuddered when the wet cloth touched me. Josie stopped, bent to pick up Paul's shirt and handed it to me, saying, "Here, you can hold onto this so you won't think about the hurt. That's what Mommy did for me when I broke my leg last year. Gave me one of Daddy's shirts to sleep with. She said it was better than a pill."

Crying in earnest, trying hard to mask that fact, failing miserably, I sniffled, "Your mommy was right, Jo. It's much better than any pill. Much, much better."

She worked in silence then, cleaning the wound and smoothing aloe over it, while I sat clutching Paul's shirt, staring at the flannel and seeing nothing. When she finished, she put everything away and spread out the pallets, then sat down beside me, cross-legged on the ground. I reached out to start braiding her hair—she's been needing fly braids for days now—and finally found some words.

"I don't dislike your mommy, Jo."

"I know. She don't you either."

"She doesn't?"

"No. When she wasn't mad at you one time, she said you were good for Daddy. Daddy said it too. He said you were funny and true, equal parts, and he thought that was good for him."

It had to be said. I plunged in, stumbling over the words, no matter. "I'm sorry, Josie. Sorry for taking him away from you. I know how much you love him, how much that had to hurt—him living off in another state with me."

She nodded, reaching for one sleeve of Paul's shirt and holding it in her hands, saying, "I missed him."

After a long silence, she whispered. "I miss him now, too."

"Oh kid, so do I," I whispered back, reaching for her hand and holding on.

"Why did those men kill my daddy?" It was a simple question, from a tiny girl with dark wounded eyes.

I'm the adult here. I should have some answers.

"I don't know, Jo. I just don't know. Wish I did."

"Daddy wasn't bothering their things. He just went to look at the water. But they caught him and tied him up to the chair and wouldn't give him any food. I sneaked him some food one time. Then that bad man said they would let him eat and they did."

"How long were you there?"

Josie shrugged, furrowing her brow. "A long time," she finally said. "They kept saying they might kill us, but they didn't. And Daddy tried to get them to let us go, but they wouldn't."

"But you got away."

Jo nodded, solemn and quiet. "I got Daddy a knife. They let me walk around and everything. The man said I couldn't do much, I was too little. But I got a knife from the table and gave it to Daddy. Then that night he picked me up and we ran to the truck in the dark."

"And they followed you."

She nodded. I held both her hands in mine.

"And Daddy said, Get down on the floor, baby girl, and then we had the crash and when I woke up Daddy was all sick and bloody like that."

I reached for Jo and pulled her onto my lap. She didn't resist.

"Tell me the dingo's story, Tally," she asked,

leaning her head back against me, so I did and when we finished, we both looked up and saw the albino standing near the sled. It felt good to have her watching over us.

Jo patted Paul's flannel shirt and said, "This was my Christmas present to Daddy when I was seven. I picked it out all by myself at the store and everything. And I wrapped it in the Sunday comics with a big red bow. Daddy liked it. Said blue made him look *good* and now he'd have to beat off the women with a stick."

"That sounds just like him."

"Yep, and Mommy said maybe he could just leave that part up to you."

"Oh really?"

"Yep, but Daddy said he wouldn't want to turn you loose with a stick in that particular situation. You might miss and hit him instead. He said you never could aim very good nohow."

"Why that—how *dare* he?!"

Josie giggled.

Struck again by how much this child had lost, at least partly because of me, I stared at her, groping for words that would atone. She spoke first.

"I'm glad Daddy lived with you."

Of all the things that could've come out of her mouth at that moment, that was the one I never could've predicted. "You are? For real?"

Josie nodded, firmly.

"But why?"

"I hated it in our house when he was there. Gave me a ache in my stomach all the time. Even the doctor couldn't fix it."

"Oh."

"It was better when he left, but I wanted to live with you and Daddy. I like your house."

"You do?" I said, shocked. I never had any idea she felt that way.

"Yep. I like living in a national park. All the kids at school say you can't do that and I tell 'em you can when you're a ranger like you and then I show pictures at show-and-tell."

"Oh."

"And I liked your bubble bath too. The one you made. Daddy said you cooked it yourself in the kitchen on the stove. Did you really do that?"

"Um hm. Sure did. Every first Sunday of the month."

Josie nodded, hands still resting on Paul's shirt. "Think maybe you could teach me how?"

"Of course. Soon's we get out of here we'll head back to the States and make wood violet bubble bath and eat ourselves sick on cheeseburgers and shakes."

"I'd rather have some of your bread, that kind you made that one time, that sour kind."

"Sourdough?"

"That. Mmm. With honey and butter, all hot and everything."

"Then it's a deal. Sourdough bread and strawberry shakes. We'll fill the tub and soak till our fingers and toes shrivel up and fall clear off. And then we'll get out and crawl around on the stubs and people will think we're tough."

Josie laughed and shook her new braids to test them. "You're funny."

"Yeah, right. Don't get out much, do you, kid?"

"Want me to wash your sore hand?"

"Nah, it's fine," I said, lying through my teeth. Truth was, I didn't want her to see my hand. Hell, even *I* didn't want to see it.

Twilight was stretching over the desert. We lay on our sides on the pallets, facing each other. It was time to get up and move on, but we were both still worn out from the sandstorm. I suggested we take a nap before leaving. She nodded, her brown eyes large, familiar. So familiar. Little pug nose and freckles. I grinned at her. She wrinkled that nose. It's an instinct, I think.

I tickled her cheek with the tail of one of her braids. Laughing, pulling the braid away from me, she said, "Quit it, you."

"Okay, kid."

Still holding onto her hair, Jo smiled again. "We're twins now."

"Twins? You call this twins. Me with hair yellow as a duck's and yours red as a fire truck? Where's the twin in that?"

"We're not the matched kind. Just sort of matched."

I nodded and we lay quiet, resting.

A while later Josie spoke again. "Daddy said you would be my second mom, if I wanted it."

"That's right, Jo. That's what I always hoped."

"Even now?"

"Even now."

Rolling away from me, onto her side, Josie yawned and said, "Two mommies. I like that. Mommy One and Mommy Two."

I slept soundly for several hours and woke with Paul's shirt pressed to my face. It was shortly after midnight. Josie was curled up beside me, one arm akimbo in an uncomfortable pose that was bound to give her a crick in the neck. Easing her pack back into pillow position, I tucked his shirt beneath her head. She stirred but didn't wake.

Warm breezes slip over the land, rustling the spinifex and soothing my skin. The sponge bath helped, I think. I don't feel quite so bruised and taut. Actually, I don't feel taut at all. Memories of Paul in a place far from here flood my mind, my heart. My body.

We were nearing the end of a two-week canoe trip in the Boundary Waters of northern Minnesota last summer, and we'd spent the day paddling and portaging hard to reach our campsite on Little Loon Lake. Mosquitoes drove us inside the tent at dusk and we lay there on our backs, talking quietly, staring through the ceiling screen at the sky, naming obscure, exotic constellations from Paul's memory, listening to the noises of a night in the north woods. After the mosquitoes retreated, Paul zipped open the door of the tent and stepped out. Comforted by the sounds of his movements, I fell asleep.

Sometime later, Paul crawled back inside, carrying our battered aluminum camp pan. The water in it had been heated with a splash of wood violet bubble bath. Our sturdy two-man tent suddenly felt like a suite at Signal Mountain Lodge, the pan shone silver in the firelight, and I sat up, drowsy, questioning, but Paul shushed me. Lifting my shirt over my head, he lay me back down and kissed the tip of my nose, whispering, "I was born to love you, Tal."

Reaching into the pan, he raised a dripping sponge and, wringing it slightly, laid it to my stomach. Tracing gentle arcs upward, he first caressed my breastbone and shoulders, neck, ears, and face, bathing me in lukewarm liquid and cool night air. Then, working back down, he scribed delicate circles over each breast, nipples constricting at his touch, and moved on to the soft swell of my stomach, easing tenderly and steadily downward, spreading my legs and bathing the inside of my thighs—fingers and sponge leaving tiny traces of moisture. Over my knees and across my ankles, he moved, carefully, slowly, down my insteps to my toes. Bathing my skin, yes, but embracing my soul.

Paul entered me then in ways I've never known a man to. And in all those ways he never left. His touch. That tent. The lake. Those stars. The keening wind.

I lie here in the darkness beside his child, feeling his hands on my body and him within me, and I ache all over again, but for a different reason this time. The warm breezes mock me now, lilting across us and capering on toward the mound of sand covering Paul. They'll pass him without comment, without feeling, without emotion, just the way the wind passed us, bodies intertwined and unaware of what lay just ahead, that night on the shores of a lake in the northern woods. The sleeping land does not remember people.

But we remember it.

Sleep brought nightmares. I finally stood up and stared into the desert. Foy's strangled death cries filled the sky and I heard his neck snap again and again. Then the sound of Paul's body hitting the ground drove me to my knees, nausea welling, ears ringing, soul as lost as one ever gets. All I knew to be true of me has withdrawn itself, and I stand naked of heart before the knowing moon.

The love of my life is dead. My wilderness skills are moot here. No rocky mountain looms above, safe and familiar. We are hanging on by the skin of our teeth, barely alive, breathing at the sufferance of fate alone. I have killed one man and maimed another, turning from my vow of nonviolence in an instinctive moment that came and went so fast I barely registered it. I killed to keep us safe, I thought, killed to make sure we got out of here. Or maybe it was just basic survival, us or them. The world would call that self-defense. Some would even call it courage.

I know better, but dare not reckon with it now. Mama's eyes are steady on me once more. For the last few days they've let me be, but now they stand guard over my listing soul. She only asked one thing of life: for her daughter to break the circle of violence that maimed us all. I did that where my father was concerned. I slipped with Dix. And then here, when I had a chance to really break it once and for all, I didn't just slip. I stormed through the damn door and kicked a man to death. Would've stabbed him if I could've gotten my hands on his knife. Shot him, if I'd had his gun. Violence rages unchecked in me, my mother's daughter, but I can't think about that now. Just cannot.

Instead I stare at this sleeping child and vow once more to get her out of this desert alive. Whatever it takes, she *will* survive.

DAY 27

90 miles, 17 gallons.

Saving Josie's life is proving more difficult by the moment.

We've moved into the territory of a new dingo pack, leaner and meaner than the one back at the research camp. In a matter of seconds this group sized us up and ranged out around our position, triangulated as if on prey, eyes locked and bodies set on lines with ours. There is something primal about that formation. The hair on my arms stood up, my neck tightened, my skin burned and buzzed in warning. Itching to run, sure if I did we were dead meat, I stopped instead and turned to face them, pulling Josie around with me. The dogs stopped too, staring at us boldly, heads up, ears cocked, every muscle alert and unafraid.

I have no experience at being prey. I don't want any experience being dinner. I ad-libbed.

Shouting, I waved my arms and the leaders backed up a few paces, then paused. As soon as we started walking again, the pack fell into step behind us in that deadly pattern. Sensing their approach, I turned to face them once more, breaking a dead stick and throwing chunks of it at the ones in the lead. They dodged the sticks but didn't retreat this time. One even stepped forward. Their lack of fear was morphing into outright aggression. We're in the middle of a drought and we look like dinner. Sticks and stones won't deter these bones.

Trying to explain all this to Josie, I reached for the Beretta and fired a shot toward the closest female. At that the whole group melted into the bush, and we've only seen them a couple times since, but I can't shake the feeling that we're being stalked. They are assessing us, even from a distance, in a way that leaves little doubt they consider us a potential food source. And since we're moving toward the next waterhole— probably the center of their established territory— our confrontations with them are just beginning.

Problem is, we have no alternative. We can't afford to bypass that water. We have to top off our supplies every chance we get. So we'll just have to deal with the dingoes.

Which means Josie has to learn how to shoot. I have put this off because I didn't want to scare her, but it is time she learns how to use this gun. Not just for the dingoes either.

Rayburn will not let us walk off without a fight. As soon as he recovers enough to muster some forces, there will be worse dangers for Jo and me in this desert than wild dogs. If something happens to me, she needs to know how to aim and fire this gun. If things come down to life and death, I want her to have as many ducks on the side of life as possible. The Beretta is a very big duck. Camel. Whatever. This gun may give her a chance to keep breathing. She has to learn how to use it.

———

Firearms are not my forte. I'd just as soon have a tonsillectomy without anesthesia as to use one. Josephine O'Malley, I found out quickly, concurs 110 percent. The moment I announced my plan, she sulled up like a Brahma bull in a doctoring chute and stomped one foot.

"I don't like guns."

"Me neither, Jo. Which means we've got a serious handicap where the men are concerned," I told her, prying open her clenched fist and setting the revolver in her hand, "So we have to work twice as hard to get over it."

"But I don't *want* to shoot the gun!" Josie wailed, squeezing her eyes shut and leaning her head back against me, arms held out stiff in front, as far as she could reach. "Why can't *you* just do the shootin'? *You're* the *grown-up!*"

"I will. But you need to know how in case something happens to me."

Josie's eyes flew open and her arms went limp, tears spilled down her cheeks. She forgot all about the gun. I had to hold it steady in her hands.

"It's okay, Jo. I shouldn't have said it like that. Nothing's going to happen to me. But I still might need your help, so you have to cooperate with me here."

Sniffling, she nodded assent, bending her head to the task of learning how to load, fire, empty, and reload the Beretta.

Cupping my hands over her ears as makeshift earplugs and turning her toward the sheet I'd hung up for a target, I said, "We can't afford to waste bullets on practice, so you only get to shoot once."

"Good," Josie snapped.

"Point and pull when you're ready," I said, feeling her face tense as she squeezed the trigger. The shot itself split through the sheet, sound reverberating through her whole body and mine. There is nothing gentle about a 9mm round.

Beads of sweat standing on her upper lip and forehead, Josie wheeled and handed me the gun. Then she walked away a few steps and brushed her hands off on her clothes. Over and over again, she scraped palm against ragged cotton, trying to erase the feel of the weapon from her skin. I know that feeling. Gunmetal seeps into your pores, the smell of the powder clings to you. Unless you like the kill that lies behind it, the need to wipe it off fast is intense. Trying not to watch Josie do the same thing I've done every time I've ever fired a gun, I replaced the spent shell. Might as well travel with a full clip as one short. Never know when you might need all seventeen rounds.

A dingo came slinking past, and Josie froze to watch, her fear tactile. I walked forcefully to her side and the dog disappeared. We scanned for the others but saw nothing.

In a bid to help Jo handle her anxiety, I suggested that we both take another sand bath, spinning a total yarn that if we decreased our body odors, we might smell a little less like steak to the dingoes. Josie raised her eyebrows and I could tell she didn't believe a word I was saying, but she threw herself wholeheartedly into the bath plan.

Her hair is burnished gold now from the sun, and I sat quietly to the side watching her roll around on the ground, like any kid in any normal situation—enjoying herself, but getting an even bigger kick out of it because an interested grown-up is near enough to be watching. Suddenly her play was cut short by a loud "Ouch!" and she scrambled to her feet, frowning at a piece of spinifex that had skinned her leg.

"I'm clean enough," she announced, annoyed.

"Feel better?"

Rolling her eyes back into her head, Jo pulled on her shirt and shorts and plopped onto the ground beside me, frowning. "Nope."

I nodded.

She continued, "I hate the desert. Everything in it has stickers." Her eyes traced the places where the spinifex was leaving a light rash. Spinifex is like that. I've gotten so used to it I don't even notice anymore. Josie's getting there too, but she's not there yet. "I *hate* stickers, Tally."

"Yeah, I know what you mean, kid. But the sharp pointy edges help the plants keep from being eaten—it's a survival strategy."

"So," she frowned, clearly not at all concerned about how arid plants survive. "Why did Daddy have to come here to study? Why couldn't he pick a place with trees and water and stuff? We wouldn't be in so much trouble if we had water everywhere like in Wyoming."

"If we were in Wyoming, love, we wouldn't be in trouble a'tall. Jed and Pony would've rescued us days ago."

"I know. So why didn't he study dogs there?"

"Your daddy likes deserts, Jo," I heard myself saying, knowing I should change the verb tense to the past, knowing, too, I couldn't. "He always told me he gets something from them he could never find anywhere else."

"What?"

Shaking my head, I had to admit to not knowing. What else didn't I know about Paul? I thought I had a lifetime to learn it all. How much of him will always remain unknown to me now?

Josie stretched her leg out to inspect the spinifex scrape. It was covered with tiny red bumps and looked like it might be stinging.

"That hurt?"

She nodded and I remembered the extensive first-aid supplies I'd left behind at the research camp. Concerned only about keeping my carrying weight down, I'd ruled out everything that wasn't absolutely essential the day I left. It never crossed my mind that I'd have someone else's injuries to worry about—or that my own would be quite so severe either, for that matter. I've moved clear out of SAR mode. Forget other folks completely. Self comes first, middle, last, and anywhere in between.

Tourist with a vengeance, that's me. Salvation's left to the better prepared. Another dingo slips past, then a second, and a third, and I stand up to create a taller profile against them. Trying not to alarm Josie, I stretch and pretend to be flexing my leg muscles. Inside, I'm seething.

—

If I could get my foot in the right angle with my backside I would kick myself for coming here so unprepared. Knew better, did it anyway. Figured I'd never need much desert know-how, so what was the point in getting any. Pretty much everything Paul told me in passing went in one ear and straight out the other, didn't even slow down. I can't remember *any*thing about dingoes today except that they're not supposed to attack people, and today that's sounding real academic, to say the least.

I don't know what's normal behavior for these animals, don't know how worried I should be, don't know what I should do to ensure our safety. All I've done so far is react, but I really have no idea how they think or communicate and so I have no clue about how best to intervene in their reasoning process. I'm pinch-hitting here, telling Jo to stand tall and act tough when they're around, "Fill up every square inch of your skinny little body with steel grits."

She interrupted, "Grits are *corn*, Tally. Everybody knows that. Nobody makes 'em from steel."

At a loss, I shook my head. Josie laughed at her own joke, and the tension began to fall away.

"I forgot. You people in Louisiana *eat* grits. The rest of us know it's a fancy word for sand and try to keep it outside our mouths."

"Grits are good, especially when you cook 'em crunchy like Gram O'Malley does."

"That's more information than I ever needed about Southern cooking, Josephine."

"And you poke holes in 'em and put in butter and let it melt all down the sides and then—yum—catch a big glob on your spoon—mmm, that's good stuff."

"Lord have mercy." I stared at the sky, gagging and calling out, *"Please.* And thank you for letting me be from somewhere besides Louisiana. I would surely have *died* if they fed me that way."

Josie laughed again, greatly cheered. The exchange was just what we needed.

"We're not prepared for this desert in most ways, kid, but where attitude's concerned, we stay at the front of the pack. And that's a point in our favor," I said firmly. "Good attitudes, strong minds—we got both. Survival's 95 percent that and 5 percent everything else, so the numbers are with us, Jo, and we need to remember it."

Josie nodded, proud, still wan and weak, but much less anxious than she had been moments before. She pursed her lips and said, "Okay, Mommy Two." Then she threw back her head and looked at the sky. It was the most natural gesture I've seen her make since we started. She was beginning to trust me at last.

"Now let's get back to preparing for those damn dogs. All we really have to do to make our message plain is stay alert and look strong, like we're saying, All right you sorry curs, we're not lookin' for a fight, but if you bring it to us, you can count on one thing—we *will* put some holes in your sorry hides before you leave."

Jo grinned and pulled an imaginary trigger.

"It's like the self-defense training we give women at rape prevention clinics back home. Act like you're the biggest, meanest bitch on the planet, and rapists won't mess with you. They don't want a fight. They want an easy mark. If you can convince them in every way possible—down to the absolute smallest detail, like how you carry your head on your shoulders—that tackling you will be the dumbest thing they could ever do, they will always choose somebody else. That's the theory anyway. And why should it be any different for a pack of mangy wild dogs looking for dinner than for a man intent on raping a woman?"

"What's a raping?" Josie asked, and I choked back a hearty expletive. I'm not used to this parenting thing. I forgot all about how young she is. It took me ten minutes and three tries to change the subject, and just as I managed it, Jo said, "Oh, I see now. I know what *rape* is. Mommy told me all about that. I just didn't know *raping*, the word."

Floored me. Just when I think I have something about this child figured out, she opens her mouth. Confounded, I suggested we practice our moves for a few minutes, and Josie turned to that with more interest than she's showed in anything lately. Whatever Miriam told her about rape, it stuck. This is a new angle on Miriam for me. It takes a hell of a lot of guts for a mom to prepare a daughter this well for life—to tell her about something so hard and yet so useful. I am impressed.

It's early afternoon now, and we've slept intermittently since dawn, but we're both working hard at not looking like dinner. No limping, no shuffling along, no apparent indecision. No slumping through any movement or acting oblivious to our surroundings. We are occupying our own skins. For now the dingoes are acknowledging our space, but I'm afraid it's only a matter of time before they come at us again.

In the meanwhile, we are staying busy.

Jo got us into this latest scheme. We still have packaged food, not a lot but enough for a few more days. We're both still enrolled in TJ's School, though, and Josie is full of ideas for her curriculum. I'll say one thing for her: she's not squeamish. Far, far from it.

A few hours ago she found a lizard—a huge one, nearly a foot and a half long from snout to tail—resting in the shade of a rock. I eyed him a bit warily and, given a choice, would've walked a good long ways around him. "I never saw a lizard that big before. Looks to me like he could eat *us*, if he was a mind to."

Josie reached for my pack, all business. She had a plan to trap and cook the thing. Children take to the fundamentals of survival a lot quicker than adults. I know lizards are edible, but the thought of eating this one made me green around the gills. Jo said she figured the meat would taste like frog legs—one of her favorite foods. That thought made me even greener.

"My book my Daddy sent me says the desert

people eat goannas all the time, Tally," she said, frowning at the piece of twine she was trying to fashion into a slip loop.

"So that's a goanna."

"Yep."

"And you're telling me we're supposed to rope him with that contraption you're fixing?"

"Yep. It works, it really does. I just have to make it big enough. Daddy showed me how."

"He did."

"Yep."

"But did you ever catch a lizard?"

"Yep. Lots. The little green ones on Gram's porch."

"And you fried 'em up in a pan and ate 'em for dinner."

Josie stopped tying and looked at me. "No, you silly," she chuckled. "You can't eat the little green ones. They're the grandparents of everybody that's already dead."

"They're *what*?"

"They're the grandparents. You have to treat 'em good or they'll hex you and hail on your crops."

I just sat there digesting that. Little city kid talking like a backwoods farmer. But she is half Cajun. That might explain some of this. Josie went back to work on her lizard lariat.

"And you don't fry lizards either, Tally. You cut 'em up in strips and hang 'em over a fire."

There was nothing in the world to say to that, so I contented myself with raising my eyebrows and holding the end of the stick still so Jo could tie her noose to it. She stuck the tip of her tongue out the side of her mouth and bent over the job with a will, sweat dropping off her nose and falling onto her hands and mine. Brushing her hair off her face, she commented, "There was a ditch in Joshua Tree where Daddy used to work called the Fried Liver Wash."

"There was?"

"Yep. Daddy sent me a picture for my wall. But I'd like to see the real place sometime."

"Well, maybe when we get out of here we can go on a vacation to the Mojave Desert and fry us up some livers in the Fried Liver Wash."

"Yuck. I don't like liver."

"What? You're tellin' me you'll eat frogs and lizards but you don't eat liver? Now where's the sense in that?"

Josie shrugged and held up her finished lasso. It was a simple thing, simple enough to work really well—nothing more than a noose attached to the end of a sturdy stick. The trick would come in being still enough to get it over the reptile's head before he got alarmed and headed south. Once it was over him, though, you could just cinch up on the lead end of the lasso and pull him in, like a catfish on a line.

This particular lizard, however, was big enough to put up a serious fight, I told Jo. "You do realize, kid, that this one's not gonna come in easy like the little green grandparents do."

"Oh, they don't come easy neither."

"Is that so?"

"Yep."

"So what's your plan *after* you get him lassoed?"

"That's your part."

"And how do you figure that?"

Jo patted her trap and shrugged, "I did all this. You need to do a part. So you can do that."

"I see," I said, proud of her for trying and absolutely certain we wouldn't get anywhere near catching the thing.

We crept into place. Josie glanced at me and said, "You better get a stick or somethin', Tally."

I just stopped and looked at her.

"You know. To beat him over the head with when we catch him."

Chagrined, I crawled off for the sand shovel, and when I got back Jo was waiting patiently, her eyes trained on the lizard. I began to understand we might actually wind up catching this lizard. She had the look of someone who had done this before.

A few yards from the rock, she stopped and whispered, "Now don't scrape on the ground or bump against anything. And don't move fast. Move slow. Real slow. Like me. You just watch me and do like I do so you won't scare him off."

I nodded and followed her to the letter. She had it down cold, like she'd been doing it every day of her Louisiana life. It reminded me of the childhood game Dix and I used to play—touch the lizard's tail. Same exact moves. You ease in, holding still for minutes at a time sometimes, gradually getting closer, a foot away, eight inches, now six and two and then less than one. Whoever could actually touch the lizard without making him run won our game. Josie had never played it, but it was obvious she had caught enough green grandparents to have beaten us both hands down. The size of the goanna didn't faze her a bit. It was dinner and she intended to have it.

Even so, when she settled the noose down around the lizard's neck, my heart was somewhere up around my throat. The goanna tensed and actually raised one foot. Jo was poised slightly above and behind. She froze. When the goanna set his foot back down on the ground, Josie pulled the cinch line taut and leaned backward, looking for all the world like a champion deep-sea fisherman reining in a sailfish.

All absolute hell broke loose. Eighteen inches of lizard cyclone picking up people parts and knocking them ascending. Jo, hanging onto her catch for dear life, landed on her backside on top of me. The lizard was everywhere. I couldn't have gotten a clean shot at him with the shovel to save my soul.

Somehow Josie kept her grip and wound up on her feet again. Before I could get onto mine, she swung the lizard into the rock. Stunned, he went limp.

Both hands tight on the stick, Jo pulled the lizard out flat on the ground and yelled, "Now hit him!" and I did exactly that.

Then we both sat down and just looked at our dinner, ostensibly catching our breath but really trying to figure out what to do next.

"Lord have mercy, kid. I hope you don't ever take a notion to rope and hog-tie me for dinner. I'd be in *trouble*."

Josie rubbed the sweat off her face like a cowboy who'd just aced an eight-second ride on a bull called the Texas Terminator and grinned. "Yep. Only you wouldn't taste good enough to eat."

———

Watching Jo roll her lariat and tuck it into her pack, I realize this child is not waiting to be saved. More than anyone I've ever met, she is holding up her end of the bargain. More than anyone I've ever rescued, she is already home.

I told her that.

She grinned at me and said, "You still have to do the skinnin'."

———

I did it. Not neat, not pretty, and sure as hell not right, but I did get the lizard gutted and cut into strips and roasted in the lee of the rock where we'd found him. To defuse the smoke we kept the fire low and hung the sheet between us and the down-wind side.

We didn't even wait for the meat to cool, just peeled it off the sticks as soon as it was done and dug in. It was tough and tasted something like a cross between chicken and flounder, very well blackened, but Josie munched hers in between satisfied Mmms. "See, I told you, just as good as frog legs," she said once, when she paused long enough to breathe. This child likes lizard. Nausea kicked me a good one, but I managed to keep it at bay by lying on my side and eating slowly.

We had enough leftovers for two days' meals. "Now *that* counts as a success," I told Jo. "All yours."

She smiled for a few seconds, but the smile died on her face and I went cold when I followed her gaze and understood why. The dingoes were back.

——

The closer they get, the more I wish I'd paid more attention to Paul's research. The information he left us about wild dogs is sketchy and mythical and of little practical value. But, then again, that's not entirely true.

He is here in the pages of his journal.

This species has endured alongside these desert people for 4,000 years, shadows at their evening campfires, partners in the hunt, pets on occasion. Stories tell of orphaned pups suckled tenderly back to life. Dingo bones show up in middens of human remains, silent testaments to ancient ties between dog and man on an endless sea of red sand. Then I arrive, weighed down with dart guns, syringes, scales, and test tubes, to learn—what?

How did you always do that? Marry heaven and earth, theory and mud? Scientist, philosopher, father, and friend, where might I have gone with you? We lived four years in an unspoken vow and now all I have to show is silence.

That and a curly redheaded girl with your eyes and my stubbornness and her own special brand of spunk.

And a ranging hungry dingo pack, not an orphan in sight among them, that wants us for dinner.

"Tell me a story, Tally," Jo says, eyes on the dogs. "One from Daddy's book. The one about me and the rodeo."

I nod. She's right. The stories take us home. And we haven't read Josephine and the Rodeo in days.

Sometimes when I look at Josie I worry about the next two years, one parent in Australia and one in the States. I wonder if it's selfish of me to leave when she's still so young and needs a dad at least on the same continent. But then I remember when she, Tally, and I went to see Dix ride bulls in Rock Springs. Jo turned six that day. Seeing her first rodeo was part of her birthday present.

We were sitting in the stands during the calf roping. While Tal explained the rules to me and told me about growing up around horses and rodeos, Josie wandered down next to the action, watching the cowboys closely and leaning against the rails along with a line of other kids. A few minutes later I heard people laughing and looked up to see them pointing toward the center of the arena. The cowboy who'd just finished his run was being dressed down by a little redheaded girl in jeans, boots, and a T-shirt. Josie. In ten steps I was over the top rail, in another ten I had snatched her up, kicking and screaming. The crowd showed its appreciation of this unscheduled event by hollering encouragement for all sides. You go, girl! Better watch your six, Dudley! She's on you, man! That's it, baby—kick him where it counts!

When we cleared the stands, I sat my enraged daughter down in the grassy shade next to a horse trailer and rubbed my shins. She had left a string of bruises on both of them. Tally watched from a distance, head turned politely away, shoulders shaking with silent laughter.

"Damnit, Josie! You can't just go around hitting people!"

"But Daddy, he was hurtin' that little cow!"

I tried logic, choosing my words carefully, articulating better than they ever taught us to do in English grammar. This was important. I needed her to hear me. "That man's been riding and roping his whole life, Jo. It's how he makes money to feed his family and pay his bills—it's his job."

"But he was hurtin' the cow and it ain't fair! All the little cow was doin' was be scared and run and not hurtin' nobody and that man throwed it down on the ground and sat on him with his knee and it ain't fair, I'm tellin' you!"

"I know, Josephine, but it's not for you to decide how people make their living."

"Just 'cause it's their job don't make it right!"

"That's not for you to decide."

"Well when I get big it will be 'cause that's gonna be my job. Stop people from hurtin' animals. I'll have a big gun like the rangers and nobody will stop me! Ever! Not even YOU!"

Mule, lion, and she-bear all rolled into one. God help any man who gets crosswise of her.

But I do believe she can survive a couple years of fieldwork.

Josie sat on the ground beside me, peering into my tin dish at my concoction of scrambled termites, leftover lizard, and noodles, and then fixed her gaze on mine, stubborn and determined to communicate it.

"I just don't think God intended people to eat bugs."

I shrugged. "Can't argue with the logic of that."

"So I think I'll let you eat 'em. Gram O'Malley says when you get on the wrong side of God, he can do things to make your life real uncomfortable, and I'm just a kid. I have a lot of life to go. You're old. You eat 'em."

"Do you remember that day at the rodeo, Jo? How you socked that cowboy and your daddy had to carry you out?"

Josie frowned and nodded vigorously, saying in the same aggrieved tones she'd used back then, "He hurt that little cow and I was tryin' to stop him, but Daddy wouldn't let me."

"Know what I thought that day?"

"No. What?"

"I thought, Now there's a kid I'd like to have on my side if we ever have to go to war. That's what I thought."

"You did?"

"Yep, sure did. Pretty brave."

"You really think so?"

"Hell yeah. Tried it my own self when I was eight. Except you made it into the arena and landed a punch before you got dragged out and I didn't make it anywhere near that far. Didn't even clear the rails before they nailed me. You did a lot better job of it. I was proud of you, real proud."

Josie smiled then and was quiet for a long time. Suddenly she said, "Well, maybe when we get back to Wyoming we can make a company and go to rodeos and hit cowboys for a livin'."

I got tickled at that, Josie did too, and we both fell out laughing. It felt good to laugh for real. We needed the reprieve. Catching my breath, I stared into Josie's brown eyes. Minutes later she dozed and I still gazed at her face, long lashes brushing her skin. She is so small and vulnerable, so strong in many ways but helpless before all this. What I did with Foy was the right thing, Mama, you have to understand. Maybe not the right thing for all time, but the right thing for here and now. I *have* to get this child to safety. If I ever needed to save a life, this is the one. I will not fail. Please understand.

Calmed by reason and purpose, I stood up to stretch and went cold with dread at what I saw.

A short distance across the desert behind us rolled the dust trail of two vehicles, headed our way.

———

There was nowhere to go and no time to do it in either. I couldn't even get the frame of the sled covered, much less our scattered gear. Clearly I hadn't been thinking enough about evasion lately, because we were camped in the middle of an open flat that didn't have a single large bush or tree, and the nearest gully was a good quarter mile behind us. In good shape, well-watered and fed, Jo and I might've been able to sprint for it. As things stood, that 1,000 yards might as well have been ten miles. No way could we get to it in time.

Frantic, I shook Josie awake, dropped the sheets, and spilled a couple handfuls of sand over them, keeping one out, plus four canteens, my pack, and the gun. Settling Jo in the lee of a spinifex clump, curled up on her side around it, I covered her with the sheet and a few hastily crumpled dry twigs and leaves. She stuck out like a sore thumb. Hunched over, I trotted to the next scrubby bush, some thirty feet away, and tried to curl myself around it too, taking care to maintain eye contact with Josie, praying as hard as I've ever prayed that the truck would pass us by without notice.

Jo stared at me as the sound of the motor rumbled closer. Sweat poured down our faces, stinging our eyes, dripping off our noses. The sun beat hard against our uncovered heads. I lost all track of time, and I'd forgotten about the dingoes entirely until they suddenly reappeared, closing in on Josie's position in swift, deadly, crouching gaits.

There was no time to plan a response, no time even to stand up and move toward them. I scrabbled for the gun, wildly. With the truck nearly on us, a gunshot would proclaim our presence, but without one the dingoes would mangle Jo in a matter of seconds. Even with a gunshot—or several—before I could make it to her, they'd have maimed her badly. On my knees in the sand, I aimed the Beretta, hands shaking so bad I was afraid I'd miss and hit Josie.

Taking a deep breath to steady myself, I

squinted down the barrel at the lead dog and was on the verge of squeezing the trigger when all of a sudden the thing I'd prayed wouldn't happen, did. The first truck came into view about seventy yards to my right. I froze.

The dingoes halted their approach in midstride, milling back, watching the vehicle with suspicious eyes. Jo stared at me, still kneeling there holding the gun in broad sight. We were both beyond terror. The moment emptied of all feeling. As the truck came steady on, the dingo pack retreated and finally turned and ran into the desert. I stayed still. No thought. No prayers. No plan. No anything. Just knees locked on sand, eyes fastened on the tiny child who was counting on me to get her out of this desert alive, mind moving into overdrive to meet that charge. If the truck stops I have to come off this ground shooting and hitting what I shoot at. It'll take them a couple seconds to react. I have to get one of them before then. If I can get one, I have a decent chance at the other. I just have to get one.

It took every ounce of strength I had to stay still.

Growling slowly by, headed toward the southwest, the first truck passed within fifteen feet of us. I know, because after they left, and I'd regained the use of my legs again, I got up and stepped off the interval. Fifteen feet, not another inch. The second truck was further out. Forty feet from Jo and me. I stepped it off too.

Two trucks, each with two men in them, had just passed right by us. Josie and I looked at each other and shook our heads. There wasn't much you could say right then. In silence we moved our gear into the nearest gully. Jo fell asleep almost as soon as we were done. I couldn't have slept right then for love nor money, not even a whole lot of both. Over and over I replayed the scene.

How could they be so close and not see us? We exist. I hurt, I bleed, Josie too. We still speak and hear and cry. We're half-dead but breathing, exhausted but sentient. So how could they *not* see us, especially perched up here in broad daylight, with not so much as a blade of grass between us and them?

There has to be a rational explanation. The supernatural is too far-fetched to comfort me. I need science—reasoned, logical explanations for material reality—and, failing that, a stab in its direction at least.

So, known facts: the two men inside that nearest vehicle—Bodley and another man—were driving into high sun. By the time they got here they'd been doing that for several hours, which means they had to be hot and tired, and the very last thing they'd have been expecting to see was a woman and child crouching on the sand. Maybe we only see what we expect to see. Maybe the material world doesn't exist until we conceptualize it. The white dingo wavers across the sand from us and I remember Grandmother Haney. She believed ghosts and spirits were as real as anything sentient. I was so angry with her for abandoning Dix and me that I disagreed on principle. Then I got a college education and disagreed on point of fact. Now I don't know what to think.

That dingo got shot. I saw it happen. Yet there she is, staring at me like always, and there's no blood on her chest. Those two trucks came within spitting distance of Jo and me, too, but their passengers didn't see us. I would like an explanation, that's all. I would like somebody to tell me what the hell just happened. More important, I'd like somebody to tell me if it's likely to happen again because I could use that little bit of data. If we're invisible, then maybe we don't need to work so hard at evasion. For that matter, if we're invisible we also shouldn't need food or water to survive, and that would cut down on our workload considerably.

No. Not going there. That's too much like Dix's religion and the Ghost Dancers from the turn of the century—Indian people praying for a miracle and believing their leather tunics were bulletproof. They got slaughtered. Just like the rest of Grandmother Haney's people. Only a few survived. She always said that's why she was so mean—life on Yankton made her that way. I'm real, flesh and blood. Foy left enough bruises and wounds on my hide to verify that.

Enough. I don't want to think about this anymore. There isn't an explanation. I might as well let it alone.

One thing I do know. If we ever had a stroke of good luck in our whole lives, it was here. It was today.

And if I make it out of this desert alive, I'm going back to Yankton, back to that shack I stalked out of so haughtily eleven years ago, back to that place whose heavy dust I was so happy to leave behind. I'm going back to apologize and ask my grandmother to tell me the story again and help me understand its meaning this time. She'll probably throw me out on my head.

Wouldn't blame her a bit if she did.

—•—

The trucks growled on across the plains, moving steadily toward Lake Surprise, our next scheduled waterhole—some forty miles to the southwest. The further they got from us, the better I felt, but the more determined I was to avoid them. All those wasted miles we walked over the last few days— going the wrong way and then having to back-track—suddenly seemed like a gift. Without those we'd have been a lot closer to the lake when these men showed up, and there's little all chance we could've avoided them then. With them in front of us, we at least had some options.

The albino rested quietly nearby. Comforted by her presence, I studied the map and let Josie sleep for half an hour, but when she stirred, I nudged her. We had work to do, and I needed her awake in order to get started. Every nerve in my body protested having to leave her alone, but taking her with me was out of the question. I talked it out one piece at a time to give us both a chance to get used to the idea.

"The campsite's a long ways away, Jo. We did a good job of masking the first section of our trail and the sandstorm worked in our favor on that too. It would take a great tracker several hours at least—maybe a day or two even—to pick up our footprints and by then we'll have covered some more ground."

Josie nodded at each point, not reassured but trying to be. I moved the sheeting to make more shade and scooted her into it, next to a small rock.

"But they're not coming from the campsite. They're working our route from the map I left for your daddy at his research camp. I thought he might find it and come find me. But it didn't work out like that. We've done pretty well so far, kid, but we've been a little careless the last couple days, so I need to go back a mile or so to brush out our tracks, just in case they pick up the trail and get within range of us. They're going to the lake now. When they don't find any footprints there, they'll probably backtrack. We're going to take a different route, but our real tracks still need to be gone before they get back here, Jo. And I need to lay a few sets of confusing ones, too, so it'll take them a very long time to catch up, understand?"

Josie nodded.

"You stay put. *No matter what,* don't you move a single inch while I'm gone or I'll skin your scrawny little hide when I get back and don't think I won't because I promise you *I will* and—trust me—you'd look pretty goddamn funny walking around this desert with half your skin missing!"

Jo didn't smile. Her eyes were dark, troubled. They mirrored the worry I was trying to hide with absurdities.

Kneeling beside her, I unshouldered my pack. "Here, hold onto this for me. That's all you have to do: stay put and hold onto this. Literally. I will be back and I need to find my pack—and you—in this exact same spot when I get here."

Josie wrapped one arm through one strap and held tight. Eyes fastened on mine, she said, "Don't you want your stuff?"

"No, kid. I can move faster without it. Stuff just slows me down."

Jo's eyes darkened. She looked at my pack and then back at me. "Don't you need to keep Daddy's book and shirt with you?"

I stopped. Something bigger was behind this question.

"What's wrong, Josephine?"

Jo eyes fell and she shook her head slowly. "Nothin'."

"Don't give me that. Something's wrong, kid, and we don't have time for me to guess. You know I'm not the brightest bulb in the package anyhow. C'mon, Josie, out with it!"

"I'll hug the rock, Tally."

Something about her bent head broke open an old memory and I found myself crouching by her side, pulling her close. She thought I was going to leave and not come back.

"Look at me, kid. I mean it, Josephine. Look into my eyes. I am not going to leave you for good. Not ever. Do you understand me?"

She just stared, wordless.

I went on. "You're keeping my pack safe for me. You know I wouldn't go anywhere without that pack unless I knew I could trust the person holding it."

Josie fingered the pack strap and nodded slightly.

"Josephine O'Malley, I will not leave you. The hell with the pack. You're my kid. I'm only going long enough to get the trail fixed."

She nodded again and said, "I know."

But her diffident tone said the opposite. I needed something more, so I reached deep inside myself and drew out the words Grandmother Haney said to me all those years ago. Those were fighting words back then. But they were as true as any words every spoken. I would leave them with Jo. They would help watch over her.

"Even when you're by yourself, Kid Jo, you're never really alone. The spirits watch over you. Kind spirits, good people. Right at your shoulder, keeping you safe."

Josie looked down her arm and said, "I don't see nothin'."

"That's because you can't see spirits with your eyes open."

"You can't?"

"No. There's too much other stuff in the way. You have to close your eyes and see with your heart."

"Oh," Josie said, shutting her eyes tight. "But what do they look like?"

I was stumped for a moment, not knowing quite what to say. I quit listening to Grandmother Haney when she got to this point with me. I didn't have any bearings. So I returned to my roots and spun Josie a yarn.

"Well, for starters, there's your daddy. You thought he had eyes in the back of his head before?

Well, he's always watching now. Front, forward and back, all sides, always."

Josie scrunched her eyes tighter as if to see better and nodded, slightly. I embellished the yarn.

"Then there's the white dingo too. This is her home, Jo, so she's never very far away. And you saw how she protected us before, just like a pet would its people. Pets do that, kid. I once saw a dog protect my mother. He wouldn't let anybody get to her while he was in the room. That's what the albino will do for you."

Josie nodded again, eyes still closed, willing to believe.

"And on top of all that, you have this," I said, drawing the Beretta out of my pack and putting it into Jo's hands. Her eyes flew open and she recoiled, but she didn't refuse to hold the gun.

"You know how to use it, kid. The dingoes were spooked by that truck and I doubt they'll come back too soon, which means I'll be here before them, but if they do show up while I'm gone, you just point it at one and shoot. And you keep doing that till they all leave. You have seventeen bullets. There's only eight dogs. You can miss every other time and still get 'em all. Can you do that?"

Josie nodded, taking the full weight of the gun in her hands for the first time.

"Good. Plus, sound carries a long way out here. If you fire this, I'll hear it and run straight back, understand? Before you empty the clip I'll be here—ready to reload for you, partner. So are we set on this?"

She nodded again.

"I need to hear you say it, Jo."

"We're set."

"So you'll get us some dingoes for dinner if they come back, right?"

"Right," she said, and a faint smile slipped across her face. "But *you* have to skin 'em and cook 'em 'cause that ain't a kid job."

"Right. Might know I'd get the bad end of the deal with my little girl setting the terms," I said, ruffling her hair. Josie caught my arm with her free hand and leaned forward to hug me. The embrace caught me off guard. Salty tears stung my eyes. I did the right thing with Foy, Mama. Rayburn too. Maybe not the right thing in the big scheme of things, maybe not the right thing for all time, but the right thing for here and now.

The repetitive words sounded hollow inside my head. Lies always echo. Patting Jo's head awkwardly, I looked at the albino, willing her to stay put and watch over this little girl, and then I set off, mind on autopilot.

—

Without the weight of the sled, I made good time. No gunshots sounded but I hurried anyway. In two hours I was back at the rock. Josie was sound asleep, head on her dad's shirt, arms through the strap of my pack, hat over her face, gun lying forgotten in the sand, one leg taking sun full force. Shedding my shirt, I covered the leg.

It was way too late. Goddammit.

How bad the burn will be I'm not sure. Lord only knows and since he isn't talking, time alone will tell. Shit.

———

So much for my plan.

I'd thought the whole thing through—how I'd make it back, roll up our gear, and hurtle us into a midday dash straight east across the next ten miles, foolhardy but necessary and doable under duress, which this is. We'd sleep at dusk and walk the night through again. Lay at least twenty miles in the wrong direction between us and here before dawn. That'd give us an even bigger lead on the men. With the clear false trail I'd laid for them a mile the other direction—and the care I'd taken to walk backward in my own tracks to do it—I was just sure we could lose them.

Had it all figured out—planned up from can to can't—only to get back here and find a kid with a leg stuck out in the sun. Shit. If it's not one thing it's four fucking hundred. Josie stayed put, the dingoes didn't come, our tracks are covered, and we were all set to move on. Now this.

Now we have to wait to see what this leg's going to do.

———

And my left hand. It's decaying by the minute. The insides of the cut have gone disgusting, oozing blackish green pus, the smell's enough to drop me in my tracks, my fingers are swollen double and stiff. When my arm even brushes against anything, I feel dizzy. With Josie asleep, I unwind the foul bandages and lay the wound open, waiting. Within seconds, flies cover it and I shudder, look away, and pray that this works. I read about it in a book one time. Maggot therapy. They used it in World War II. God, let it work on me. Please let it work or I'll be done in by the greatest irony of all: a stab wound I can't even remember getting.

I hear Justin, my sensei back at the dojo, giving his spiel about weapons. "If they've got you cornered so you can't get away and they're armed, you might as well count on getting hurt. Knife? You'll get cut. Lay money on it and forget it. Do what you're trained to do. Gun? You'll probably take a bullet. So lay your money on the table and do the best you can to come in under their radar while you're still breathing. Whatever—whichever way it goes down—if they're packing, you *will* get hurt so don't waste time and energy trying to avoid it. Just take 'em to the ground. *That* belongs to *you*. That's what jiujitsu's all about. Once they're in your guard, you have the odds on your side no matter what kind of weapon they came in with, so concentrate on getting them to the ground and then just do your thing."

I can't remember when Foy's knife got me. Somewhere in that crazed struggle, I guess. I believe it had to have happened on the ground, though. And if I ever make it out of here and back to the dojo, I intend to share that little tidbit with Mr. Justin Stephens. Did all I could do and still took a knife: that spiel about weapons you do is so right on, it's scary.

I'm seething inside. As tired as I am, I stand up and pace. Twenty steps one way, twenty back. This is crazy. I'll have to work twice as hard to brush these tracks out, but I can't sit down. There are things from my life back home that I need to sort out. I have to survive, have to make it back there, to find Dix and Grandmother Haney. To see Pony just once when I'm not trying to help her make good choices. To see Jed strictly because I need to see a friend. To see me alive and finally free of my past. To see Josie safe and well and getting free of hers. That's what I need.

I think I'll visit my mother's grave too and tell her some things I never had a chance to say. Like I *don't* see any way around what I did. None. He *was* going to kill us. It *was* us or him, just like it was you or John Nowata all those years and you wouldn't raise a finger to protect yourself. You protected Dix and me— stood between him and us every time, shielded us with your goddamn frail little body. But you wouldn't stand up for *yourself,* Mama! *Why?!* How useful do you think it was for you to practice nonviolence right into your fucking grave and leave everybody who needs you still alive? Why didn't you fight back so maybe you could've stayed with us— like I fought for Josie? How hard would that have been? I wanted you to keep me safe for always, but you didn't. Couldn't or wouldn't, which one? Why the fuck did you leave me? Why wouldn't you stay?

The words sound hollow inside my head. I am screaming at a ghost. Arguing with a dead person.

But you can't do this with them. They know all sides of the story and they don't have to explain anymore.

It's clear. I am crumbling on the inside. This struggle is breaking me into little pieces. I feel myself clutching at what was solid only to find nothing there and the terror rises strong. Stubborn cheerfulness, once so easy to summon in the outdoors, limps in now on a whim but fades quickly. All the dangerous emotions—apathy, anger, discontent, and complaint—the ones I spent my whole life avoiding, lie at my surface, threatening to erupt any moment. I'm going from calm to petty for no reason. Resignation to anger, no rhyme. Must find a way to center. If I lose it we're done for. Nose over your toes, Nowata.

———

Josie believed my tale about the dingo. Too well. She even spun me her own yarn about how the albino came and sat beside her all the time I was gone.

"So they didn't kill her, Tally! Just hurt her leg. She limps on it, but it's getting well. And now she's like a pet, so I think we ought to name her, don't you think?"

I nodded, midgulp, hot water coursing down my throat. If fairy tales make this situation more bearable for this child, so be it. I'll participate. Not half Indian for nothing.

Then I looked off to my left and there she was. The albino. Staring me steady in the eyes. I was so glad to see her again that I broke off a piece of cracker and tossed it to her.

"Eat up, kid," I tell the dingo, and Josie looks at me and smiles. She liked that. She'll be doing the twins thing with this animal soon enough.

Now it's official. My mind's toast. Sharing hallucinations with a child is one thing, but tossing it a cracker and *talking to it*? Son of a bitch. The men at that camp are the least of our worries.

Suddenly there's a blur of brown fur behind the white, and that is confirmed.

The neighboring dingo band is back, leaving me no time to worry about mirage dogs. These are real enough to make dreams unnecessary. They are hungry too, and hostile. We can no longer nap at the same time. When I sleep, Josie has to keep watch. When she does, I do.

I'm trying to put a positive spin on this but am coming up short. The posturing we've been doing isn't enough. The dingoes keep pushing the boundaries, one or two of them within sight at all times, openly keeping track of our situation. The only thing we lack is buzzards overhead and a grave digger on the right.

Worse yet, Josie's leg needs medical attention. I know how to make a field dressing for burns from tree bark back home, but am clueless here and can't risk adding a weeping rash to her problems. The tube of aloe is practically empty. She used most of it on my back. I think her leg is worse anyway, and I'm afraid to risk breaking it open. She can't afford an infection. She is too weak as it is.

The day has stretched long. The trucks stopped moving by midafternoon, well this side of the lake and well before dark, probably making camp, and even that bothers me. Worry is debilitating, I know, but I can't help it. I am worried sick about everything.

If only Paul were here. He always knew how to make me laugh. You can't worry very effectively when you're laughing.

We were rushing out the front door, arms full, late for the potluck Tally's crew was holding for Jed's birthday. Tal had spent the whole afternoon cooking and we each had two heavy, steaming dishes stacked atop the other. She could barely see over hers.

I made some imprudent remark about that and Tal shot a dark look over her shoulder. The next thing I knew, she'd tripped and food was flying, then I tripped trying to avoid her and the rest of the food went south. When everything came to rest, one casserole, a pot of baked beans, and two salads were spread over our lawn and us, Tal was sitting flat on the ground looking bemused, holding onto a stack of paper napkins, and I was standing up, barely, still gripping a six-pack of beer.

Tally looked at the food and the napkins and her spattered legs and then up at me.

"Nice to see you've got your priorities in order," she said. "I cook all day long and when there's a choice of things to rescue, you save the BEER."

Extending my hand to help her up, scanning the area around the steps for obstacles with as straight a face as I could muster, I said, "What did you trip over, hon?"

"Shut up."

Careful not to meet her eyes, I kept studying the ground, saying with exaggerated concern, "I really don't see anything, babe, so I was just wondering what you got hung up on."

There was a long silence, a deep sigh, and then she said, "My feet. Thanks for bringing it up. And what did YOU trip over?"

"You."

That much food going that much to waste—it's hard to fathom now. All I cared about that day was all the work I had put into it, only to have to show up at Jed's empty-handed anyway. Effort and community was it for me then. The food itself was beside the point.

Not anymore. I think if I spilled two pots of food today I'd sit down and bawl my eyes out.

Now it is official. Now I know I am in trouble. If the memory of me sitting sprawled on my behind amid all that food—and Paul teetering above me, holding onto that damn beer for dear life—can't make me laugh, then I don't know what can. Something important is turning loose inside. And the worst of this thing lies just ahead.

I unwind the bandages on my hand and heave uncontrollably. The smell is disgusting, but I hold my nose and look anyway. No maggots yet.

DAY 28

115 miles (unless we can figure out how to get around the men on a straighter line), 15 gallons.

Josie's skin is paper-thin, and her immune system is nosediving. Even the slightest scratch festers, and the burn on her leg looks ominous now. Sleep is supposed to be healing, but she's sleeping too much, and her reflexes are slow and fuzzy. All the same could be said of me. I feel numb and empty, like I'm sleepwalking under water, and every movement, every thought takes enormous effort. I've forgotten what it feels like to laugh. Putting words on paper helps to capture reality, gives it substance long enough that I can tie myself to it. Journaling always used to do that for me, but I haven't written a word since the day I found Paul. That was twenty-one days ago. Three weeks. How can it be that one swift moment erases the habits of a lifetime?

The trucks split up before dusk last night. One went on toward the lake. The other started scribing a slow circle west and north. They were cutting a perimeter back toward their base camp, seeing if they could raise our tracks. For more than an hour I watched their dust crawl toward us, trying to remember Jed's party that night. After the food wreck Paul and I sat on our porch steps and drank two beers apiece before going inside to make love and shower and start over, minus the food. We laughed all the way to Jed's. If Paul was here now, we'd find something funny in this too, I'm sure of it. When the sound of the truck's engine finally reached us, I stopped watching and remembering and settled down on the ground beneath the sheet with Jo.

"Hey you, it's gonna be okay," I whispered.

She nodded, reaching for my bandaged hand. I closed the other one around the hot steel of the Beretta.

We lay quiet then, listening to the truck putter in the distance. Suddenly a rifle blast split the night, a second one followed close on its heels, and a series of yelps trailed off into silence. Someone in that truck had shot into the pack of dingoes.

Josie trembled at the sound of the gun. I whispered, "It's okay, kid. They don't know we're here. They just saw that crew of dogs—who knows? Might be in our favor—maybe they scared 'em off."

We listened hard then, straining to hear, not sure what was coming next. Gradually the noise of the motor faded, and we crawled from our hiding place, sore and cramped. They had gone beyond us, well beyond us. They appeared to be heading for Rayburn's camp. We were safe for now.

"We did it, Jo!" I exclaimed, attempting a little victory dance for her benefit.

She stood quiet in the night, some small part of her wanting to smile and dance, but the rest too tired and dispirited to do it. Seconds later I understood.

"They prob'ly killed her this time, huh?"

"Killed who—oh, you mean the white?" I asked, tentative, wondering how wise it was for me to encourage Josie's fantasy about having a dead albino for a pet.

Jo nodded, staring at the ground in the moonlight. I used to believe adults owed kids the truth in all circumstances. Not anymore. I lied straight through my teeth. "Course not. She's invincible. Spirit dog. Can't kill her. It's a rule of nature."

Josie looked up at me. I drove the lie home harder, saying something about how spirit animals can move about the world in different forms but nothing can really hurt them, echoing a line I'd once heard from Dix. Back then it sounded like the worst kind of delusion, and I'd taken it with a bucketful of rock salt. Here I almost believed the story myself.

Jo nodded and said, "You sure?"

I said I was, and for the briefest moment I wasn't lying.

"So you'll be needing that name. Did you come up with one yet?"

"I'm thinkin' Eli."

"Eli?"

"Yep."

"Any particular reason?"

"Eli's my best friend at home and I miss him."

"Good reason for a name. Eli who?"

"Eli Walker. I'll have to tell you about him some-time when it's not so hot."

"Deal," I said, reaching for the waist harness. It was time for us to move on. "We'll start covering some serious ground over the next few days, Jo—we're gonna make it out of here, kid. Just you wait and see."

Josie nodded and bent to pick up her pack. "Let's go then," she said. "Which way?"

I pointed toward the southeast horizon and strapped on the harness. Josie limped forward, ahead of me for a couple hundred yards and then alongside for another fifty. When she finally agreed to sit on the sled and brush tracks behind us, her burned leg was so swollen it hurt to look at it. Even with the red lens on my flashlight—to cut the glare and save our night vision—the burn looked omi-nous.

"I'm takin' a little break. Then I'll walk some more," she said.

"Having you sit there actually works just fine. Makes it easier if you erase the tracks as we go. Saves me some steps."

"I'm gonna walk. I'm just restin' a minute or two, I said, but I'm gonna walk. Soon."

"Okay," I agreed, hoping she'd see reason later.

We're going to make it out of here. We are both stubborn enough to beat this place. We just need some more food. Some more water.

And the luck of the Irish O'Malleys to breed a crop of maggots in my left hand and keep that pack of dingoes at bay.

Yala (desert yam). Miracle food of the desert people, who trust this place enough to travel through it empty-handed, knowing the land always provides whatever they need. The buried tubers put on runners above ground when water is plentiful. During droughts, when resources can't be expended on such excess, the yala simply waits below the searing surface, its presence marked only by a few withered stalks.

Fuck luck. I don't need luck. I need brains in working gear.

I can't believe I forgot about the yala. That's one of the first plants Paul showed me when I arrived. We didn't dig one up, but he pointed out the dead stalks and talked about how miraculous the desert yam was and how important it was to native peoples here. "Tasty, too," he said, "Not like sweet potatoes, but close." All that information and what do I do? Forget it clean and practically starve to death, probably walking all over tons of yams. Damn.

I've been so used to getting my food from a store or my own little garden patch or even stealing it from the men's camp that I just didn't process what he told me about this wild vegetable. Damnit. Tomorrow we will have yala for dinner, come hell or high water.

Hell's already here, no chance of high water—evens things out. Yams for dinner it is.

But right now, before I take another step, I skim the whole of his journal. I need every single bit of information I can get on this place.

DAY 29

110 miles, 13 gallons.

Life is perception. Nothing exists outside how we see it.

Bullshit.

Josie's leg is cooked. Fried, to be more exact, covered with huge oozing blisters and one diagonal scrape, bloody and raw, from when she fell against a rock in the night. You can perceive that anyway you want, O'Malley, it's still goddamn fucking real, and we have to deal with it—no, make that me. *I* have to deal with it. The hell with perception.

The burn was bad enough. The scrape was flat out unnecessary, and it wouldn't have happened at all if this child had listened to me and rode on the sled like I tried my dead level best to get her to. But no, not Josie, little knothead.

"Forget the twin thing," I told her, "Anybody with my genes wouldn't be stubborn on a bad leg." She gritted her teeth and stuck out her tongue at me.

"I met your brother."

"So," I said, not yet picking up on the connection. Children always think wide looping circles around all the adults in their lives.

"Which body part did he lose from the bull?"

It was beginning to come clearer. "Spleen. In three parts over three years."

Jo nodded. "He was kin to you."

I shook my head and leaned into the harness and kept putting one foot in front of the other. Josie was chuckling behind me on the sled. Suddenly she sang out, "So I reckon you're stuck with me now, Mommy Two!"

After about a fifteen-minute rest, she crawled off to walk—limp, to be more precise, dragging that swollen leg every step of the way—chin set at an angle that said, Don't even mention me riding again.

I honored the chin. Figured it was best. Kept my pace slow and took more breaks than normal, said I was tired and meant it twice. Josie's whole body reflected the pain, all of her held rigid, hunched, trying to ease the pressure on that limb, but she wouldn't even consider sitting on the sled until she tripped. She wept silent tears then, and let me ease her onto it. No complaints.

Not one. All night long.

Furious at our lack of supplies—I had nothing to ease her throbbing leg—I pulled on into the darkness, telling jokes and singing silly songs until she went to sleep, still crying. The sight of that, her lying there unconscious with tears rolling down her pale cheeks, kicked me in the teeth every time

I took a break, and I pushed too hard. Tried to cover too much ground too fast. Thought I could just power us through. Wound up tripping my own self near dawn.

In the process I twisted a goddamn ankle. Congratufuckinlations, Nowata. Now you've really done it. Perceive the situation now.

DAY 30

107 miles, 11 gallons

Instead of the six miles I'd planned, we might've covered four—if we're lucky, that is, and I don't even have the energy to say how not lucky we are anymore. What a pair we make, sprawled out here in our sweltering shade, both hobbled by a leg. There's a potential water source less than a mile away, marked by a line of scrubby trees. If we could get to them, we'd at least have decent shade. But I need to stay off my ankle for a while, so we're holed up on the flats.

At least we have dinner. If you can call a shriveled-up excuse of a yam and a leftover lizard and a cup of powdered soup dinner, that is.

I saw the yala stalks not long after taking to the ground with my ankle. Digging up the tuber while sitting wasn't the easiest method, but it worked. Eventually. I spent almost an hour following the root line to the yam—two feet down—and freeing it. But even before I had it out, I knew this wasn't going to be a very big miracle. Softball size, it could've been. Better water and it would've. Instead the lemon-size skin was dry and cracked, wrinkled, and the flesh was tough and stringy and barely moist. Tasty my sore, cracked, tired, ugly old foot. I wish Paul was here so I could say, "Another case of your stories being bigger than the truth. You people from Louisiana stretch *everything*. Sweet potato, my ass."

We soaked it in water and ate it anyway—beggars can't exactly be choosers—and I will hunt them again. Josie pronounced my efforts a success, but she was so weak she forgot to give me a grade. I threw up the first helping and had to eat the second one lying on my side to get it to stay down, but it is food and if nothing else it'll keep our insides from caving in on themselves.

The nausea rides hard now, and I lie flat on my back, willing it to subside. I'm so sick I can hardly think straight. The strange food we've been eating just must not agree with me, but you'd think I would've gotten used to it by now. I keep trying to, but I don't know what else to do, and I'm sick to death of being sick.

Grandmother Haney always claimed she was a healer. Well actually, she didn't say that, but other people said it about her. Dix, for one. A few years ago he said he saw her do a ceremony for a man with a broken leg and when it was over the man got up and walked away and never even had the bone set. I told him the old fool was probably faking it, him and Grandmother too, both probably in cahoots.

I can't believe I said that. "The old fool was probably faking it." I cannot believe those words crossed my lips. I was angry with my grandmother, yes, but how could I speak of her with so much disrespect? So much venom? Dix asked me that then. I fired back that it was easy because I wished the old bitch was dead. My little brother paled at that. Much later in the day he said quietly, "One day you will need a miracle, Tally. I hope Grandmother is still here so she can help you find it."

I thought he was a bit touched in the head, so I laughed at him and said, "I make my own miracles, bro."

Today I could use a miracle. Today I could use my mother's mother. And my brother. God, let me get out of this place alive.

—

When we move again, I'll watch for the other three "miracles" I found in Paul's journal too: witchetty grubs, dry riverbed frogs, and seeds buried in ant dens. Josie found a couple letters about them as well. I'm also still doing my homework, testing plants we pass if they look even remotely capable of being eaten. One dry stalk I found yesterday seems promising.

I've cut down the time on that toxicity test, though. Don't have 24 hours to waste on every plant that needs testing out here. I still do the skin and tongue thing, but once it's swallowed I don't wait for eight. The head instructor of TJ's made a new rule to respond to the realities of our situation: No reaction after two hours is good enough. If I don't fall out dead by then, another six probably won't get the deed done any better.

Josie and I are writing our own survival manual

now. People with 24 hours to spare on every plant can take the leisurely course. We can't. But this is not as idiotic as it sounds. We are learning to come alongside this place. Our educated guesses are starting to pay off. Two hours is plenty long enough for plants we've roughly identified using Paul's descriptions and line drawings. It's also long enough for plants with similar stem and leaf structures. Kinship is a useful tool for plant classification.

Jo rummaged through the letters yesterday, looking in vain for one that mentioned a celery-like plant, so we extended that taste test to four hours instead of two. We needn't have worried, though, because the stalk settled fine on my stomach, as fine as it could given the normal state of my stomach these days. And when I put some of it in a cup of water, it plumped back up and really tasted like celery—not my favorite vegetable, by any means, but I could get to liking it here.

The frogs and witchetty grubs are another story. I'm having to work to get my head around just the concept of them. The mere thought of a plump frog or footless worm making the trip from mouth to stomach makes me gag. I gag after I quit thinking about it, too. Josie is not helping. She read the journal entry about frogs, took one look at my face, cooed out her trademark "Mmmm," and assured me they at least would be good eating. But the grubs, I was proud to see, made her a little queasy too. Little fat feetless worms have a place on the planet; we're just not sure our stomachs are it.

On a theoretical level anyway, despite the fact that our filched supplies are almost gone, our food situation is looking up. But we're still hobbled—Jo by that leg, me by this ankle—and our lack of movement with the men and the dingoes still in the picture has us tense. Moving helped us feel like we were getting somewhere, more ways than one. Sitting still is hell. Time drags, nothing recedes from memory or eye, and we're worn out from resting so much. Body parts hurt worse. We want to be back on our feet again. We need to be back on our feet again. How are we ever going to get out of here if we can't walk?

To keep Jo from getting too worried, I dragged out the map and made a big production of plotting the rest of our route. "Somewhere between 100 and 110 miles," I told her, "110 if we have to angle. That's how far we have to go. About the same distance from New Orleans to Osyka, Mississippi or from Moose to Dubois and halfway back again."

"But there's water everywhere both those places," Josie reminded me, her voice thin and plaintive. She's exhausted, starting to fret. "Enough water for a boat both sides of the road sometimes, like on Lake Pontchartrain."

"What're you saying? That we don't have enough water for a boat? You see that line of trees ahead? Right up there—the spot where all the animal trails are converging? Means there's water. Enough for a boat and when we get there I intend to build you one just to prove I'm right."

Josie squinted in the direction of the trees and finally mumbled, disinterested, "Bet it won't be a very big boat."

"Well, size isn't the point and when you get as old as me you'll have heard that said by enough men you'll start believing it too," I snapped, trying to rouse Josie's interest by any means possible, even adult sarcasm. She used to respond to that back home.

She sniffed, "Bet it'll be a little boat. A real little one."

"Fine, but it'll still be a boat and seaworthy too. Which means you will owe me bigtime. Now here, help me get the rest of our trip planned so we can move on as soon as our legs let us."

We drew our route in a dotted line across the paper then, and Jo used her forefinger to measure each segment and calculate the total miles. She figured 100, ten less than me, and we worked it out in days by her numbers since we both liked them better. Ten miles a day is ten days. Eight miles a day is thirteen. Seven is fourteen and a few hours. Five is twenty.

At that Josie held up a frail hand and said, "I don't think we can be out here twenty more days."

"And why ever not?"

"Because every day one of us gets another hurt. And we don't have twenty more parts left."

"Well maybe not on just one of us, but between the two of us we do. Sure do. Nothing's wrong with our noses yet. So how about that? Our ears. That's six. Our eyes. Ten. Plus I have one elbow that doesn't hurt, which makes eleven."

"My stomach isn't sick like yours."

"Good. That's twelve."

"And my back's not burned. Thirteen."

"See there. Told you so. And my little toes feel just fine, so that's fourteen and fifteen."

"Mine too. Sixteen and seventeen," Josie giggled.

Next thing I knew we'd both stripped to our ragged underwear, minus my hand bandage that is, counting every conceivable unbruised and unbloodied body part, until we'd come up with forty-six. Way more than enough to last twenty days. We could have two injuries apiece every day and still have six unhurt body parts left over. Jo seemed comforted by that. I definitely was. More important, we hadn't seen sign one of the dingoes since the truck left, and *that* felt like seriously good luck.

But when I saw two emus stroll across the simmering sand toward those trees, I could've sung hallelujah in a Full Gospel choir, which would be a considerable achievement since I can't carry a tune in a bucket. Food. Serious food. All I had to do was hobble my way over to those trees and bring it home.

"Now here's a job for a gun. Which we have. And we can use it because both those trucks are a good twenty miles away either side so they could never pin down the location of the sound. And that," I declared, "can't mean but one thing. Our luck most definitively has changed, kid."

———

The emu plan seemed brilliant on the face of it. Geniuslike, armed-and-dangerous half-breed stalks and shoots wild animal just like they do in the movies except ecologically sound: one bullet, one bird, no waste, no fuss, no muss. That was the brilliant plan on the paper in my head. Dinner for minimum effort. *Right*.

Out here in the real world it took four hours, three bullets, and a hell of a lot of straight pain to execute and in the end both birds hightailed it for parts elsewhere, not a single feather ruffled, leaving me to limp back to Josie in empty-handed defeat. She met me with a cup of water and an unasked question in her eyes.

I shook my head and said something about trying again tomorrow.

She asked, doubtfully, "Will that help?"

"If you mean will it improve my aim, no. Probably not."

"Maybe you need to shoot at somethin' littler."

"Oh right. Even less to point **at**. That would fix everything."

"And maybe do it from closer. Like maybe from here over to there," Josie continued, ignoring my tone, gesturing toward a small hillock a few feet away.

"Yeah, I might could hit that bush dead center, if I tried real hard."

"Then it would work."

"Yes, if you count skinned and roasted bush as dinner, which I don't. Not yet anyhow. Waste of a good bullet."

"But Tally, there's a rabbit livin' there."

"Oh. *There is?*"

"He came up twice while you were gone."

"He did?"

"Yep."

"So. If I get us a rabbit you'll eat it?"

"Yep. Aunt Dilys and Uncle Fred, they live in Slidell you know? They grow rabbits for people to eat and it's good. Almost good as chicken, if you know how to cook it. Do you know how to cook it?"

"Well no, can't say as I do. But I bet between the two of us we can figure it out."

Josie's whole body perked up. She was proud and it showed. I patted her on the back, and she tolerated a few seconds of a hug before pointing out where she thought we should position ourselves.

I thought about making a trap for all of ten seconds. "This gun will blow that rabbit all to pieces," I said aloud.

"Oh."

"But it'd take us several hours to make and rig a trap and then, if we didn't get it set just so, we'd miss the rabbit anyway. Lot of energy put out for not much meat in the long run and, I don't know about you, but I'm about sick of failing at stuff, so let's go with the gun. The men are far enough away not to hear it, and it'll be quicker."

Jo nodded. Neither one of us has the patience or strength to be tying a bunch of sticks together with twine right now.

"I just hope you hit him on the first time, Tally, because he won't never come back up once he's heard that thing," she said, motioning toward the gun as if it were the vilest demon she'd ever laid eyes on.

I promised not to miss. And prayed about it a couple times too, for good measure. Anybody who's too good to pray just hasn't been in enough trouble yet. That's one of the last things Grandmother Haney said to me before I hurried out to my brand new red Mustang. I thought she was a simple-minded old Indian woman that day, but on this one I understand she was right. So right it hurts.

We laid in wait then, Josie's eyes locked on the burrow entrance, mine running parallel to hers. It didn't take long.

When the rabbit poked his head up again, I held my breath, ready to squeeze off one shot. When he set his feet on the ground outside the den and started to tip off to the west, I squeezed. And, saints be praised, sinners too for that matter—hit him. Square in the center of his body.

Josie gulped, audibly, then shouted, "Yay!" but she changed all that to a hearty "Yuck" one slim minute later as we stood over our kill.

I seconded the yuck. Sincerely. Sure enough, our pending dinner was a mess. Guns like this aren't meant for small things at close range. Hollow-point bullets aren't meant for any game but humans either. The rabbit's middle was blown all to hell and back.

No matter. We still had fresh meat. And the second good reason to feel proud of ourselves since we started.

<hr />

Josie got two more reasons to feel proud of herself out of the deal. It was right-hand man time. She worked as my literal left hand the whole way through, and it's clear: nothing is better for a kid's self-esteem than to step in where grown-ups are falling short. I could see it in her shoulders and the way she held her chin. I count, they said. Tally needs me and I can do this.

We cut the rabbit's throat and hung it by its heels from a branch, letting it bleed out into a cup. There wasn't much to catch and it didn't take long, but blood's very nutritious and we couldn't afford to waste a drop. Josie went a bit green about the gills when I said we'd be boiling it for soup, but even then she didn't quit on the job or me. Holding the upper paws secure, she watched intently while I slit the hide from tail to throat and worked it loose, then gutted the carcass, tossing aside the gallbladder. I remember when Dix was skinning deer he'd always say, "Don't eat that." When I asked him why, he shook his head and said, "Just don't. It's not meant for eating." It was so tiny on the rabbit it didn't matter much, so I figured I could heed Dix's advice. But everything else we would use somehow.

"Pretty damn good work for a city kid," I said, threading a sharpened stick through the dressed cadaver, and Jo smiled, self-satisfied, and retorted, "New Orleans is a special city. Gives good people to the world."

I laughed aloud at that, her sounding like a commercial for a tourism campaign for the state of Louisiana. "Next thing you know you'll be hawking beignets and Dixieland jazz. Pralines and gumbo, the such, kid."

Josie persisted. "It's true. Where you're from makes a difference, Gram O'Malley always says. It does."

"That so?"

"Yep."

"Why?"

"Because it sets how your feet hit the ground and how your eyes see the world. Gram says where you're from fixes some things and you can't change 'em. Ever."

"Ever?"

"Ever. You're stuck bein' where you're from no matter where you go or what you do, so that's why it's important to be from a good place like New Orleans."

"I see."

"Because we have a history and people need a history. And in New Orleans it's everywhere, so even if we forget it, all we have to do is bump up against a buildin' or trip on a cobblestone or somethin' and there it is right there, all our history. It never goes anywhere so we can't get too lost."

"Hm, must be nice."

"Yep. Where're you from, Tally?"

"Nowhere in particular."

"Daddy said Oklahoma."

"That's right, far as it goes."

"Well, that's a place."

"Yep. Place with no history. None of mine anyhow. It's new and it's forgot itself. Not like New Orleans."

"How can you forget your history?"

I didn't have an answer to that, so I just shrugged and Josie didn't push the point. She's far more insightful than I ever knew, a lot more like Paul than I ever could've guessed based on the way she used to act back home. Spoiled was all I ever saw from her then, all I could ever let myself see, I suppose.

Here she's a constant surprise, a different child entirely, helpful and interested instead of balking and howling when things don't go to suit her.

What is it about adversity that makes some people function at their best—and the rest at their worst? I wondered, eyeing Jo from beneath half-closed eyelids, not wanting to give the impression I was staring. She was busy laying out the rabbit skin to dry. We don't really have a use for it yet, but TJ's School has a few hardcore rules and Do Not Waste is near the top.

Moments later, she asked, "Can I make the fire? Daddy showed me how."

"Sure, just set it in the lee of this rock, so the smoke will be defused a bit."

I watched her openly then, small head bent over her task, limping on that swollen, festering leg, hands shaking but still gathering dry twigs, sticks, and limbs and lacing them atop one another into a flawless tent—designed to draw in just enough air to catch the flame beneath the lighter kindling, but not enough to blow it out before it'd had a chance to involve the heavier fuel on top. It was a Paul fire. Absolutely perfect. Lit every single time. Never, ever failed.

"Not many people can build a perfect fire, but your daddy was one of them and you are another, kid," I told her, and she smiled so big I thought her face would break. Then leaned back against my pack, pale around the edges of her mouth from the effort.

With the rabbit skewered and hung from a homemade spit close enough to Jo that she didn't have to move to reach it, I left the turning of the meat to her and limped to the spring to gather a cluster of spinach and two stalks of celery, then came back and spread a sheet, determined that this would be a special meal. We're in desperate need of some ritual. Josie, delighted at the fuss, folded filthy bandanas into triangular napkins and set out battered bowls and cups, saying, "It's almost like we're back in Moose, huh?"

I nodded.

"Only you always have candles there. I wish we had one for here."

"Ah, but we do," I replied, rummaging around in my pack for the stubby little household candle I never leave home without. It's misshapen now, because of the heat, but still functional. "Nothing is better for starting a fire in wet conditions than *this*, Josephine."

"Wet?" Josie asked, archly, looking all around as if to say, And where the hell would the wet stuff be?

I tickled her then with my one good hand, trying not to hurt her leg or shudder at the sight of it. Second-degree burn. Bad at home, dangerous here. Josie laughed and for a moment forgot about the pain. I forgot the spinach and nearly burned it, but it didn't matter. The meal raised our spirits.

We ate slowly, stopping to talk and sit quiet between bites. I was trying to keep my food down. Jo, I think, was just savoring the taste of a home-cooked meal again. She smiled twice for no reason at all and soon insisted on saving the albino a leg bone, saying it was only fair since we had all the rest to use for soup. I agreed, remembering the meat I stole from the white that saved my life, dropping iodine tablets into yet another canteen of water.

The flow here is modest—it takes almost a half

hour to siphon one quart out of the rock crevice the water's hidden in (thank God we didn't jettison that piece of tubing when the load felt too heavy last week)—but we need all we can collect, so I'm working steady at it, as steady as I can with only one hand and a bum ankle.

Back and forth I go between our camp and the water. A couple hours here and then one over there. It's not good for my foot, but I don't know what else to do. We can't camp at the spring. It's illegal, for one thing. One of the conditions of Paul's permit was that we would not camp within 1,000 yards of any water source. It's good practice too. People scare off the animals, foul up the water, and generally make nuisances of themselves. But that's all a little beside the point today. Far more important, for us here and now, camping away from the water is just flat out smart. When the men get systematic about their hunt, they'll check all the known waterholes first, so we can't risk a lengthy stay at any of them. My ankle will just have to cooperate.

My left hand could kick in on that cooperation thing anytime now too, and you wouldn't hear me complaining about that either.

I've done my best to keep Jo from knowing what's up with it, but she's noticed it isn't much use. I keep it bandaged while she's awake and pretend to use it some, but I'm not fooling her. Every now and then I can feel her looking at that arm, worry palpable, a warm buzz of anxiety stretching between us, but so far she's letting me get away with the lie, not saying a word about the fact that my bandage now reaches up to my wrist and covers my fingers all the way to the tips. They are so distended and discolored they're beginning to look like those tourists' hands we pulled off the Skillet Glacier.

Or Paul's, the way they were last week.

Can't have Josie seeing them. Just can't. I feel sick to realize I can't remember what Paul's hands looked like before last week. Searching for his face, I draw a fuzzy blank there too. This can't happen this fast. Cannot. I will not let him go. Think, Tally, *think*. Think about something else. Get your head back on the track. Get inside the *now*.

Josie and I *are* managing this gig pretty well. So that's something. We're functioning as a team, pooling our liabilities and talents, picking up each other's slack. I have a lot of faith that we will make it, and for the first time since I stumbled onto her at the Land Rover, I actually mean that. Before now I've been bluffing, saying everything would be okay, but not ever sure it would. Now I'm serious. We just made dinner from our own wits alone—no grocery store, no stealing—and served it up in style, with napkins and candles, no less! We are *living*.

The odds are still hellish, yes, but we are holding our own, controlling every aspect of the situation we can get our fists around. That has to be a point in our favor. I believe it.

And if I keep saying it, surely it will prove true.

—

We cleared our dishes, tended the leftovers, and folded the sheet, with great care. Rituals demand attention to detail. Even tidying after our meal felt momentous. Comforting.

Then we crawled out of our clothes and hung them up to air dry. "They are so stiff now they could almost stand up by themselves," I said, and Josie immediately tested it with her shorts. It worked and we laughed.

"That's pretty sad, Jo. Clothes so filthy they don't even need us in 'em to stand up and salute the flag."

She nodded and cupped her chin in her hands, staring at the shorts.

"Maybe we oughta give our clothes a dirt bath too," she suggested.

"Can't hurt."

Bunching our outerwear into bundles, we pummeled each piece into the sand, rolling and kneading and finally shaking it out and hanging it on a bush. Laundry done, we rested.

Josie curled up on her pallet and stared into the fire, yawning, and said, "Do you miss your history, Tally?"

It took a long time to come up with an answer for that one, but she waited patiently.

"Not really."

"No?"

"No. I think maybe I'm making my own history, kid. You know, in all the little things I do, the kind of dumb stuff, lighting candles and making bubble bath and bread and growing vegetables and flowers and cooking food nobody really likes anymore in these days of TV dinners and drive-through windows."

"*I* like it."

"Well then, that makes two of us. In a world of about five billion. Not exactly a majority yet, is it?"

"Two's all you need. Daddy says. One person can't do nothin'. But two, two people workin' together, well they can do everything that ever needs doin' in the whole wide world. That's what he says."

"That sounds like something he'd say. Always has it figured out, doesn't he? Thumb on the pulse of the big picture all the blessed day long. Man lives on the mountaintop, the rest of us scurrying along in the valley—but not him, no, not Paul O'Malley. *He* always has a handle on the big idea for how it all works, what it all means."

"Yep."

I pause, realizing I just had Paul in the present. Maybe I should fix that. I don't want to make it harder for Jo to turn loose of him. But she's about to fall asleep right now. Fixing what I've said would be hard to do and might make her sad. I'll wait till next time. Next time we talk I'll be sure to use the past tense.

The fire has died down to a soft sizzle, blackened wood murmuring against glowing coals and silky ash. Jo's lying on her side with her head next to my leg, eyes closed, breathing soft. I start unwrapping my bandage. Suddenly she speaks again and I freeze.

"Daddy liked your things too, Tally. Your candles and dinners and stuff."

"Like's probably too strong a word, Josephine, tolerate's more on the money. But I'll grant you that much. He did tolerate it all pretty well."

"So that's three of us."

"That's three."

A smile flits across Josie's face and she whispers, "So you do have a history. Like New Orleans. With other people to remember it for you when you forget. It's kind of like a buildin' to bump into, ain't it? That's the way Daddy always says it." As quickly as it came, the smile fades and Jo is asleep.

This child just spoke of her father in the past, present, and future tenses. I understand now. I don't need to save her from the knowledge of Paul, present or past or future. She will choose the path she needs to choose for herself on that. Sometimes she will speak of him as present, sometimes as past, and sometimes as always. That is how it should be. No one needs rescuing from her own story of the truth. And no one needs to sidestep her history.

———

As soon as Jo fell asleep, I peeled the bandage off my hand, and spread the wound to check it. Maggots. Working alive, deep in the seams of my rotting flesh. Shuddering, sick, alarmed and elated all at once, I rewrapped my hand. Didn't even get finished before the heaving started. Tried desperately to will it away. Failed. Lost all my supper in the sand and collapsed face down for how long I don't know. Can't do this. It's too much. Cannot. Past, present, future all collide. Cannot do this thing.

Have to.

Reaching for Paul's shirt, I tried to steady myself but found only sheer terror. It's starting to smell more like me than him.

Then I reached for his journal and browsed

through it, looking for something, anything, specific to now. What I found stunned me, left me numb and torn, drowning in a screaming sea of silent grief. I missed it before. Missed it in this book and missed it in our lives. Paul saw it all along.

Tally and her kitchen. There's a simple, elegant beauty to it all. Wine bottles and tall candles stand amid pasta and spices. Heavy handmade pottery, blue on gray, offsets an ancient well-seasoned cast-iron skillet. Bunches of dried herbs and flowers hang from the ceiling, interspersed by brass-bottom pots and pans. One pewter hanging rack holds fruit. Another, root vegetables. A battered recipe book lies forgotten on the counter. A large silver colander cradles the bright yellows and reds and greens of her summer garden. Something is always bubbling on the stove. And in the midst of it all, small frame clad in cutoffs, a T-shirt, and a huge canvas apron that falls below her knees, is the woman at the center of my heart. My Tal.

She is so angry at me right now. I've never seen her this angry before, and for so little reason. One block of cheese. They were giving it away in town—some social service commodities being gotten rid of because more had arrived unplanned—so I took one and brought it home. The instant she saw that plain wrapper, she lit fire and ordered me to get it out of the house. I set it on the counter and she backed up, eyes blazing. I've never seen her so enraged. "Out!" she yelled. "I mean it. This isn't funny."

"But hon, what's wrong? It's just cheese! If you don't

like it, I'll eat it, but there's no need to throw it away."

"Get it OUT of my house this instant, Paul O'Malley. NOW."

Stunned by her tone and her words—she's always said it was our house before—I did as she asked and set the cheese outside the door. Tally wasn't satisfied. She pushed open the screen and kicked the block of cheese off the stoop.

Trembling, she returned to the counter and propped her hands on it, staring at me. Her voice was low, gravelly. "That's the kind of shit they used to feed us on the rez. That's the kind of shit they're still feeding my grandmother. We buy our cheese from the STORE, do you understand me? We do not take government commodities. I would rather DIE than eat that stuff again."

I nodded. Tal reached for a carrot and began slicing it on the diagonal, clearly through talking to me.

Her eyes are still dark and incensed. I know so little about her past. She shuts down when I ask about it. All I know is that she hasn't seen her father in seventeen years, her grandmother in ten, or her brother in fourteen months, and her mother is dead. I don't know the how or why of any of it. She refuses to speak of them. A pain too deep to speak lies at her core. Some nights she cries out in her sleep. Some days she flinches for no reason. Sometimes I see a silent shadow of sadness cross her eyes. If I ever bring it up, she makes a joke and moves on, keeping me outside.

It breaks my heart to see her in pain. If only I could take it all away.

One thing I know. I was born to love this woman, to hold her close and keep her safe, and this I will do as long as I live. I pray one day she will trust me enough to tell me these things that eat her alive, for when she does, I will kiss away the hurt and give her heart the space to heal . . . and then I will stand aside and watch my Tally fly. And I will live forever beneath the canopy of her sheltering sky.

My heart is screaming no in the face of your words. Timeless, speaking the unspeakable, saying to me on paper what I could not let myself hear when you were at my side.

I reach back, ears turned toward us, in vain. So much we left unsaid. I didn't want to hurt you with my past. Didn't want to risk scaring you away. Most people leave when they see it. I couldn't stand the thought of that with you. So I shut down on it and you, denied my history and my people. And myself.

But you stayed and loved me anyway. I thought we would walk together till the end of time. I thought somewhere in that I would be saved from all that was lost.

And now you are gone on without me, and I'm losing everything we were. I can't hear your voice anymore. Can't remember your face. It's a soft blur in my mind. Can't feel your hands. Can't see your smile or our sky. Can't steer for home by the light in your eyes. I'm losing you, Paul.

Losing us. Me.

I knew not to read big chunks of this journal. Knew it. It's one thing to skim the whole looking for something concrete like food suggestions. It's another entirely to read big chunks searching for something to hang onto, looking for hope at the point of a pen. That on top of the maggots and the vomiting and everything else is too much. I can't afford to do that again. I'll go back to reading one thing a day, no picking, no browsing.

No, one's not enough. Two's better. Two it is, then. One in the morning and one in the evening, like a set of parentheses around our nights.

A frilled lizard pauses in the shade of a grass stem nearby. Collared and puffed, doing territorial push-ups aimed at me.

"No need to worry about me trespassing on your turf," I feel like saying, "I'm too tired to move," but then I remember we're out of stolen food and change my attitude and stance.

In another life, I'd have been doing this for fun. Touch his tail without making him run. Dix and I played that game since we were knee-high to nothing. Evenly matched, we tried it on every type of lizard, turtle, or snake we could find. In this life, I should be able to use that skill for better reasons, but I am weak and tired and not very skilled anymore. Jo's noose worked a lot better, I think. My way takes more effort, a good deal more than his little dab of hide is worth.

But even a dab of meat isn't to be sneezed at now. I am so frail I can hardly function. Josie is noticing. It's not that we haven't found some edibles because we have. The goanna. Termites everywhere. My spinach and celery. That dadgum yam. The acacia pods. The rabbit. I even scraped down the inner bark of a scrubby tree the other day and we gnawed on the pulp, so we have found food. But I still can't seem to beat the nausea. I'm throwing up everything about as fast as it goes down, so I'm skin and bones and a smidgen of willpower on the hoof and not much more. If I can't find some way to master this land it's going to kill me. And her.

And then I really will have lost him.

I cannot let that happen. *Will not.* Do you hear that, Mama? Grandmother? *I will never give up.* I will never turn my head and walk away. I will fight this desert every step of the way, if that's what it takes to bring Josie home.

Survival: 95 percent brain, 5 percent circumstances. There's clarity in struggle. All that warm, fuzzy stuff about living with the land is fine and good for folks who never got into trouble on it. Forego the fight and be a part of nature's a perfect little ditty if the land's not trying to munch you for dinner, but if it is you better roll up your sleeves and get ready to do some damage yourself.

———

I should not have talked so tough. Things were good a while ago. As good as they're going to get out here anyway. Now they've worsened again.

The dingo pack is back. Minus one. Seven hungry dogs to one woman and a girl at the ends of their tethers.

No, make that two hungry women and one of

'em's mad. The dogs are laying out a ways now, not pushing up so close like they were before, and when I stand and walk toward them, they retreat slightly, but it's clear they're only biding their time. Fine by me, we'll do the same. Sooner or later, they'll come in close again, and if I get half a chance I intend to kill one this time. We need the meat. So there.

If it takes whipping this land into submission to get us out of here, I'll do that too.

You hear that, Tanami—you red-hearted, yellow-livered bully? It'll take a hell of a lot more than you've handed out so far to beat *us!*

—

The truck to the southwest is moving our way. The truck to the northeast is doing the same. They are beginning a systematic sweep of the land between that camp and that lake. We are right in the middle. I stand and watch them move and feel my bones go weightless in my body. We are outnumbered, outthought, and outgunned. I can posture all day long and it won't help us evade these men or this place.

And now I'm crying again. Spent two decades of my life almost tearless and now, here, I cry several times a day.

I miss Paul and Pony and Jed and Dix. I miss the aspens and alpenglow on the Grand. I miss dancing at the Rancher and rafting on the Snake. I even miss paperwork and having the people in Admin fuss at me because I forgot to cross a T or dot an I on one of the 900 official forms they make us fill out every damn day. I would give my right arm to have a form to fill out right now. Or maybe my left arm. Yes, definitely the left. It's about to rot off anyhow. Might as well trade that one in for something of value.

I used to have a life that made some sense to me. At least in the Rockies, I knew enough about what I was doing not to waste energy yelling at the land—calling it a bully, for crying out loud in a bucket! There the earth speaks to me, gives me clues, and I move through it agile and confident, no matter what the weather or season. Here I just struggle through one night and day and then struggle through the next. No competence. No dexterity. Sure as hell no elegance. Just slog and scrabble and drag all your body parts from one task to the next and try not to fall down in between 'em.

What I wouldn't give to have Pony here. Pony Sutton knows desert better than most people know the backs of their own hands.

Bless her heart, she *did* try to get me to come better prepared.

"Don't even go if you're not prepared to rise above the level of tourist, Tal," she said, and I grinned and retorted, "Everybody needs to be a fool at least once in her lifetime and this is mine. Don't worry, I won't make a habit of it—I like water in my world, deserts are for people like you and Paul—this is just a vacation for me. One puny little vacation, and I'll be back before you even notice I'm gone."

Famous last words.

"Keep your head covered and your skin out of the sun and be careful where you put your hands and feet." That's the only thing I can remember

Pony saying about dealing with the desert. That and "You can't get potable water from a cactus so don't even try. People who think you can have just seen way too many movies."

I have been keeping my head covered and my skin out of the sun, for the most part. And watching where I put my hands and feet—well, except for that thing with the brown snake and I did manage to finagle my way out of even that in the end.

But there's no barrel cactus here to even try on. I need to remember to tell Pony about that. We've managed to collect almost two gallons of water, but we drank one. My mouth is sore from siphoning, but I can't quit. I need to remember to tell Pony about that, too. TJ's top desert survival tips. Shoot from the hip and count on sore lips, hon. They're a hell of a lot more reliable than cactus.

No cactus here, but ant dens galore. Paul was intrigued by how the Aborigines collected seeds stored by ants in heaps around their dens. So am I.

Using the end of a stick sharpened with my knife, I cut into one of the small mounds and pick out a handful of seeds. Working on the theory that if the ants consider them edible we can too—there is no way in the world I'm fixin' to test all those different seeds for toxins, Jo would be ninety or dead before I got done—I lay them out on a stone and use a smaller rock to grind them into a coarse meal. Josie watches, nodding approval. Altogether the handful amounts to about a tablespoon of gritty flour. I brush it into my bowl and stare at it.

"Hungry for a pancake, kid?"

She crawls over to peer at my rock-strewn flour and skinned knuckles, raises her eyebrows, and says, way too polite, "Well, if it's all the same to you, I'd just as soon wait till I get back to Louisiana for *that*. But you get a A for effort."

You're not supposed to stick your tongue out at children, this I'm fairly sure of, but mine is out of my mouth before I can think it back. Jo giggles. I turn around, treating her to a view of my departing backside, tossing my head dismissively, fly braids swinging. She laughs out loud.

"Fine then. Don't eat my pancakes. Just leaves more for me." I mutter all the way back to the ant den. Jo laughs till she cries, clutching her stomach and rolling on the ground.

"I'm collecting ants this time, Teach. Movin' up from seeds to raw protein. I expect an A+ on this project."

That was about three hours ago and about ten steps too far over the line. Toasted ants taste exactly like they look walking around: leggy, brown, and a little bit bitter.

I am really in the mood for an extended visit to the IGA. They sell chocolate-covered ants on the ethnic aisle. Paul used to tease that I ought to try them.

Over my cold dead body.

Well, may be.

DAY 31

107 miles, 14 gallons.

"Let go, Tally girl," Grandmother Haney used to say when we were very small and lived with her on the rez. "Don't fight the land. If you do, you will lose every time."

She was elegant and dark and tall, Lakota and always leaning west no matter how far east she was trapped. I was clumsy and short and fairskinned, Potawatomi and other stuff too mixed up to remember or name, and I could lean west all I wanted but it wouldn't make me more real, more Indian, more her. I prayed she'd rub off on me till the day my mother died, but then she looked at Dix and me and gave us to the state, and I was stuck inside a skin that didn't look a bit like home anymore.

I saw Grandmother Haney only once after my mother's funeral—six years later, when she was toothless and haggard. Whatever had been elegant had worn away. She was clumsy and shorter than I remembered and her hair had gone steely gray, and I stood tall in my fine clothes and listened to her talk without hearing a word she said. And then I turned my car's nose to the west and eventually wound up in the Tetons with a brand new life.

I never spoke her name a single time after that day. Only here in the Tanami have I finally let my soul come to rest enough to reckon with her.

"Trouble makes an idiot of the wise man, and a wise man of the fool," she used to say.

The truck to the north is getting closer—five or six miles out, steadily combing the land for sign. The albino sees me watching. Josie sees us both. We exist in a web not of our own making. To call it trouble is putting it mildly. I look to the heavy brush and pray for more cover.

———

Josie saw one of the acacia bushes Paul described in a letter as the place where witchetty grubs could be found, and we both set in to digging at its base, aiming for the swollen roots that encased the grubs but not sure exactly what said grubs would look like or how deep they would go. Disgusting and not far were the answers.

"Oh mercy," Josie said, when we got the first root broken in two and I started extracting the grub. Its bulbous orange head lolled my direction and I dropped the root. Then Jo and I both rocked back on our heels and just gawked at this thing we technically could eat. It was bigger around than my thumb, sort of pale and fleshy and plump, wriggling like a worm in a can but nowhere near that fast. Sluggish. Truly disgusting.

"Your daddy said they were really nutritious. Tasty."

Jo wasn't convinced. "He said that about the yala too, Tally."

"Yeah. Maybe men lose their taste buds early on or something."

"How are we supposed to eat that thing?"

"Raw or cooked."

"Raw?" Josie gagged and crawled backward.

"Or cooked."

Jo jumped to her feet and shook her head. "I can't eat that."

Determined that our work wouldn't go to waste, I reached for the grub. When its soft fat body touched my fingertips, my stomach nearly came out my mouth and I landed on my feet somewhere by Josie.

"Me neither."

We left the grubs exactly where we found them. There is a limit to what sensible women are willing to do to survive. Grubs sit square in the middle of our line. We will not cross them.

—•—

But what would Grandmother Haney have said about all this?

Tears sting my eyes as I remember that last day, watching her pour ketchup on that stale slice of white bread, fold it over, and raise it to her mouth. Her only granddaughter was standing in the middle of her home, clad in disgustingly expensive clothes and fed disgustingly well, and still Bess

Haney had the grace and fortitude to simply eat her ketchup sandwich and say nothing untoward. Nothing unkind. Nothing mean. That was never her way.

Her cupboards had no doors and no need for them. They were empty. It was the middle of the month, two weeks to go till the commodities came again. Half a loaf of bread and half a bottle of ketchup would have to do till then. The roof had small holes in it. The walls had bigger ones. She had patched those with clothes so worn and filthy they should've been burned, but the cold air still crept round them and through her. Her bed was a pile of tattered blankets on the floor. Her only chair had a broken leg so it listed to one side. But she was an old woman with nowhere else to go but this one-room shack and so she stayed and ate her ketchup sandwiches with dignity and told her stories to those who came to hear and helped anyone she could and she never, ever was unkind or mean. To anybody. It simply was not her way.

She abandoned us to the state, yes, without so much as a whiff of an explanation, but she never said anything unkind to me. Not even that day— when I was so far out of line I deserved it.

Weeping now for the years we have lost, wishing I had not let my pride and my fear and my anger drive me away from this woman who probably knew me better than anyone else, I think about Grandmother and what she would say about these grubs.

"Live with this land, Taliesin. Claim it as your

own not by force but by submission. Let go, Tally girl. You fight, you lose."

I will try this. Today I will try to let go and move with this land. Rest on it, sleep through the heat, and by tonight we should be able to travel again. Josie's leg is still too bad for her to walk more than a few feet, but my ankle's better. Swelling's on the way down, pain's close to manageable. I can pull her. Not far maybe, but a ways. We've tanked up on water, and still have some meat left. This morning I'll collect those grubs and roast them, make a soup, and look for another rabbit. If we keep a slow, steady pace, we still have an excellent chance of making it out of here. And today I want to go home for more reasons than ever before. I want Josie out, safe and happy. But I want me out too.

Let go and live with the land, Tally. Chin up and breathe.

——

That lasted all of ten minutes. Which is exactly how long it took for me to close my eyes and relax with the land until my ears picked up the drone of a plane engine.

Instantly the rest of me snapped into high gear, adrenaline surging. A small fixed-wing, Cessna something, was circling low, deliberate. There was no time to think. I yanked the sled into the shade of a small scrubby tree, as much out of sight as possible, and crouched there, helpless to do anything else, torn between wanting to signal and knowing they might be unfriendly. The longer I watched, the surer I was about the latter. This plane wasn't on a pleasure cruise or working holiday. It was tracing wide looping circles in a clear search pattern. They were looking for us, working with the men in those two trucks. I drew further back into the shade. Josie hunched on the ground, silent. Neither one of us reached for the binoculars. We couldn't risk a reflection.

"It's hard to see people from a plane, Jo. Helicopter's worse, but a plane's not easy. I've done it before on searches. Tough."

"Is it them?"

"Don't know for sure."

"But you think it is?"

"Yes."

"Will they find us?"

"Depends how bad they want to and how bad we don't."

"Oh," Josie said in a small voice, reminding me again just how young she is. I've been treating her like a pint-size adult. I tried to fix that.

"I tell you what, though. If it was me, I'd put my money on us women. Seen what we did to that rabbit, didn't you?" I was lapsing deep into the vernacular, using the language of a hick to reassure this child. And myself. If you're confident enough to fuck with the language, you're pretty damn confident. Josie responds with a small smile.

"Uh huh, seen it. But those men are a lot bigger than that rabbit and you have trouble hittin' big stuff."

"Why you little—"

Josie grinned and the moment of terror receded in both of us just far enough that we could make a plan and prepare to execute it. I talked it out loud to keep us calm.

"Wouldn't be easy to land that thing out here, so I expect they think they'll pinpoint our location from the fixed wing and then radio those trucks. Pretty good-size operation they're running, Jo. They're burning some serious money on us, kid. And drawing some attention to themselves to boot—or they would be if anybody besides us was out here watching. We have to go to ground."

"Go where?"

"To ground."

"How?"

"Put ourselves inside their heads, for starters."

"But how, Tally?"

"Think it out as if we're them and they're us. Like, if it was me, I'd do flyovers of the main water sources in this area first. Means they'll get to this one soon. We have to blend in with the dirt by then, Josephine."

"With the dirt?"

"With the dirt. Be best if we could have a few miles between us and this spring, but we don't and we can't risk moving now with them up there— they might catch a glint of sun off our gear or something and spot us. So that means we have to wait till dark to clear out of here and in the meantime we've got to lay like dirt and do it without raising any dust."

Our work cut out for us, we set to it, the dull moan of the plane's engines staking a claim to the land several miles to the northeast, looping ever closer. We stayed focused. Josie unlashed the gear and tucked it under scattered bushes. I dug a sand cave barely big enough for two into the side of a small ravine and balanced the sled crosswise above to form a stopgap roof. Then we covered it in sheets, camouflaged the whole with sand, twigs, and brush, and swept out all the tracks we've made around the spring since yesterday. Crawling inside, we stretched out flat to wait.

Peering out, I nudged Jo. "See how normal it all looks? Only a really good tracker could see signs of us here. And he'd need to be on his feet to do it, not in a plane. So now all we have to do is endure being stuffed in this cave like a couple of fat juicy grubs in a root till that plane leaves."

Josie nodded, stared outside a while, and then turned over and lay on her back. I did the same.

The metal of the revolver digs into my right leg. It's worthless, but invaluable just the same. If they do spot us, this gun may be the only thing we have on our side in the encounter.

There's been no sign of the dingoes. I'm praying they stay out of the equation. We have enough on our plates without adding them to the mix. Just as I say that there's a scuffling outside and I turn over to see the albino rush past in a blur of white fur. Two of the dingoes are tearing into our packs. She's chasing them off. Or trying to.

—

We've 107 miles to go, at best, on our current route. We're still pinned down about a quarter mile from the waterhole. The white backed the dingoes off, but the men are all over us. Trying to walk around them isn't going to help much. They're mobile and can circle as wide as they like. We have to do something different.

Echoes of the proud child I was at sixteen run through my head. I was wrong that day, but the principle of the thing was right. Grandmother did abandon us and she refused to share her reasons; I was furious at her and wanted her to know it. The first thing she said to me when I walked in the door was, "You've grown up. Got a backbone of steel and a heart to match, I can see. Hang onto them if you can, Tally girl. They'll do right by you when nothing else will."

Whatever else has been true of my life, I have kept my backbone and heart intact. And just as soon as that plane lets up, I am going to use them to march Josie and me out of this goddamn desert. Straight down the middle, no more detours. We will evade as best we can, but we won't do it by walking extra miles. I have seventeen bullets in the clip and another forty in the box. If it comes down to it, I'll use them all. In the meantime, I'm going to get us out of here.

DAY 32

85 miles, 13 gallons.

Each mistake carries within it the seeds of truth.

The shelter we made yesterday nearly killed us. Kept us hidden from the men, yes, but almost killed us in the process.

I didn't position it to take advantage of the wind. Ground temp went to 139. We nearly died.

I realized the mistake fast, but not fast enough. The plane was circling our location by then, growling soft in the sky above, and we couldn't afford to draw their attention. If it hadn't been for the seven quarts of water we had inside, I really think we'd have collapsed from heat stroke. In one hour I drank four and Josie downed the other three. The dead, sizzling air weighed heavy on our bodies, Jo dozed and I listened, struggling to breathe, trying desperately not to feel buried alive one thin floor above hell's middle.

It is a feeling I cannot evade. Or shake, even temporarily. When the plane finally eased away from us to the south and disappeared, we hauled ourselves out on our stomachs and lay there in the sun, gasping and spent. Every inch of our clothing was wringing wet with sweat and the wind blew against it, cooling us, but I still feel like I'm smothering. Josie does too. It's done something to both of us, I think, broken something important on the inside. We're silent. Have been all night long.

Talking takes too much effort. I can't remember any songs. Wracked my brain to think of something funny to say for hours and didn't come up with one thing so finally quit trying. We collected more water and set out. I walked till I couldn't, then walked some more. We're going through water like it was air. I'm so thirsty I could scream anyway. Found a rabbit at dawn but the men were too close to risk shooting the gun. Dug another sand cave, deeper, head into the wind so it can tunnel through and over us during the day. At least this time we won't smother.

But I don't intend to get inside unless I absolutely have to. I'd rather sit out here. I've stared at the map and our route till it is burned on my memory for tonight, ready to lead us through the long dark hours again. The albino hovers close like a ghost sister, waiting to walk us to the other side. She stayed between us and the ranging dingo pack all night, working the line between them and us like a patrolman on an assigned beat. I'm so bleary I can't even wonder about that now. Jo's leg is going south. I have to get her to a doctor. The maggots have sucked up the decayed tissue in my hand and started on the healthy flesh, drawing blood and hitting nerves, bringing my hand back to life enough to hurt again, clear to my elbow. I took a stick and picked their heavy bodies out, cleaned the cut with fresh urine followed by a quick dash of water, not a drop more, and wrapped it shut. No idea if it'll hold. Numb now. No pain anywhere. I gaze at the white and try to hold onto my steel.

DAY 33

75 miles, 10 gallons.

Home. That's all I can think of today.

We shouldn't be here, none of us.

Every day I wake hoping we aren't, and maybe if I sleep a little longer we won't be. Things will change. Josie will be in school, playing with Eli (the boy, not the ghost), sleeping in her bed, saying goodnight to her mother. Paul's dissertation will be done and defended and he'll be back home at Moose, sitting in his chair reading or splitting wood in the backyard or reaching for me gently in the night. I will be in the park, working a rope rescue on granite instead of sitting in a desert with faces that haunt. I'll be curled up with a book by the fireplace, paging through the latest Seed Savers' Catalogue, dreaming of my spring garden. Sleeping in our bed, old nightmares gone toothless in his presence. Pouring coffee in the morning and wine at night. Comfort, safety, rest.

We none of us should be here in this desert.

Except the white. She's the only one that

belongs here. The only one that doesn't struggle. She who watches everything and says nothing is the only one that's real.

━━━

We crossed a dry riverbed last night, and I wasted valuable time and energy and the last of the flashlight batteries stopping to dig for frogs. They bury themselves in the ground in the riverbeds, Paul wrote, and survive right through the drought.

I thought if we could find frogs it might cheer Jo up. She's been getting quieter, too quiet. The strain of watching for the men is wearing on us both. The plane hasn't been back, but both trucks are still out here, still crawling across the plains, still searching for us. So I lit on the notion of the frogs and lured Josie into a bet about who would have to cook them. She lost.

I dug then, thinking surely we'd find one or two. Two hours later with a hole two feet deep and about that wide, still nothing. The look in Josie's eyes said it all.

Quit while you're still ahead.

DAY 34

69 miles, 8 gallons.

The truck to the north crossed close to us late yesterday evening and made camp for the night about a mile to the south. I'm hoping this means they haven't a clue where we are. If so it'll take them days to run across signs of us and by then we may already be out of here.

We're still in evasion mode and will stay that way. Laying up midday in a shallow trench, camouflaged by sheets, sand, and small limbs to stay out of sight. No fires, no potshots at bunnies, no laughing aloud, no singing, no camping near water, no walking without thought. Every move now must be calculated by where we can best hide if the men show up unexpectedly. I am pissed as all get out and a part of me wishes they'd just come on so I could blow holes through their hides, only the rest of me knows I'm so unsteady I'd probably miss. I've no bravado left to draw on and I am so tired of myself that I could scream. Would, if it'd do any good and I knew for sure the sound wouldn't carry.

"Tell me a story, Tally," Jo says, face flushed from the heat. It must be 125 degrees in our little shelter right now. "One from Daddy's book."

"Good idea, kid. Been a few days since we went to the rodeo. I've missed it."

"Me too."

While I locate the place in the journal, Josie stares outside.

"Those dingoes keep followin' us, Tally."

"I know."

"But Eli Two won't let 'em get us, right?"

"Right."

"Good."

"Okay, ready for me to read?"

"In a minute."

I waited. Jo turned over on her back and clasped her hands on her stomach. Suddenly she looked at me and said, "You think those men in those trucks are cowboys, Tally?"

"Well, I don't know. Why?"

" 'Cause if they are I was thinkin' maybe you and me could just go on out there and beat 'em up."

"Now *there's* a plan. Both of us shaky as foals on the third day of a bad case of the scours—takin' on four grown men. I think we better stick to beatin' up ants and lizards, Josephine. More our speed."

She laughed and said, "I know. Now *read*."

———

Jo trapped and toasted termites this morning, and we both ate. I kept them down too—an important point in our favor. I thought hard about shooting the albino since she's of a size to keep us going several days, but caught Jo's eyes on me and couldn't. And then I realized I was thinking about shooting a spirit and that was so damn messed up that I didn't know what to think anymore.

Josie saved the day by announcing that it was never going to get cool enough to tell me about Eli Walker, her best friend from school, when it was cool. So she was going to tell me about him while it was still hot.

"He's in my same grade but he's shorter and skinnier than me. He's got white hair and glasses and I told him he could be my boyfriend while I was gone if he wanted to."

"That a fact?"

"Yep."

"And what did he say?"

"That he'd think about it for a while."

"Oh really? And what did *you* say to *that*?"

"I told him he better hurry before I changed my mind."

"You did?"

"Um hm. And he went to the water fountain to get a drink and came back and said he reckoned he'd say yes if it was all the same to me and I said it was so he did."

"Ah, young love."

"Why do you say that?"

"Because I think it's sweet, Jo. You have a boyfriend. Isn't that sweet?"

Josie considered that for a couple minutes and

then said, "Nope. Not really. He just has a puppy that I like, so if I'm nice to him I get to pet his dog."

Puppy love. Literally. Still, Eli Walker is the person Josie misses most today. More even than Paul, I think. She's slipping into the habit of seeing everything in reference to her friend. "Eli would like that," she says to the albino. Or "Eli would think that was funny, wouldn't he?" Or "Is it the weekend yet? I wonder if Eli's going to the movies today?" It's almost as if by thinking of him she can get outside what's happening here.

—

We covered a lot of miles last night—five at least, maybe six. Weight's down. I've jettisoned everything possible, buried stuff all along the way, trying to get the load light enough that I can still pull it. My feet feel like lead. Water's going fast and Josie's a rack of bones. That means she's easier to pull, but nerve-racking to reckon with. Sometimes I get scared she's just going to disappear before my very eyes.

Sixty-nine miles or so left on eight gallons. One last shot at surface water between us and the settlement. All bets are off. I wouldn't put a nickel on our chances either way.

Or take a million dollars from somebody who wanted to lay a wager against us.

Tally once jokingly said to me, "Don't bother to try and run or hide from me either, because I'm a T-10 tracker and I WILL find you." I remember thinking later that the funny thing about that conversation was, I believed her.

Skills and will. Until the Tanami yanked me up short, I thought that was all you needed for whatever needed doing. Until I stood at Paul's grave twisting that ribbon around those sticks I thought I could fix anything, find anybody, rescue everyone, and carry them all out on my own goddamned back if necessary—in short, save the world entire or at least my little corner of it. Paul believed it too, but he was wrong. *We* were wrong. I couldn't even save him.

But I did manage to save my left hand. It's healing. The maggots worked. And, so far anyway, I have saved Josie. And she's saved me.

I've pulled this sled so long it feels like part of my bones. We are going home.

And I know what Paul would say if he were here. *Everything's going to be all right, Tal, you'll see.*

In our life together he was never once wrong about that. Over time I got so I believed him, hands down, no questions. Now he's left me to run across the rest of the truth on my own.

Clutch skills and will with both hands, stand strong into the wind, pray for rain and dream of water, and keep moving. Nose precisely over your toes.

DAY 35

67 miles, 6 gallons.

Follow on hard the ghost of your dreams. Let each trailing breath pull you past each disappointment, each loss, each day's small death. No one ever yet died on the trail of a dream. Suffocated on the stench, maybe. Died? No.

Waxing philosophical. It's a bad sign, the worst, a clear attempt to compensate for my loss of control just about everywhere else.

Especially on the smallest points.

Of all the bum raps that could've gut hooked me here, it's the least one that's causing the most trouble, my ankle. The thing swelled up to twice its size last night and cut the forward end off the miles I was intending to cover. Made two instead of six. One of the trucks turned north and headed back for their base camp. I thought they might be giving up. Prayed they were. But the other one crawled along an east-west line south of us till almost midnight. They camped a couple miles away, and they can't have gotten our trail yet because we haven't gotten that far, but they're crosscutting the area systematically so it's only a matter of time till they do. Going to that next waterhole will increase our exposure, but we can't afford to skip it. Sixty-seven miles to go, six gallons. These numbers are not in our favor.

I'm trying to bury my awareness of how precarious our situation is in a fog of work: walk, pull, brush out tracks, dress wounds, guzzle water, memorize route, make shelter, sleep, get up, do it all again. Routine dulls the edges of everything. We're way past hungry. Jo and I keep looking for food, but except for termites and another shriveled yam, keep coming up empty-handed. I'm so unnerved I even built a ramshackle trap yesterday morning using sticks and lashing it with strips of rabbit hide and sinew, but couldn't get it situated so anything would come near it. Don't have skills for this level of survival. Can't control all these variables.

Josie worries me too now. Her leg is gruesome, swollen and purple and infected. I'm keeping it as clean as I can. She doesn't complain, asks for a story, sits quiet and listens and watches the white or me, then slips away again. Sleep is supposed to be healing, I keep saying it, but this doesn't look like healing to me. She's too pale, too weak. When she rouses I talk about Eli and she listens, dogged, but doesn't offer anything new and I have so little to go on I can't get very far on my own. I should've worked harder to get to know her over the last four years instead of running off, telling myself I was doing it for her good and Paul's. Not true.

I ran because they scared me. I knew if he ever had to pick between us he wouldn't pick me, so I was making sure he never felt he had to pick. I also ran because I scared me. In Josie's eyes lurked an echo of my past and I was afraid she would get too close and I'd hurt her or maybe I wouldn't and one day she would just walk out anyway. So I didn't even try to get to know her when I could. I was too busy running.

And now my running is over and I find myself hobbled to this child, heart and soul, and needing every last detail I can get from her life to hold her in it, and I'm coming up empty-handed there too.

Hopscotch. A child's game, one of Jo's truest loves. She never tires of it. The simplicity of that—strong loyalty to such an ordinary activity—always makes me wonder. What is it about adults that we lose our loyalties to the common so quick?

Thank God for this journal.

Josie and I played hopscotch with sticks and leaves this afternoon while we waited for the sun to go down. Neither of us could hop, so we let the rubble do it for us, fingers for feet, and we played by rules I never heard tell of. Low score wins first round and teams—the dingo and Jo against me and the sled.

"Might know you'd pick the only other live thing here," I grumbled when Josie chose E-Two for her team. "But I bet she can't hop worth shit— I mean *sin*."

Josie giggled softly at my attempt to clean up my language. "You're funny."

"And you're fixin' to lose this game, kid, because that sled partner of mine can jump like nobody's business."

Jo laughed out loud, then clapped her hand over her mouth. We're trying to be quiet. That one truck is still only a couple miles away. Jo's smile beamed through her fingers. Then she and her team beat me and mine into the dirt and I made a big pantomime of howling and moaning in despair and she fell over on her side, laughing till she cried. Then rain clouds gathered high above and far to the southwest, and that made us both happy.

Daft happy. We forgot all our troubles for a few minutes. Even the glimmer of the sun off the men's windshield, puttering its way ever closer to our hiding spot, couldn't dampen our spirits right then. We know what the clouds mean. One day soon it's going to rain. Maybe not today or tomorrow, but soon. Rain means hope, and nothing could tamper with how good it made us feel, not even the presence of the men.

But when the albino rose, silent, crouching, to stare over the plains toward the next waterhole, and I saw what she was looking at, I felt a tingle of sheer joy. Water *and* food. Now that has to be heaven.

———

Tanami IGA.

The dingo pack was harrying a kangaroo our

direction. We were upwind and they hadn't spotted us yet. The animal was hurt, one back tendon severed along the way, but still fighting to escape. About twenty yards out, the leader pushed it into a sharp turn and the rest closed in fast, lean bodies flying at their quarry, teeth gnashing, drawing blood and forcing it into submission at the throat. Three of the dogs milled around, aware of me suddenly, while the other three hung on. The roo struggled for several long minutes and finally went limp.

Without conscious thought, Beretta in my pocket, heavy stick in my right hand, I plunged in. Arms raised, body as formidable as I could make it look, I stomped toward the frenzied mob. The white trotted along about thirty feet from me. The pack looked startled, confused, angry at my approach, but they stood their ground. I kept charging forward, just like I had good sense, swinging the stick, determined to back them off the kill without having to use the gun—which might work, but would risk bringing the men to us too. The dingoes held on, crouched, necks taut, eyes burning with equal resolve. I never paused, never slowed down, just locked eyes with the male and stormed in like I owned the place and everything in it. Some part of me was terrified they'd call my bluff. The rest knew I couldn't deviate from the effort. We had to have that meat and we had to have it without making any noise. Possession is nine-tenths nerve.

It worked. Once at the carcass, I kept walking,

waving my stick, missing the dingoes but not by much. They held my gaze, not ceding a thing. I kept swinging, turning first toward one and then another. They feinted backward at every swing but stepped in as soon as I turned to the next one. Suddenly the largest female rushed me from behind and I swung wildly, on instinct, and somehow, miraculously, hit her. With a yelp she ran off and the others gradually wandered after her. The hot steel of the Beretta burning my thigh, I dropped the stick and picked up the kangaroo's hind leg to drag the body back to camp.

So now we have fresh meat, and the only price is an annoyed set of Canis neighbors. No matter. I can sleep with one eye open while we're inside their territory. What counts is we have more than enough food to get us out of here if we're careful. We have six gallons of water left and we're getting close to the next waterhole. Rain is getting close to us. The one truck is still a couple miles away. The other one is still gone. My left hand is healing over and my ribs don't hurt. Josie's leg looks awful, but we're only sixty-seven miles away from a village with a medical clinic. We were right, Paul O'Malley. Everything *is* going to be all right. It really is.

DAY 36

65 miles, 4 gallons.

She inhabits her name like an uneasy cloak, suspicious of it, I think, worried that it may say something about her she doesn't want said. Taliesin. Welsh for shining brow, but better known as the name for Frank Lloyd Wright's home. I once suggested we visit there and Tally looked at me as if I were proposing a midnight raid on an animal cemetery. I actually think she might've agreed to the latter.

Well, one thing's for sure. Human neuroses are, at the very least, entertaining. Josie had to be prodded awake to read from Paul's journal this morning, but by the time she reached the end of this passage, she had curiosity written all over her gaunt little face. Where *did* my name come from?

Hanging the kangaroo from an acacia limb by its back feet, I stood in the growing darkness and told her the truth. How I had a dreamer for a mother, a quiet, kind woman who always wanted to be an architect or a writer—which is the reason for my name and Dix's, Taliesin and George Sand Nowata. When life crushed her dreams, she made them live again by naming me after a house none of us ever saw and Dix after a woman author none of us ever read. Grandmother Nowata called it an act of faith—useless as tits on a boar hog—and everybody made fun of us for it. Then Dix got old enough to understand where his came from and begged me to rename him, so I did. Dixon, after a pet frog and a town I'd never seen but liked the sounds of. The slimy green frog gave him warts before the summer was over, and neither one of us ever went to Dixon, but Dix hung onto his name and refused to answer to anything else ever again.

Josie grinned and wrote Taliesin in the sand with a stick. I watched and tried to swallow down the rest of the story by slitting the kangaroo's belly, groin to neck. All I can hear is that soft, kind voice. *Violence isn't the way to fix violence, Tally. You don't fix anything by breaking it again. To end the circle you have to be bigger than your pain. Promise me you'll end it. Promise me, Taliesin.*

Jo draws on and I think, opening the center cavity and gutting the kangaroo, searching for something to say to break the silence. Nothing comes.

The kangaroo swings from the limb. I sit down to rest, blood on my hands and heart and soul. There's no real way to run from life.

— — —

Mama saved the ice cream man his head, and Dix a few childhood thumpings I was pretty sure he'd earned fair and square, and my father his life. I didn't hit the playground bully or slap the first boy who kissed me. That's all Mama's doing. She is not going to let me off the hook now.

Josie gets tired of practicing her cursive and stretches out flat on the ground, head nearly touching my knee. I rest my sore left hand on her curls and the feel of her hot sweaty scalp helps me feel safe. Safe enough to hit it head on at last.

I am the daughter of Joy Nowata. What I have done she would not judge. Would not *do* either, but would not judge.

Rising again, I slit a strip of thigh meat off the roo. I must reconnect with the center Mama begged me to keep. I need the balance that was second nature to me in the Tetons, need the control—the control of myself and my surroundings—that I relied on back there. I'm teetering here, listing from one side to the other, holding on by the skin of my teeth. But this is no time to reinvent Tally Nowata, no time to throw out my core beliefs and disavow my own history, no time to throw up my hands and quit on myself. I need to face me head on.

I lay the strip over a limb and cut another.

Mama was right. Nonviolence is the strongest stance you can take in a crazy, violent world. It gives you a center no one can ever threaten. If I hadn't been so scared and angry, I could've taken Foy down and disabled him. I know a hundred ways to do that. At the end I even had him down, so I definitely didn't have to kill him outright. I could've left him, moved in and got Jo, disabled Rayburn, and gone on. Saying I killed Foy for Josie or even for me is a lie. I didn't kill him for us. I killed him for what he did to Paul.

All the justifications in the world can't change that.

The knife slices through the meat, smooth and habitual. Honesty has no cost. I broke my promise to my mother because I wanted Foy to pay for taking Paul from me. And if it hadn't been for Jo showing up when she did, I'd have killed Rayburn too, I was so far gone, so far from my center, so far from everything I've always held onto as truth.

Any way you cut it, that is revenge, and there is no way to justify it. To get back to my center, I have to quit lying to myself. I cannot be strong if I'm swaddled in untruths, head buried in the sand of my own excuses.

No more.

I have ten strips now, laid side by side, pulling the limb low. I stop to rest again, letting my hand rest on Jo's shoulder.

It is time to release my grip on the past and move forward. The only future we ever have is the one contained in the steps we're taking right now.

Sometimes we need to be reminded that the future is as real as the past.

Josie walked back into her life today. The combination of fresh meat, rest, a win at hopscotch, and her dad's stories started it, but the accident I had with the knife brought her to her best self.

We had the kangaroo skinned and gutted, hung and partly dressed. The men's truck had just made another long pass south of us, the sound of their motor fading and rising, moving away, coming closer, then moving away again. We're used to them now and evasion is second nature. We've come onto a plain of very heavy brush, which works in our favor, but at dawn we still dug a hideout a few yards from the tree and stocked it with water, bandannas, journals, and the gun, and stashed the rest of our gear a little farther off.

"If those cowboys get within a mile, we'll hide," I told Josie when we finished, "but till then we work." She agreed. Having a job makes everything—even being stalked—easier to bear.

It does not make you proficient.

I'm not sure how it happened. Early in the afternoon I broke concentration for a split second, I think, easing my hips enough to move the seam of my shorts off my hipbone—I'm so emaciated now that it hurts for the seam to brush against the bone, so I'm constantly squirming inside my baggy clothes, and I've actually gotten pretty good at moving that seam without using my hands. But when I reached for the next strip of thigh meat and started slicing it off, I slipped somehow and the knife wound up buried in the palm of my left hand. Everything stopped but Jo. In a blurred haze I watched her run to our shelter and return with our bandannas, while I crouched my way to the tree trunk and leaned back against it.

"Hold still, hold still!" Jo exclaimed, "We have to stop it bleedin'."

Small hands trembling, strong with fear, Josie wound one bandanna around my hand.

"Tighter," I said, and she cinched it down as tight as she could get it. Blood seeped fast through both wraps. Jo wrapped the second bandanna around the first, fastening the last wrap of it around my wrist, and sat down next to me, exhausted, her eyes locked on my hand. My two middle fingers lay useless, their tendons severed. I didn't explain that to her. The blood was more information than she needed anyway. Gradually the bleeding decreased and she stood up again.

"I'm gettin' our medicine stuff. We have to clean it. Daddy said animal blood mixed with human makes people real sick. You can die. So we have to clean all the insides out, Tally."

"We don't have anything to clean it with, kid. If we had any medicine stuff, I'd have been using it on your leg."

"My leg's better, see? I'm not even limpin'. I don't need it cleaned anymore," Josie said.

"The only thing we could use to clean it is fresh urine. Want to pee in that cup for me?"

Jo looked at me as if I'd lost my mind. Speaking in an ultrapatient tone, the sort you'd use for a hysterical child, she said, reprovingly, "Tally, that's not clean."

"Yes it is, kid. Clean as you can get. Been cooking inside your body for hours. I'm serious, Jo. That will work."

Shaking her head, she walked off to where we'd hidden my pack. What it took for her to cover that ground without limping a single time, I'll never know, but she did it. All the way there and all the way back, stubborn as a little she-mule. Then she knelt down behind the tree and peed in the cup.

When she came back around she was frowning and looked a bit sick. There was less than a cup of bright orange liquid.

"Not much there, kid."

"I missed the cup."

"That so?"

Josie didn't meet my eyes. She was evading me. I pushed. "And it's bright orange, Jo. Remember what I told you about water? You need to be drinking more."

"I'm not thirsty."

"And what did I tell you about that?"

"That that didn't matter."

"Right. So why aren't you drinking more?"

Josie stopped then and set the cup on the ground before looking into my eyes. "We don't have enough water, Tally. And you are bigger than me, so you need more."

Using my right hand, I cupped her grimy little chin in my fingers and said, "That's not a decision you get to make, kid. Like I told you before—way, way back when we started this thing—we're partners here. Fifty-fifty. You promised me then you'd drink your share. When did you change your mind?"

"Yesterday."

"Why?"

"Because, like I told you, I think you're bigger

so you need it more. Plus you have to pull the sled. So I changed my mind."

"Unchange it. From now on every time I take a sip of water, you're going to take one too, do you understand me?"

Jo nodded, subdued, but it was clear she wanted to argue.

"Now would you please pour that urine into the palm of my hand?"

Unwrapping the makeshift bandages, Josie cleansed the wound as best she could while I gritted my teeth and sweated bullets. The cut went clear through.

"Makes it easier to clean," I joked, feeling sick.

"Yuck," she disagreed, brow furrowed over her task.

When she finished I started to get up, intending to tear a strip off our sheet for a bandage, but Jo pushed me back down.

"I'll get it. You stay put," she said, heading for our shelter. A few steps away, she stopped and hissed over her shoulder, "You better hug that tree, Taliesin Joy Nowata, or I'll skin your hide and don't think I won't and you're already in real bad shape, you can't afford to be skint, too. So *there.*"

Red hair flaming above the most self-satisfied little set of shoulders I ever saw on a human, Josie marched on to the sheeting and came back a few minutes later with my bandage.

"At this rate we won't have a sheet much longer," I quipped to keep the nausea at bay.

Josie drawled, "Then I reckon we'll have to sleep under our shirts."

She is bending to this place the way her father did. Living with the land, not against it. Adapting. Flexibility—it's crucially important to survival. People who can't bend break. Maybe that's what my grandmother and Paul were talking about. Maybe the issue never was one of control, the way I always saw it, but one of remaining pliant, open to possibilities, acquiescing to change and doing it cheerfully. Well, why didn't they just say so?

Don't fight the land, Taliesin. Let go, Tal, and you'll find the land bears you up in ways you never could imagine.

Josie is letting go, bending, working with this desert. She is a survivor, the truest kind, one who understands that survival itself is beside the point. It's how you take each moment that counts. Nothing more, not one thing less.

——

Dressing the rest of the kangaroo was out of the question. One cut was enough. Josie offered to slice more meat, but I vetoed that so loudly she didn't mention it again. We had a sizable pile of thin strips anyway, enough for several days if we could get it sundried before it spoiled. A fire would be faster, but with the men so close on us, we couldn't risk one. Salt would work too, if we had any. But with those two quick curing methods out, more meat isn't to our advantage. More to carry, that's all. More to defend from the dingoes.

Working together, three good hands to the task, we severed the head and upper arms and tossed them to the albino. Then I salvaged the heart, liver, and kidneys, in case the men left soon enough that we could cook them, while Jo spread the thigh strips out in the sun. Finally we each grabbed a hoof of the kangaroo's remains and dragged it out near where we'd last seen the ranging pack.

"After all, they caught it," Josie said, wiping her hands off on her shirt as we turned to leave, walking backward to our site, both of us sweeping branches over our footprints as we went. With only a few minutes of this steady afternoon wind, the ground would look as if we'd never been here. The dingoes moved in on the carcass moments later. Dust rose behind the crawling truck to the south.

We stretched out flat on our backs and sucked on raw meat and neither one of us gagged. Somehow the value of cooking is lost on us now. I think we'd still prefer cooked meat to raw, but we can't have it until the men leave, and we're so ravenous at this point we'd be willing to eat a cow on the hoof. Not a grub, but a cow. Taste buds are pliable, willing to deal with certain contingencies. Ours can stomach a ruminant in any form, but a grub in none. That wild-haired notion I had to eat some the other day has gone permanently to roost.

So here we sit, sated and quiet, bending with the land. The next waterhole is less than a mile to the south. In spite of my sore hand and Josie's sore leg and the men and the miles ahead, we feel good, strong inside ourselves. Strong enough to hatch a plan, the most normal plan we've had this whole time.

"We'll take a short hike over to collect water, leaving our stuff here," I tell Jo. "It'll be almost like we're on a backpacking trip back home, minus the mountains and a few other details. We never camp near water there—it's environmentally unsound, for one thing, fouls the water for the animals, and, way more important, dumb, since it puts us in the moonlit paths of grizzlies and such. Same here, no grizzlies but the men. Camping near this spring would put us at risk where they're concerned, so we'll stay back like before. But it won't hurt anything to walk in and tank up on water. That's normal."

"Yep," Josie agrees, grinning. "We're all normal again."

DAY 37

---

64 miles, 6 gallons.

Normal fled.

We made it to the water, a bug-strewn puddle in a shallow rock tenaya or depression. A seep normally feeds it, according to Paul's notes, but only pale stains on the rock hint at where it used to be. I dug a shallow hole a couple feet behind the seep and, sure enough, groundwater pooled in, quickly at first and then slowing. We collected all we could and sat back to rest a few minutes before returning to our hideout. I told Josie this was the homestretch and all we had to do was pull back and play it smart, keep our wits about us and walk ourselves home.

"Six gallons, sixty-four miles, give or take one or so on either side. Not a soul alive would think we could make that, so we'll just have to do it and show 'em all. If there's a God she's cutting us a break," I said. "Lord knows we could use one. We've earned it, kid, you and me."

Jo nodded and turned to the south, eyes bright with hope. Rain clouds were piled up on the horizon again. The truck was at least a mile away, working a long east-west line through heavy vegetation. We weren't hungry or thirsty for the first time in too long to remember. We had a good camp close by and the strength we needed to get back to it. And then the wasps hit us.

———

I still don't know where they came from. One minute was quiet, the next they were on us. I took the most stings, six or seven on my face and neck, but that means nothing because I'm not allergic. Jo is.

She got three, one on her neck and two on her left arm. Any one of them was enough to kill her. Before I could even get the stingers out of her skin, she was wheezing, and before I had a light tourniquet above the bites on her arm, her eyes were swollen shut. We had to have the epinephrine—from Jo's backpack—but that was at camp, half a mile away. We'd forgotten it in our delight at being normal. I ran. Harder than I've ever run in my life. Both ways, but it wasn't fast enough.

The men, tired of tracking, had decided to stop for the night—at the nearest waterhole. They came in from the southwest.

I managed to reach Josie, administer the shot, and drag her around the backside of a large boulder seconds before they drove up. There was no time to brush out our tracks. Holding Jo's head on my lap, trying to mask the sound of her labored breathing with my bandaged palm, my own head pressed hard against stone, I sat on the ground, one arm holding Josie close, the other holding the Beretta. We waited.

—

Not for long.

As they made camp, one man said, "Check around, Bod. See if the bitch's been here yet."

Bodley muttered, "Doubt it."

"Check anyway."

—

My tracks shine like searchlights. I stare at them, sick, knowing what they mean. If this man knows footprints at all, he'll read everything we've done for the last three hours in a matter of minutes. And he will walk straight to us about ten seconds later.

Back against the rock, I hold Josie close with one arm and click the gun's safety off, then wait, eyes locked on those glaring signs.

He'll see the leisurely pace we came in on first, my right foot taking shorter steps because of the sprain, my left one overcompensating and hitting the ground harder and turning slightly outward as I picked the right one up again. If he's any good, he'll know I'm injured and how—and be able to make an educated guess as to when it happened too, because my tracks didn't look like that back at their camp or Paul's. He'll see Jo at my side, her burned leg causing her to drag that foot anytime she's not specifically thinking about picking it up. He'll see the way the toe of her other shoe digs in when it lands—she's instinctively rushing to get it on the ground to relieve the pressure on her sore leg. He'll see where we stopped and turned to each other for a high five when we glimpsed the shallow puddle of water: both of us standing firm on the good legs, letting the hurt ones take a break, one strong track and one faint one apiece, facing each other toe to toe, the albino at Jo's side, waiting patiently through this odd human ritual. He'll see where Jo hurried ahead of me and got down on one knee next to the tenaya. He'll see where I dug a shallow hole a few feet away to collect water for us without fouling the pool itself. He'll see where we stretched out for a rest before we headed back to camp and where we were when the wasps hit us. I was sitting cross-legged in the sand. Jo was standing. When the wasps got her, she tried to run but fell down, fighting the whole way. He'll see all that, too.

She is struggling to breathe now. There is no sound from the men. I ease her head into my lap and hold her close with my left hand, right one still cradling the gun. She holds onto my arm with both hands, shaking, scared, crying silently. I nod that it will be okay, and she closes her eyes to listen. I wish I could do the same, wish I could believe my nod enough to close my eyes on what is happening here.

The place Jo went down is torn up like a newly plowed field. Dry grass stems broken and ground into the sand, dead leaves half buried, a rock kicked a few feet away, an ant den busted open. And now a man's boot.

Bodley.

I can't see all of him, but I remember those boots from the Land Rover. Vibram-soled and lightweight with canvas uppers, size twelves or thirteens, worn down hard on the outer front thirds of both soles. He favors the left leg some—maybe from an old knee injury. He doesn't stand long for indecision. At the Rover, his tracks were purposeful, no hesitating. His stride is shorter than you'd expect from a man his height: he is capable of much more than we have seen, and he knows deserts, probably has had some training in wilderness survival, maybe in the army; he can bide his time. And follow through when need be.

He's facing away from us, just standing there. Now he's moving again. Out—on the track I made heading for our camp to get the epinephrine. It's clear as a bell. Maybe he'll follow that and I can make a break for it—drag Jo into the bush the back way.

No, it's too sparse in the immediate area, open and parklike under these trees. The other man would see us sure.

Josie catches her breath. I pace my own breathing slow and touch her cheek so she'll look at me. She understands and slows hers. We breathe together a few seconds. She closes her eyes once more, calmer.

"Find anything yet?" The man at the spring yells.

Bodley shakes his head, still walking out. He's not looking at the ground anymore, just around, almost disinterested. Either he's such a good tracker he doesn't have to stick to the ground or tracks mean nothing to him. I am sick of praying, but I do it again. Please God, let this man not know footprints from fungus.

Please.

━━

He knows footprints.

As well as me or better.

Well enough not to have to waste steps or hurry. He has made a short half-circle of the spring, staying on this side where all our tracks are, trailing me partway to our camp. Now he's coming back here.

I press against the rock as hard as I can, holding utterly still, clutching the gun's grip, palm sweating, finger slippery over the trigger, praying desperately that he won't find us. Even if I do shoot him, there's no way I can get to the other one before he has a gun out. All this work, all this way, almost normal, and then this.

The place Josie went down now has a clear set of footprints through the middle. Vibram-soled man's boot. Bodley on his way out. He had to've seen the marks I made pulling Jo back here. There's not a single good print left between us and there, but the drag marks are as visible as an interstate highway. A very short one, eight feet tops.

He sees it.

As he reaches us, I raise the revolver to a line with his chest and freeze, holding the gun as steady as I can.

He stops and stares at me, unafraid, and then at Josie for several long seconds.

The albino rises from where she's been lying in the shade nearby, and he glances at her, then looks back at Jo's swollen face.

Without warning his shoulders drop and he raises a finger to his lips as if to say, Shh. Our eyes meet, no words pass.

Cold and still inside, chill bumps racing down my arms, I wait.

He turns and goes back to the campfire, shuffling his feet through our tracks, saying, "Nothin' but old dingo scat, Den. Bitch ain't been here yet."

"Shit. Means she's somewhere between this hole and the last one," Den says, slamming something down at the truck. "Yank fuckin' cunt."

"We head north in the morn, we'll prob'ly pick up a trail by noon," Bodley says, as calm and measured as if we don't exist.

Under cover of them making dinner, I picked Josie up and carried her far enough away that her breathing wouldn't draw attention. I didn't understand it and didn't have time to try to then, but Bodley had done more than overlook us and shuffle his feet through some of the most obvious tracks we'd left. He'd as good as told me they'd search to the north tomorrow. We had a chance to escape. All I had to do was dismantle our camp up there without leaving signs and get us started south.

It didn't work out that way.

DAY 38

After mixing a small amount of dirt with water, I pasted it on Josie's stings. Mud packs help relieve the pain. If I hadn't had so much work to do, I'd have done the same for mine. Instead I schlepped gear, brushed out tracks, and laid misleading ones all night long.

The albino stood watch over Josie, and I came back and forth to check on her several times too. The swelling decreased slightly, but she had bad vomiting spells twice. Every time I had to leave again, plain terror rose in me, but I swallowed it and trusted the white. She never moved an inch from Jo's side all night. I worked and worried.

Why did Bodley let us go? Is he sick and twisted, into the chase? Or just biding his time? What if he changes his mind? Will we have a chance then? What possible reason could this man have for letting us escape after all these days of searching for us? What do I really know about him anyway?

Four things. One, he didn't shoot Paul. Two, he dug Paul's grave. Three, he saw us and pretended he didn't. Four, he deliberately pointed Den toward the north, which would give us a chance to move southwest. It was confusing and strange, and I couldn't figure it out, but something in me wanted to believe in the good of this man. Maybe he wasn't a killer at heart. Maybe he got into this thing over his head and couldn't get out. Maybe— I don't know. All I know is to focus on the work ahead of me. I just don't know the rest.

It's near dawn now and I've finally finished and am slipping back to Jo. All I have to do is get her on the sled and move out. Loud angry words stop me.

From the back of the rock where we hid a few hours ago, Den shouts, "I thought you said they weren't here."

Bodley doesn't reply.

Den is quiet a moment, then says, "So Rayburn was right about you then."

"Right how?" Bodley asks.

"That kid never could've got away in the first place if you'd done your job. And now what do we have here? Three sets of tracks on this ground. *Three.* Means you saw 'em, had to've. When?"

Bodley is silent.

"Last night?"

"That's right. Last night."

"Fucker. Like it out here in the sun, do you, chasin' bloody tail?"

Bodley waits a beat, then replies, quiet, "Didn't sign on to kill kids."

There is a long empty moment. Then a gunshot cracks over the desert and someone groans and hits the ground. Den snarls, "You signed on to do what Rayburn fuckin' paid you to do."

Bodley forces out a reply, "Went too far."

Another shot echoes, silence ensues, and then I hear the sounds of packs being thrown into the truck. Minutes later it peels out, headed north, with Den at the wheel this time.

Josie, pale and in shock, stays with the sled. I go back to the rock. Bodley is lying on his side, shaking violently, blood pouring from his stomach and mouth. I try to stem the bleeding with my hands but can't.

"I'm going for help," I say, not really knowing why. "If you can hang on for a few days, I'll get somebody to come for you. I'll leave water and some meat. You'll be in the shade here. You just have to hang on."

Bodley shakes his head and struggles to speak, "No. Get out. Now. He's gone for help, too. They mean to kill you both. Go."

"Fine, we'll go. I'll just leave you some water," I reply, slipping my canteens free of my waist belt.

"No."

Setting the two full canteens next to his hand, I stand to leave, and stop. I have to ask.

"Why? Why'd you do this for us?"

Bodley's answer is slow in coming and so weak and hoarse I can hardly hear him, "Have a daughter myself."

"Oh," I mumble, not knowing what to say.

"Same age, same hair," he says, face contorting in pain, blood slurring the words.

His next words are barely audible, but they'll never stop ringing in my ears.

"Kids are supposed to be exempt from all this."

Moments later, his head lolled back. There was no need to feel for a pulse.

I stand silent over this stranger, my right foot next to the last tracks he made. For the first time here, he was standing with his weight evenly distributed, not angling to the outside edges of his shoes as usual. Before Bodley fell, he was afraid. But he was standing strong and he went down without ever shifting his feet like most people do when they're nervous. Unable to help myself, I stare at the footprints. They are clear and tell a lot—his height and weight, how well he knows this land—but all the most important things, they say nothing of: that he was the father of a little girl who looked like Jo; that somewhere inside he had a kind enough heart to give life to two strangers he was hired to kill; that we all owe our lives to someone else. In a move more intuitive than instinct, I bend and brush those two final tracks away.

Then I gather the canteens and stumble back to the sled. Josie is out cold, face flushed and still swollen. The white stares at her and then me. There's no confusion about what has to happen in the next few days. I have to get this child to a doctor no matter what it takes. Kids are supposed to be exempt from all this.

DAY 39

3.5 gallons, 44 miles.

Both trucks are back. Close on us. Made out three men through binocs, then buried the glasses next to a mulga. Can't afford one ounce extra. Living with the land, no need for stuff. Walk until I'm shaking so bad I can't walk another step, rest, do it again. Covered maybe twenty miles. Used up both gallons of the water we got at the spring. No more water between here and the village but what I have with me. Vegetation heavy in the unburned areas—trying to stay with them as much as I can.

Josie not responding to anything, I'm having serious difficulty getting her to swallow, her temp's rising, so is mine. My urine's dark orange, which means I'm not getting enough water, but I'm drinking as much as I can. Not much left, but rationing is dumb. Belly makes the best canteen. Just need to cover more ground faster. Let go. Nose over your toes. Get this gig into debrief.

Don't have time to read from the journal. Must draw from the memories in my heart.

*Ask me to remember who we are and trust me not to
leave when we forget.*

Passed an old grave this morning. Mounded like
the one over Paul sometime years ago, it's sunken
now and nearly level with the surrounding land. Set
in a small acacia grove, it would've gone unnoticed
but for the rickety wooden board standing at its
head and the fact that I walked within six feet of it.

For the first time, I was glad Josie was asleep. To be
safe, I pulled the sled past the grave and turned it so
that even if she woke she wouldn't see anything, and
then I just sat down, too tired to move another step.

I couldn't make out the letters on the board. It
made me sad. Who remembers the person lying
here? Family? Friends? Acquaintances? Whoever
put up the board? Does anybody really remember
us when we're gone?

And what about Paul? What if I can't make it back
to take him out? He doesn't even have a board, just
two sticks tied together with ribbon buried in the
sand next to him. It isn't right. Death should count
for more than that. His death for sure.

The only person in the whole world I could
never imagine living without, and now he's gone
without a trace. It just isn't right.

The white looks at me in silence.

I cross dry rivers in my mind, following the
tracks of a stranger—myself yesterday—home. The
wings of my heart are tethered to a tall man with
kind brown eyes and the grin of a boy not yet
turned bitter. Where do I go from here?

Leave no trace. Our one and only lasting argument. Tally says no one goes anywhere without leaving signs. I say we at least must try.

Today I stand here, a part of this place. But one day I will be gone and even the land won't remember my name, and I draw comfort from that. Tal argues the point to the ground. She is a tracker and tied to signs. "The land may well forget you, O'Malley, but I will always remember your name."

Sometimes, in spite of myself, I believe her.

I carry this stranger's grave in my heart as I walk on. I carry Paul's grave and Mama's and Grandmother Nowata's and all the graves of everyone who ever died. I fought Paul tooth and nail on that Leave No Trace concept. He had some fuzzy ecologically correct notion of leaving only footprints, taking only photos. He said footprints would vanish and photos would fade and eventually nothing would remain of anyone and that's how it should be and didn't my ancestors think that way too? "Now is all we have, Tal," he used to say, "And now is enough."

I can't get Jo to wake up. I can only get water down her by sitting her up and blowing in her face to get her to swallow. I hear a truck rumbling near, but my eyes are so weepy and tired I can't see where it is. I don't know what my ancestors thought. And I don't really care, either. Now is not all we have. And now is never enough.

When I look into her eyes I see only one word. Tomorrow.

There is no tomorrow separate from yesterday.

I cannot go faster without rest, cannot push beyond my limit one more step, must give my body a chance to recoup. When I close my eyes, I feel Paul beside me, warm and strong, smiling in his sleep the last morning we shared. I see the tent flap swaying in a hot, gentle wind and hear the song-bird trilling us awake with his simple melody. I feel the albino pass the camp, a white shadow tied to us in ways we could not imagine then. I hear the spring water gurgle into the sand and the spiny grasses rustle along the path. I watch as Paul turns to leave and then the dust rises and falls quickly behind the Land Rover. Nothing in me calls him back. I have all faith, no fear. I know he will return, sure as the sun comes up to scour the Tanami.

Other images roll in on the blinding heat. Paul hanging from his seat belt. Josie whimpering in a pile of filthy sheets. Foy's cable and tow, Paul's bloated body dragged over the sand, the white shot and wheeling red into the night, then Foy and Bodley and Rayburn and my stark terror when Jo walked into their camp. The weight of Foy's heavy body on mine, the sound of his neck breaking, the steel in Rayburn's eyes and the hard slashing of his tendon, Jo's anger and fear, the nausea and disgust and aching pain of it all. Days and days and nights on end of walking and sleeping, vomiting and cry-ing, fighting to exist and keep Josie alive and not answer or forget my Mama's eyes. The dingoes, the white, the brown, the kangaroo, a blue ribbon sway-ing in the warm wind, the stories and bad jokes and raw meat and filthy water. We became scavengers, taking the dead to stay alive. Scavengers of memory, too, people long gone and forgotten, Dix and Mama, our grandmothers and friends. Scavengers of places, New Orleans and Jenny Lake and the Grand Teton in winter. Scavengers of events, Josie kicking a cowboy in the shins and us forming a company to do that full-time. And scavengers of souls, Paul's especially. We drank him in from the journal and the letters and the shirt and held on as tight as we could. In the process we became saviors, flawed and stumbling yes, but saviors all the same, rescuing ourselves as we rescued each other.

Bodley dug Paul's grave, saved Josie's life and mine, and gave his own. I wish Paul could know that. Jo saved me and I saved her. I wish he could know that, too. The songbird and the wallaby saved me. The scrounging pack of dingoes and the albino saved us both.

The bird and the men and us, scavengers all, no need to fight the land, each gives its existence when needed, each takes in return, the whole an unbroken circle of life. I wish Paul could know me now, now that I carry the songbird's melody quietly within, now that I really have let go.

The true survivor is one who has finally learned that survival itself is beside the point.

DAY 40

1.5 gal., 20 mi.

I heard the truck two hours ago and hit the ground on instinct, face first. The men were so close I could feel the engine rumbling.

"God please, not now, not like this," I whispered into the sand. "Not like this." The sound rolled in and over me and the world went dark in the straight sun of high noon.

After a long while, I eased onto my knees, sure it was over, sure we were finished. Three men, all armed. We don't have a chance. Trembling, I stood up, afraid of what I would see, terrified of what I wouldn't. The trucks were about a mile ahead, crosscutting a set of parallel lines between us and the village. They had passed us. Missed us. The white was standing next to the sled.

Taking up the harness again, I reached back to lift the sheet protecting Josie from the sun and said, "Let's go, kid."

She never stirred.

The dingo fell into step beside me and we walked toward home.

Dreams wake us to the truth within and save us from the truth outside.

Dead men don't dream. Neither do dead women. The hell with let go. I won't let go till this child is safe.

Paul was a big believer in dreams. I hated them. Always have. Always will. Spent most of my life running from them. Earnestly. Would rather get up and stay up than risk dreaming. Have gone days on end—48, 72, even 80 hours at a stretch— wide awake on purpose. But now, even waking, every time I close my eyes, the dreams crowd in and I am undone.

Water. They all speak of water somehow. Rain, sleet, snow. Ice, rivers, and streams. Fog on my face, mist on my cheeks, sea spray wild against my limbs. Oceans, tidal waves, and thunderstorms. I walked into a room, thought I saw a mirror and turned to leave but couldn't. Found myself staring into it, not a mirror at all but a clear sheet of water, suspended vertically in the dark, and in its depths I saw nothing. Nothing at all. Just shimmering liquid, deep and bottomless, lost in time. I have no reflection. I don't exist.

Wish Paul was here so I could tell him that one. He once asked me if I'd ever seen my reflection in a mirror while dreaming and I snapped, "Hell no. I don't even look in mirrors when I'm awake. Why would I do it in a dream?"

Well, now I've looked, O'Malley, and no one was there. What would you say to that?

Woke this afternoon to rain clouds gathering

heavy in the south. Thought they were part of a dream at first. Rain. If only it could be real for us. I could resign myself to the dreams if real rain would fall. Time to walk. Enough rest.

———

I have fought this moment all day long, doing everything I can to come up with another option, raging at fate. We've come so far, we're so close, but the end is closer and closing fast. The men are less than a mile away. They worked their way to the village and now they're coming back. I know I need to leave Jo behind and go for help, but can't bring myself to do it.

She woke once, long enough only to whisper, "Mommy?"

I bent over her and whispered back, "It's Mommy Two, kid, and we're almost home."

Then she was out like a light again. I don't even know if she heard me. I held her in my arms anyway, trying to let her know everything would be okay, saying it the way Paul always did, like a promise not a prayer. The praying part I must leave to action, making a plan and following through. Words are no help in times like these.

Beyond hunger. Nausea's all I know anymore. Digestion uses up too much water anyway. Can't afford to eat, so I jettisoned the meat we prepared so carefully a few days ago, gave it to the albino. The sled didn't feel any lighter. Both water tanks are gone and all the canteens but six. As each goes empty, I'll toss it. Along the way I've buried everything but those, the gun, our journals, Paul's shirt and letters, one sheet, and one flare. Survival at this level is ecologically unsound. We've left not just traces but a hell of a lot of stuff all over the place. They should put that in a SAR manual somewhere. Maybe I should do that when we get home. Write a real survival manual, tell it like it really is instead of cleaned up how we'd like it to be. Yes, I think I'll do that.

Meantime, I need to go on. It's getting dark and the men will stop to sleep. I think I can pull a ways more. In fact I'm sure I can. Nose over your toes, Nowata. This child is depending on you.

I saw them walking closely together, so attentive to each other it was hard to tell who was leaning on who. Slightly stooped, bundled in blue, arm in arm, eyes searching the snow-packed sidewalk before them, each intent on easing a lover's journey. Two smiles that meet as one. Two hearts, a single soul.

When they pass, I see Tally and me in forty years. I only hope I have more hair.

Paul is leaning on me. I am leaning on him. No small matter like death can sever a love this large. Together we will get his daughter to safety. Together we will watch her grow into the woman she was meant to be. Together we will still grow old and, as I always told him, with no little measure of glee, together we will still watch him go bald and I will love him anyway, to my very last breath.

DAY 41

.5 gal., 10 mi.

Fell down over and over last night.

Gave up covering tracks, just walked and prayed for a good hard wind. One came at dawn and blew all day, leading a brief rainstorm this afternoon. The water was cold and shocking, but it didn't revive Jo. Or me. All this time praying for rain and now when it comes it's another danger. I got chills. Josie did too. We have nothing to warm us but the sun.

At least the wind and rain helped us with the men. They're a mile or so behind us now, working hard to find our tracks, cutting for our signs on a line that ought to raise us and would, if our prints hadn't been beat up so bad by the weather. Pony could find us. Bodley could too. And Foy. Nobody in that truck is as good as them. But they are good enough to know the basics, and if they keep at it, they'll get to us soon.

I'm surprised they didn't stay between us and

the village. Surely they know that's where we're headed and that we're too busted up to get there by any but the shortest route.

They think we couldn't have gotten this far.

They are wrong.

DAY 42

4 mi.

If you could name the beginning, what would you say?

If you could name the end, where would you go?

I have to leave her here, Paul. If I don't get help, she's not going to make it. Hidden next to this rock, the men won't find her. They haven't picked up our trail yet. They're working back a ways. It's just four miles to the village. Maybe less.

If only I could pull her I would but I can't. When I lean into the harness my knees buckle and I hit the ground. I can barely stand up now, but if I leave everything here, surely I can make it to that village. The white will keep watch over Josie.

I'll put our journals in her hands and cover her with your shirt. I won't wait for dark. She won't last till dark unless I get help.

So this is it, Josephine. We are almost home, kid. Nose over our toes just a little while longer.

It's going to be okay. It really is.

DAY 42

YANGAARA, NT, AUS
17 JANUARY
9:00 P.M.

I didn't make it to the village on my own. I got close—within a mile—but finally fell down and couldn't get up again. The last thing I remember thinking was that now Josie would die for sure. And then I passed out.

In 129 degrees, full sun, that should've been it for me.

But, according to the Aborigine family who rescued me, the white tipped fate in my favor once more. I didn't even know she'd followed me but when I went down, she ran on into Yangaara and set to howling outside the home of Ruby Piljara. Two neighbors tried to chase her away. She refused to leave, just kept up that awful howl until the woman and her two sons, Japanangka and Janswira, responded, and then she led them quickly to my location.

I was too far gone when they arrived to know it, but Ruby and Janswira carried me into the clinic.

The dingo wouldn't let Japanangka leave. She harried him until he turned in Josie's direction and then led him to the rock where I'd left her.

She wasn't there.

Josie.

That was the first word to leave my mouth when I woke up at the Yangaara clinic this afternoon, eight hours after leaving her at the rock. It's late now and her name is still the strongest word in my mind. I will spend what's left of this night mobilizing every resource I can lay my hands on to help me look for her.

We have to find this child.

—

Japanangka found the journals, the sled, Paul's shirt, the gun, and one canteen, but Jo had vanished without a trace.

When I came to, a heavyset woman in a brown dress was sitting in a chair by my bed.

"Ruby Piljara," she said, explaining in broken English what had happened and her role in my rescue.

I was hooked up to an IV and a bunch of monitors and every single body part was hurting. The cool air in the room felt like sledgehammers against my skin and my bones felt thin and rubbery. All I could think was Josie, so I interrupted and Ruby finally shook her head.

Her sons had been looking all afternoon. There had been a heavy downpour with localized flash flooding. No one could locate any of Jo's tracks.

Unhooking the monitors, I turned off the machine, then pulled out the IV and the central line the doctor had put in my chest as prep for surgery. He'd planned to try reconnecting the two severed tendons on my left hand this afternoon, but there was no way in hell I'd let anybody put me under while Jo was still missing. When I reclaimed my tattered, smelly clothes, the nurse protested.

"I've been functioning fine with two dead middle fingers," I said, stumbling over the words, hearing them come out fuzzy and slurred like a drunk, only I was stone-cold sober. "Too late to reattach the tendons. He'll have to go on a fishing expedition up my left arm for the ends and I'll wind up looking like a gutted pig."

"Just let him try," she said, concerned and kindly, left hand reaching for the call button.

"Later. Maybe."

She hit the button and took her eyes off me to speak to the doctor. Without a word, Ruby took my arm and we left. I didn't need permission to do what I had to do but I was grateful for Ruby's support.

———

I knew better than to do what I did next. Know better.

Did it anyway—got Ruby's sons to drive me out to the PLS (point last seen). Crazy damn fool thing to do—hurry off to the rock where I left Josie in hopes I'd be able to raise her footprints, even though both Japanangka and Janswira had tried to do just that all afternoon. Some part of me couldn't believe she'd gone without a sign. Even if the men had gotten to her, they would've had to leave signs. I was sure if I could just get back there I could walk right to her. After all, I am a tracker.

And yes, Aborigines track, but who knows how well? I'm the one with all the reasons for finding this child. That's what I kept thinking all the way there, that and praying the rattletrap vehicle we were in wouldn't break down and leave us stranded. Ruby and her sons watched me with keen, knowing eyes, and I pushed what I knew about those kinds of looks to the back of my mind.

How many times have I looked at desperate family members that same way?

There were no tracks. *None*. Not Jo's, not the men's, not the truck's, not the white's, not even mine. Josie had vanished into the last downpour without so much as a scuff mark.

I tried anyway. Cut a perimeter ten yards out from the center. Crossed several sets of Japanangka's prints and two of Janswira's. They had done a good job. Probably better than I was capable of. But I still had trouble breaking from the site and returning to town.

Now I understand why people who lose kids don't come for help as quickly as they should. Any second, just around that bush or that rock or near that gully, she'll show up, and if I'm not here—

Eyes so blinded by love they can't see the truth if it's slapping them upside the head with a two-by-four.

Enough.

Back to base. There are people here, resources. We can run this just like a search back home.

DAY 43

Lyle Cade, the local constable, had already left his office when we arrived, so we went to his house and got him out of the shower to report Josie missing.

He and I headed back to the police station to work out an initial response plan, Japanangka went to muster trackers, and Ruby went home and came back with a big sack of various remedies. Then she built a small fire just behind the station and brewed a noxious tea that nearly gagged me going down, but made me feel stronger than I've felt in weeks. I asked for a second cup.

Ruby shook her head and handed me a handful of roasted witchetty grubs and two bright green leaves steamed to a soft pulp. Too concerned about Josie to fret about dinner or even ask what it was, I ate it all. And kept it down. That's the thing about lines. They keep moving. As near as I can tell, grubs have no taste whatsoever.

We have mapped out a search strategy. Six men from the village are camped behind the station, waiting to help track Jo—that gives us enough for four hasty teams at dawn and if these people are all as good as the Piljaras, that's worth about sixty park rangers starting ten hours before Jo got lost. At first light Japanangka and the trackers will go with me to the PLS and work outward from there. Lyle Cade and Janswira will visit all the sites—the research camp, the accident location, the meth lab, and the spring where Bodley was shot—to see if they can raise any clues about the men's identities in case they got to Jo first.

Ruby listened in silence as the plans were made, but as soon as they were finished, she motioned for me to follow her outside. Near the fire she'd made a pallet. I needed no more bidding. Humming a low chant, she put a dry, withered branch over the flame and fanned its pungent smoke my way and I drifted off to sleep, wondering. Something about this woman is familiar to me, but I cannot think what it is. She hasn't said ten words since we met, but I understand her on a level I can't explain. I feel safe when she is near. That's it. With Ruby I feel safe.

4:30 A.M.

The day is nearly on us, and I've already had my cup of tea. Ruby made me a bowl of dark soup too, and I drank that while rechecking the sites I marked on the map for Lyle last night. Between my memory and Janswira's knowledge of the area, they should be able to find them all. When they left we promised to stay in touch by radio. Technology and manpower can't guarantee success on a search, but it goes a long way toward it. I can't help but wonder how different this all would've been had Paul been operating on a budget the size of the Northern Territory's instead of a grad student's. We at least would've had a working radio.

Can't go there.

The high yesterday was 129 and it dropped to 60 after the rain. Hypothermia city. Whether or not Rayburn's men found her, Josie is in serious trouble. Can't go there either. Just run the gig.

I called Miriam and explained things the best I could over the phone. Brusque as ever, but this time with good reason, she said she'd catch the next plane. I put on my ranger voice and told her we were doing everything in our power to find Jo and that I hoped we'd have her back safe and sound by the time she arrived.

Miriam snapped, "You'd better."

The relatives of lost people lose all their manners. That's normal. Miriam never had many to lose in the first place. I dread seeing her again. As near as I could tell, the news of Paul's death didn't make a bit of difference to her.

The trackers are up and packed, ready to go. They're quiet and mellow, but their eyes miss nothing. They remind me of Pony in the field. Informal, relaxed, strolling along, glancing at the ground occasionally. And deadly effective. If any group of people ever had a chance of finding one little girl, it's this one.

The local shopkeeper offered us his four-wheel drive and himself as driver. As soon as he arrives we'll head out.

DAY 44

Noon straight up. No sign yet. Not a footprint, not a broken branch, not a single scuff, no tire treads. No dog prints either. Even Eli Two has vanished.

No one but the people looking for Josie have left prints since yesterday's rain.

Straight-up sun is next to impossible to track in. If you already have a good trail, you can backlight tracks using a hat for shade and a mirror to reflect sunlight over the shaded ground, but it's slow as hell and not very effective, and here we don't have a trail. As much as it kills me to admit it, I know we need to lay out an hour or so to let the light angle work in our favor again. The men do what we always did in the field, lie down in as much shade as they can manage, cover their faces with hats or hankies or arms, and sleep. Ruby gave me more tea and indicated that I should sleep too, but I can't.

Huddling in the shade of a bush, praying that Jo has the presence of mind to be doing the same thing, I wish I could write in my journal. That's what I used to do to keep from thinking too much. When you think too much, you can't see shit. I need to be relaxed and calm to do this child any good out here. But I can't write. Since I found Paul, the words won't come. My pen sits lifeless in my hand, struck dumb by my grief. Everything about him pours into me and nothing will emerge. Nothing takes the edge off the memories.

The sled was still at the rock. It reminds me of Paul too.

He's a dull, bitter ache today. If it weren't for Ruby, I'd work myself right into the ground looking for his daughter and trying to forget him, but Ruby reminds me to be wise. When she thinks I've had enough and need a rest or a drink or a nap, she stops and motions for me to sit down. Then she feeds me some concoction and I rest a few minutes and get up feeling a bit stronger than before. She has a special herb that helps the nausea. I haven't thrown up since I met her. That's a point in my favor. *Our* favor.

We will find Josie, Paul. I promise.

3:00 P.M.

Lyle called in. They picked up a few usable finger-prints at the meth lab, though it's deserted now, and several more at the Land Rover. He's coming back into the office to run those and leave the trip to the research camp till later. If the men who left those prints have records, we'll at least know who we're after and where they're from.

We had much less to report from our end. We've been working a series of perimeter cuts of the PLS, four concentric circles steadily expanding outward from the rock. Ruby and Japanangka are walking with me. The rest of the men are working in pairs. Still no sign.

Everyone looks calm but beneath the surface lies a tense steel spring. No one here needs to be told how long a child can survive without water and shade. Especially one who was already weak, sick, dehydrated, and nearly comatose.

I smell death again, the way I always do when it gets near, but reject it strongly. Losing Paul is enough. I can't lose Josie too. Not now that I've found her. Not now that she has given me back my life. My history, my family, the parts of me I tried so hard to scrub clean. I just can't lose her now.

And not like this—ever.

We *have* to find this child. Every minute we don't she's that much closer to gone.

My eyes stray back to the land and then to Ruby. She nods. It's okay to move again. I've rested long enough.

6:00 P.M.

The second team found Jo's T-shirt two hours ago. The third found her shorts ten minutes after that. We all picked up the pace, even me. Ruby gave me an extra cup of tea.

Josie is shedding her clothes. That means she's going down. In this heat, too confused to stay dressed and seek shade, she doesn't stand a chance.

There's no sign of the men, so it's just her against the desert. Naked, that's no contest at all.

Son of a fucking bitch. Josephine O'Malley, sit down and hug a goddamn bush!

———

Japanangka found one shoe twenty minutes ago, and we just came across the other. I am steeling myself for what's coming.

I have done this before, not in a desert, but in the mountains. Eight years ago, I worked point on the tracking team that found a child who'd wandered away from his parents' campsite in a freak summer snowstorm, the kind that comes so regularly in Wyoming nobody there bothers to pack winter clothes away at all.

Ethan was his name. Ethan Williams. He was eight, going on nine, blond hair, blue eyes, small for his age, diabetic. After three hours in the storm, he got hypothermia. Thinking he was burning up, he shed every stitch of his clothes. We found them all in a neat sequence of blowing snow. A light green Patagonia jacket first, a Nascar T-shirt and Levi shorts next, then a pair of Adidas tennis shoes so new they had no distinguishing marks on the sole, and finally, two tube socks taken off and folded neatly together and left at the base of a tree.

The only thing Ethan was wearing when we found him—frozen stiff at the foot of a talus slope—was his ball cap, cinched up to the smallest setting. Dale Earnhardt's car number—3—emblazoned on the side in trademark black.

As we carried him out in a body bag gone stiff with sleet, the only thing I knew for sure about Ethan Williams was that he was from the South. And that on Nascar Sunday afternoons, he used to stand in his folks' living room and cheer that number three car on.

DAY 45

Eli Two found us. And led us straight to Jo.

She was curled up in a gully 600 yards from the rock. There is an excellent chance that we would've walked right past her, if it hadn't been for the white. Search and rescue is never a done deal. There are too many little cracks on this planet for people to fall into unseen. Josie was in one of those.

Even a grid search, shoulder to shoulder by a battalion of Marines, might not've worked. It's the least effective way to search for somebody anyhow, but it looks impressive to people who don't know anything about SAR. Family members of the lost person, especially, usually feel relieved when they see a gang of searchers marching out in unison— systematically combing the area. What they don't know is that the grid really means only one thing: the SAR boss is desperate enough to risk destroy- ing all relevant signs. Since signs are all you have to lead you to the subject, walking a grid—and stomping them all into the ground—almost never locates somebody like Jo. But a white, half-tame wild dog did.

And did much more to boot. The dent E Two's body made in the sand next to Jo's showed that she stayed close through the rain, lying on the lower side of the gully, keeping Josie from sliding into the water that ran hard through the wash right after the storm. Then she stayed on through the night and yesterday, standing to shade the sleeping child from the sun and keeping watch until we finally showed up. That is a mystery I cannot explain. Or question. I don't understand this dog. I only know I'm grateful for her. Because of her, Josie will live, I will live, *we will live*.

———

As Japanangka was carrying Josie into the hospital, she roused enough to say, "I found my dog, Daddy," and then slipped away again. So far she has not reawakened. Her condition is stable, though, and the doctor says there'll be no permanent damage. I keep saying this to myself to make sure I hear it, and every now and then I stand up to stare out the window to where Eli Two is lying in the shade of a bush. Several times children from the village have come up, trying to get her to play. She ignores them, waits patiently for them to leave, and stays silent, eyes trained steady on this window. When I turn back to my chair, I feel her, still out there, still keeping watch. It helps. So does seeing the sled propped up against a tree trunk near her.

I need to keep that sled. Objects never mattered to me before, but now they do. That sled, Paul's journal, his shirt—these are things I cannot lose. The sled leaning against that tree reminds me of Paul puttering in the garage all those days till he got it built so it suited him. The shirt recalls his smell, however faintly, and the care package he left with it. I laughed until I cried at the contents of that box and the yellow Post-its Paul had included: a bottle of wine ("for next Friday night, love"), a candle ("for your Tuesday bubble bath"), Rilke's *Letters to a Young Poet* ("for advice on the moral benefits of solitude"), and two C batteries ("for your vibrator—but please don't get too attached to it, babe"). I slept with that stuff on his side of the bed from the day he left till the day I boarded a plane for Australia. And now all I'm left with are these pieces here.

The sled, the shirt, his journal. Traces of his life. They're all that's left.

Those few things and Josie.

The adrenaline that surged in me when I learned she was missing is leaching from my body now. I feel shaky and a little bit sick, but looking at Jo helps it to subside. I never thought I could love a child. Never wanted to. Didn't want to get that close. Didn't want to be that responsible for someone else, especially a little person. I was afraid I'd blow it with my Nowata genes and ruin a life just by breathing, so I intended to leave child rearing to people like Paul who had it all figured out. Yet here I sit by this ornery little girl, and my heart is no longer mine because I would do anything in the world to keep her safe. No search I've ever worked has meant more than the one we did for her.

She is resting quietly in a hospital bed with an IV to match mine. Ruby has the chair on the left side of the room; I'm on the right. We've spoken less than five words to each other since they wheeled Josie in, but I am glad Ruby is here. She understands me, knows the center of my pain, gentles it with her quiet ways and simple remedies.

9:00 P.M.

They want to try the surgery on my arm first thing tomorrow morning. The doctor suggested that they get the Royal Flying Doctors Service to transport me to Alice for it, since I could get the services of a specialist there. I told him I wasn't leaving Yangaara until Josie wakes up and if it was going to get done he'd have to do it, so he should go bone up on the procedure in his medical books if necessary. He shook his head. I looked him level in the eye and he didn't say another word.

11:00 P.M.

Ruby shook me awake. Jo was up, asking for me.

The light in her eyes said it all, everything that couldn't be said for lack of words. I promised her cheeseburgers and strawberry shakes just as soon as I got back from having my arm fixed, and she asked about Eli Two. Ruby lifted her up where she could see the white, silhouetted in a dim street-light, and Josie grinned and lay back against her pillows, finally content, eyes drowsy.

"Tell me a story," she whispered. Remembering how Paul used to tuck her in every night with a long rambling tale, I started one about a white dingo and a rabbit, but Josie stopped me.

"No Tally. Tell me the one from Daddy's book like when we were walking."

Nearly undone, I started Josephine and the Rodeo. Before I'd gotten to the part where the crowd was shouting encouragement, the story's real heroine was sound asleep, a healing sleep this time. Paul was right again. Where Josie was concerned, it was going to be okay. It really was.

For the longest time I sat by her bed and cried. Ruby stood next to me with one hand on my shoulder. Neither of us said a word. Words run dry on the rocks of human grief.

DAY 46

They're set to put me under at 8:00 A.M. The surgery should take only a couple hours. Another two or so in recovery and I'll be back here. I'll have a cast and a nonfunctional arm for about six weeks, but after that, with a lot of physical therapy, the doctor says, I'll be good as new. I just listened and nodded.

I don't really know how to talk to people anymore. Aside from running the search for Jo, which was based on instinct alone, everything else I've said has come from a numb tongue. My mouth doesn't work quite right—it's almost like the parts don't fit together—so I'm saying very little. But that's only a fraction of what's wrong with me now.

I feel strange, out of my element, disoriented. I'm not sure exactly why, but after two months of struggling over the sand, everything here makes me uneasy. These smooth tile floors, for one. My body doesn't trust a surface this polished and level.

I keep feeling like I'm about to trip and fall, so I tense and pick up my feet too high, like a horse forced onto ice. Then I catch myself doing it and try to stop, try to walk right, normal, but as soon as I forget to think about it, I'm tipping around like a circus pony again.

And then there's the noise. My ears buzz and my neck hurts clear down my backbone from all the sounds. Like when I walked past the nurses' station last night. They had a cassette player on and turned down low to one of my all-time favorite songs, "Sweet Home Alabama," so I stopped to listen, but couldn't manage it. Between the music and them talking about a patient's chart and a constant beeping coming from the nearest room and the whir of the air coolers in the hallway, I felt like I was drowning. There were days over the last month when I thought the silence would burst my eardrums. Now I'm desperate to hear nothing. And I don't know if I'll ever feel music again.

And finally, there's the water. Even that bothers me. All those days in the desert I longed for a cold shower, and then when I get here where I could have one ten times a morning if I wanted, I can't bear the feel of water on my skin. After we brought Jo in, I was looking so forward to it—to getting really cleaned up at last—but then when I stepped into the tub and turned on the faucets and the water hit me, it hurt so bad I nearly screamed, and I stumbled and banged my knee getting out. I tried once more, later, but even with the flow turned on the gentlest setting, I couldn't stand it.

It's not just the injured parts of me either, but the whole. Every drop surged down my limbs, beating me into the ground. Water doesn't weigh enough to cause pain, I would've vowed back home. Here it feels like the heaviest substance on earth. Tons and tons of liquid squeezing the life out of me. I didn't get clean. I'll have to try again tomorrow.

But whether I'm clean or not doesn't matter much now. There are all these people here, but it's like Grandmother Haney used to say—"Ain't sleepin' with 'em, wouldn't like to be"—which means she didn't give a good goddamn what they thought of her, and neither do I. Never did care all that much, but really don't now, especially not enough to endure that water again too soon.

Or the people. That's maybe the worst. All that time in that vast, empty land does something to you, I think. I've gone quiet inside, too quiet to know how to relate to the rest of my species. People are curious about us. They have heard about the white woman and kid, and several have stopped by the clinic. I'm shrinking from everyone but Ruby and Jo. When anyone else even says hello, I wince and find myself yearning for the spinifex plains again, glimpsing a frilled lizard scuttle from sun to shade and back again, hearing the simple, true notes of the songbird's melody, feeling the white close by as we walk through the starry night. Several times in my mind I've slipped outside to a bench near her waiting spot and sat there in silence. It is the only place I really feel safe. This building smothers me, hurts my eyes and ears and skin. The bench looks quiet. When my surgery is over and we both feel up to it, Jo and I will have to go sit out there and have a picnic. I can't think much beyond that today. The sled stands mute beside the bench, waiting for me to load it and move on.

It feels as if I'm being pulled back to this place I fought so hard to escape. There were lessons I didn't know I was learning till now, and I wish I could go back and move through it all at a different pace. But I can't. Jo is here and she needs me, and my life is calling me back. I'll have to find a way to pick up the pieces and let the Tanami go to seed in my memory. But how can I leave, with Paul still here?

Josie. That's it. She needs me, and what we've been through has forged a bond so strong nobody will ever be able to break it. Just seeing her makes me glad, but knowing she needs me—well, that feels right.

She's slept all night. A couple times she whimpered with nightmares, and I gentled her back to sleep, using her father's words and my new name.

"It's going to be all right, Jo. Mommy Two's here."

I like that name. Mommy Two. I may not have what it takes to be a real mother, but I intend to be a hell of a Mommy Two.

Maybe I should request a transfer to a park closer to Louisiana. Maybe in Texas or somewhere. Big Bend perhaps. But I don't like Texas. Only good thing I ever knew to come out of there was

Pony, so maybe moving isn't such a good idea. I don't know. We'll have to see.

Lyle called at 5:30 this morning. He got a hit on three sets of prints. The other two came back zero. Rayburn didn't show up anywhere. Lyle thinks that may not even be his real name, which means we'll have to find him through the men he hired.

For that at least, we have good information. Both Foy and Bodley had records, Earl Foy for a string of aggravated assaults and armed robbery, David J. Bodley for grand theft auto at age eighteen. Denys Wilhoit had too many offenses to count, ranging from petty crimes like shoplifting and resisting arrest to transporting stolen property and drug trafficking. Foy and Bodley are from the Melbourne area, but Wilhoit grew up in Alice Springs. Lyle plans to travel there today.

I should be intensely interested in what he's doing about the men, but I'm not. Somehow I just can't summon the energy to care what happens about that. All I want is for them to leave us alone. The quicker I can recover the better it'll be. Miriam is supposed to arrive today. Then we can get Josie out of here—back to the States. We'll be safe there.

But first there's the little matter of this surgery. The nurse has been hovering for ten minutes, ready to start prepping me. I have probably ignored her as long as she's willing to be ignored. Time to submit. Lights out for a spell.

I do wish you were here, O'Malley. The only other time I had surgery—for that ruptured appendix—you were there until the anesthesiologist ran you out of the room. Yours was the last voice I heard on my way down and the first one I reached for on the way back. How I wish I could hear you now.

Enough. I can't afford to wallow. Your daughter needs me to be strong.

And anyway, I can do this on my own. All they're doing is sewing two tendons back together. It's not like a major reconstruction project or anything. Nose over your toes, Nowata. Let's get this gig into debrief.

2:00 P.M.

I'm out of surgery. Still here in the recovery room.

I feel groggy and sore and my left arm is like a lead weight, but it's over now and soon I'll be good as new.

Except for the news.

If they hadn't told me that, I'd have been hounding them to get me back into Josie's room two hours ago. As it is, I've been sitting here stunned, trying to come to grips with it all.

"And the great thing is, your baby's fine, dearie," Meryl, the floor nurse, said a while ago, breezing in to take my blood pressure and temp and check my O2 levels.

"Yes, at least I got Jo out of that desert alive."

Meryl looked at me funny and said, "Oh no,

hon, I wasn't talking about her. I was talking about *your* baby."

"Mine?"

"Why yes, yours. About two months along, we think, and a regular miracle it is—all you've been through and your baby's still fine!"

I didn't know what to say. Meryl suddenly looked worried, "Oh, you didn't know? Nobody's told you?"

I managed to shake my head and register that Meryl was apologizing—profusely—to me for spilling the beans in such an informal way, but I couldn't hear her anymore. My ears were ringing and I felt sick.

Paul's child.

Good Lord, all this and now that too?

It can't be. I can't do it.

How can I possibly manage to be a mom without Paul? I never thought I could do it even *with* him, so how the hell am I supposed to do it alone?

I asked Meryl to close the door and leave me by myself for a while. I need to go back to Jo, but first I have to come to terms with all this. The white howls outside the clinic and I'm grateful for the sound. It helps me center. Maybe she understands what's happening in here.

4:00 p.m.

So that's what the nausea was all about.

Me, pregnant with Paul's baby and on foot in the Tanami and thinking the iodine wasn't setting well on my stomach. Lord have mercy.

One thing's for sure: when this kid gets here, it'll be one hell of a fighter.

I can do this. If I have enough guts to be a Mommy Two, then I can certainly be a mom. I may not be my mother, but I am my mother's daughter. Still, I wish you were here, Joy Nowata. I will need more than your eyes to see me through the next twenty years or so. I need Grandmother Haney. I will call home today and make arrangements to go see her. Maybe she would agree to come live with me. Maybe I could get her out of that damn shack and into a warm house. Ours is big enough. We have that extra room, and the sublet will be up in a couple months. In the meantime, I'll get us an apartment in Jackson. Surely she will agree to come live with us. She probably knows where Dix is too. Yes, I need to call home.

But it's time for me to get back to Josie now. I rang for the nurse fifteen minutes ago. Meryl still hasn't showed up. I'll give her another three and then I'll get up and go by myself.

DAY 47

Meryl never showed up. I went down the hall on my own.

Josie's bed was empty.

Ruby was standing near the window, staring outside. She turned when I came in. I wasn't enough with it to be alarmed yet, so I joined her. The white was on her feet, every nerve alert, ears cocked and quivering, eyes fixed on the horizon. I tapped on the pane and she flicked one ear, nothing else. Something was wrong. I looked back at the bed.

I didn't have to ask.

Ruby looked at me, dark eyes gone infinite with sadness, and I knew.

I sat in a chair for a while then, looking at the empty bed. They had already mopped the floor and changed the sheets. The new ones were freshly laundered, no wrinkles, no places where she'd kicked them free of their tight, neat hospital corners or bunched them into a wad against the rail because she was too hot. The bed and the room were ready for their next occupant.

They had already forgotten the last one, a tiny redhead with big brown eyes and her daddy's crooked smile. Not even a hint of her smell was left.

I couldn't think, couldn't speak, couldn't move of my own accord. Waves of exhaustion swept through, tears did not come. Sometime later they put me in a wheelchair and took me down the hall to another empty room waiting for its next occupant—me. Ruby came along and I could feel their eyes on me, the nurses' and orderlies' and hers, could feel the warm buzz of their concern, their kindness to this broken stranger, but I couldn't look at them, couldn't hear them, couldn't let any of them get too close.

I just drew inside myself and sat in the chair, staring out the window at the white dog, both of us lost in longing.

———

"Josie threw a fit," Meryl said later. "She didn't want to leave without saying good-bye, but her mum wouldn't be swayed. She just bundled her up and off they went."

I think I nodded, I'm not sure.

So when the dingo howled, it wasn't for me. Jo was leaving. I was deep inside myself, huddled in my room, figuring out how I could ever be a mom while the little girl who taught me I could actually do that was going away for good.

Ruby leaned over and set our journals—Paul's

and mine—in my lap. Tucked inside Paul's was a letter from Jo. I just stared at it, too numb to think, much less read.

I should be a bigger person about all this.

At least Josie survived. She is going home with her mother, home to Louisiana and Gram and Gramps O'Malley, home to Eli and gumbo and pralines and sleeping safe at night in her own bed. She is alive and one day she will recover and be well and all this will fade into an ugly childhood memory, mean edges dulled by time. That was the whole point, wasn't it? That I get her here so she could live her life out like she was meant to?

Then why am I so sick inside?

Why does everything in me ache to see her just once more, to share one of our sideways hugs, a touch in passing without direct intent the way we both were prone to do it? Why does my hand yearn to feel her small fingers snugging its bandage tight? Or my eyes beg to watch her lashes flicker above her cheeks when she sleeps? I thought this thing I feel for Josie was about keeping a part of Paul alive, but I see now it wasn't that at all. It was about her and me. Us.

I found a long-lost part of myself in this little girl child and I liked having it back.

They lost the shirt too. Paul's shirt. That sent Jo right over the edge, according to Ruby. She wanted to leave the shirt with me so it would make me feel better, but some helpful orderly had tossed it in the trash and no amount of turning the hospital upside down could locate it.

So now even that little piece of him is gone.

I am not meant for this world. Not meant to be clean, not meant to have family, not meant to have home. There was something in the moon on the day I was born, wrenching my loved ones away even then. Everybody leaves.

Sitting on this bench with the white at my feet, I stare into the desert and the past. What was it all for? Four years ago I sidestepped my own memories and pain, dove headlong into a deep pool of perfect hope, and now all I'm left holding are the remnants of a soul. A mirror with no reflection.

But then I looked down the road and saw a rental car coming my way. The passenger door was opening before the driver even got fully stopped and a little redhaired girl was crawling out and coming straight for me. Josie, on her own two feet. Unsteady, but strong of will, arms outstretched for me. I rose and hugged her close. Her hair was newly washed and dried, its curls falling in soft ringlets. Her face was thin and freckled, all the dirt of our trek long gone. Her baby body clung tight to me and I knew that I was home.

Miriam walked up quietly and waited a few steps away. I sought her eyes, tears in mine, thanking her for letting us say good-bye. She nodded and walked unsteadily to the bench. Jo and I joined her.

Josie was all words then, remembering the high parts of our trip, asking me if I remembered this or that detail and telling her mom about it. Miriam nodded and smiled, weeping openly. I had never seen her cry. Josie was the only one of us who wasn't bawling. So she did most of the talking. Suddenly she stopped and turned to her mother.

"Did you forget, Mommy?"

"Forget what, babe?" Miriam asked gently, letting her fingertips touch Jo's cheek.

"The surprise!"

"Oh that. No, I didn't forget. Here it is," Miriam replied, reaching for one of the paper sacks she'd set next to her on the bench and handing it to me.

Josie beamed. "It's our present for you, Mommy Two."

Startled, I looked quickly at Miriam to see if she was offended by that, but she smiled and said, "Open it. She swore it was what you wanted."

Inside the sack was a cheeseburger, fries, and a strawberry shake. I broke out laughing. This is a complicated world we live in, but *this* is what it means to have family. We had cheeseburgers, fries, and the thin milky substance that passes for strawberry shakes in Australia then, the three of us perched on that bench in the warm sun. I did my dead level best to eat all of mine. Jo, too. We managed quite nicely. Josie told me about seeing our names in the newspaper—a local reporter had got onto the story and we'd made the front page of *The Territorian* the day before—and Miriam and I talked about getting Jo out of Australia and back home and working something out so she could spend summer vacations with me in Moose.

Holidays too, sometimes. I told them about the baby and Josie finally cried, squealing, "I'm gonna be a big sister! Yay for me!"

And then we talked about Paul, not long but long enough. Two women and the daughter who'd loved him shared a wooden bench and a meal and remembered his quirks together. My heart ached but felt full when Miriam agreed that I should arrange to have his body cremated and asked if she and Jo could come with me to the ridge above Jenny Lake where he wanted the ashes scattered. Our grief was being dispersed in the terrible mundane details of his death. And life. An hour earlier I hadn't known how I could go on. Now I did. Family makes all the difference.

When the rain clouds moved in, they got ready to leave. Jo hugged me tight, while Miriam stood aside, waiting. I reached out my one good hand for hers and drew her into the circle. This is the woman who loved Paul and lost him too, the woman with enough courage to warn her daughter about rape while she was young enough for it to make a difference, the woman who hid her pain behind sharp witty comments and bore it alone. Since the day Mama died, I've never hugged another woman. Never wanted to. But this felt right. We stood together, drawing strength from our shared love for a man no longer technically here but with us always in our hearts, until raindrops spattered our heads.

Then they turned to leave, with Josie shouting, "Bye Eli Two!" and Miriam looking quizzically around, not seeing the dog her daughter was calling. Then Jo hollered, "And bye for today, Mommy Two!" and they both waved until the car was out of sight, heading for home.

I sat on the bench for a few minutes more, enjoying the feel of the warm rain on my head and the silence of the white's company. Then I got up and headed into the clinic, looking for a phone.

DAY 48

I'm running another search, from a hospital bed in central Australia, trying to locate my brother somewhere in rural South Dakota. He left a message for me at my house in Moose a month ago—Lanes gave it to me when I called to check in and tell her I'd be home soon—but the number he left is no longer in working order. So I've put in calls all over the place, to some of his old rodeo buddies and girlfriends. I'd call Grandmother Haney, but she doesn't have a phone, and I don't know the names of any of her neighbors, so I'm stuck, waiting to hear from Dix.

In the meantime I checked in with Pony and Jed. It felt good to hear their voices, disembodied and groggy—it's early morning there. I didn't tell them the whole story, just enough so they know about Paul and that I'm all right. Jed said I could bunk with him till Laney's sublease was up on our house, if necessary. "But Lanes called me a few minutes ago, Tal, squealing that you were coming home early and maybe the two of you could be roomies, so you'll have your pick." Pony offered too. I thanked them and said I'd let them know, but I'd been thinking about having my grandmother come live with me so I'd probably take a place in town till Laney moved out. That shocked them both silent. Pony recovered quicker than Jed.

"You have a what? A *grandmother*? I thought you sprung free from the blessed womb of the earth, Nowata. Immaculate conception of the agricultural type. Soil, water, a bit of manure and the such. Sure didn't figure you for any long-term family ties with *humans*."

When I didn't take the bait, she continued, "So when do the rest of us get to meet this miracle woman?"

"As soon as I can arrange it and get back home."

I hadn't been off the phone ten minutes before it rang again. Dix was on the line. With news that ripped my world in two.

DAY 49

Grandmother Haney is dead.

Bess Haney. She died in her sleep, on that ragged stack of bedding, the morning of January 6. Day 31 for me and Jo. That's the day the plane came, the day of the grubs, the day I remembered my grandmother making that ketchup sandwich and eating it while I stood in her house, distant and judgmental, angry and wanting to hurt her the way she had hurt me.

Dix was with her at the end. Sober, for two years, eight months, and three days. He hasn't taken a drink since the day I slugged him. I asked him to forgive me. He said he did that two years, eight months, and three days ago. He's getting married this fall, to a girl he went to high school with—Shelby Greer. I don't remember her. They're going to live in Artis and Elaine's house for a while. We inherited that and rented it out all these years. Neither of us ever planned to go back, but now Dix says he is. He wants to have children. He's given up rodeo, says he no longer has a spleen to lose so he's afraid they might start taking more vital organs next. He's doing construction work and has a new truck.

I asked him to tell me about Grandmother. He said she wrote me a letter and everything's in there. He'll send it out by courier tomorrow. I asked if she was in pain.

"No, Tal. Sleepin' like a baby. She knew you were all right. She told me she finally knew you were going to be all right so she could go. And then she just went to sleep."

"How could she know I'd be all right—that day even *I* didn't know I'd be all right!"

"She knew."

"And even if I am all right, didn't it ever occur to her it might be nice if *one* of our family members *stayed the fuck around for a goddamn change?*" I was yelling. Meryl poked her head in the door to check on me.

Dix listened in silence, the line long and heavy between us. When I stopped ranting, he finally said, "She talked something about you meeting your family soon. Something about a woman with the name of a jewel taking up where she left off and teaching you how to live on the land and leave the signs you were meant to leave. I think she put all that in the letter, sis. I'll send it this morning."

I thanked him.

Dix said, "And whenever you get ready to come home, Tal, you call me. I'll come get you."

"I don't know when that will be."

"Don't matter, sis. You call and I'll come get you. We're family, you know. So promise me you'll call and let me come bring you home."

I promised.

And one day, though I don't know when right now, I will keep my word.

DAY 54

Lyle stopped by and sat on the bench beneath the tree for a few minutes. The white watched him warily. I listened.

They've arrested Denys and managed to get a lead on Rayburn. That is his real name. Adrian Rayburn Smythe. "Dangerous man," Lyle said. "Dangerous and very slick. Runs beneath the radar. Took me a while to track it down, but he's on several people's lists. Including your DEA."

"He's operated in the States?"

"Apparently."

"Any arrests or convictions?"

"One. Minor drug charge and battering of an old girlfriend twenty years ago. Nothing firm on paper since then. But lots of fingers pointing his direction for lots bigger things. Drugs, guns, even some homicides—ugly stuff. He runs in a fast crowd." Lyle glanced at me to see how I was taking all this.

"You'll be going after him for Paul, right?"

"Right."

"And Bodley?"

"That too. Though Denys will go up for the actual hit."

"I'll testify."

"Rayburn'll be motivated to stop you doing that. You should probably leave here. Go home. Get among your friends and the people who know you. That way if he ever shows up, you'll have protection."

Lyle said it like an older brother would. I nodded while he was talking and then shook my head. "I'm staying here."

Lyle sighed. "I had a feeling you were going to say that. And where will you stay?"

I shrugged.

"All right. We'll make the case, you can testify, then you can leave. Meantime, let me know if you need anything. Money, contacts. We don't have much of a budget, but I could probably get something together for you." Now he's back to sounding like a law enforcement officer.

"I'm set for money," I said, thinking about my inheritance. All these years I never touched a dime of it. If I'd been my better self I could've made my grandmother's last years a hell of a lot more comfortable. The thought makes me wince. Lyle puts his hand on my arm, concerned, and gives me a couple minutes to collect myself.

"You'll need to lay low. Real low. That damn newspaper yesterday—I don't know why they feel the need to do that!" he said, brotherly again.

"No worries."

Lyle grinned and then his face went still. Hand

still on my arm, he said, "I arranged for Paul's body to be brought in. The M.E. in Alice will do an autopsy."

Face frozen, I managed to mutter, "We want him cremated. Can you arrange that?"

Lyle agreed. After promising to keep me apprised of the situation, and making me vow to keep in touch, he left.

Ruby came back then, with a big leather bag. Opening it, she laid out all the contents on the bench between us. I recognized many of the ingredients she's been using to feed me and nurse my wounds as well as a couple of the plants Jo and I learned on our own. After I'd had a chance to look at everything, she carefully placed each item back in the bag, cinched it shut, and handed it to me.

"For your journey," she said, standing up. "I will meet you there."

Then she turned and walked away, never pausing, never glancing back. I held the soft leather close and watched her disappear down the street.

———

When this is all over, Paul, when the bruises fade and the burns and cuts heal, I will still have you.

But I won't. Night will stretch into an endless abyss and I will be alone.

That's what hurts the most, being separated from the one person who taught me I was beautiful just the way I am. No longer the homely little half-breed a drunken father cursed for the color of her hair and eyes or the distant nerd at the head of the class, just me, graceful in my strengths and lovely in my flaws. I wanted all that, forever.

And I wanted the little things too. Making coffee in the morning or giving back rubs in the evening. Preparing meals together, immersed in Beethoven and REO or extravagant silence. Tying shoelaces and splitting wood. Hearing you breathe at night and watching you wake at dawn.

I wish I was more prepared for this.

But how do you prepare to lose the love that gives your life meaning? A love that was first easy, then natural, then right.

I vowed forever.

I will see it through.

I'm just so tired I can't think right now, too tired to hold on. I've stumbled through these last days and nights aching for your touch, not knowing whether I knew you at all, wondering how I failed you and what I missed and what I could've done better and, most of all, why you had to leave. I've argued with you and talked back to you and been sassy to you to keep myself upright and moving, dragging your daughter to safety. I fought this desert you love, fought it tooth and nail, with everything I had in me to fight with—and all the while you lay quiet and cold beneath its heavy red sand. It is too much.

But this much I know. One night soon I will again lie next to you and your voice will ease me to sleep. And as our wings take flight, you and our child will live forever beneath the canopy of our sheltering sky.

DAY 55

I keep coming back to this bench, looking for an answer, waiting for my grandmother's letter to arrive. The courier just brought it a few minutes ago. Quiet of heart, I hold the plain white envelope in my hand. I tried to open it, but burst into tears at the sight of the paper. I made stationery for Mama and Grandmother for their birthdays the year I was six. Grandmother wrote her letter to me on a piece of that paper. It is so old and yellowed, her penciled letters so carefully laid down. I cannot read it now, so I slip it back inside the envelope and just sit holding it.

There's an explanation here for why she abandoned us, I know, but I don't need to read it. Not yet. And maybe not ever. Grandmother's reasons don't really matter to me anymore. They were hers and wisely chosen for what she knew to be true. I understand this now. I only wish I could've told her that before she left. But I held my anger close like a shield and shut her out of my life until now, when it is too late. So I must face my life, as a mother myself, birthed and set into this world by tough women with gentle hearts. Their choices were the best they could make with the hands they were dealt. Will my child one day feel the same about me? And will her understanding lessen the anger she feels for my mistakes? No answers. They will only come from the living.

Ruby's bag sits beside me on the bench. The white stays close, we watch together. The sled's rails glint in the late afternoon sun, and I remember dragging it over bumpy ground, mile after mile.

The noises of the hospital hum behind us. I hunch away from them and the people and the town. I don't fit here anymore. Turning my eyes north, I see the sandy plains opening out on the heart of the Tanami. How I fought that bloody red desert. But we were safe there. I didn't know it then, but the Tanami was the safest place I've ever been.

Suddenly the white alerts. The hair on her spine stiffens and she rises to her feet in a slow, deliberate move. Following her gaze, I look across the street. There, beneath the awning of a shop's entrance, stands a man in khakis and white shirt, leaning on a pair of crutches.

Rayburn.

He moves into the street, heading my direction, and I stand up, mindless, not sure what to do or where to go. Our eyes lock and I know. This man will never stop until I am dead.

The white growls and steps in front of me. Rayburn keeps coming.

All of a sudden, a group of children pour down the street, arms and legs flying in pursuit of a battered old soccer ball. As they come between us, Rayburn backs up and I see Paul's shirt pass on a little boy not half the size of Josie. He's got the blue flannel pulled up, wrapped, and tied around his waist, but it's still trailing in the dust and flapping against his knees as his bare feet pound the dirt to keep up with the bigger kids. I smile and wish Paul was here to see this. A piece of somebody else's history getting a new lease on life—on the back of a child. A trace of a life well lived if there ever was one. I make a mental note to write Jo and tell her about that.

Rayburn stands still, momentarily thwarted. I look him level in the eyes and feel the truth. I carry another life within me. I will not yield to this man's violence or anyone else's. Ever.

At last, I know what I must do. Taking up Ruby's bag, I slip between two parked cars and head away from Rayburn and the clinic and the village. Back into the Tanami. The white paces alongside. We move quickly but without fear.

Minutes later I see Ruby up ahead.

"It's going to be all right, Eli Two. It really is. C'mon, baby Bess. Your grandmother's waiting for us."

EPILOGUE

MAY 27

Departing Alice Springs, Ansett Air Flight #419.

Thwarted by Ruby's neighbors that day, Rayburn disappeared. I haven't seen him since. Lyle built an airtight case against Denys and, while waiting to testify, I lived with Ruby at her camp in the Tanami.

The desert turned green around us as heavy rains broke the drought and pummeled the earth. We sat in our cave in front of a warm fire and listened as food and water became plentiful again. I learned to tolerate the taste of grubs and then to taste them—nutty, simple, nothing either to write home about or gag over, truth be told—and to relish desert tomatoes and raisins and yala cooked soft in warm ashes. The morning sickness ended as my cuts and bruises healed. I put on weight, gathering desert foods alongside Ruby, living with the land. And everywhere I turned, I saw Paul in the gentle red hills he loved.

Then two weeks ago I came here to Alice for the court case. It was over quickly. The one against

Rayburn remains open, but there is nothing more for me to do here now. I can finally go home.

Bess stirs inside me. I shift Paul's urn to one side so that I can quiet my daughter with my palm, and remember sitting in the light of the campfire, the white's eyes resting on us, and Ruby showing me how to gentle Bess when she kicked. The first time it happened, I was surprised. Ruby laid her hand on my swollen belly and smiled.

"She runs," she said.

That was an understatement. Bess is in training for the damn Boston Marathon. We might as well be boarding a plane for Massachusetts.

Dix stands in line behind me, one hand cupped strong on my shoulder. Having him here for the trial was a godsend. I told him so. He brought me new tobacco for my pouch and fussed over me like a mother hen. I told him that too and he frowned but kept right on fussing. His wife-to-be sounds like a nice person. He'll be glad to get back to her, I think. I like seeing him sober. He spent most of our adolescence and all of our early twenties on a buzz. I barely knew my brother the day I slugged him on the cheek. Now he seems familiar again, and I feel my old fears for him quiet and step softly aside.

We surrender our tickets and move outside, down the wide covered sidewalk, toward the commuter plane that will take us to Sydney. As we reach the tarmac, I pause to look back one last time. Ruby is not here, but I can see her in the desert with the white by her side. Josie is not here, but I feel her in Louisiana, laughing hard with Eli over some new prank they've pulled. Mama is not here, nor either of my grandmothers, and yet they all are, taking shape in Bess's bones. We have come full circle. Eucalyptus and acacia trees grow close to the buildings. Their smell is strong. I know these trees now, know their names and fruits and flowers. I know what they heal and what they help. I know when they grow and what they do to wait out the dry. I have lived with this land.

Dix steers me onto the plane and we settle in, me next to the window, with Paul's urn held tight. My photo has been in all the papers, so the stewardess recognizes me and, bending the rules of the air for this flight, doesn't insist that I stow the urn. Without a word, she leans over Dix and tucks a blanket around my knees, her eyes two dark, knowing pools. Light skin like mine, blue eyes dark with the knowledge of shared sorrow. I never realized before how strong family is among all humans. I never could've guessed that even strangers speak the silent language of grief and yearning. Until now I'm not sure I ever saw strangers as people. I was locked too tight inside myself. Even working SAR couldn't save me from me. It took the Tanami to do that.

Dix takes my hand and I grip his, staring out the window. Suddenly a man steps away from the sidewalk and stands facing the plane, unafraid. Rayburn. Lyle's crew left his organization in shambles, but he has managed to elude them so far. How did he know I was here? His eyes meet mine and I understand: one day I will have to reckon with this man.

But not today.

As the plane taxis, raindrops spatter my window. We climb high above the fog-draped land and I hold onto the urn. I have loved a man of constant heart and steady soul. I carry his child within. What we had will never die. I hear his voice, a whisper.

Ask me to remember who we were and trust me not to leave when we forget.

I, Taliesin Joy Nowata, am finally home. What lies ahead does not matter. What is within will see me through.